GHOST
OF THE
GRAY

GHOST
OF THE
GRAY

J. JONES

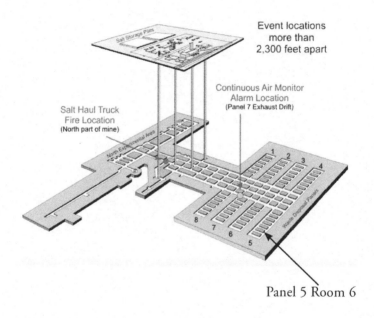

Event locations
more than
2,300 feet apart

Continuous Air Monitor
Alarm Location
(Panel 7 Exhaust Drift)

Salt Haul Truck
Fire Location
(North part of mine)

Panel 5 Room 6

WIPP Underground courtesy U.S. Department of Energy

To my mother.

CHAPTER 1

A LOW RUMBLE

CHUCK WHIPPED HIS head toward the sound of the rumble just in time to see a puff of salt dust billow into the corridor.

"Not tonight," he groaned. "Not again."

He threw the transport into reverse and backed up 300 feet to the entrance of Room 6 in Panel 5 of the Department of Energy's Waste Isolation Pilot Plant. Mined out of salt beds 2,150 feet beneath the New Mexico desert, WIPP's expansive system of rooms and corridors provided permanent protection from some of the nation's most dangerous radioactive waste.

The transport skidded to a stop, kicking up another puff of salt. Chuck shined his light deep into the room. Darkness devoured the beam. He rocked back and forth, nervously considering options.

"*Shit. Shit. Shit.*"

Nobody was around. Of course not. Nobody was supposed to be in the underground at this hour—and never alone.

Twenty minutes earlier, the night safety coordinator had his feet on the desk and earbuds delivering country music. Swinging his lanyard to the beat of Hardy, he noticed his radiation monitoring badge, usually connected to the lanyard, was missing. A quick check of the office confirmed his fear. He left the dosimeter underground while inventorying hardhats and miner's lamps for decontamination after the day's entry. Already on thin ice with management, he sure as hell wasn't going to self-report a lost dosimeter.

The rocking slowed. The smart choice would be to leave. Erase all evidence he had been in the hole, and let the dayshift figure out what happened. But maybe the rumble could work in his favor. If it was another ceiling collapse, he could report it to Mel discreetly. Give the boss a chance to fix the paperwork. Maybe then Mel would finally stop ragging on him for misplacing a fifty-five-gallon steel drum of radioactive waste last month. With hundreds of drums shipped to WIPP weekly, one was bound to be misplaced once in a while.

Chuck stepped from the transport and looked both ways down the long empty corridor. Though he had spent much of his life hunting and hiking by himself in the desert, he never felt so alone. At the wide entrance to Room 6, a precision cut in the solid salt wall two feet thick from floor to ceiling, he strained to see inside. Darkness.

The clipboard on the wall provided no indication a collapse was expected, but it had to be a ceiling collapse. With nobody working the late shift and nothing living in the underground, a collapse was the only explanation for the rumble and puff of salt dust.

Small blocks of salt fell from the ceiling once or twice a year causing more of an inconvenience than a problem, but since the fires of 2014, salt creep was supposed to be monitored more closely. Collapses were to be predicted, identified on the room inventory sheet, and, of course, immediately reported to the Department of Energy, the government agency responsible for WIPP.

Another glance at the clipboard.

"Shit."

The last thing he wanted to do was enter Room 6 alone. Waste drums in that room had been nothing but trouble. Mel had ordered everyone to stay out unless he approved the entry. But something else was keeping him from zipping in to check it out. There were rumors about Room 6.

He maneuvered the transport to face the entrance. Dim headlamps on the electric vehicle lit the room wall to wall but struggled to project deep into the waste tomb. The collapse could be anywhere. He sucked a deep breath through the respirator, squeezed the steering wheel tight, and crept toward the drums against the back wall. The nearly silent electric motor of the dual-seat transport seemed to amplify the sound of salt crunching under the tires. Two hundred sixty feet into the room, he lifted his boot from the accelerator. The transport stopped with a lurch.

"What the hell?"

He wiped a sleeve across his face mask.

"No freakin' way."

Forty feet ahead, a pair of eyes glared at him over the top of a fifty-five-gallon steel drum. Cobalt-blue eyes reflected in the dim headlamp.

He shook his head, ripped off the respirator, and rubbed his eyes clear.

"Not possible."

Muffled sounds of gnashing, chomping, and slurping permeated the room. A second pair of eyes joined the first.

Crack!

The chomping stopped.

Chuck's eyes darted upward in time to see salt crystals dribble from a narrow crevice in the ceiling. He slammed his foot on the pedal, swung the transport around, and fishtailed into the corridor, speeding toward the elevator.

"Come on! Come on! Faster, damn it. *Faster!*"

Panel 5, the farthest panel from the elevator, and Room 6, the second-to-last room in the panel, made the drive in the electric cart almost a mile. A quick look over his shoulder. Obscured in a trail of salt dust, something was following. Halfway to the elevator, radiation alarms began to wail. Sirens blared in the corridor. Red strobe lights bounced off white walls.

"*I'm fired. I'm fired. I'm fired.*"

He hadn't had *that* much to drink. Not enough to be seeing things. Nothing lived in the underground. With no outside access, no food supply, and no water, *nothing* could survive in WIPP.

A cadence of galloping feet overcame the high-pitched whine of the motor. He pushed harder on the pedal, already pasted to the floorboard. His respirator slid off the seat as the transport skidded through the turn into the main corridor. Though every fiber in his body was telling him not to, he had to look.

"*Shit!*"

Two very large somethings were catching up fast.

"Be there. Oh, God, please be there."

He hurled himself from the transport, tumbled once, and came to his feet, hitting the elevator call button in stride.

"*Open. Open. Open.*"

Inside the conveyance, he pounded the ground button.

"*Close! Close! Aaaaaaagh!*"

Chapter 2

Only in New Mexico

"Would you answer that already?" groaned a groggy Mrs. Martin to the sound of the cell vibrating like a rattlesnake on the opposite nightstand.

"This is Mel," her husband mumbled into the phone. "Uh-huh. Uh-huh. And the monitors? Good... *Wait.*" He sat upright. "Say that again. I'll be right there."

The WIPP corporate site manager slipped on yesterday's jeans, splashed lukewarm water on his face, and ran wet fingers over his head to hold down the mess of salt-and-pepper hair that every day was losing more ground to intruding gray. Mel grabbed his keys and was in the truck in less than two minutes. With no traffic on the deserted desert road, he cut ten minutes off the drive to the isolated government complex forty miles east of Carlsbad, New Mexico, but that still left plenty of time to worry about what his longtime friend had just told him.

Domingo Chavez, the waste manager at the site, just reported a series of underground alarms that indicated the ceiling in Room 6 of Panel 5 might have collapsed. That particular panel was being closely monitored. As best Mel could remember, a collapse was expected later in the year. Not now. Not while the room was still active. Not before the next special shipment. A shipment that would make the rest of his life quite comfortable, or cost him his life if anything went wrong. That was the reason Mel jumped into the truck so quickly that he left his security badge on the kitchen counter. At three o'clock in the morning, the guard would let him pass.

He dialed Dom's number.

"Any news?"

"What can I say, Mel? Ceilings collapse. But since the accidents in 2014, DOE's watching everything. This one could be on us, though, because I suspended the mine stability operations in Panel 5 and two other panels."

"Nice try. I made that call. If there's a problem, it's on me."

"Don't put this all on yourself. With contamination in half the underground, regular maintenance was stopped long before we showed up at this godforsaken site. I swear, I don't know how you ever talked me into moving here. Tyvek suits and respirators slow everything down. When things slow down, cost goes up. Especially maintenance on restraints to keep these collapses from happening."

"Preaching to the choir, friend. I request the budget, the Department of Energy turns it down, but DOE still expects us to do the work. Trucks roll in every day with drums that need to be moved underground. Hell, the only discretionary funding I have, if you can call it that, is maintenance. Sure as hell can't turn away trucks. I had to cut the restraints budget."

"But it was my study that justified biennial tightening instead of quarterly."

"Good study too." Mel chuckled. "Almost believable. The only mistake in all this is that you and I expected to be long gone before the next collapse. Gotta go, I'm coming up on the gate."

Mel slowed in the last turn to allow a herd of tumbleweeds to cross the road. While crushing through a swath of the prickly round weeds was satisfying, it was also potentially dangerous. Something he learned the hard way when a large dry tumbleweed stuck in his grill and caught fire. One of his first "only in New Mexico" events after moving to Carlsbad.

He shook his head as the illuminated waste handling building came into view. "Freakin' Los Alamos." A phrase often uttered aloud, referring to Los Alamos National Laboratory, the DOE lab that sent the drum that caught fire on Valentine's Day 2014. Of course, Los Alamos wasn't entirely at fault. Sure, they sent the drum, but a dozen people in the chain of custody had an opportunity to investigate the contents and challenge the waste manifest to make sure the contents met the waste acceptance criteria. Supposedly, the drum met all required criteria. At least that's what the final report suggested, but Mel knew firsthand, documentation was easy to manipulate. Los Alamos had nothing to do with the WIPP salt truck that caught fire a week before the Valentine's Day drum burned. Two fires in one week had brought a lot of unwanted attention to WIPP.

He stopped at the gate and again mumbled aloud, this time with a sarcastic snicker. "Haven't forgot a Valentine's Day since."

"Accident" was the official designation for both fires, but many workers at the plant were not convinced. Release of radiation from a single drum that *spontaneously* combusted had contaminated so much area underground the repository was shut down for three years. Mel was brought in from Savannah River to bring the facility up to the impeccable standards of the large engineering and construction contractor operating WIPP for the DOE. Too many previous site managers had been geologists or hydrologists. They knew everything about salt, creep, and hydrologic transport, but not one had operational experience.

It took a half-billion-dollar screwup for somebody in DC to finally realize an experienced operations manager was needed. A person who knew how to get things done, understood radiological risks, and had actually generated radioactive waste. Someone with practical application of regulatory requirements, logistics, and knowledge of the intricacies of packaging, transportation, and disposal. As an international expert in the life cycle of radioactive waste, Mel was a perfect choice. The only thing he knew about salt was the doc told him to stop using so much of the shit.

He steeled himself as he peered through the chain-link fence. The 'perception over compliance' management style that had served him well over his career was about to be tested. The management and operating contractor had been warned that another accident would put the entire contract in jeopardy. If radiation levels were as high as Dom reported, DOE and the contractor were about to be in deep shit. Heads would roll from DC to Carlsbad. Paperwork alone would keep the site busy for six months, but none of that worried Mel.

Why did it have to be Room 6?

Chapter 3

Reset the Alarms

THE WIND HOWLED outside as Mel watched the uniformed man hand a clipboard to the TRUPACT-II truck driver on the opposite side of the guardhouse. Papers clipped to the board fought to escape in the wind while the driver signed. This was no time to be waiting. It was also no time to cruise through the gate in a flagrant violation of procedure that might be observed by staff. Impending violations would need to be much more discreet.

Mel rolled the window down and shielded his face from windblown grit. A smell of rain from the dry thunderstorm filled the cab. Another blustery night producing just enough rain to pepper dust on the truck. Julio, one of the first people Mel hired when he arrived in Carlsbad, poked his head out from the guardhouse. The young man had worked security at the JCPenney until the store closed. He practically begged Mel for the guard position. The badge would not be an issue tonight.

"Little early, Mel."

"Hell, Julio," he replied in a coarse morning voice, badly in need of coffee. "I'm just getting back from lunch. Speaking of, I left my badge on the counter right next to the microwaveable slop the wife set out for me. I hate that shit, but what are you gonna do, right?"

"No problem. Just hold your hand sideways like you're showing me a badge in case the cameras are watching. By the way, you were right about taking my Maglite downhole."

"Downhole?" Mel's attention refocused. "Were you in the shaft tonight?"

"Nah, this was a couple-three weeks ago. Dom needed a warm body for the two-man rule, and I got the pleasure. I had just bought a new Maglite, best security flashlight they make. You warned me not to take anything downhole that I want to keep, but I had to see that high-powered beam blast those dark rooms, you know. Worked great, but a week later the switch rusted. Gave the damn thing to my little brother."

"Salt will do that. The light would have worked fine if you left it downhole. Bring it up, the salt corrodes it almost overnight. Ruined three cell phones that way. You'd think by now I'd remember to leave my cell in the office."

"The salt left a bad taste in my mouth too. Kind of a salty metal. Hell, you know that. You're down there all the time."

Mel had a bad taste in his own mouth as he entered the site, making a mental note of the first procedure violation: access without a badge. A violation that would be untraceable because employees do not log in at the main gate, and nothing would show on the video, which had been disconnected for a month.

He continued into the fenced complex of surface buildings that supported the cavernous operations 2,150 feet below. Pulling the truck into the site manager space, he turned the engine off and listened to the howling wind whip up dirt that pecked the windows. A prelude to the DOE storm headed to Carlsbad if he was unable to contain the situation. A nauseating feeling crawled through his twisted gut. Once again, procedures and site logs would be scrubbed by auditors and outsiders who were bound to find something. With so much documentation, all managed in prescriptive detail, they always found something. As long as he could keep DOE away from Room 6, he might survive the impending onslaught of inspectors. Rumors about that room being haunted were more real than people knew.

He slipped a silver flask from his jacket and primed the pump for what was sure to be the last carefree moment for a long time. He pulled his collar up and fought through the wind to the aluminum-framed glass door of the administration building.

Dom had already gathered staff in the conference room. A good move. They couldn't afford to have people digging into alarm logs or going downhole to satisfy curiosities over a possible ceiling collapse. But something that haunted Mel the entire drive in was what the staff already knew. Was anyone downhole when the ceiling collapsed? Had anyone reviewed the radiation alarm log? Any chance of containing the incident rested on hope that the graveyard shift of handpicked inept employees did exactly what Mel paid them to do; sit on their hands, sleep at their desks, and make midnight purchases online. A lack of ambitious, motivated self-starters on graveyard was not an accident.

He glanced through the window as he passed the closed door to the conference room. Four people sat at the table reading their phones. One man was writing on the whiteboard. Mel entered Dom's office and closed the door.

"What the hell is Rip doing here?" he asked Dom, who was the same six-foot height as Mel but projected a bulbous gut almost too far over his narrow waist to maintain balance.

"I know, Mel. Steve called in sick the last two nights. Rip's been covering."

"Sick? What does that ass have, the casino flu again?" He squeezed the back of his neck. "This could be a problem."

"I got Rip into the conference room as fast as I could, but he wasn't in the admin building when the alarm sounded, and I'm not sure he's being straight with me."

"Go back to the conference room," directed Mel. "Have everyone write down what they were doing tonight. That should keep them occupied until I finish. It'll also tell us what we have to work with. Collect the papers and shred them later. I'll join you in a few minutes after I check some things."

First stop, the security room. Cameras had been discreetly disconnected a month ago, but he needed to be sure some overzealous employee hadn't fixed the system on their own to impress management. Obviously, Julio believed they were still working.

"The dependability of the government contractor," uttered Mel upon confirming the video recorders were still disconnected. His stress level decreased a notch. Another swig from the silver flask. "I deserve this one." Next stop, the health physics office where the night HP manager, Steve, should have been napping had he been at his post.

The HP manager was responsible for monitoring radiation levels around the facility. More than just a meter swinger, the HP manager implemented the dosimetry program, cleared trucks from restricted areas, and performed random sampling of surfaces to check for contamination. The manager also verified alarms from radiation area monitors that detected radiation in the immediate vicinity of the monitor, and alarms from continuous air monitors that collected air samples and alarmed when concentration of a particulate exceeded a pre-established limit.

Data from all radiation sensors passed through the HP office. In a multiple-alarm condition, data from the sensors could be correlated to track movement of contamination through the facility. With few trucks scheduled for late offloads and the rarity of off-hour alarms, the night shift HP manager could complete most activities without leaving the office. Exactly what Mel hired Steve to do. But Rip was not Steve.

Mel plopped down at the HP's desk, effects of the flask beginning to pay off. He studied the alarms to fully grasp the extent of the problem. Flashing magenta and yellow radiation symbols covered the screen with "ALARM" and the sensor designator underneath. On a separate monitor, a map of the underground illustrated the location of each alarming unit. A third monitor displayed a map of exterior radiation sensors and those in the surface facilities.

Not terrible. Three units alarmed in Panel 5, all in the vicinity of Room 6. One unit alarmed in Panel 7.

Daily alarm activity frequently included false alarms in panels and rooms. By themselves, alarms were not reportable to the Department of Energy provided they were promptly remedied. Only the alarm in the elevator and the radiation sensor along the fence were disconcerting. He could not recall ever having observed alarms at those locations.

Mel grabbed a bottle of cleaning solution, abrasive pads, and a pack of clean cotton rags. *Time to manage compliance.*

An hour later, having cleared all alarms from the computer and scrubbed the elevator, Mel returned to the admin building. Managing compliance had taken longer than expected. Staff inside the conference room were bored stiff, but Mel was not about to apologize or show any sign of weakness. He took one more swig from the flask and opened the door.

"Hey, boss," said Dom in a lighthearted voice intended to establish the conversation tempo. "I'll fill you in. Brandi, Gabe, and Emilio were all at their desks reviewing procedures and working on the five-year license renewal update."

Mel nodded, mentally translating the description. Those staff had either been asleep or too wrapped up in some cell phone game to leave their office. That left Rip Anderson as the only bogey.

"Rip had just finished taking swipes and readings on the truck you saw on your way in. But—"

Rip jumped in with the crisp, overly authoritative voice of a young army sergeant, though the man was north of fifty. "But when I heard the alarm and saw the emergency light flashing on the Waste Handling Building, per procedure, I went to my office to check dose levels remotely and silence the alarms. Not knowing the precise whereabouts of other staff at the time, I went to the Waste Handling Building to confirm nobody was inside."

Mel recalled resetting that building alarm in addition to the other alarms. He hadn't noticed anything unusual in the area.

"I had my GM meter, I mean my Geiger-Muller radiation detection meter."

The meter clarification was unnecessary but typical of Rip. Radiation protection training was mandatory, and all technical staff understood basic operation of the GM meter, a device Mel operated daily the first five years of his career.

"I entered the room cautiously, scanning in all directions, but was unable to confirm an elevated dose."

Mel breathed a quiet sigh of relief. "That's what I suspected. Another false alarm."

"Until I got to the shaft elevator."

Shit.

"I was getting an increased zing at the door. Not much, but clearly a radiation level above background. I pushed the call button to see if something in the elevator may have been contributing to the elevated dose. The door was beginning to open when the emergency speakers notified personnel to report to the muster point. Per procedure, I left immediately and came here."

Mel stood at the table, unconsciously squeezing his chin with his thumb and index finger. He needed a drink.

A sketch on the whiteboard illustrated each alarm location Rip had described. Still, maybe it wasn't so bad. A few false alarms, but no physical confirmation. Maybe the calibration of Rip's meter was off. That could explain why he saw higher readings outside the elevator door. Doubtful, the dutiful health physics manager probably calibrated his equipment on the hour. Still, as long as Rip hadn't seen the inside of the elevator, the problem could be gone by morning.

"So to confirm. You did not go into the shaft."

Rip pursed his lips. "That's correct."

Mel breathed another sigh of relief.

"I guess that about wraps things up. This incident does not meet the criteria for a reportable occurrence to DOE. I cleared the alarms and made a quick run through the underground. Everything is fine. I'll track this with our other alarm metrics. If we have any more trouble with these sensors, we may need to recalibrate or replace a few." He smirked. "That's what happens when we're forced to buy equipment from the lowest bidder. In the meantime, everybody stay topside until Dom and I check out Panel 5 more thoroughly."

He and Dom needed to figure out exactly what had happened in Room 6 of Panel 5 because there was no simple way to explain all those alarms, or the blood he had just cleaned from the elevator.

Brandi raised her hand like an overzealous third grader.

"Does anyone know where Chuck is?"

CHAPTER 4

INSPECT THE UNDERGROUND

WITH THE EIGHT o'clock Friday workday fast approaching, Mel and Dom had just under two hours to contain anything in the UG that needed to be contained. A hundred and twenty staff would be arriving on-site, not counting an untold number of daily visitors from the national labs, DOE, and other government agencies, plus a host of contractors for commercial maintenance, equipment suppliers, vending machine operators, and even the porta john cleaners for the three units in the far corner of the site.

"Basement, please," said Dom as Mel pushed the elevator button. The oversized car capable of accommodating seventy-five people started the lengthy descent.

Mel tipped the flask. "Now's not the time to be funny, old friend." He handed the silver container to Dom. "The operating contractor brought me in for one reason, maintain compliance. We've done pretty damn well, considering the fallout from that fire."

"One drum of combustible kitty litter." Dom shook his head. "It's still hard to believe. Millions in fines, millions to upgrade procedures, and hundreds of millions to clean up the mess. A half billion dollars to clean a spoonful of radioactive material dispersed from one lousy steel drum." He took a drink and passed the flask back. "Remember when we used kitty litter to absorb nitrate salts at Savannah? Easiest way to turn liquid waste into solid waste. Hell, we never had any trouble."

"Let's keep what's behind us, behind us, and figure out what the hell happened. I don't want to go to jail for a freakin' ceiling collapse, if that's what caused the alarms."

"Hell, Mel, nobody ever goes to jail for these things. Insufficient training and lack of management oversight. I could write the after-action report before the elevator door opens."

Mel rocked his head, lips pinched tight. "Corrective actions are the least of our worries. More alarms went off last night than went off for those incidents in 2014, but that wasn't the only problem. Keep this between you and me." Flask in one hand, he held his arms out wide and turned a circle. "This entire corner of the elevator was splattered with blood. Not a little blood. The floor and chain-link up to my waist were a mess."

Dom eyed the chain-link enclosure. "What the hell?"

"Never seen anything like it. That's what took me so long to get back to the conference room. I wiped as much as I could off the cage, but I need you to scrub this later."

"Where'd the blood come from?"

"No idea, but we need to be extra careful. I'm not about to let a block of salt falling from the ceiling and a little blood disrupt the success we brought to this shithole. We've got one more special shipment before we can leave." Mel closed his eyes and leaned against the rail. "I can't wait to get out of the desert and back to green pastures. The smell of wet hay. Galloping clop of my friends."

"I'm as ready as you, but I don't ever want to see another horse." Dom grimaced. "But Panel 5, Mel. Room 6."

"That's what's kept me on edge since you called. We gotta make sure those three drums weren't involved. Then we have to do whatever is necessary to keep anyone else from surveying the damage down here."

"Is it possible this was just a freak series of false alarms?" asked Dom.

"Not a chance in hell. The alarms went off in sequence. You could track the radiation from Room 6 to the fence. The weirdest part of the whole damn thing, aside from the blood, of course, is the ventilation alarm never went off. Any contaminated particulate would have been picked up long before the fence alarm. Almost like somebody carried a sealed radioactive source or something else radioactive from Room 6 to the fence."

The steel-framed conveyance hummed the entire four-minute descent. When the door finally opened, their eyes adjusted from the bright light of the elevator to the dimly lit underground. Straight ahead, a long dark corridor invited them into a shadowed tunnel. Salt crunched lightly underfoot as they walked to the electric transport. With three rows of seats, the vehicle looked more like an amusement park shuttle than a repository conveyance.

Mel pushed the start button. "My training's expired on driving down here. Add that to the list of insufficient training."

A dull hum of the transport and soft crunching of tires on salt provided the only sounds on the half-mile drive to the transition line that designated the start of the contaminated area. Mel parked the cart in front of the red heart-shaped box of chocolates that someone had tacked to the wall, reminding staff of the Valentine's Day fire. Both men stepped out of the transport just long enough to don personal protective equipment, slipping into slick white Tyvek suits, booties, and nitrile gloves, taping all connections. They pulled their full-face respirators on, tightened the straps, and pressure tested the seals. Preventing inhalation of residual americium or plutonium remaining from the drum fire was paramount since even the tiniest amount of the alpha-emitting man-made elements could cause lung damage or worse.

Room 6 was typical of every other repository room. Thirty-three feet wide, a thirteen-foot ceiling height, and as long as a football field. The walls and ceiling were covered with a chain-link fence material anchored in place with heavy bolts and buttresses drilled into the salt; the restraint system, maintenance of which Mel had suspended.

Everything appeared normal as they drove deep into the room until they neared the back wall. The transport headlamps illuminated fifty-five-gallon radioactive waste drums stacked neatly to the left, much like cans of soup stacked in a circular pattern in a pantry. Large chunks of salt were scattered to the right intermixed with a handful of toppled drums. The chain-link mesh restraint draped from the ceiling, clearly insufficient to hold back the weight of the salt.

"That could be why the alarm went off," muffled Dom through his respirator. He pointed to a boulder-sized salt chunk, slightly larger than his gut, that had ripped a gaping hole in a drum.

"Why isn't my meter singing?" Mel slapped the side of the radiation detector. "I should be seeing something at ten feet, but I've got almost no increase in dose."

Dom shrugged. "Keep that probe out front. Had all my kids, but I don't need any extra problems down there, if you know what I mean."

Gripping the eight-inch handle with a three-inch pancake-shaped sensor at the end, Mel moved forward. He passed the silver disk across the gap in the damaged drum. The needle pegged when the namesake sensor neared a torn yellow plastic bag protruding from the hole.

"Stay a few steps behind me. If I jump back, I don't need you on my heels." Mel continued past the drums.

Dom stopped to study two toppled drums. Scrap metal, tools, and discarded PPE, typical of much of the waste deposited in WIPP, lay scattered on the ground next to one drum that had popped its lid. The second drum had a large hole in the side. A shredded yellow plastic rad bag, commonly used for radioactive waste, lay half in and half out of the hole. The bag was coated with a congealed gel. He rolled the drum in a half circle and wiped off the label.

"It's one of ours," said Dom. "But the damn thing is empty. How the hell did the contents get out?" He looked around as though the answer might be nearby. "And what's this goopy shit dripping down the side? Smells…ugh." He gagged inside his respirator. Though the cartridge filters captured the tiniest of particulates, his head had been close to the drum long enough for noxious vapor to seep through. "Never mind. I know what it is."

No response from Mel. His eyes were fixed on something else. "Look at this."

Dom skirted around the drums and stood next to Mel. "That's not supposed to be there."

CHAPTER 5

NEW CHAMBER

DOM DIRECTED HIS flashlight beam through the opening in the back wall of Room 6. "It's a cave or something." He stepped over rubble, squeezed through the hole, and panned the beam side to side and high and low. "What the hell?" His boots crunched a pebbly mix of limestone-like material as he stepped deeper into the dark. "It's like we're in the caverns. Only this room is dry and brittle."

The men gazed at geologic features that extended into the chamber well beyond the light. They pulled off their respirators and walked deeper into the dark, staying next to the wall shared with the repository.

Dom half chuckled. "Guess that Burro guy was right, and they blew him off."

"Burro? Like donkey?"

"Dr. Burro or Barrow or something like that. He documented that karst geology around here was conducive to sinkholes and caves. There was a write-up on karst in the site characterization package they gave us when we came here."

"Right. Like I have time to read that shit." Mel rubbed his hand along the wall. "Kind of surprising they never hit this with one of their drill holes during site characterization."

A few hundred feet from where they entered, the two avid hunters stood next to bedding of what appeared to be a large animal or family of animals. The radiation meter clicked faster. Mel pushed the probe to the wall above the bedding. The staccato beat increased.

"That can't be what I think it is," he said.

Dom nudged dry scat with his boot. "I don't know what it is." He picked up a matted piece of fur the size of an entry rug and moved it toward the pancake probe. The meter zinged. He dropped the fur like a hot potato.

"Something made a bed at the base of the wall," said Mel. "Looks almost too big to be a coyote den." He placed an open hand against the salty stone. "Warm. Judging from the distance to the opening, I'd say this wall is the backside of Room 3. There's a lot of remote-handled waste in those walls. Hot on contact."

"Makes a nice place for an animal to bed down," added Dom. "Something's been bedded down in a radiation field for years. Look at this matted fur. Gotta be a foot thick." He directed the light to an enclave a few yards to the side. "And what are those? Bat bones maybe? And larger bones over there."

Though sweating in the PPE, a cold chill crawled up Mel's spine. "Let's get the hell outta here." He slipped the respirator back on.

An hour later, they had moved the slimy, smelly, empty drum through the opening in the wall and filled the hole with salt blocks that had fallen. They refilled the drum that had spilled then covered the back row of drums with bags of magnesium oxide, the standard filler material used for gaps between waste containers, and left enough undamaged toppled drums to satisfy an investigatory team.

"Haven't worked that hard in years," said Dom, removing his respirator the moment the electric transport cleared the buffer area. "I'm getting old, friend."

"Don't say that. I'm three years older than you. With a little luck, we can convince DOE they don't need to enter the room. Just to be safe, make a new drum and put it somewhere in case we need to 'find' it later." Mel added finger quotes.

"No problem. I'll have it done before DOE shows up."

"We can handle getting dinged for a misplaced drum. Blame it on labeling. We wouldn't survive a breached container." Mel donned a more serious face. "I trust you know the importance of this staying between you and me. If this gets out, there's no way in hell we can bring in that final special shipment. Our bonus disappears, and I don't mean the official bonus."

Dom replied in a bad German accent mixed with a hint of Spanish, "I see nothing! Nothing!" He slipped his legs out of the protective white Tyvek and slid the suit to the side with a shove of his foot. "Do you think Joel will come through? I mean, after…"

"If he wants those three drums at WIPP, he'll come through. He understands that we're the gatekeepers for everything entering this repository." Mel shoved his Tyvek next to Dom's. "But to tell you the truth, it wouldn't break my heart if he called the shipment off. He should just have his guys sink those cans in the Savannah River. Of course, we'd be out of a payday."

Dom bit the inside of his lip. Mel could afford to miss the bonus. He didn't have three wives breathing down his neck for child support or heavy loans accruing interest faster than the national debt.

They dropped their respirators and gloves onto the pile of contaminated clothing. "What do you want to do with our waste?" asked Dom.

"Bag it. Throw it in the bed of my truck with the stuff from this morning. Make sure it's covered with the tarp."

"You can't trash it in town. The city dump has a radiation detector. This crap will set off the alarm the second you drive under the sensor."

"It's not going to the dump." Mel spread a wolfish grin. "There's a lot of desert out there, and I've got a shovel."

Back at Mel's desk, they discussed the day's activities, beginning with a healthy pour from the flask into their coffee.

"I need you to run the plan-of-the-day meeting and the safety meeting. Keep staff on the clean side for a few weeks. Pick a room over there, and we'll start filling it with the truck that came in last night."

"Chuck may have been down there," said Dom, eyebrows raised. "Nobody knows where the hell he is."

"Well, he wasn't there when we cleaned up the place. Until we hear otherwise, we work on the assumption that Chuck left early to go hunting."

"How do you explain blood in the elevator? You said it looked like a butcher shop. That's not somebody slicing a finger on the jagged edge of a drum."

Mel rested his elbows on the desk and buried his face in his hands. "I can't explain the blood. You wouldn't believe how much was on the floor. But if it will make you feel better, I'll track Chuck down." He sat back upright. "Do you think he might have brought his dogs in again?"

"In the shaft? Not even Chuck would be that stupid."

"He's pretty close to those German shepherds. Late shift, bored stiff. I wouldn't put it past him." Mel flipped open Chuck's personnel folder. "He's been written up twice for bringing them on-site."

"Hard to believe he would take them into the underground, but you could be onto something. I'll check with Rip. See if he issued any verbal warnings to Chuck about the dogs. He doesn't always write people up if the issue isn't safety related."

"Let me handle Rip. After you get the staff organized, bring over the current creep log. I want to see what kind of salt movement we've been observing in Room 6. How much have those walls shifted over the last few months? When was the last time we calibrated the micrometers?"

Dom sputtered spiked coffee with a snort.

"I'm serious, Dom. When was the last time you checked them?"

"Micrometers? Are you kidding me? We're talking about deflection that can be measured with a yardstick. That room's been moving, Mel. I've told you a dozen times. Had it in my Friday summaries for at least two months."

"You know I just scan those."

"That's why I've been telling you every Monday morning in our plan-of-the-week. We knew this was coming. We should have been on top of it."

Mel slumped his shoulders more. "I hear you, but that ship has sailed. If we have a paper trail, we'll have to weave our story around what's in place. That's easy enough. Start documenting that we expected a failure. In a few weeks, we'll bury the failure notice in a report to Washington."

"I'll work the documentation."

"Thanks. Can you walk by the fence sensor when you go outside? That sensor had to be a false alarm, but one of us should at least take a look. I need to make a call."

When the door closed, Mel opened the bottom desk drawer, retrieved a bottle, and refilled the flask. He had known Dom since their days at the Nevada Test Site, north of Las Vegas, working at the DOE disposal facility for low-level radioactive waste. NTS was one of few commonsense decisions the government had made, burying radioactive waste in subsidence craters created by underground nuclear tests in the fifties and sixties. The work became so routine, the men found themselves filling their days away from the office. Between the drinking, gambling, and clubs, Mel lost one wife and Dom two. Child support for Mel's two kids and Dom's four, combined with alimony payments, didn't slow the men down at the tables. It wasn't long before they were forced to supplement their income.

Financial opportunities came in the approval of unique radioactive waste items that required a special analysis for one-off waste streams that didn't entirely meet the waste acceptance criteria. Special analyses provided opportunities to work with specific individuals rather than teams of people. Personal relationships were developed. Agreements made. The men justified the clandestine activities and accompanying payments as saving taxpayers money by streamlining approvals to dispose of dangerous materials. Everybody won.

Cockiness, more than greed, caused their downfall. Word got out, and they agreed to leave before a formal investigation was conducted. Resignation letters made no mention of illicit activity.

A month later, both men were working on the Consolidated Incinerator Facility at the Savannah River Site. The CIF was DOE's answer to disposal of tens of thousands of gallons of highly contaminated liquid waste. Though it had been many years since Savannah, the memories were vivid, the disappointment fresh. After treating 10 percent of the planned inventory, CIF operations were suspended. For a decade, advocates had pushed cost effectiveness of incineration and increased site safety through elimination of liquid radioactive waste. After a few short years of operation, those same people complained about safety and cost. The CIF was closed. Mel and Dom maintained their management positions, which, for a dormant facility, required little effort. Mel kept himself busy orchestrating side jobs while Dom dug himself deeper into debt in ill-fated equestrian ventures.

A blast of wind slammed the back door of the admin building shut, startling Mel out of his visit to yesterday. He smiled at the CIF logo on the coffee cup. Over the years, he had developed his own axiom for government facilities: "A world where so many do so little so safely."

"Now that would make a good cup."

It was time to make a call to somebody much closer to that world than himself. He should be calling his DOE counterpart, but that conversation could wait. Mel picked up the phone. Joel was not going to be happy.

*

On the way back to his office, Dom walked by the fence-mounted radiation sensor. A single piece of flannel hung on the lower rung of the three-strand barbed wire atop the chain-link fence. A remnant from the windstorm. With a Phil Mickelson jump, he snagged the cloth.

Rubbing the fabric between his fingers on the way back to the admin building, he never noticed drag marks in the dirt or paw prints the desert wind had nearly erased.

"Looks like something Chuck would wear."

CHAPTER 6

COYOTE CAVERN

BRIAN POKED HIS head around the back end of the truck and yelled, "Trip, hurry the hell up."

In hundred-degree desert heat, sweat dripped from Trip's forehead as he sat cross-legged in the dirt. "Can't do it. Don't you have any tools or anything? Something long that I can stick inside."

"That's not how we do things. Move your ass. We gotta go."

Trip leaned his head forward and peered into the dark opening. Sprinkles of dirt fell into the circular access, rippling the black water below. Dense air hung above the hole, preventing the dank organic smell from dissipating. He held his breath one more time and lowered his face an inch below the rim.

"Nope. Can't do it." He pushed himself back from the opening. "Are you sure there's no spiders in there? You know I don't do spiders."

"Dude, it's your job, and there are no freakin' spiders."

Brian tried to sound convincing, but when he removed the cover, a black widow web loaded with egg sacks coated the underside of the rim. He cleared the erratically spun web while Trip was uncoiling the hose. His friend would have freaked and quit on the spot had the sticky mesh entangled his hand like it had Brian's.

Returning to a pretzel position a foot back from the opening, Trip tossed a handful of gravel into the hole. "Then you do it!" He pulled a can of dip from his hip pocket, smacked it twice on his leg to compact the contents, removed the shiny aluminum lid, and pinched two fingers of menthol-smelling ground tobacco. He placed the pinch between his cheek and gum, wiped his fingers on dirty jeans, and spit into the hole, dribbling a brown line back to his leg.

"It's your freakin' job, Trip. I worked my ass off to get where I'm at. When you're driving the truck, you get to be the boss, but today ain't that day."

Trip spit again. "You know I don't want to be a driver. Stand behind the truck as long as you want. I ain't putting my head in that hole again."

Brian didn't move.

"Seriously! I don't know how to do it. I'm starving. Come over here and show me so we can finish up and get some food."

"You puss," Brian grumbled. "Get out of the way."

The six-foot, square-shouldered cowboy with wiry sandy-red hair tossed his crusty ball cap onto the ground next to the septic tank access hole. He scrunched the left sleeve of his flannel overshirt all the way to the shoulder, got down on his stomach, and leaned deep inside. Half his body was engulfed in the dark.

"Hold my legs." The damp hole muffled his voice.

Two inches shorter than Brian and thirty pounds lighter, Trip held Brian's legs with one hand and tugged on the hose with the other.

His long arm stretched deep into the black water, Brian unsnagged the suction nozzle. The metal fitting released with a *pop*, flinging black droplets in every direction.

"My bad."

"Thanks, asswipe," mumbled Brian as he pulled his head out. He'd been splattered before.

He removed the flannel work shirt and used the dry right sleeve to wipe speckled spots off his chin. While he wiped, his gaze drifted into the distance, beyond the vast expanse of desert. The nozzle clanking against the truck brought him back to his small New Mexican town.

"Got shit in my mouth again." He spit. "You're doing it next time, dickhead."

"You should be thanking me. I coulda let go of your feet." Trip whiffed his hand across Brian's shoulder. "Let's go."

Twenty minutes later, they were at Coyote Cavern, the local

watering hole for redneck locals and blue-collar workers from the radiation dump. Grady and Arturo were already parked at their normal table in the back corner when Trip and Brian walked in.

Arturo looked up from his iced tea. "Rich texted. He and Fernie are on the way."

"Gives us time to eat some fries before Fernie wolfs them all down," replied Brian, his eyes on Cathy as she made her way to the table.

"Just a pitcher," said Grady, adding with puppy dog eyes, *"please."*

"And a large red chile fries," said Trip. "With cheese, please."

"Sure thing, hon," replied the voluptuous thirtysomething waitress wearing a stained baby-blue uniform.

She leaned toward Brian. All eyes at the table followed movement of her chest, each boy praying for the thread securing the bulging top button to give way.

"You gotta little sumpin' sumpin' there, darlin'."

Cathy licked her thumb and wiped a black spot off his cheek. "Got it." She tousled his hair and returned to the kitchen to drop the order.

Brian caressed the cheek. "Hope she doesn't lick that thumb."

"Why's that?" asked Grady, his tanned, callused hands cradling a beer.

"Just had my head inside a tank. If that was a black spot, it was shit."

No repulsive reflexes around the table. Growing up in New Mexico towns, they all had septic tanks at one time or another and had their own stories of working in the black water.

Arturo gestured to Trip. "Thought that was his job now."

"Nozzle got stuck." Trip diverted his eyes to the hardwood floor. "I don't know. Something in that hole felt like bad news…"

"Yeah. It was full of shit." Grady pinched his nose. "Candy ass. What the hell did you think the job was? You work for a septic pumper."

"I know. I know. Seen Brian do it a hundred times, but it's different when you're right there. Looking into the dark. It's creepy. Like something's hiding in the shadow, waiting to…" He shuddered. "I don't want to think about it. I can pump them okay, just can't put my head in the hole."

Brian leaned back in his chair and donned an authoritative manner. "I told you, it's all in the approach. A septic tank is like a bottle of fine wine. Once you open it, you have to let it breathe for a minute, *before* you stick your freakin' head inside. It just needed to air out."

Arturo snorted. "What the hell do you know about fine wine?"

"I had a little trouble in the beginning," continued Brian, ignoring the remark. "I'll teach you the tricks of the trade. Won't be long, and just like me, you'll love this job."

The waitress returned with the pitcher and a pile of fries smothered in a classic New Mexican red chile sauce. Rich and Fernie arrived at the same time, gawking at Cathy as they fumbled with the chairs.

"I should wash my hands." Brian grabbed a handful of fries, stuffed the wet pile into his mouth, and licked his fingers on the way to the restroom. He stopped for a moment next to the bar when pictures of Big Ben and the London Eye flashed across the television in prelude to a soccer game that was about to begin. The clock tower and oversized Ferris wheel looked exactly like photos in his old high school history textbook.

"Can we get another?" asked Fernie Montoya, pointing to the pitcher.

Rich gestured to the TV above the bar. "Cathy, can they change that to a real sport?"

"Leave it there," pleaded Fernie in a light Hispanic accent. He and Arturo the only ones at the table with copper skin not entirely attributed to the desert sun. "Soccer is the most popular sport in the world. We should have had a team in school."

Grady snickered. "Didn't you get your ass kicked enough in high school?"

"Man, you don't know what a real sport is." Fernie turned to Arturo. "What'd I miss?"

"You missed them kicking the ball on that side of the field." He pointed left. "Then you missed them kicking the ball on the other side of the field."

"Ass," replied Fernie, eyes locked on the game.

Brian returned and nudged Trip on the shoulder. "Now's your chance. Sylvia just came in. Go ask her out."

"I can't just walk up and ask her out."

"Sure you can."

"What if she says no?"

Arturo snorted again. "Of course she'll say no, *ese*. You have to play the odds. Ask a hundred girls, eventually one of them will say yes."

Rich wiped beer foam from his lip and added, "For you, maybe one-fifty. Better get started."

"Like you're doing any—"

Fernie shot his hand up. "*Shhhh! Càllate.* Did you hear that?"

"What are you babbling about?" Brian started to turn his head, but Fernie's rapid nod suggested he shouldn't.

In a nearby booth, four men wearing light-blue short-sleeved shirts with embroidered names above the left pocket were talking about the nuclear waste dump. Three men were trying to keep the conversation low, but the fourth man didn't own an inside voice.

"It's happening again," said one man, the name Marcus embroidered on his shirt. "Mario heard it. Exactly the same as last time."

The man across from Marcus pulled the brim of his ball cap down and shook his head in disgust. "Every time something like this happens, we get more training. I'm tired of it. Why can't they just let us do our jobs?"

"*It's not a training issue*," hissed Marcus, his Spanish accent prominent. "Something is going on down there. Mario told me."

The loud man huffed. "Mario's full of shit. You know he's still seeing a shrink from the last time."

"I would too," replied Marcus, "if I got contaminated like he did. We don't know what is in that waste. Radiation causes cancer. He was down there breathing it in while we were all topside."

"I was topside," said the smallest man at the table, the name Craig on his shirt. His hand trembled lightly as he raised his glass for a drink. "Still got dosed from the vent. A few millirem of radiation. The DOE guy told me it wasn't much. Not to worry. Said a little dose never killed anybody."

"Nothing to worry about *now*." Marcus scoffed. "Cancer is like a cougar, man. She'll stalk you like a big cat and pounce when you get older."

"Marcus is right," said the loud man. "You can't believe the government. They're covering their ass. They still won't tell the truth about the last time. We know damn well that wasn't an accident. WIPP went fifteen years without a single problem, and then a salt truck catches fire. A week later, a drum catches fire. *Spontaneously!* Something is not right."

Ball Cap looked from one man to the next. "We all know the last time wasn't an accident, but who cares? We got a good gig going. Mario telling people he hears a dog down there will cause nothing but trouble. If he paid attention to his job, maybe he wouldn't be hearing things. Nothing can live in a salt mine. What the hell is his game, anyway?" He mocked a howl. *"Arruuuuu. Arruuuuu."*

The loud man's face turned serious. He lowered his voice. "That's not how it sounds."

"How would you know?" asked Ball Cap.

"I wasn't going to tell anyone this 'cause, man, I need this job. *Swear you won't say anything.*"

The men leaned into the center of the table.

The loud man leaned in and whispered, "I heard it too."

CHAPTER 7

FIRST SIGHTING

FERNIE GRABBED THE "oh shit" handle above the door as the truck bounced over the rutted dirt road. His coal-black hair scraped the top of the cab with each jolt. "Do you believe those guys at the Cavern?"

"They had to know we were listening," replied Grady, sitting in the middle of the bench seat, Arturo driving.

"You didn't see their faces. The look in their eyes. Like they were scared, *ese*. Really scared."

Grady bounced into Arturo, then back into Fernie. "My dad works at WIPP. He never talked about the accidents, but he was real quiet after they happened. I think it was classified or something."

"Classified?" Fernie laughed. "It's just radioactive waste they put down there. Why would a pile of waste be classified?"

"I've dumped a few waste piles that I never want anyone to know about," said Arturo. "If you get my drift."

"I'm being serious." Grady elbowed Arturo in the side. "You remember a few years ago when they had those fires. Nobody believed two fires were a coincidence. They never had an accident, then two fires in one week. Come on. I think Dad was spooked, and you know my old man, he doesn't get spooked. He's been kind of weird about his job ever since. When he leaves for work, he's just different. Like he doesn't trust anybody."

"I don't remember much about the fires," said Fernie. "But the howl that guy made. My grandma tells us stories about a howling wolf.

Those guys. Their eyes. They had the same wide eyes as my grandma when she tells her stories."

Arturo shoved Grady enough to push him into Fernie. "Don't be stupid. My mom tells the same stories about a lone wolf that followed the family up from Mexico. None of that shit is real. Think about it. Sometimes the story is about a wolf that protected the family on the long walk. Howled in the night to scare off bandits. Sometimes they say the wolf has crazy eyes and is looking for lost kids or kids who don't behave. They used those stories to scare us when we were little."

Fernie leaned his cheek against the glass and whispered, "*Fantasma del Gris.*"

"What the hell does that mean?" Grady asked as Arturo pulled to a stop in front of a large mesquite bush at the edge of a dirt clearing.

Before Fernie could answer, Brian slapped an open palm against the hood. "Damn, you guys are slow." Beer in hand, he moved back to the blazing fire and pushed at the embers with a stick, sending glittering orange sparks into the night, the closest thing to fireflies in New Mexico.

Grady hollered to Trip after relieving himself in front of the truck. "Yo, *Pop-a-Top*, toss me one of those."

Trip tossed a can. "Don't call me that, asshole." His dad, a long-haul trucker, had given him the handle when he was six. He hadn't seen the old man since he was seven. "And move away from the truck next time you gotta piss."

"It's still a good handle," mumbled Grady. "Even if your old man gave it to you."

Trip held out a second can. "Arturo?"

"Don't offer that to him," snapped Grady.

"I'm just kidding. The good old days. Remember?"

"I remember some of them," replied Arturo. "But I don't miss them. Doc gave me a choice. Said if I liked beer, I could have beer. If I liked birthdays, I could have birthdays, but I can't have both."

"I like birthdays," said Trip.

Fernie covered his face with his hands. "He doesn't mean it like that. If he drinks, it'll kill him."

"I thought that only happened to old guys and alcoholics."

"Something about me having a weak liver. Didn't help that Fernie and I drank a case a day the summer before I quit high school."

Fernie twisted a grin. "And maybe a little vodka."

"When Fernie went back to school that left me alone to drink by myself. Doc said my liver looked like an eighty-year-old alcoholic's." He placed a hand on the right side of his stomach. "Was an El Paso doc too. Knew what he was talking about."

Brian crushed his empty and tossed it into the fire. "You girls gonna stand around yapping, or we gonna shoot?" He reached into the truck and retrieved two .22-caliber rifles from the gun rack mounted across the back window. He popped the clip out of the first to make sure it was full, then popped it back in, checked the safety, and handed the rifle to Trip. He repeated the process with the second rifle, handing it to Fernie, who forced a frown.

"Ahh, man. Why the twenty-twos? I wanted something with a little more *umph*."

Brian pulled his pockets inside out. White pouches hung empty. "Rabbit ears, dude. When you're buying the ammo, I'll bring the ought-six. Forty bucks gets five hundred rounds for the twenty-two. The ought-six cost ten times that."

"Dad's got ought-six shells in the shed," offered Rich. "A couple hundred rounds, but he don't have the rifle anymore. I'll bring 'em next time."

Brian swiveled the truck-mounted spotlight toward the dark desert. Sets of red eyes began to glow in the mix of creosote and mesquite shrubs at the far edge of the open area.

Pop! Pop! Pop! Trip fired at eyes to the left. Fernie popped a few at eyes on the right.

Red-eyed targets disappeared as soon as the gunfire started, leaving the shooters plinking at shadows in the distance.

"Got one," said Trip.

Fernie raised his rifle. "The hell you did."

Brian reloaded and handed the guns to Rich and Grady, who commenced plinking at their own dark spots. Both stopped at the same time. Silence replaced gunfire. Rich, Grady, Brian, and Fernie stared dead ahead. Nobody said a word.

Reaching into the truck bed for another beer, Trip hollered, "Y'all ain't out. I only counted seven."

"What the hell is that?" asked Brian in a nervous whisper. He adjusted the light, but whatever was across the clearing was obscured in the brush, leaving only the eyes reflecting in the night.

"Aw, shit," said Trip, returning from the truck. "Is that a horse?"

Grady transitioned to full hunting mode. He lined his sights, ready to shoot the moment he identified the target. "Horse. No way. Eyes are too close together."

"I think it's a coyote," whispered Fernie. "It must be standing on a rock or something."

An ominous rumble rolled across the dirt clearing. The rumble increased in intensity.

Arturo grabbed the rifles and handed them to Brian. "*We gotta go.* We're in deep shit if we hit a horse."

They jumped into the trucks and spit dirt and gravel from the rear tires as they sped away.

"Man, did you see those eyes?" asked Brian when they were almost to Trip's house. "Freakin' cobalt."

"I only saw blue eyes."

"Yeah, dipshit. Cobalt blue. From art class. Didn't you have Miss Muller in tenth grade?"

"Naw, I took Spanish with Mrs. Cordova. My mom always wanted me to be bilingual. I speak a little French too. Remember Ms. Leroux?"

Brian rocked a grin. "Everybody remembers Ms. Leroux, but I never had her for a class."

"Had her in ninth. Transferred out 'cause she was too hard, but I still know some words." Trip stepped out after the truck stopped in his drive. "See you tomorrow."

Across town, Arturo dropped Fernie off then continued to his trailer, the sixth slot in a small mobile home park nearby. Grady grabbed a six-pack from the cooler and followed Arturo inside. They sat at a wobbly table in the paneled kitchen, a bag of chips between them.

Confidence building with each beer, Grady emptied the last can. "Let's go back and shee what the hell we were shooting at."

"Dude. It was a horse. I don't want to be anywhere near there if we hit it."

"It was shtill shtanding when we left," replied Grady, alcohol in full control. "Most we did wazh wing it. Let's go see if there's blood or tracks or anything. Come on. What the hell elsh is there to do?"

"Fine," huffed Arturo.

"I been drinking all night." He hiccuped and belched at the same time. "You better drive."

"Like you had a choice."

Grady yanked another six-pack from the cooler and finished the first beer before they exited the trailer park. A few minutes later, they pulled into the same spot next to the fire pit. Heat still radiated from red coals.

Arturo reached behind the seat and pulled out a twelve-inch steel-handled flashlight.

"You got a marg…a Maglite?" asked Grady.

"Fernie left it in my truck. His brother gave it to him." He blasted the bright LED beam into the desert.

"More to the…to the…to the…there."

Grady staggered in the direction of the light, Arturo a few feet behind. At the edge of thorny shrubs, Grady's feet stopped short. His body swayed forward.

"*Do you see something?*" whispered Arturo, stopping just as quick. The flashlight blinked out.

"I gotta take a leak." Grady swayed forward and back.

"Ass. You scared the shit out of me." He slapped the steel cylinder into his palm. The light blinked on for a second and went out.

"Gotta take a leak. No…No…I'm gonna throw up. No…Gonna piss, then throw up."

"Just do it, and let's go. There ain't no horse out here."

Grady stepped behind a cluster of mesquite. A zip followed by a hose stream broke the stillness.

Chomp!

The stream stopped. A bloodcurdling scream jolted Arturo backward.

"*Aaaaaiiiiiii! Myyyyyyyy...*"

Arturo smacked the light against his leg, trying again to turn it on.

Another *chomp!*

Silence.

"*Grady?*" Arturo's voice was quiet, shaky, and two octaves higher than normal. "*Grady?*" Nervous anger mixed with fear. "Stop dicking around."

He backed up, flicking the switch on and off repeatedly. Nothing.

"I'm going to the truck."

Arturo turned around just as the light clicked on. He turned back and pointed the beam. No Grady.

"Come on, asshole." He panned the light from left to right while shuffling short steps toward the brush. The light reflected off a pool of urine in the center of muddy sand. He stepped around the mess and started to raise the beam. A glimpse of four cobalt-blue eyes level with his own forced him to backpedal and fall into the newly created mud. The light fell to the side. The beam vanished.

Thick, heavy breathing consumed the silence. Short inhales and long exhales accompanied crackling of dry bushes being pushed aside. He tried to move, but his body questioned the command.

Come on, legs, get the hell out of here.

Words resonated in his mind, but jellied legs refused to comply. Petrified arms rejected orders to cover his face. Eyelids refused to close, forcing him to watch two mammoth animals creep forward, ears back, pinned tight against matted fur. Angry, narrow eyes. Grady's arm hanging from the mouth of the larger beast, complete with the flannel sleeve of his best friend's shirt. Blood dripping to the ground absorbed as fast as desert rain on dry sand.

Another chomp. The arm disappeared.

Both animals crept closer, their long noses coated in blood. Grady's blood. The terrifying, hairy beasts were so close they peppered Arturo's face with droplets of bloodied saliva. Hot breath blasted a smell of warm flesh. Enormous fangs pushed drooling lips to the side.

Arturo stretched out, grasping for anything, finding the flashlight. He pounded it into the ground. The high-powered bulb blasted on. The light zipped across the ground, passed over what was left of Grady, and shined directly into glassy eyes. A chorused yelp. Both animals disappeared in the darkness.

He pulled the light to his chin. Trembling hands squeezed the life out of the steel casing. Chattering teeth, the only sound in the desolate dark. Tears flowed. He wanted his mom. Would she believe him? Would anyone believe him?

CHAPTER 8

TOWN HALL MEETING

SATURDAY EVENING, BRIAN and Trip occupied two chairs in the middle of a large conference room at the local motel, both eyeing the pretty lady standing at the podium. With the voice of a teenage girl, the dimpled professional thanked four men sitting at the table, then began her presentation.

"As Dr. Bradford mentioned, my name is Rebecca Olsen, but everybody calls me Becca. I am a project manager with the US Fish and Wildlife Service, which I will refer to as 'the service' throughout my presentation."

She squeezed the sides of the podium, trying desperately to steady knocking knees.

"Let me start from the beginning. In 2002, the service initiated a reintroduction program for the *Canis lupus baileyi* to return Mexican gray wolves to their natural habitat in southeast New Mexico and southwest Texas. NEPA for this effort has been completed, as required by the CFR, and we received a ROD for the FEIS earlier this year."

A voice from the crowd carrying the drawl of a local interrupted. "Excuse me, miss, but what does all that there mean?"

"I'll be happy to take questions at the end of my presentation," replied the junior project manager, standing in front of the largest crowd of her career.

Becca had left nothing to chance for her first solo assignment. A successful meeting and subsequent wolf reintroduction would finally command respect from a boss who acted as though she didn't exist. She had organized the meeting, developed the slides, and practiced the talk a dozen times in front of the mirror. She even videoed the presentation to critique her performance. She had not, however, practiced interruptions. Butterflies flocked in her stomach. She lost her place. Her throat grew hot and dry, like desert sand in the afternoon. Nervous fingers reached for the water bottle. She took a quick sip, then fumbled with a cap that refused to screw back on.

After an eternal moment of silent fidgeting, she continued. "My name is Rebecca Olsen. Oh. I said that already. Um. The Fish and Wildlife Service is located in Falls Church, Virginia. They, I mean we, or the service, actually, first reintroduced wolves into the area under this program in 2002. After one year, all the wolves had been killed or died of natural causes or other human interface causes, like getting hit by cars. In 2012, we introduced two additional groups of wolves. Those ten wolves disappeared in less than two months. Nine carcasses were recovered. One alpha female was never located even though she had a tracking collar."

She gazed professionally over the top of the crowd, eyes focused on the upper portion of the back wall, heeding a friend's warning to never look directly at the audience.

"Because the last wolves were deliberately killed, we delayed this final reintroduction for five years, which, as you can tell, has turned to ten. During that time, our studies have shown that an increased human presence, use of guard dogs, spotlights, and alarms, combined with turbo fladry can be very effective in controlling loss of livestock. We now have the resources and infrastructure in place to assist any farmer who makes a request through our website. This brings us to why we are here today. Very soon, we will make another reintroduction of three males and three females. The alpha pair in this set has three subordinates."

A hand raised in the back of the room, causing an inadvertent squeeze that popped the cap off the water bottle. Once again, she lost her place. This time, stage fright together with audience murmurs compelled her to pretend she was finished.

"Are there any questions?" Her doe eyes locked on the lone extended hand.

Boots scuffed the floor as the man moseyed up the center aisle to the microphone.

"Miss, what are some of those terms you were floatin' about?"

"May we have your name for the record?" asked Becca, further irritating an already suspicious crowd.

"Yes, ma'am. My name is Vernon Marshal," he replied with a slow drawl. "What are some of those odd terms and such? And that turbo thing."

"Turbo fladry is a system we can install to keep the wolves separated from active livestock areas."

"Uh-huh. What kinda system we talkin' about?"

Becca straightened her five-foot-six frame and brushed away a short strand of chestnut hair that had escaped the slicked-back bun. Having worked on turbo fladry systems, she was relieved to have a question to which she could reply with confidence.

"Well," she began with a self-assured smile, "turbo fladry is an electric wire with red plastic flags. We—"

Vern interrupted. "A wire and a plastic flag. That what we're callin' a system these days?"

A hearty laugh burst out.

"No offense, little lady, but that don't give me a whole lotta confidence that *your* wolves won't be killin' *my* cattle. I was around these parts the last two times y'all set those bastards loose on us. A little wire and a red flag ain't gonna keep them outta my herd."

Becca defaulted to defense. "Depredation is a natural act, sir. The wolves are just defining their territory. They were here first. You need to remember this is their rightful habitat."

Dr. Bradford stood and shouldered Becca to the side. "Thank you, Mr. Marshal, for the excellent questions. First, let me try to help with the 'terms and such.'"

Bradford's nauseating fake drawl was obviously intended to appease the crowd. Standing uncomfortably at his left shoulder, Becca didn't know whether to walk behind him and take her seat on the opposite side or stand still and wait for direction. Her feet made the decision, choosing to stay put. She clasped her hands in a fig leaf posture and forced an awkward smile.

"CFR is the Code of Federal Regulations. It's another way of sayin' 'the law.' NEPA is the National Environmental Policy Act, a review of which is required for any environmental disturbance on federal lands. We received a Record of Decision, also called a ROD, for the Final Environmental Impact Statement, which is the FEIS mentioned by our little Miss Olsen."

Little Miss Olsen? Becca's smile faded behind a clenched jaw.

"Oh, and GPS is, of course, the global positioning system."

Over the next ten minutes, Bradford provided vague answers to specific questions, leaving the crowd suspicious and unsatisfied, but quiet.

"Basically, it's all your government BS that we didn't get no say in," said Vern. "And what's that there depredication the young lady got so upset about?"

Bradford turned to Becca, who whispered, "Depredation."

"Depredation is what we call it when a wolf attacks livestock," explained Bradford. "The service treats depredation very seriously. We monitor it as closely as we monitor animal movement, and in rare instances we will relocate aggressive wolves to more suitable areas where we are better able to control the animal's behavior."

"Then relocate them bastards to your own backyard," yelled someone from the back.

Bradford ignored the remark, shifted to the side, and nodded for Becca to continue.

Next in line stood Stan Cady, an old cowboy with perfect posture, a leather face that matched his boots, and little trust in the overdressed professionals at the front table. Stan cleared his throat too close to the mic, blasting a phlegmy throttle through the room. "How come nobody told me y'all were planning this? Didn't work out so great the last time, like you said."

The room reverberated agreement.

After the not-so-subtle admonishment from Bradford, Becca was not about to ask the man to state his name. "Sir, we sent multiple notices to every registered address in four counties in New Mexico and twelve counties in Texas. More than forty thousand notices were distributed in the last six months to farmers all over this part of the country."

The rolling grumble frustrated Becca. During the entire time Bradford stood at the podium lying to these people, nobody made a sound.

"We ain't *farmers*, miss," snapped Mr. Cady. "We're *ranchers*. I run cattle on sixteen sections smack-dab in the middle of that there spot where you want to release those cattle-killin' wolves."

Trip whispered to Brian, "What's a section?"

"One square mile of land."

"Why didn't he just say that?"

"*Ranchers*," continued Becca. "Sorry about that. But, still, the service has provided all the information on our website for more than a year."

Dub Phillips stood erect three seats down from Trip. With a booming voice, the man had no use for a microphone. "I lost six head the last time you yahoos come out here all the way from DC and did this to us. And now you want to go and do it again." He pointed up two rows to an older man sitting quietly. "Samuel there lost ten head. And I heard a guy in Texas lost twenty-six."

A weathered old man with skin a shade darker than Fernie's leaned into Trip and whispered in his ear, "*Fantasma del Gris.*"

"Let me tell you plain and simple, miss," continued Dub. "You put those wolves out there with my cows, and I'll kill every damn one of 'em."

Dr. Bradford again shouldered Becca to the side. She secured her position on his left, unconsciously coiling a loose strand of hair around a finger and chewing her bottom lip.

"As Ms. Olsen is trying to explain, though not very well, the purpose of this meeting is to *gather* your input. We are here to *listen*. To understand all of your issues and concerns. We will gather data to include in a formal assessment *before anything is decided*. A second meeting will be held right here next Tuesday. In the meantime, I *assure you* we will be taking everyone's comments into consideration."

As the meeting ended, a line of individuals gathered in front of Bradford. Brian and Trip headed toward the back where Becca was standing alone against the side wall.

"What'd that guy whisper to you during the meeting?" Brian asked.

"Something in Spanish. I'm pretty sure he said, 'phantom from Greece.'"

"That doesn't make any sense."

"I could barely hear him. The guy looked like he spent all day in the sun. Kind of smelled like it too."

"Like we smell any better." Brian held out his hand. "Ms. Olsen, I'm Brian, and this is Trip."

"Are you *ranchers* too?" she asked, pent-up anger still brewing from her failed attempt at running the meeting.

"Naw. My mom owns a half acre north of town," replied Trip. "She wanted me to come and see what's up. We don't have any animals or anything, so I don't think we care. But Mrs. Olsen, Brian and I wanted to ask you something."

Trip's crooked smile helped relieve her stress. The junior project manager, impeccably dressed in a tan pencil skirt and a ruffled black blouse with tiered sleeves, uncrossed her arms and began to relax.

"It's *Miss* Olsen, but call me Becca."

"We wanted to ask you a question about wolves," said Brian. "We might have seen one last night not far from town. It was dark, and some of us were spotlighting rabbits."

"Spotlighting? What's spotlighting?"

"Just shooting rabbits at night," replied Trip matter-of-factly. "You know, shine a light and shoot at their eyes when they glow in the dark. Having some fun on a Friday."

"You shoot poor little bunnies *for fun!* What did they ever do to you?"

Trip backpedaled faster than a wide-eyed deer mouse bumping into a rattlesnake. "We don't hit too many. I mean, we just shoot at them. They're hard to hit in the dark, and they usually scatter when they hear gunfire."

"Good for them!"

"But last night, we saw some blue eyes out in the desert," said Brian. "They didn't move, even with guns blasting. What kind of animal would have blue eyes? I've seen yellow and red. We thought it might have been a horse, but could it have been one of your wolves?"

"Did you shoot it?"

"We're not stupid," replied Trip, disappointed Becca didn't share their enthusiasm for the nighttime activity. "You can get in real trouble for shooting somebody's horse."

"Well, it wasn't a wolf. We haven't released any yet. Dogs, coyotes, wolves, they can have blue eyes, but it's pretty rare. They are almost always a gold or yellow. Same with a horse. Blue is not very common. The eyes glow because animals have a layer of tissue at the back of the eye that lets them see at night. It's called a tapetum lucidum."

Trip grinned. "That's what I told Brian."

"Yeah, 'cause you're the smart one."

"Do you guys want to get out of here? I need a bucket of ice cream and a spoon, but I'd settle for a Froyo."

Trip raised an eyebrow. "That's like ice cream, right?"

"Yes, but I haven't seen a place in town yet."

Both boys pursed their lips considering the alternatives: a popsicle at the gas station or a tub of ice cream from Walmart. Before they could offer a suggestion, she modified the request.

"Or maybe somewhere we can get a beer?"

"We know just the place."

Inside Coyote Cavern, dull yellow lighting hung in the air like dust behind a pickup truck on a dirt road. A strong whiff of stale beer nearly pushed Becca back out the door, but after spending the day with Bradford, even a dimly lit dive was welcome relief.

Trip and Brian went straight to their regular table, a thick slab of dark wood that matched the cowboy-infused greasy burger joint decor. Heavy wooden chair legs scraped the wood floor as the two quickly sat. Both watched Becca struggle with her chair, Brian realizing too late he should have assisted their new friend.

"Thanks, guys. I had to get out of there. Dr. Bradford is an ass. A pompous ass. Interrupting me like that and taking over *my* presentation. I hate him."

"Who was that guy anyway?" asked Brian.

Becca placed her elbows on the table and cupped her hands over her face. "My boss."

Trip shoved Brian and laughed. "Bosses can be like that. But, I mean, you were using a lot of big words and things I never heard of. Brian graduated in the top ten of our class, and he didn't know 'em either."

"He's still an ass," she said, allowing a soft smile to expose shallow dimples and perfect teeth. "Okay, I'll dumb it down next time."

The boys shrugged.

"I don't mean it like that. It's just…the meeting didn't go anything like I expected. I worked so hard to pull this release together, and it can only work if the public trusts us. After Bradford's BS…" She released a dejected sigh. "All I ever wanted to do was help wolves. I've loved them my whole life. I talked about them so much as a kid, my dad took me to a forested wolf sanctuary just so I could play with wolf pups."

Brian sank away in a vision of lush green forest that disappeared when clinking glasses were placed on the table.

"For as long as I can remember, I always played Ranger Becca games. My dollies were the bad people who attacked wolves, and I was the ranger who protected them. We moved east when I was nine, but I never lost that feeling of wanting to protect wolves." She sighed and returned to the topic at hand. "Maybe I should have assumed nobody read the website."

"You can definitely assume nobody read the website," said Brian. "Those ranchers are in the field most of the day. They come home at night and work in the garage or the barn, but they're not sitting around on a computer reading government notices."

Becca pinched the bridge of her nose to squeeze away a headache. "That explains the blank stares. When I presented this in Odessa and Midland, nobody complained about the website."

"'Course not." Trip snickered. "Texans don't care if you release wolves in New Mexico, just like we wouldn't care if you were letting them loose somewhere in Texas."

"I was wondering why the crowd was so small at those venues. We had eight people at one place and eleven at another." She sighed again. "Everybody was so nice."

Becca took a sip of beer. "I've been thinking about what kind of animal you saw in the desert. What's more interesting than the eye color is that it didn't leave when you were shooting. Most animals would have scampered off at the first shot. And you said four or five feet above the ground. That's small for a horse and way too big for a dog or coyote or even a wolf, but like I said, there aren't any wolves around here. Did you look to see if a boulder or something was in the area? Maybe a coyote was standing on something? Sometimes they'll hold their ground, but only when they are far enough away. They pretend to be tough, you know, but coyotes are skittish. If you would have walked toward her, she would have run away. I can't imagine a horse sticking around either, though."

"Tell her about the noise," said Trip.

Brian cradled his beer in both hands and leaned in. "After we stopped shooting, the thing just stood there. We couldn't see it, but we could feel it glaring at us. Like it was angry. Then we heard a low rumble. Kind of like a growl maybe."

"How far away did you say it was?"

"Sixty yards. Maybe fifty."

"I'd be surprised if you heard a growl at that distance. I mean, first of all, coyotes don't growl a lot. They yap a kind of high-pitched bark, and they howl, but they only growl when they're threatened. I don't think one would feel threatened that far away."

"It wasn't a regular growl." Brian tightened his grip on the glass. "More like rolling thunder. Loud, long, and low. Kind of made us want to leave."

"You have me super curious. I'm free tomorrow morning before my flight, if you want to go back and look for animal signs. We could try to figure out what you saw."

CHAPTER 9

FIELD TRIP

A DULL-EYED TRIP, hair still wet from the morning shower, climbed down the steps of the single-wide trailer.

"Why'd you say seven? You know today is Sunday, right?"

"Ain't nothing wrong with mornings," replied Brian, almost too spry for the early hour. "Best time of the day."

"I got nothin' against mornings. Get some of my best sleep before noon."

"You're driving," said Brian. "My truck's acting up. Yours better not break down on us again."

"There's nothing wrong with the Suburban."

"Right. Tell that to my elbows. They've been covered in grease the last two times we took your truck."

They climbed into Trip's 1982 dull green Suburban. The camouflage pattern a result of too many beers and excess paint in the shed. The brown stain on the driver's door, a product of Trip's smokeless tobacco habit. On more sober occasions, they had modified the exhaust, installed a lift kit, upgraded the stereo, and added a dual gas tank and a three-foot-long high-intensity LED light bar on the roof.

The Suburban rumbled up next to the cold fire pit where Becca's compact rental was already parked in the dirt. She sat on the hood, feet resting on the bumper, fingers texting on her phone.

"I lived in the desert for two years," she offered as Brian stepped down from the oversized SUV. "Texas desert near Dallas. A lot greener than this."

Brian turned his head east in the direction of the big city. He closed his eyes to the morning sun and once again pictured himself in the top row of the Dallas Cowboys stadium.

Becca slid off the hood and shook a pebble from a yellow sandal that matched her three-quarter-sleeve cotton blouse. "I still miss it sometimes, but the grass in DC is super gorgeous, and the rivers are huge. What does New Mexico have, the Pecos and the Rio Grande River? Honestly, back east, we hardly call those creeks."

"That's redundant," said Trip. "Rio means river in Spanish. So when you say Rio Grande River, you're saying 'river grand river.'"

"Trip speaks Spanish." Brian pointed across the open area. "We were right here, shooting at the rab...Shooting in that direction."

When they approached the shrubs, Becca moved in front, slowed her pace, and studied the ground. "You said Friday night, right? Did it rain or anything since then? I got in Saturday morning."

Trip shook his head. "Nah."

"How about any wind?"

"Lots of wind. It's windy almost every night this time of year."

"Hmm. I don't see any evidence of a horse. That would be pretty obvious, but here's a paw print. Must be windblown because it's wider than any canine. No rocks around for a coyote to stand on." She held an open hand above the imprint. "This is super big."

Trip picked a sweat-stained camouflaged ball cap from the thorns of a mesquite bush. The team name "Chihuahuas" embroidered on the brim, and a baseball above crossed dog bones embroidered on the face.

"This is Grady's hat, Brian. Did the guys come back after we left?"

"They never said anything about coming back, but I haven't seen them since Friday. You sure it's Grady's?"

"Know anyone else who likes the El Paso Chihuahuas?"

"Is that a team?" asked Becca.

"Triple A baseball." Trip slapped the cap against his leg to knock off the dirt.

"I don't see any other footprints," said Becca. "Maybe the wind cleared them out." She followed a clumpy trail of sand into a bush. "Here's a little blood. Whoa! A lot of blood." She glared at Trip. "Looks like *one of you* shot a rabbit or something larger. And here are some scratch marks, like a coyote was pawing at the ground. It's a pretty wide area. Maybe a couple of them were scratching the same place. Weird there aren't any more prints, though."

Becca reached carefully between slender thorny branches of a dead ocotillo plant to free a clump of fur from the inch-long spikes.

"This has to be coyote, but it kind of looks wolfish." She rolled the fur in her fingers. "I'll have a friend look at this when I get home. Maybe you have some large coyotes around here that didn't turn up in my research." She studied the fur. "I'm pretty thorough when I investigate a site. Don't know how I could have missed a species."

The trio walked back to the vehicles and leaned against the side of Becca's rental.

"I better head to the airport. We have another meeting on Tuesday, so I'll be right back." She slid the toe of her sandal back and forth in the dirt. "Dr. Bradford lied when he said we were here this week to gather information. Everything is in motion for us to release the wolves. Next time we come out, it's to let the farmers, I mean, *ranchers*, know that we're turning them loose."

Brian scraped his own toe in the dirt, lightly bumping Becca's sandal. "Seriously? You mean Bradford just lied to everyone. That's why nobody trusts the government."

"Can you guys come to the meeting? I know you said the release doesn't affect you, but it would be really nice to have friendly faces in the crowd. And maybe I'll know something about this fur by then."

"Yeah, we'll be there," replied Brian before Trip could make an excuse not to go. "You leave today and come back Tuesday. Why don't you just stay?"

"I could have stayed through the weekend, but my secretary would have made me fill out paperwork to justify how staying saves the government money. Kind of a pain in the butt. I prefer sleeping in my own bed anyway, and after last night, I have a lot of work to do to ensure the next meeting is perfect."

"Is it really that important?" asked Trip.

"It's super important. I have to prove myself if I'm ever going to get any respect in the office. Bradford treats me like a high school intern. I have a master's degree, dang it." She kicked dust off her sandals. "So you guys work on Sunday? What do you do?"

"I drive a honey wagon." Brian pulled his shoulders back. "Someday, I'm going to have my own truck."

"And I'm his assistant. We don't usually work Sunday, but we had an emergency call."

"That's super cool. I love all that natural stuff, you know. How many bee farms do they have around here? Maybe I can get some honey on my way to the airport. The bottle can't be more than three ounces, though, if I'm going to carry it on the plane."

Trip glanced at Brian, not quite sure how to correct their new friend.

After saying their goodbyes, Becca checked her phone on the way to the airport. Still no reply from boyfriend, Ashton. Once again, she wouldn't know whether he was picking her up from the airport until after she landed.

Brian and Trip stopped at the office to pick up the pumper truck, then cleaned out the Marquez tank a few miles outside of town. The septic system had overflowed so much the pumper truck nearly got stuck in the mud when they were trying to leave.

"Arturo was supposed to bring my jack stands by yesterday," said Brian an hour later when they were back in the Suburban. "I wanted to do the transmission on the Jeep."

"You ain't ever gonna do the transmission. Face it, Bri, the blocks on that Jeep are permanent. Just paint the things."

"If you give me a hand, we could get it done in an afternoon."

"Soon as you have the parts."

"Rich went to a junkyard in Roswell last week to get parts for his truck. He pulled a yoke for me while he was there. That's why I need the jack stands. Swing by Arturo's, and we'll pick them up."

Trip crept through the trailer park to the last single-wide. Lack of rain kept the grass yellow in the small, cluttered yard. Lack of maintenance kept it tall enough to hide tools and parts scattered on the ground.

Arturo was the first in their age group to own his own place, a white trailer trimmed in faded sky blue. The friends moved the mobile home onto the lot by themselves, bending the trailer skirt in the process. The mangled aluminum siding they had pushed underneath the trailer was not helping in the search for the jack stands.

"It's too quiet," said Brian. "He always comes out when we pull up."

"Sunday, dude. If he sleeps like me, he ain't up yet."

"Nobody sleeps like you. Where the hell has he been, anyway? Not like him to blow me off yesterday. He usually calls if something comes up."

"Maybe he's in the Guadalupes," suggested Trip, referring to the nearby mountain range that ran along the New Mexico and Texas border. "Scouting places for deer season. Maybe the Lincoln National Forest? I scouted with him last year about this time."

"Doubt it. Lincoln is a long way to go without telling anyone he left."

Brian pointed at the pair of dirt-encrusted jack stands half hidden in the grass next to the trailer axel. "There they are. You want to throw them in the truck?"

Trip reached for the first one and yanked his hand back with a whip. He bounced backward, wiping both hands feverishly on his jeans as though he were trying to put out a fire.

"*Shit! Spider webs! They're covered in spider webs!*"

Brian rolled his eyes at the familiar dance.

"*Get it off me! Come on! Get it off!*"

"If he was asleep, he's up now." Brian swooshed an open hand across Trip's back, ridding his friend of the imaginary eight-legged killer.

"Did you get it off?"

"Just get the jack stands and let's go."

"Give me a second." Trip cringed. "You know I hate those things."

He stepped back to load three fingers of dip into his mouth and gather his nerves. With half of an old broom, he brushed the web away, then stuck the broom handle through the opening in the jack stands and carried them at arm's length to the Suburban.

"Knock and see if he's home," said Brian, sitting on the bumper and picking goathead stickers from his shoes courtesy of the flat vines sprawling on the ground. The namesake stickers that resembled two pointy horns on the head of a goat had punctured tires on every bike he owned and punctured his bare feet more times than he could count.

"He's got some kind of sewer leak over there." Trip spit and gestured midway along the trailer.

"Sewer's not on that side. It's on the back end. I helped him with the connection." Brian waded through the grass and looked underneath. "There's a stink all right, but it ain't sewage. Tell him it smells like a dead animal, maybe a dog."

Trip climbed the rickety wooden steps and knocked on the thin metal door that bowed outward at the top. Paint on either side blistered from the hot desert sun, not quite as bad as the blistered paint on the shorter vintage single-wide he called home. He glanced at the blue trim along the roof. Someday, he and his mom would have a place as nice as Arturo's.

"He ain't answering." Trip drooled a pool of tobacco mucus over the railing. "I'm going inside."

He opened the door a few inches, slammed it shut, and stumbled down the steps.

Brian inched the door open. An odor of decomposition combined with a scent much like the tank they had just pumped stopped him in his tracks. He pulled his shirt over his nose and moved farther inside. His eyes glazed over, stinging from the ever-present smell of trailer formaldehyde mixed with the new odor. He glanced from the brown paneling in the living room to the chipped Formica countertop to an empty vodka bottle on a chair. A pair of shoes on the floor next to Arturo's lifeless body. A bottle of vodka on his chest. He backstepped out the door.

"We gotta call the police. I think he's dead. *Arturo's dead.*"

Trip reached for the doorknob, but Brian grabbed his wrist.

"Man, don't go in there."

CHAPTER 10

HEALTH PHYSICS SOCIETY

BRENDON TRACY CHECKED his watch from the side aisle of the sparsely crowded conference room on the lower level of the Hyatt Regency in Bethesda, Maryland. The annual Health Physics Society meeting ended at noon, immediately after his presentation. Only 22 of the 140 seats were occupied at the unprecedented Sunday morning session.

He moved quietly to the back wall to refill his coffee and study the remaining attendees. No surprises in the nearly vacant room. Out-of-state attendees had already left to travel home. A few students from local universities stayed for extra credit. One or two overly ambitious kids might ask a question. A small group of professional boy scouts were clustered near the front. Those "do my best to do my duty" employees who had yet to experience corporate downtrodding. Fingers of the future middle-managers tapped excitedly on tablets and laptops, logging notes that would never be used. Three beltway bandits sat on the left. Employees of private companies located within the sixty-four-mile Interstate 495 loop that surrounded Washington DC; the Beltway. Lastly, two men and two women representing non-governmental organizations.

Brendon topped off his cup.

"You're up next," said Ted Anders, a beltway bandit refilling his own cup.

"I'll be quick, Teddy. They've given me an hour, but I've only got forty minutes of slides and could cut that to thirty if you don't ask any hard questions."

"Not today. I've got a report due in the morning. I'll be honest, I haven't paid much attention all week. The only ones you have to worry about are the antinukes. Sorry, I should more politely refer to them as nongovernmental organizations or NGOs. They're the only ones left that could keep you from wrapping up early."

Brendon nodded agreement while he stirred in two sugars.

"The NGOs are on a mission," continued Teddy. "Close the nuclear facility. Doesn't matter which one. Reactor, incinerator, repository, or anything else they can complain about. Guess I should show a little respect. Writing these reports to justify our industry keeps me in business."

Brendon gestured in the direction of three regulars. "They're not bad guys, just different agendas. I expect they'll ask the usual questions. Try to get me to slip up on the record. That's the game we play."

When the meeting facilitator finished reading the introductory bio for the final speaker, Brendon stepped up to the wooden podium and set his cup on the inclined stand. Coffee sloshed over the brim and dribbled down the varnished oak surface, dripping onto his pant leg. A whispered curse boomed through the microphone, echoing among empty seats.

"Sorry about that. Seem to have spilled coffee on my knickers. May need to stand behind this until they dry, if you know what I mean. So start thinking of some questions."

A courteous laugh ruffled through the room.

Brendon delivered his routine opening line intended to grab the audience's attention and imagination.

"Two thousand one hundred and fifty feet below an isolated desert landscape in the middle of an ancient geologic salt bed, a small army of staff busily place radioactive waste into rooms mined out for disposal."

He had given the same presentation at least thirty times, adjusting only the status of operations, which had been continuous from the time the facility opened on March 16, 1999, until the drum fire of February 14, 2014.

"Let's go all the way back to 1957, when the National Academy of Sciences determined that placement of radioactive waste in salt beds provided a promising permanent solution. You geologists in the room know that salt beds creep over time. In a thousand years, the salt will permanently encapsulate everything in the facility. A slow creeping entombment. The perfect solution for dangerously radioactive waste."

He was thankful the facility had finally reopened, having spent three years explaining why an event determined to be "unlikely" by the best scientists in the world had not only occurred but had a disastrous impact. Still, every time he stood behind a podium, most questions were related to the billion-dollar bag of kitty litter.

"For the first eight years, contact-handled waste was disposed at WIPP. As the designation implies, workers move contact-handled containers by hand. In 2007, the first containers of remote-handled waste arrived. Remote-handled drums have a higher surface dose, which requires personnel to employ shielding or other measures when working with the containers. These cans can be warm or hot to the touch, providing a mild heat source in rooms where they are placed."

A student raised her hand and asked about other activities conducted in the repository.

"The underground, or UG, facilities include the radioactive waste disposal panels, a research area, mine safety area, maintenance shops, and the ventilation systems. There are only four access openings in the entire facility. The air intake shaft, exhaust shaft, waste shaft, and salt handling shaft. Staff can use the salt hoist but generally use the waste hoist to enter the UG, which I'm told makes sense. They are government employees, after all."

Another courteous laugh.

"In fact, the elevator car in the waste hoist is a dual conveyance carrier. People on top, waste underneath. Staff and waste are never transported in the same trip."

Another student asked why some waste was low-level and some was designated remote-handled. The question provided a perfect entrée for Brendon's canned monologue on the Atomic Energy Act, the Nuclear Waste Policy Act, and other federal policies. Heavy eyelids began to droop. Perfect. Maybe next time they wouldn't extend the conference until Sunday.

A familiar NGO representative walked to the microphone in the center aisle and spoke before being called upon. "Are you operating at full capacity, and are all areas in the UG open? I've heard that ceiling collapses, which are documented as high risk to staff and the repository, are occurring at a greater frequency. What are you doing to prevent these collapses? Also, six vehicles were contaminated and abandoned after the fire. Are they full of gasoline as reported? If so, are there plans to remove the gas and oil from those vehicles to prevent additional fires?"

Brendon leaned back from the mic and released a professional sigh. Typical. One NGO rep could easily ask six questions in a single breath. But receiving an onslaught of questions in one burst gave him the upper hand. He could choose which questions to omit in the lengthy, boring response he was prepared to provide. In this case, he preferred not to address gas in the abandoned vehicles, for which analyses were ongoing.

He began the response with a discussion of fiscal allocations, comparing current numbers with those before the fire. He explained that budgets and staffing were higher and allowed the audience to come to their own conclusion with regard to what that might mean. He talked about the well-publicized ceiling collapse in Room 4 of Panel 7 that had occurred eighteen months ago. Employees in the underground heard the noise and saw the salt dust. A precautionary evacuation had been implemented. He informed the audience that today's robust preventive maintenance program was keeping everything stable. He neglected to mention a ceiling collapse that occurred a few months before the conference and did not talk about increased salt movement, which was being monitored closely in multiple rooms.

More NGO representatives queued at the mic, waiting to ask their own multipoint questions, most related to safety, environmental releases, the cost of remediation, and, of course, the kitty litter that caused the fire. Like the proficient tennis player he was, Brendon batted back answers to each question, lengthening volleys as needed to avoid controversial rebuttals.

The moderator stood, implying time was up. The latest assault on the government operation was over.

As he stepped down from the dais, Brendon again looked over the room. The senior DOE Headquarters expert on WIPP was confident in his performance until he saw Joel Weiss standing in the back corner. A consultant to DOE and any other agency with deep pockets, Joel was a regular whenever big-dollar decisions were being made. His fingerprints could be found on everything from site management contracts to decisions to build incinerators, vitrification facilities, and other high-value assets.

Brendon packed his bag and headed diagonally toward the exit.

The most expensive suit at the conference intercepted Brendon at the door. "Let's take a walk," said Joel, a John Lovitz doppelgänger complete with receding hairline and nasal voice but lacking the sense of humor. "How have you been, Brendon? Jamie's doing well, I trust? And the kids?"

Consultants. Always dropping family names. Anything to help with small talk before the punch line.

"She's fine. Thanks for asking. What brings you to the HP conference? Isn't this a little low on your radar? You're usually at higher level activities. The ones not open to the public."

"Well, I was at Forrestal this morning talking with Donna about the budget cycle and fiscal year commitments."

Dropping the name of Brendon's boss, another clear sign Joel was after something.

"She mentioned you were up here for the conference, and I thought I'd stop by. I was hoping your talk would cover more on the ceiling issues. We're working on some things that could be useful in that area, so I thought I'd gather firsthand knowledge from the man in charge."

"Wow, Donna knows I'm working another Sunday. Think that will improve my performance bonus?" The quip sailed over the consultant, clearly focused on himself. No reason to put off the inevitable. "What are you wanting to know, Joel?"

"I've read about the ceiling failures over the last few years. The last documented collapse was about eighteen months ago."

"As a matter of fact, I did speak about that."

"Yes, but why didn't you mention the two collapses since?"

Few people knew of both collapses. The larger of the two was public knowledge, though little information had been disseminated on the event. DOE considered the second collapse to be minor, not severe enough to require a formal report from the contractor. Thus, information on the second event, though not classified, was not disseminated to the public and not easy to find.

Brendon shrugged. "What's to say? Salt creeps. It's one of the main reasons the WIPP site was selected. We know it. We plan for it."

"When the ceilings collapse, what happens to the containers in the room? If one drum fire shut the place down for three years, what will happen when a dozen drums breach because a slab of salt crushed them?"

"You're in luck, Joel. The ceiling problems have been in empty rooms. Knock on wood." He tapped a closed fist to his head.

"Yes, but what would you *expect* to happen?" Joel asked, finding it hard to maintain composure. "Has that been studied? Have you postulated the scenario? Conducted one of your feature, event, and process analyses? Assessed the potential consequences?"

"I'm sure FEPs was completed on a ceiling collapse years ago. Everything's been studied to death on WIPP. I've certainly postulated the event you're suggesting, but the sky is the limit when it comes to *postulating*. Big boulders of salt and a few drums. Small chunks and a lot of drums. Remote-handled or contact-handled? Specific contents in the drum? I can't give you a straight answer because there are too many possibilities to recall from memory. Heck, it would take a month to write up a response to that question."

"Maybe I can narrow down my interest." He growled under his breath. "Suppose you had a ceiling collapse and a few drums were impacted. I'm talking about drums that breach. Say the drums release enough radiation to trigger alarms in the underground. Obviously, you respond according to procedure, but once the situation is contained, do you have a response plan to go back inside what would now be a contaminated room and repackage the drums?"

"You're asking how we would recover damaged drums? That's a good question, Joel, not unlike the issues we're facing with the contaminated vehicles that were abandoned after the fires a few years back. I can tell you we've developed recovery procedures. We've trained on those procedures and performed cold mock-ups at full scale. We haven't recovered the vehicles yet, but we're prepared for a minor incident where drums need to be secured or stabilized."

At the Bethesda Metro Station, Joel headed south toward downtown. Brendon headed north but only one stop. He couldn't stomach the nasally voice for another twenty minutes. At Medical Center, he crossed the track and headed back to his Forrestal office. Standing on the southbound platform, he squeezed a fist.

What does Joel know?

CHAPTER 11

CARLSBAD CAVERNS

"*Auuoooooohhhhhhh!*"

"*Dad,* tell her to stop," cried Robbie from the back seat of the minivan. "She's hurting my ears."

Seven-year-old Amber pulled her lips back with her fingers and bared her teeth. "I'm a wolf, Dad. Did I scare you? Wolves hide in caves. They might get us."

"*Uh-uh,*" whined Robbie. "Dad, will there be wolves in the cave?"

"No, son. I don't think so."

"*Auuoooooohhhhhhh! Auuoooooohhhhhhh!*"

"*Make her stop.*"

"Knock it off, Amber. We are almost there."

"Oh, Bill, she's just excited," said Joyce.

The restless children had played, bantered, and fought in the back seat for five hours on a Sunday family outing that began in Las Cruces, stopped at White Sands National Monument, then continued through Carlsbad. The closer the family got to the caverns, the more apprehensive Robbie was about entering the cave.

"Is it gonna be dark? I don't want to go if it's dark."

"See the sign for Whites City?" Bill pointed out the window. "That means we're only a few miles from Carlsbad Caverns National Park." He glanced at Joyce and said, "Slow, winding miles."

A childlike grin spread across his wife's face. "I think I'm as excited as Amber. You and I haven't been here in years."

Scanning the desert on both sides of the road, Bill said, "Doesn't look like much has changed. Yuccas, dirt, cactus. Except for the caverns, this isn't any different than home." He turned into the visitors parking lot. "Here we are!"

Bill stuffed his cell phone into the oversized fanny pack hanging under his gut, then helped Robbie climb down from the car seat. Amber and Joyce were already entering the visitors center.

"Four, please," said Bill, after corralling the family at the ticket window.

"My shoulders hurt, Mom," whimpered a reddened Amber.

Joyce placed a hand on her daughter's bare shoulder. "She's sunburned, Bill. I hope you're happy. I told you we should have skipped White Sands."

He turned from the counter. "It's not my fault we left Las Cruces at ten. I wanted to leave at eight, do White Sands before the sun got hot, and have lunch in Alamogordo. That would have got us to the caverns two hours ago, with no sunburn."

"Would you like the ranger-guided tour or self-guided?" asked the ticket agent.

"I'm sorry," replied Bill, fumbling with the fanny pack.

"Y'all want the ranger-guided or self-guided tour?" repeated the teenage girl behind the glass, rolling her eyes at the same argument among families she'd heard a hundred times.

"Self-guided, please."

"Are you sunburned too?" Joyce asked five-year-old Robbie.

"No, Mom."

"Of course not. You wear that sweatshirt day and night. I have to wash it as soon as we get home." She turned back to Bill. "Are we taking the elevator or walking down, dear?"

"I don't know," he replied, struggling to zip the overloaded pack. "Hmmm. Found the sunscreen."

"Damn it, Bill."

"The kids are already complaining," he said, oblivious his wife was also beginning to sour. "The natural entrance stinks pretty bad. That's a smell I'll never forget. And it's a long walk down."

"Elevator, then. That way, we can come back up when the kids reach their limit. Follow me." Joyce led the way.

Bill held Amber's hand for the speedy ride to the bottom. "You'll be fine, sweetie. I used to be sunburned the entire summer when I was your age."

"That was before we all learned about M-E-L-A-N-O-M-A," said Joyce.

"What's 'melonema,' Mom?"

"Nothing to worry yourself about, little lady."

"The air is cooler inside the cave." Bill gave his daughter's hand a little squeeze. "That will help cool you down."

"Fifty-six degrees," said Joyce, closing the brochure as the elevator door opened. "Maybe we should have brought sweaters."

Bill popped an eyebrow. "It's a hundred degrees outside. I am not wearing a sweater."

"Says here they've only mapped twenty percent of the caves. That's not very much, really. What do you suppose they would find if they mapped the rest?"

"More caves," replied a disinterested Bill, focused on damp rock formations ahead. "See that, kids? Those pointy rocks hanging from the ceiling are stalactites. The ones growing up from the ground are stalagmites."

Robbie wrapped a tight arm around his father's leg. "Will the slagmites fall on us, Daddy?"

"Stalagmites are on the ground, growing up. Stalac*tites* hang from the ceiling. Like they are holding on *tight*."

"Would I die if the pointy one fell on my head?"

"Why are all your questions about dying?" asked Joyce.

"They won't fall." Bill patted the child's head. "Not if you don't touch them. And they're pretty high up, so I don't think we have anything to worry about."

Joyce pointed to a unique shape suspended from above. "That one is called the Lion's Tail. See how it's bushy at the end?"

"Where's the rest of the lion, Mommy?" asked the inquisitive five-year-old.

Twenty minutes into the route around the Big Room, Amber, who had been quiet much of the walk, said, "I'm cold, Mom. Did you bring my jacket?"

Joyce rubbed her daughter's arms briskly. "We'll head back in a minute." She hoisted Amber onto the rail. "That's the Doll's Theater, honey. The sign says the ones hanging down are called soda straw stalactites."

"Like I use in my coffee?"

"Exactly." She tousled the youngster's springy hair.

Amber pointed to another feature. "That looks like icing dripping from a gingerbread house."

"I'm thirsty," whined Robbie.

"Me too," added Amber.

Joyce opened the brochure again. "The cafeteria is back by the elevator. We can get a bottle of water there. It's seven-hundred and fifty feet underground."

"Is that a lot, Mommy?"

"Yes, it is, Robbie. I think we should turn around now."

Bill looked down the stone path. "One thing has definitely changed since the last time we were here. The walls weren't dotted with flashlights during the tour back then." He lowered his voice as he unlatched a wooden gate. "Let's scoot to the side for a minute, where it's nice and quiet."

"What are you doing?" Joyce whispered, holding the kids back. "It says do not enter."

"This path was always open before. Nobody will care." Bill led the family down a small, isolated trail far from the main path. "Now, isn't this better? Nobody bumping into us. No lights dancing on the wall."

Joyce smiled in the dark. "Yes, dear. You're right, again. Just don't get us lost."

"If we are all really quiet, we'll be able to hear water dripping from above."

Drip...drip...drip.

"*Auuooooohhhhhh!*"

"Amber, I told you to knock that off."

"That wasn't me. *I get blamed for everything.*"

"Well, it wasn't your brother. Get over here." Bill hefted her onto his shoulders. "Stop horsing around. You can get hurt in a place like this."

"*Auuooooohhhhh!*"

The chilling howl emanated from down the isolated path. Joyce gripped Bill's arm. Vibrating fingers bit into the soft bicep.

Bill panned his phone light toward the howl.

Nothing.

Silence.

The light faded to black. He willed a trembling, "We…should… go."

A tiny voice atop his shoulders sang out, "Told ya it wasn't me."

CHAPTER 12

A LIVID DOE

AT 7:45 A.M. Monday morning, in a large office on the seventh floor of the James V. Forrestal Building in downtown Washington, DC, Steve Simon, consultant for a large defense contractor, gazed out the window of the undersecretary for Environmental Management admiring the rust-colored Smithsonian Castle across the street. The anchor structure of the National Mall.

"Great view," said Steve, when he heard Donna's heels click across the floor as she returned with her morning espresso. "That's not paint, you know. It's red sandstone from the Seneca Quarry out by Germantown. That stone can be found all over DC, especially around Dupont Circle."

The receptionist entered with a freshly brewed cup for Steve.

"Kind of ironic, really." He thanked the receptionist and sat in the leather visitor's chair. "You get a view of that gorgeous stone across the street. The DOE complex in Germantown is down the street from the big hole in the ground where the stone came from, but your job is managing holes in the ground. Never really thought about it before."

"I'd trade that view for a competent staff," replied Donna, who had only been in the appointed position for five months.

"You don't really mean that."

"Eh." She downed her espresso and nibbled on a chocolate éclair, fully dependent on caffeine and sugar to make it through the day. "Not entirely. It's just so different up here than it was in corporate life. Everyone is so busy kissing my ass they don't get a damn thing done.

In my staff meeting last week, we were talking about shipments. A dozen different sites, all with shipping activities underway. A routine conversation, Steve. I mumbled something about why a particular container design was taking so long. An off-the-cuff statement, not an action item. The next day I got a seven-page report explaining the delays. How do I work with people like that?"

He chuckled. "Next week, mumble that you need a certification for the new D62 waste package."

"You're not helping," she replied in an I-have-work-to-do tone. "So why are you here anyway? I know you didn't stop by to give me a lesson on architecture and geology. I've got an eight o'clock and a ten o'clock that always goes long, but we could do a late lunch if you're still around."

"We'll have to do lunch next time. I'm in Rockville the rest of the day. Just wanted to give you a heads-up on WIPP. Another ceiling collapse occurred last Friday. Triggered multiple alarms but nothing was reported. Not surprising from that crew. I've informed Carlton, and he'll be calling Mel Martin after the site opens. They're two hours behind us in Carlsbad."

"Damn contractors," snipped Donna. "No offense."

"None taken."

"I swear, Steve, if they had a reportable occurrence and didn't call it in, Mel's out of there."

He nodded agreement. "You have to be tough on flagrant violations, but let's wait to hear what they have to say."

"How did you find out about it?"

"I hear everything, Donna," he replied, exiting the room.

Later that morning, three floors down from the undersecretary's office, Carlton Banks placed a call to WIPP.

Mel recognized the phone number, bit his lip, and put his game face on. He needed to control this call by leading the conversation in a light-hearted direction, but headquarters never called just to shoot the breeze.

"Hey, Carlton. How's things back east? It's nine o'clock in Carlsbad. Shouldn't you be at lunch by now?"

"This is all business, Mel. What the hell is going on out there?"

The steely voice put Mel on the defensive. DC was bound to find out sooner or later, but Monday morning was pretty damn fast for the feds to be on top of anything that happened Friday.

"I'm not sure I know what you mean."

"You know damn well what I mean," Carlton yelled into the speaker phone on the corner of his mahogany-veneered, metal-framed desk. His voice bounced off the walls in the cramped office. "This is no time to blow me off. I know you had a collapse last week. Radiation alarms. A man is missing."

Mel maintained a stoic voice over the phone, while his gut dropped to his knees. His mind raced as fast as the remaining brain cells allowed. Who the hell would have called headquarters? The call hadn't passed through the official reportable occurrence network, or he would have received an automated notice and a dozen emails by now. It must have been one of the staff that worked that night. *Rip!*

Mel pinched his lips to keep obscenity-laden thoughts from escaping. He needed to say something, anything, to keep Carlton from sending an investigatory team to the site. Ever since those damn fires, DOE wanted to send a team whenever a staff member was constipated and didn't report it.

The main reason Mel had agreed to run WIPP was the proximity of the site *to absolutely nothing*. It took headquarters staff a half day to travel to Carlsbad and a full day to return. A one hour meeting required two days of travel. With ever decreasing budgets, Mel depended upon the lack of oversight to accomplish his job. Limited oversight had allowed he and Dom to flog the hell out of staff to get the site back up to standards. Still, the intense operational readiness reviews conducted prior to restart of disposal operations had been almost too much for the old veteran. He couldn't go through that again. Especially now with another midnight operation coming up. The final midnight operation.

After an overly long pause, he replied, "I really have no idea what you're talking about. Can you give me a little more detail?"

"What the hell, Mel? More detail on a ceiling collapse? A guy missing? How much detail do you need on missing staff? Want me to send you his yearbook photo? Alarms went off, Mel. That means you had a release! You know damn well I am to be informed immediately upon *any* release. *Then* you call the occurrence hotline."

"Carlton...Carlton," replied Mel as calmly as he dared. "I was in town all last week. Even came in a few nights to get some extra work done on the recertification. Thursday night, actually it was the wee hours of Friday morning, we had a couple alarms, maybe that's what you heard about. The alarms were investigated immediately and confirmed to be false. Procedure dictates that false alarms are not to be reported via the hotline. You'll certainly see them in the quarterly report, along with a dozen other false alarms we've had in the quarter."

"I'm sending—"

Mel cut him off. "Hey, I'm supposed to be in DC Wednesday." A blatant lie he hoped would keep a DOE team from hopping on a westbound plane. "Let me have an all-hands meeting this afternoon. I'll get to the bottom of this. Honestly, this sounds more like a disgruntled employee than a reportable incident. DOE doesn't need any more fake news in the papers. If anything happened, I would know. Especially if a man was missing, but let me dig a little."

Now the pause was on the other end. Mel could almost hear the DOE twit huffing in his tiny office.

"Damn it, Mel. Be in my office at 0900 Wednesday. If you find any of this to be accurate, call my cell immediately."

Mel tilted his chair back. He had just bought a few days to scrub the site and make sure records, alarms, and residual contamination were dispositioned. His DOE counterpart would wait until after the Wednesday meeting to decide whether an investigation was necessary. But now he had a new problem. He would have to fly out Tuesday afternoon to make a morning meeting at Forrestal on Wednesday.

*

Joel Weiss stepped into the office at the sound of the phone slamming on the cradle. His presence, not by accident. He too had been informed of a ceiling collapse, but how had Carlton become aware of the incident, and what was the talk about a missing man?

"Good morning, Joel," said Carlton in a tepid voice. "What brings you to the fourth floor? Shouldn't you be upstairs?"

"What makes you think they had a problem at WIPP?"

"How much of that did you hear?"

Standing in the sterile off-white tiled hallway outside the office door, Joel had listened to the entire conversation.

"Most of it, I suppose. Didn't want to interrupt."

"Just something I heard," grumbled Carlton.

"Well, he didn't exactly deny it."

"No. He didn't. I've known Mel a long time. He runs a pretty tight ship. The problem is he's colorblind. Everything in his world is gray. If something happened out there, he knows about it. Either nothing happened, which I doubt, or he's buying time to cover it up."

"Mel's always been a pretty straight shooter." Joel bit the inside of his lip, hoping he wouldn't have to defend the man who had nearly ruined everything. "Guess he deserves a chance to talk to his people before you rain down on them."

Carlton released an exasperated sigh and, along with it, months of frustration from arguing with his management team about the need for closer oversight of WIPP operations.

"To tell you the truth, Joel, I'm tired of this shit. If he can cover it up in three days, it saves me another year of nightmares. That'll give me time to transfer to a DOE slot where there's no accountability."

The man's openness caught Joel by surprise, but he understood how the stress of maintaining a safe operation in a remote desert almost two thousand miles away had worn on the DOE middle manager. He threw the dejected civil servant a bone. "You just defined every other job in DOE except yours."

Leaving Forrestal, Joel crossed the street to the National Mall. In the gardens on the backside of the Smithsonian Castle, he took a seat on a bench next to a man wearing an oversized navy sport coat but no tie. Unlike Joel, the man's thick neck was not built to accommodate such an accessory.

Surrounded by fifty varieties of roses with daisies, delphiniums, and foxgloves intermixed in the renowned garden, the men sat quietly while tourists and commuters flooded the path with clear distinction. Commuters zipped by without a glance at the floral arrangements, while tourists stopped to read nameplates and smell each flowery exhibit.

The pleasant breeze died without notice, bringing out heavy droplets of sweat on large foreheads. Joel finally spoke after convincing himself they were alone.

"This might work out better than I hoped. Martin is coming to DC for an early meeting Wednesday. He'll have to fly out tomorrow, which gives you at least two days to make sure our drums are secure."

The thick-necked man turned to Joel and asked in a Brooklyn accent, "Why don't we have Mel or Dom check the drums? Quick and easy."

"Talk slower, Tony, before you hurt yourself." Joel gazed over at the red stone castle and released some of his pent-up stress. "Mel called *me*, remember. That's how I know the collapse breached one of our drums. He said he took care of it, and that is exactly why you are going. I am *not* betting my life on Mel's word. He's not sure he can fend off an investigation, and after listening to Carlton, I'm not either. That's the problem."

"Understood," replied Tony Valastro, Joel's go-to man for under-the-radar work.

"Your job is to make sure DOE doesn't have any reason to question what is inside those drums. And we can't have them questioning anyone who may have seen the contents of the breached drum."

Tony swallowed hard. He and his men were radioactive waste experts who could make drums appear or disappear on command, but they only recently began dealing with people, and they weren't very good at it.

"Carlton also mentioned something about a man missing," added Joel. "Need you to check that out. Make sure he's not a loose end."

Tony nodded. "Got a name?"

"Figure it out when you're there," growled Joel.

"No problem. You'll have us on the unescorted access list for the site?"

"Already done. Take your own gear. Pack out everything you pack in. Don't interact with *anyone* that you don't have to. I don't like sending you out there this close to the next shipment, but that's why you have to go. We can't afford to have DOE increasing oversight when our final shipment is next in line." Joel rotated his head toward the big man. "Don't screw this up."

Tony gritted his teeth. Joel just wouldn't let the last job go.

CHAPTER 13

TRAFFIC ACCIDENT

THE LOOK OF shock on his wife's face was priceless. Served her right. Dan had just swerved to miss a strip of tire in the road and nearly lost control. An overcorrection that scared him as well. Hopefully, Diana got the message that he was still pissed off at having to drive so late Monday night.

White knuckles gripped the steering wheel as tight as his hands could squeeze. "That's why I wanted to leave earlier. I can't see shit at night. You know that."

Diana had put up with the complaining since they left Boulder and had long since given up trying to calm Dan down.

"You *could* slow down. Maybe do the speed limit *for a change*."

"Don't tell me how to drive, woman." He accelerated just enough to remind her he was in control. "I *would* do the speed limit if we weren't in a hurry. And we wouldn't be in a hurry if you didn't take so long to get ready. Damn, woman, we're only here for two nights. What the hell did you pack? You got three bags!"

The question was rhetorical, but Diana answered anyway. "I couldn't decide what to wear." She teared up for the umpteenth time. "I haven't seen my sister in two years. I can't show up in jeans. You wouldn't understand."

"No. I wouldn't. It's a funeral, not a fashion show. Deb isn't going to critique your outfit. She's going to cry her eyes out." He took a deep breath, struggling to maintain his own composure. "Arturo was a good kid."

"Just last week, she told me he wasn't drinking." Diana sniffled. "She saw him at the tavern with all his friends, and Arturo was the only one with iced tea. He was my favorite nephew, and now he's gone. I can't believe it. I just can't believe it." She blew her nose into a wet tissue. "Please slow down."

"Just let me drive," replied Dan, his anger subsiding. "It's flat as a pancake out here. Not like I'm going to miss a turn in the road if I go a little over the limit. If we hadn't missed the Denver flight, we would have arrived before dinner. I told you it would have been faster to drive from Boulder."

"With your driving," she huffed, then raised her voice. "Now damn it, Dan, I said slow down."

Now was not the time to remind her husband that they missed the flight because he insisted on taking a shortcut to the airport. A shortcut that got him lost. They arrived at the Denver airport just in time to see their plane being pushed back from the gate. Reroutes and delays had them both on edge after an exhaustive day that eventually landed them in El Paso where they had picked up the rental car.

A shadowy figure appeared a mile ahead, almost beyond the reach of the headlights. Dan tightened his grip. "What do you think that is?"

"I don't know," Diana replied. "But there's two of them."

Two dark shapes moved across the oncoming lanes. With enormous strides, the large animals seemed to fly over the wide median and were in front of the car so fast all Dan could say was, "*Look out!*"

A hideous face passed through the headlights, mere feet from the car. A rabid horse, maybe? He slammed the brakes and turned the wheel. The two-door sedan skidded to the left. Tires smoked in the night. A smell of burning rubber engulfed the vehicle as the car skirted precariously along the inside shoulder. The tires slipped from the pavement. The sedan tumbled into the shallow median.

Forty minutes later, five state troopers, one volunteer fire department truck, and two police cars from Carlsbad were scattered over a quarter mile of roadway on the outskirts of Whites City.

"I don't get it, Cole," said Officer Benny Montoya. "We got all this blood on the car doors. Driver's side and passenger side but hardly any blood on the seats or dash."

"It's like they cut themselves climbing out of the vehicle," replied Officer Cole Millard. "How the hell does that happen?"

"Odd," replied Benny. "But that's not the weirdest thing. Where did they go?"

CHAPTER 14

LIST OF LIES

"DOM, I OWE Carlton a call this morning," said Mel, first thing Tuesday. "I'll tell him we had the all-hands meeting yesterday, nobody is missing, and the alarms from last week were verified false. Maybe he'll cancel the meeting he scheduled for tomorrow in *his* office at 0900."

"Not Carlton. He never cancels anything which means you're on the afternoon flight today."

Mel leaned back in the chair and pulled his hands down his face. "The last thing I need right now is a trip to DC. I'm going to try like hell to get back tomorrow night, even if I have to fly into El Paso and drive from there. If I can keep this between us and Carlton, we're still okay, but if he pulls his management in, all hell will break loose." Mel looked over the weekly schedule to see what else he needed to shuffle to get out of town. "We have two trucks coming in tomorrow. Place those drums as far away from Room 6 as possible. Got another truck coming in Thursday, but I'll be here for that."

"That reminds me," said Dom. "When I checked the fence, I found a piece of flannel stuck in the barbed wire."

"Not surprising. The wind blew like hell last week. I got peppered with grit coming in."

Dom rested an elbow on his bulbous gut and rubbed his chin. "That's what I thought at first. Just a piece of trash, but it sure looked like something Chuck would wear. Have you heard from him?"

Mel had neglected to follow up on that particular action, mostly because he didn't give a shit. He was pretty sure Chuck had been in the underground that night with his dogs, which brought in another string of violations that he had no desire to expose. He had begun to convince himself that Chuck was near Room 6 when the alarm sounded. Blaring sirens and flashing strobe lights probably caused the dogs to panic. Somehow he got them back into the elevator, where they either bit him or attacked him. The piece of shirt could very well be Chuck's, but he still didn't care.

He steepled his fingers. "Not a word. When you get back to your office, create an all-hands attendance sheet that I can give to Carlton. Date it yesterday. Make sure to omit Chuck's name, obviously. For now, list him as being on vacation."

"I better keep Rip's name off too. He's been in and out anyway since his kid run off."

"I spoke to him yesterday. He didn't mention anything about Grady running off, but he confirmed two verbal warnings to Chuck last month. Evidently, Chuck's got a couple new dogs he's been working, and get this, the last verbal warning was inside the Waste Handling Building. Rip made it a point to tell me he issued that warning in front of the shaft elevator." Mel lifted worn cowboy boots onto the corner of the desk and shook his head.

"You don't look convinced," said Dom. "I'm not either."

"I wish we had kept a wad of fur from that big mat we found behind Room 6. I could compare it to this fur Rip bagged from the elevator." He pulled a baggie out of his desk and studied the contents. "Looks like shephard to me. Old shephard. There's a lot of gray in this."

"Coyote maybe?" Dom asked. "That would make more sense. Think about it. The coyotes that created that mat of fur would have entered the opening we found in the back wall of Room 6 the second they felt the fresh air flow. If Chuck was down there with his dogs, there would have been a heck of a dogfight." He leaned back with a satisfied smile. "That's where your blood came from. Chuck's dogs were bleeding from the dog fight. He got them back to the elevator and took them straight to the vet. Probably had to go to El Paso."

Mel felt a wave of stress slip away. "Mystery solved. Sometimes I think you're smarter than you look." He downed a gulp of spiked coffee. "That explains the blood, explains why Chuck is gone, and explains the fur. And any coyotes that entered the repository would be dead by now or real soon. Think about it. No food or water for four days. They would have been licking salt the entire time. That'll dry those scavengers out. They probably curled up and died behind a pallet of drums. If we ever do find a carcass, at least we'll know where it came from." He placed the baggie of fur back in the drawer. "Now, don't you have some work to do? I've got a call to make." He flipped to a blank page in the spiral. "I better take notes. My list of lies is getting long."

CHAPTER 15

BLISTERING HANDS

As THE SUN crept over the horizon Tuesday morning, the honey wagon lumbered up the dirt drive to a dilapidated trailer. Brian pulled to a stop next to Trip's Suburban parked in the weed-ridden front yard. He learned long ago it didn't do any good to rush his friend in the morning. He and Trip had grown up together in Jal, seventy miles east of Carlsbad. Though Trip was a year younger, they hung out every day. After high school graduation, Brian and his dad moved to the city. A year later, Trip and his mom followed. With eighteen thousand dollars and a promise from Trip to fix the place up, his mom bought the single-wide on a half acre of land.

Trip did what he could on the fixer-upper, but not having a father around was evident in the DIY efforts. The awning above the kitchen window pulled fiercely on the trailer siding, trying to free itself and fall the last three feet to the ground. Wood screws that Trip used to secure the aluminum trim were not only the wrong type, they were at least two sizes too small. A siding panel next to the steps flapped whenever the wind blew. Duct tape had held it in place through the spring, but after a summer exposed to a scorching New Mexico sun, the gray tape was nothing but frayed string. The yard wasn't any better. Even with Brian's help, they were unsuccessful in efforts to till the caliche-laden hardpan soil deep enough to grow more than goatheads and foxtails, a grassy weed known for leaving herringbone stickers in every sock in town. Trip's mom eventually resigned herself to a raised vegetable plot that ended up full of the same local flora, because she seldom remembered to water. Still, the trailer and yard were in much better shape than Trip's adobe house in Jal.

He gave another short honk. The bedroom drapes moved. A good sign.

Brian's eyes drifted to the deflated football that had landed on the roof with a thud when Trip shanked a kick last summer. No surprise. Trip played defense on the Jal football team, never receiving the accolades gushed upon the quarterback, Brian, after hometown wins. Always the smarter and stronger of the duo, he could depend on Trip to do almost anything, except get up on time.

Another honk. Lanky legs shuffled down rickety steps and climbed into the passenger side. "Hey." Trip leaned his head against the window and closed his eyes.

"Tomorrow's the funeral. You ever been to one?"

"Naw." He yawned. "All my grandparents are still alive, but I don't see Dad's much since he left."

"I only went to one," said Brian, diverting his eyes. "My mom and sister. I just remember everybody crying afterward, but not me. Don't know why, but I couldn't cry."

"That was the year Dad left. Mom wouldn't take me to the funeral. Said I'd been through too much already."

"I was only eight, so you would have been seven." Brian took a deep breath and let it out slowly. "Mom and sis were just driving back from a shopping trip in Odessa, you know. I don't think Dad ever got over it. Maybe I didn't either. I don't know. Dad never really talked about it. He just started hanging out in the shed after work. At least he was at home." He shook the depressing thoughts aside and tugged at Trip's sleeve. "Gotta dress nice. We'll need to work after, but we can go home and change. Old man Jenkins said we could have a half day off, but he ain't gonna pay us for it."

"Figures." Trip pulled his sweaty cheek from the window. "Think Grady will be back in time?"

"Hard to say. I mean, he doesn't even know anything happened to Arturo. Kind of weird, because Grady usually tells us when he's going out in the desert. Fernie thought he was fishing, but not for four days."

"It's not that weird," replied Trip. "Grady spent a week alone in the Guadalupes last spring."

"Yeah, but he invited you and told everyone he was going. I checked with his old man. Grady didn't take any gear. His dad figures he's just hiking in the desert or scouting for deer. It's possible, but he would have invited us."

Trip shook his head slowly. "I'd rather be scouting deer than going to a funeral, that's for sure."

"If he doesn't come home pretty soon, we need to help his dad look for him."

After another hot, dry afternoon of pumping septic tanks, they pulled up to the final stop of the day. Brian punched the brake a little too hard, stopping the truck with a lurch. Sludge in the tank sloshed a wave action that rocked the truck forward and back.

"Let's get this done," he said, peeling his sweat-soaked shirt off the vinyl seat as he slid out.

Trip made his way to the front of the truck. "Do you think my right arm is redder than my left?" he asked, stumbling over a rock as he studied both arms.

"'Course it is. You hang it on the door all day. It's gonna get a better tan than the other one. Just like my left arm is redder than my right. If old man Jenkins would fix the AC in the pumper, we wouldn't have this problem."

While they compared respective arms, Brian said, "The wolf lady gets back tonight. I want to change before we go to the meeting."

"*Ooooooo*. You like her." Trip sang out, *"Brian's got a girlfriend."*

"What are you, six years old?"

He backed up. *"Brian's got a girlfriend."*

"I just don't wanna smell like shit, and we promised to be there. You better go, too, or I'll kick your ass."

Finished with the last job, they climbed into the cab. "*Shit!*" Brian yanked his hands off the scalding steering wheel. "Did you move the window shade?"

A guilty face provided the answer before Trip replied. "I might have shifted it to my side, on accident."

"Accident, my ass." Brian brushed blistering-hot hands back and forth on his thighs.

"I burned my back on the seat when we finished the last tank, so I moved the shade."

Brian draped a soiled rag across the top half of the steering wheel to insulate his hands from the hot polymer. "It's not your fault. Jenkins should have given us a new windshield shade at the start of summer." He cranked the engine to life and headed back to the office. "Things'll be different when I have my own truck. I'll get a shade that fits."

After dropping Trip at his trailer, Brian rushed home to clean up, entering through the back door. The wood-framed screen door smacked against the jamb, formally announcing his arrival.

"Dad, I'm home."

"Hey, son. Good day?" asked his dad from the fully reclined Barcalounger in the living room, three steps back from the television.

"Always a good day, Dad. Cashed my check this morning."

Brian set five twenties on the counter next to the avocado-green push-button telephone, then flipped the calendar to the current month, swapping the skyline of Dallas with a beach barbeque on South Padre Island. Each destination only a day's drive from Carlsbad, but a million miles away.

"How's your back, Dad?"

"Same."

"Did you get out today? Do the shopping? Stop at the hardware store to get those washers for the faucet? I want to fix that leak in the kitchen."

Brian had purposely not picked up the washers, though he and Trip passed the hardware store twice on the way to different jobs. He needed to give his dad a reason to leave the house. It had been ten years since the old man hurt his back while shouldering steel pipe in the oilfields. Brian suggested moving to escape the small-town complacency of Jal and give the old man more opportunities to get out. They sold their double-wide and bought a small house on a large lot in Carlsbad. The plan seemed to have backfired because his dad stayed home most of the time.

"Couldn't make it today." His dad spit a load of brown mucus into a cup on the TV tray. He and Trip shared the same tobacco habit. "Maybe tomorrow."

Brian tousled the old man's hair. A maybe was better than a no.

"Got a date tonight," said Brian, exaggerating the evening event. "New girl in town."

His dad muted the TV and pulled the recliner upright.

"A date? Good for you, son. Treat that girl nice, you hear? She could be the one. Gotta start off on the right foot."

It worked. He had his dad interested in something other than the pain in his back and reruns of *Gunsmoke*. That alone would get the old man through the night. Tomorrow, he could make up some interesting details about the evening to get his dad engaged again.

*

"How's Pop?" asked Trip, climbing into Brian's truck, which had been fixed just enough to putter around town.

"Not so good. Stayed home all day again. I got him to perk up when I told him about Becca."

"At least he don't drink like Arturo's dad."

Brian shuddered. "I couldn't handle it if he was a drunk. Don't even want to think about it."

"Remember in the third grade? You were in fourth, but Arturo and I were in third. We all used to stay at his house."

"I remember. It's kind of cool we all moved to Carlsbad after graduation, but I miss a lot of those days in Jal." Brian looked out the side window. "At least in Jal, Dad would go for coffee most mornings. Now he won't even go to the kitchen and get his own coffee. Might have to drive him to El Paso next week to see a doc. He won't take pain meds, but he needs something, otherwise he may never get out of that chair."

"You could disconnect the cable. That's why Mom gets out every day. She's got nothing to watch on TV."

Brian laughed. "Good idea, but Dad would have a heart attack."

"The meeting is at seven, right?" asked Trip. "That's enough time for a couple beers and something to eat. We can ask Fernie about that crash last night. His brother, Benny, was one of the officers who responded."

"I don't know if I want to hear about that. The funeral tomorrow is bad enough."

"You'll want to hear this. He told me blood was everywhere, and nobody could have lived through that crash."

"Okay. You just filled me in. I don't need any more details."

"But, Brian, they didn't find any bodies."

Chapter 16

Small Plane

Tony took full advantage of free drinks offered in the first-class seat from Reagan National to Dallas-Fort Worth. His two-hundred-sixty-pound frame required the extra leg room, and his proportionately sized liver was accustomed to large quantities of alcohol. The connecting flight to Carlsbad departed from DFW Terminal C, where he joined Augie Benedetto and Jack Reust, who arrived from a job at Brookhaven National Laboratory on Long Island. The longtime friends had spent years together decommissioning radioactively contaminated buildings at Department of Energy facilities around the country.

Growing up in challenging neighborhoods of Brooklyn, the big men had few limits on what they were willing to do. In the early years, they made honest money as dose sponges, a blue-collar term for men and women who worked in hot areas where receiving a radiation dose was part of the job. Eventually, acknowledging the increased risk of cancer drove them to find opportunities with less direct exposure to radiation. To supplement their income, they hired themselves out for midnight operations where they made highly contaminated materials disappear. They perfected the art of hacking into waste inventory databases, doctoring waste manifests, and creating counterfeit drum labels.

An introduction to Joel brought more lucrative work applying their skills to influence outcomes of government procurements. Initially, the men were successful with simple intimidation. Few auditors could resist their imposing charm. But an increase in government oversight groups that mandated transparency of site operations had made the jobs much more difficult. Convincing auditors to modify reports began to require more physical efforts.

Tony lumbered down the terminal, soda and sausage sandwich in hand, and stood next to his team.

"Boss, I don't like the looks of that plane," said Jack, his three-hundred-pound, six-foot-one body punishing the steel frame black leather airport chair. "How the hell is it gonna carry the three of us?"

Augie, a few pounds lighter and two inches taller than Jack, had watched the miniature version of a small plane stop on the tarmac. "I got a drone bigger than that. Wanna draw straws for who lays horizontal in the cargo hold?"

The twin-engine turboprop plane sat alone on the apron with the door opened downward, doubling in duty as steps into the aircraft. The men climbed the four steps and took their assigned seats. Tony and Augie faced Jack and an empty seat. Two additional empty seats were behind the men.

As quick as Augie sat down, he bounced back up, bumping his head on the low ceiling. He cursed the three strides to the lavatory, where he fumbled with the door.

"I knew I shoulda gone in the terminal. This is ridiculous. My fingers are too big to open the damn door."

Jack chortled. "Ya got fat fingers. Don't blame the door."

Standing in the lavatory doorway with his back to the cabin, Augie drained the last of the large coffee, aiming as best he could at the center of the blue plastic commode.

"You better hang on to that burrito you had at La Guardia, Jackie. Ain't no way you're depositing it here. I'll call in a bomb threat if you even think about dropping your pants and dumpin' a load."

Focused on his aim, Augie did not notice the young lady scurrying up the steps and taking the seat next to Jack.

"I ain't even going to try to wash my hands. I'll break the freakin' faucet."

He turned around tugging upward on his zipper and immediately noticed the new passenger.

"Sorry, miss. I thought we were alone." He offered a hand to the new acquaintance.

Becca pinched a smile. "Think I'll pass. I heard more of that conversation than I needed to."

The flight attendant came back on board and looked over the passengers. "Tuesdays are always a little light. It's just you four today," said Christine, who was using this job to gain enough experience to work on grown-up planes.

"Gentlemen." She pointed to Tony and Jack. "Could I have you switch places? We need to balance the weight as best we can on this aircraft."

Augie huffed a heavy laugh. "They ain't no gentlemen." He batted black eyelashes at Tony. "Jack's cuter than you anyway, *big boy.*"

Christine pacified her passengers with a smile as she stepped back onto the stairs to give Jack room to stand in the doorway while Tony happily moved to the seat next to Becca. Only then was there enough room for Jack to squeeze by and sit next to Augie. The small aisle between the small seats again filled with husky legs, knees resting against each other.

"Keep the lights on, miss," said Tony. "With those two that close to each other, ain't no telling what they might do." He pointed at the connected knees. "They're starting already."

Augie winked at the petite attendant, in love with the woman's tiny blue eyes. "If we need to lighten the load, I'd be happy to toss that one off the plane. Can we wait until we're at altitude?"

The plane bumped along the runway to its position in line for takeoff.

Tony leaned into Becca. "Do you hear that?"

"I don't hear anything," she replied, trying desperately not to give any impression she wanted to talk.

"Listen real hard."

He leaned closer to the pretty lady. The armrest creaked with the movement.

A rancid smell of sausage sandwich combined with flat cola and bourbon pushed Becca into the window.

"You'll hear it. There it is again."

She cocked her head but still didn't hear anything unusual.

"It's our little plane asking the one in front, '*Are you my mommy?*'" He hacked a throaty laugh that caught in his chest.

With an obligatory smile, Becca adjusted her shoulder into the crevice between the seat and window and opened her book. The low drone of propeller soon transitioned to a high-pitched roar, and the plane lurched forward, accelerating down the runway.

The small aircraft seemed to hit every atmospheric pothole on the way to Carlsbad, bouncing and bumping its way through an empty sky. As much as Jack wanted to rid himself of the oversized burrito, he held it in. But he was only able to hold in the solids. Gas snuck out intermittently, drawing the ire of Augie and Tony.

Becca buried her head in the book and pulled her sweater over her nose. She directed the air nozzle above her head toward the men, pushing the pungent odor back to the origin, though she was unsure exactly which of the three men were contributing most to the stench.

"When we land, do we go to the site first, or do you want to check in?" Augie asked Tony.

"I think we should check in first," replied Jack. "Need to get the package I sent to the hotel. The one we didn't want to check as luggage."

Tony gave them both a hard look and gestured discreetly toward the lady with the book, indicating there were ears aboard not privy to their conversation. "We'll go to the hotel first. Now I'm gonna get some sleep." He leaned his chair back the allotted two inches, grunted, and closed his eyes.

"Could be a long night," replied Augie.

Tony opened one eye and gave Augie another glare.

All four passengers waited on the tarmac next to the plane while the attendant unloaded their bags from the cargo hold. Becca picked out two large bags. The men picked up equally large bags, along with corresponding black backpacks.

Tony graciously pulled Becca's largest bag to the rental car counter and motioned for her to go ahead. The twentysomething agent offered a choice of two vehicles. She selected the full-size sedan. Tony was handed keys for the last available vehicle, a subcompact. They left the counter at the same time, a now disgruntled Tony pulling Becca's bag as well as his own.

"Thanks, but you didn't have to do that," said Becca as Tony hoisted the suitcase into her trunk.

"No problem at all, ma'am. What the heck do you have in here, anyway? This might have been the weight problem on the plane instead of Augie." He again laughed at his own joke.

"Just shoes." She smiled politely and started backing out. "You can never have too many shoes."

"What the hell is this?" Tony and the men stared at a yellow, subcompact lemon drop in the last row. The only vehicle in the lot.

He opened the door, releasing a hot plume of confined air that had been waiting to escape.

"*Ow! Hot! Shit!*" Jack popped back a step from the car. "Freakin' handle burned my hand."

"Get in the damn car." Tony climbed in, wrapped his fingers around the steering wheel, and repeated Jack's soliloquy. The men carefully clipped their seatbelts trying not to touch metal parts in the process.

Becca drove to the Stevens Inn, where she had stayed the week prior. The men headed to the local Towne Plaza.

"You two clean up." Tony pointed out the window to a plain white "Restaurant" sign across the street. "We'll meet there in fifteen minutes to go over the plan. Jack, take this package to your room. Load the weapons and bring them across the street."

*

Becca hoisted her suitcase onto the double bed closest to the window in the ground floor room. She didn't remember the bag being so heavy. Exhausted from the turbulent trip, she lay flat on her back next to the suitcase, arms spread wide. The meeting was in three hours, and she was not looking forward to it. The farmers, *ranchers*, were going to be upset when they realized Bradford had lied at the previous meeting.

She showered and returned to the suitcase, one towel wrapped around her body and a second wrapped around her hair. Odd, the zippers were dangling from the bottom of the bag. She always zipped bottom to top, leaving the zipper tabs readily accessible. TSA must have searched the bag. Another disappointed agent now knew she wore department store shoes and could never decide which ones to pack. Hopefully the agent at least appreciated her taste in clothing when he pawed through the three outfits. Three outfits for a two-day trip had brought accusing questions from Ashton, who couldn't appreciate all the factors she had to consider when ultimately deciding what to wear for the public meeting. The weather, temperature, and even her mood affected the final choice, which was why she packed so heavy.

She slid the zippers around, flipped the bag open, and backed into the television. The face mask for Ant Man, or something very similar, was staring straight at her.

"*That jerk!*"

The slob from the airplane had accidentally loaded his bag into her car. No wonder the suitcase was so heavy. She opened the second bag. At least the supplies for the conference were intact. Thank God she traveled in a pantsuit instead of the fluorescent exercise outfit she had changed out of at the last minute. Keeping the towel on, she ran a quick iron over her blouse and slacks and slipped them back on. She then called Jenny Lopez, the meeting facilitator, for a quick update.

"Hey, Jen. Is everything ready?"

"Becca, I'm glad you called. The venue's been changed. Evidently, city hall received too many complaints about the crowded room on Saturday. So tonight, we're meeting on the second floor of the Riverwalk Recreation Center. It's about five minutes from your hotel."

Back in the bathroom, Becca applied makeup, hot curled her hair, dabbed perfume in all the right places, then examined herself in the plastic-framed mirror on the back of the closet door.

"That's as good as it gets, people."

She rolled the heavy suitcase down the hall and loaded it into her car in hopes the men from the plane were in town for the wolf reintroduction meeting.

*

Jack and Augie heard the yell from down the hall and ran to Tony's room.

"That *bitch* has my bag!"

The three men stared at the open suitcase filled with polyester pants, pastel blouses, a variety of lady's underthings, and at least six pairs of shoes. Jack and Augie tried, but failed, to contain snickers.

"Maybe some of that'll fit," said Augie, stepping quickly out of Tony's reach.

"*Does this look like a joke?* Do you know what's at stake here? This is not a job where failure is an option."

Augie wiped the grin away and directed his eyes to the floor.

"We got two choices," said Tony. "Find the lady and get my suitcase back, or use equipment at the site. They have everything we need, but it'll be locked in a building we didn't plan on entering. We don't know how many people are on-site. There's a risk of running into somebody."

"There's a third option, but it's not any better," said Jack. "One of us could go without a respirator."

Tony's look told Jack he should have kept his mouth shut. "Unless you're volunteering, I don't like that option. Bring your gear to the car. Let's find that bitch."

Tony was kicking his own ass all the way downstairs. The screwup was entirely his fault. He had hoped the night would go well. Talk to the pretty lady, and tomorrow, when the job was complete, maybe they could hook up. When the lady buried her head in a book, he should have accepted the fact that he had no chance. Still, if they could find the little lady quickly, the problem would go away, as long as she didn't open the bag.

CHAPTER 17

FANTASMA DEL GRIS

BECCA DROVE PAST the unappealing restaurant with the cracked, aged, off-white stucco front. The Chinese diner two blocks farther down the street sounded more inviting. A handwritten note taped to the glass door listed chop suey as the Tuesday special. She entered to find the interior less appealing than the exterior. Food scraps lay under the tables, and a thick smell of old fryer oil hung in the air. Flies along the windowsill made no attempt to flee as the door closed behind her. Grease-stained pictures dotted the walls. The Spanish nameplates suggested the art had been there at a time when a more local cuisine was served.

Her elderly waitress was pleasant but slow, considering only three patrons were dining. A clear view through the kitchen pass revealed beads of sweat bubbling on the extended forehead of an old-looking young man wearing more tattoos than clothing. The cook.

She said grace before the food arrived, praying the chop suey was straight from a can, the sweat missed its target, and the few hairs remaining on the cook's head held on for another day.

Pen in hand, she began reviewing the small pile of index cards for her presentation. Something she had planned to do on the plane but had no opportunity with a rancid row mate stalking her every move. She had spent half of Monday annotating each card with sufficient detail to ensure there would be no repeat of the Saturday stumbles. If butterflies flocked tonight, she would simply resort to reading directly from the cards.

She dipped an eggroll in duck sauce squeezed from a packet and flipped through the cards one by one. With each card, she seemed to find new words to better explain the benefits of wolf recovery. Powerful words the local ranchers were sure to grasp. Compassionate words certain to bring understanding among the many stakeholders. A new perspective about recovery of a species that at one time had lived in harmony with the surroundings. Her newly crafted approach emphasizing harmony over intrusion just might get the locals to forget some of the promises Bradford had made. On the second pass through her notes, an unidentified gelatin picked up from whatever the previous diner had dripped on the table speckled the backside of the index cards.

Dang it.

She wiped the cards with a single-ply napkin that shredded at the first sign of resistance from the glue-like substance. The momentary confidence from the new perspective began to fade. Her stomach turned slow somersaults, either from the chop suey or from nerves that understood the most important meeting of her life was ninety minutes away. She pulled in a deep breath to push down the queasy feeling.

You've got this. You can do this. Confidence returned after repeating her favorite mantras multiple times. She squared her shoulders and allowed her eyes to wander back to the pictures; a descriptive nameplate tacked to the frame of each.

The first picture, *La Llorona.* The Weeping Woman. A tormented lady dressed in a long white gown hovering over an acequia. The wailing woman of the ditch, searching the night for wandering children to drown in the black water.

The second picture, a colorful parade of skeletons. Bony structures with flowered hats and headdresses. White faces colorfully decorated except for the deep black eyes. Were the eyes inviting, or daring anyone to come near? *Dia de los Muertos.* Day of the Dead.

The last picture, a large transparent wolf with teeth twice the size of a normal Mexican gray. Huge jaws. A sturdy haunch. Deep blue eyes. *Fantasma del Gris.* Ghost of the Gray. A lone wolf howling in the night, warning all to stay away.

Becca arrived at the venue early, finding the doors to the back hallway and foyer open but the meeting room locked. She set up the trifold displays and placed brochures on the exhibit tables. She signed the visitor logbook on the first line, immediately noticing the erratic script. Her anxious fingers had balked at penning a crisp cursive moniker. Illegible squiggles provided a reminder that as the senior member of the service, she needed to control her nerves tonight.

Finished with incidentals, she glanced at the time then walked briskly down the entry corridor, checking each side room for Jenny. Her pace increased between empty rooms. The meeting facilitator was nowhere to be found.

A nauseating tingle crawling up her throat met resistance from the heavy weight on her chest and forced shorter breaths. She extended her right hand arm's length and watched jittery fingers dance faster than they did on a frozen day in DC. A neon sign could not have provided a more obvious warning of the anxiety onslaught.

"I've got a few minutes," she muttered, two fingers on her wrist measuring a throbbing pulse. "Get it under control, girl."

In a quiet corner in the empty entry hall, she slipped her heels off and took three deep breaths, holding each to the count of ten. She stretched her arms above her head, palms pasted together and leaned to the left, then back to the right. Breathing exercises and yoga, recommended by a fellow Toastmasters member, were supposed to be the perfect cure for premeeting nerves.

Most of her short career had been spent assisting managers with their meetings. Bradford had only assigned her to lead the Southwest Wolf Reintroduction Program because no senior staff wanted to travel to Carlsbad. Prior to the Saturday meeting, her largest audience had been a group of fourteen at an early morning Toastmasters session. That embarrassment cost her twelve quarters, one for every "uh" uttered in the five-minute talk.

Though her nerves were providing fair warning, with the new perspective succinctly annotated on the note cards and no Bradford to hover over her, a hint of confidence returned. In the middle of the tree pose, eyes closed, hands folded above her head, left foot resting against her inner right thigh, rapid steps echoed down the hall. She opened her eyes to Alejandro's wispy black hair and toothy smile; his hand extended straight out. She wobbled her left foot back to solid ground and shook the hand of her IT man.

"What do you need first?" he asked.

"I'd really like to see the room. Make sure my presentation works on the video and get the head table set up. Then…"

Before she finished the sentence, he darted down the hall, quickly unlocking the remaining doors, then zipped in and out, connecting microphones, video displays, and a bridge-line for guests to call into the meeting. He popped her flash drive into the computer situated at the facilitator's chair. The title page of her presentation promptly displayed on the large screen over her right shoulder just as residents began filling the seats.

Wearing their best flannel long-sleeves, Brian and Trip secured inconspicuous middle row seats among the locals.

Only when Trip flashed a hip-level wave did Becca notice her friends had arrived. She mouthed a "thank you," took her place in the center chair, and set the stack of neatly organized index cards on the worn red table runner next to a bottle of water. With fingers inter-locked to quell relentless vibrating, she gathered just enough nerve to peer out over the crowd still pouring in through the main doors. Careful not to make eye contact, she observed weathered bodies of all shapes and sizes. Men arriving from sunbaked jobs began to line the walls on either side, deferring the last open chairs to the ladies. Had the venue been in DC, the room would have surely smelled of perfume and cologne. In Carlsbad, a waft of blue-collar sweat drifted in the air.

The room presented a billboard for hard life in the blistering desert. Wiry women wore crusty faces that generally matched those of their husbands. Prominent wrinkles cast shadows in deep canyons on haggard cheeks seldom treated to fresh dust of a powdered blush. Thinning dry hair, baked from decades in the sun, barely covered pink scalps. Still, a youthful fight glistened in most ladies' eyes.

Dust and dirt from whatever their callused hands had been heaving, hauling, and hoisting coated jeans and boots that dominated the men's attire. Cowboy hats rested on half the men, equally split between ragged straw and black beaver pelt. Nobody beyond the front table had dressed up for the meeting, though the men wearing black hats might beg to differ.

The mayor and county manager were the only two men wearing ties, one of which was a bolo. They shook Becca's hand and took their respective seats. Jenny offered a quick smile, adjusted the microphone, and directed the versatile Alejandro to close the doors. She quieted the room with brief introductions and mandated instructions for government meetings. Much like a flight attendant, her arms extended toward exits to the sides and rear of the room. Locals offered their first snicker, fully able to find an exit should there be any need to leave in a hurry.

The mayor received a courteous applause as he stood and spoke. The county manager followed to a similar applause. Both men talked of local amenities and the upcoming election, deferring the wolf reintroduction program entirely to the junior project manager.

The dreaded butterflies awoke when the county manager wrapped up. Nerves shot to high alert. A twitch that had matured in college returned to Becca's upper lip. With shaky knees that no doubt could be seen from the back row, she stepped to the podium.

"Our next guest," announced Jenny.

Becca's brain did not register the rest of the introduction. Her eyes were locked on the crowd of men lining the walls. Not only was the room larger than Saturday, it was packed to the limit. When the facilitator left the podium, Becca moved mechanically into place. She read the first index card verbatim, a practice she learned the hard way to prevent flubbing the first sentence of a presentation.

"Thank you, Jenny, for that wonderful introduction. As Jenny mentioned, my name is Rebecca Olsen. I am a project manager with the US Fish and Wildlife Service. I am excited to meet with you, our stakeholders, to discuss how we, as a community, can live in harmony with the Mexican gray wolf."

She looked over her right shoulder, happy to see her introductory slide displayed on the screen. She looked at the audience, who seemed pleased to be referred to as stakeholders, people with a vested interest in the decisions before them. She had the audience right where she wanted them.

First card complete, she attempted to shuffle to the next but found the second card stuck to the first. She pulled at the edge with no success. Duck sauce cemented the cards together in a tight paper brick.

Her skin began to tingle. Sweat swelled on her eyebrows. Panic attacked with a vengeance. Wide-eyed and head down, she worked desperately to separate the cards, cursing fingernail nubs that proved useless in the effort. Just like Saturday, she found herself fumbling with the water bottle as she tried to regain her composure and continue—off script.

After a much too long delay, she looked up from the podium. Big mistake. Her eyes connected with angry faces in the front row. Every word of her new perspective evaporated in a room that had become suddenly hot.

"Um, I...I recognize a lot of faces from a week ago. I mean Saturday. That wasn't actually a week ago. Um, I would like to thank all of you for taking time to educate yourselves on recovery efforts implemented with the Mexican Wolf Reintroduction Program. Next slide, please."

She glanced over her right shoulder to a visual of the DC headquarters office. *What was that slide doing in the set?*

"Um. It is only through knowledge and understanding that you can appreciate the importance of reintroducing wolves back into their natural habitat where they can live in harmony with your cattle."

What? That wasn't right.

"Next slide."

A graph of green and red lines appeared on the screen. She had planned to discuss the history of wolf reintroductions across the Southwest, impossible without the corresponding note cards, but the slide reminded her of a field agent who was present in the room.

"Before I continue, um, I would like to introduce our federal wildlife officer, Daphne Bender, who is standing against the back wall."

Daphne rocked her tall frame away from the wall and tipped her service-issued circular-brimmed brown hat to the crowd. Light flickered off the gold badge centered above the hatband.

"Officer Bender and I will be coordinating the release efforts." She lowered her voice to a whisper. "This week."

Even without slides and note cards, Becca was still able to bore the room with mind-numbing details of flora and fauna in southeast New Mexico and west Texas. She carefully avoided the many acronyms introduced at the previous meeting but was compelled to again explain the preferred alternative identified in the Environmental Impact Statement: a sustained Mexican gray wolf population in the designated habitat.

Forty minutes into a one hour meeting, she tired of hearing herself and inadvertently glanced at people in the front row. Inflamed faces scorched flocking butterflies. They fell with a thud to the pit of her stomach. She increased her tempo to get away from the podium as fast as possible.

"This brings us to why we are here today. Very soon, we will make another reintroduction into the secondary zone. Three sets of adults. One pair with three subordinates. Are there any questions?"

An old man rose in the second row. "What do you mean, you *will* make a release into that there secondary zone?"

"There's nothing to worry about, sir," replied Becca, interpreting the question as concern over the zone designation. "Release into a secondary zone is routine." Having nearly memorized the service manual during all those months Bradford kept her behind a desk, reintroduction details had become her specialty.

"It is a common misconception that the secondary zone is for troubled wolves that didn't work out in the primary zone. That's not really why we release in a secondary zone. In this case, it is purely for a better dispersal. You know, to even out the distribution over a large area. I mean, like, we do translocate wolves that are, let's say, a nuisance. But, um, that can go either way. Primary to secondary or secondary to primary. The decision really depends on the animal and the location of nuisance incidents."

The man's scowl hardened, vaporizing Becca's momentary confidence. Alone at the podium. A hundred people in the room. Two hundred angry eyes. Her voice trembled as an unseen force compelled her to continue. Talking seemed to be the only way to keep her body from collapsing at the podium.

A voice from the middle of the room shouted, "Damn right the decision depends on the wolf. Those bastards go wherever the hell they want."

An old cowboy stepped up to the microphone in the center aisle. She was thankful for the interruption from Vern, whom she recognized from the Saturday meeting.

"Miss, I'm going to need some help with this. Maybe I'm not so smart as some of my neighbors here, but I think of primary and secondary as a first choice and a second choice, where first is always better. That's why it's the *primary*. So when you try and say the primary isn't really more important than the secondary, you start to confuse people. I'm confused just askin' you about it. When y'all say 'nuisance,' is that another word for killing cattle? If it is, why not just say so? And what exactly is translocate? It sounds kinda space-like. Maybe y'all could translocate those bastard animals to Roswell with all them damn aliens and just leave us the hell out of it."

Laughter-filled applause engulfed the room prompting Jenny to stand up and motion the crowd to settle down.

"It's funny, yeah," continued Vern. "But that's the kinda talk people down here are tired of hearing. Everybody thinks ranchers aren't too smart cause we just raise cattle, but we know you're trying to hide somethin' when those big words start poppin' about."

"Excuse me, miss," interrupted Cal Eggers, replacing Vern at the microphone.

"Would you please hold your question until I answer Vern's?"

"No, ma'am, I won't. When you were talking so fast, you said the wolves 'will be released.' That doctor fella told us last week that no decision had been made, and now you're standing up there talking like you got 'em in a truck out back. Where do we send our comments on this, and when do y'all figure on making that final decision on the release?"

Becca stared blankly at the old man, unsure how to reply. The truck wasn't out back, but it was on the way. Bradford had flat-out lied to these people, and shit was hitting the fan. A fan pointed directly at her.

"Well, Mr. Eggers, Dr. Bradford couldn't make it this week, but he wanted me to clarify some things that he mentioned. You may have left last week's meeting with an understanding that the process is quite lengthy. Indeed, it does take a long time to select a pack of wolves and prepare them for release. There are many activities that you wouldn't begin to understand."

"Try me," came a deadpan reply.

"Well, um, no. That was a figure of speech. My point is we started the process years ago. As I explained, we are finally in a position to release the last grouping."

"What about our due process? What about submittin' the comments Bradford said you would address?"

Becca's fingers picked nervously at the cards. "You may have misunderstood."

"Let's get somethin' straight. I didn't *misunderstand* anything. What are you trying to tell us?"

Unable to put off the inevitable, Becca let it out, albeit quickly. "*We are releasing a pack of wolves tomorrow.*"

Thunder rumbled through the room. Profanity-laden shouts came from every direction. Chairs scratched the floor as a dozen men and women stood up and yelled at Becca. With questions coming all at once, she couldn't decide who to answer.

"People, people, please listen to me. The last time we had a release, the wolves were killed within two months. I'm here to inform you that Federal Wildlife Officer Bender has been assigned to monitor the movement of this new pack."

The noise dissipated slightly. Cal flipped her off and left the room.

"Won't take that long this time," shouted a voice from the back.

Becca wiped her forehead and gripped the podium. "Be advised," she yelled, which exacerbated the puberty-like crack in her voice. "Officer Bender is armed and will be in the vicinity of the wolves at all times. She is trained to live in the field and will closely monitor the wolves until the agency is confident the animals' safety has been established."

She was almost thankful when another old man said, "I'm outta here," and walked down the center aisle. Half the crowd followed while the other half talked angrily among themselves. With nobody paying attention and no one in line to ask questions, Becca slipped over to Brian and Trip. The three made their way to the stately officer still standing against the back wall, shoulders square, hands clasped behind her back.

"Look at the size of her," said Trip. "She looks mad. I don't think she liked those old guys."

"Just don't say anything stupid," replied Brian, sizing up the officer who was at least two inches taller than him and broader at the shoulders.

"Cool hair. It's as square as her chin. How do you think she gets it to stick straight up?"

Brian bumped Trip with a "shut up" nudge as they approached the larger-than-life woman dressed in olive-green pants and a short-sleeved sage-green shirt, likely the largest size available. A polished brass name bar pinned above the right pocket read "D. Bender." Overhead fluorescent lighting reflected cleanly off the top of impeccably polished black boots, a shade darker than her skin. A gold badge on her left shoulder and a service belt loaded with accessories rounded out the ensemble.

A hand twice the size of Trip's shot out. "Daphne Bender, federal wildlife officer," she said in a smooth, husky voice.

Tongue-tied and in awe of the statuesque woman, Trip shook the hand and spouted a conditioned reply to anybody in uniform. "Thank you for your service."

Daphne raised an eyebrow at the little man, then shifted her gaze to Becca. "Well, bless your little heart, and I thought it was hot *outside*. You just fired up enough trouble to keep me in the desert for a month."

"Let's get a drink," said Becca, the weight of failure pulling her shoulders down. She stared at the crowd and shook her head slowly. Her first solo meeting had been a disaster.

Daphne draped an arm over the junior project manager. "After this mess, you're buying."

CHAPTER 18

FIND THE DRUM

FINISHED WITH THE greasy meal, Tony and the men were back at the hotel inventorying equipment. Three Sig Sauer nine-millimeter handguns lay on the dresser, courtesy of the package Jack shipped to the hotel. Grouped together on the bed were respirators, white Tyvek suits, gloves, booties, duct tape, flashlights, and miscellaneous accessories for work in the repository. Two of everything.

Jack flicked on his pager-sized self-alarming dosimeter. A three-second high-pitched screech sounded the warning they would receive should they encounter radiation exceeding the safety threshold.

"Turn that thing off," snapped Tony, still fuming over the loss of his suitcase.

They stuffed the equipment into their backpacks and headed out.

"Drive around town and find that lady's car," Tony ordered Augie. "I need my shit. If we can't find her in twenty minutes, head to the site."

Jack gazed out the window from the back seat, reading signs of mom-and-pop shops along the sparsely populated main drag. "We can cruise this town twice in twenty minutes."

After three passes, they gave up, never seeing Becca's car parked behind the Riverwalk Recreation Center.

Forty-five minutes later, Augie pulled to a stop at the WIPP guard-house. The setting sun blasted his eyes through the windshield as each man displayed their credentials. The guard grinned at the yellow sub-compact, touched each badge, and motioned the car through the gate.

"Wait here," ordered Tony. He slipped in the back door of the administration building, returning a few minutes later with a bulbous respirator in hand.

"Dumbass was watching a movie on his computer. Didn't even see me take it. Couldn't find the Tyvek."

"Night shift at a government facility," said Jack, his hand covering a jetlag-induced yawn.

Augie parked behind the Waste Handling Building to keep the car out of sight. The men entered a rear door and made their way to the elevator.

"This I find hard to believe," said Tony, impressed with the over-sized elevator cage and the long smooth descent. "We've conducted a lot of midnight operations, guys, but slipping into this hole unde-tected beats them all."

Voices echoed and ears popped during the long ride down. Augie and Jack used the time to don Tyvek protective outerwear, stepping into paper-thin white jumpsuits and zipping the front from the crotch to the neck. The big men began sweating immediately in the impen-etrable suits. In black slacks and a short sleeve button-up, Tony leaned against the opposite wall, his angry eyes boring into the Tyvek.

The elevator came to a smooth stop at the bottom. As the doors opened, a rush of cool air from the underground blasted past, making its escape up the elevator shaft. Jack, Augie, and Tony stepped out shoulder to shoulder, staring in awe at the deep, dark corridor that beckoned.

Jack kicked at the ground while Tony verified the route to Room 6 of Panel 5, the location of the ceiling collapse giving Joel so much heartburn.

"Didn't expect this," said Jack. "The ground is smooth as a tile floor." He bent over and ran his fingers along the off-white surface, then licked the tips. "Salty."

"Ya think," said Augie, turning on the LED lamp strapped across his forehead. Jack did the same.

"No safety briefing here," said Tony. He gestured to Jack's dosim-eter. "Let me know if we run into a hot area."

Tony pushed the start button on the electric transport and headed toward the restricted side of the UG. The men had seen their share of oddities in the world of government operations; H canyon at Savannah River, entombed reactors at Hanford, hot cells at Oak Ridge, but the underground world of salt was like nothing else. An ominous yellow glow, courtesy of periodic light fixtures, pushed forth from the walls. The fifteen-foot-high, thirty-foot-wide corridor seemed to narrow the farther they drove. Salt crunching under the tires and a steady whine of the electric motor provided the only sound in the waste tomb, reminding the men that they were alone deep below the desert floor. Nobody on the surface knew three men were in the restricted access area. If anything went wrong, it could be weeks before anyone found their bodies.

Few signs provided direction in the main corridors, further evidence, if any was needed, that visitors were never underground without an escort. Tony found himself backtracking twice before making the correct turn to Panel 5. A warm feeling of success replaced some of the heat sucked away by the cool depth.

Panel 5 consisted of multiple rooms of identical size. At the entrance to Room 6, Tony stopped to surveil the surroundings. According to the drawings, the room was three hundred feet long and thirty-three feet wide. From the entrance, all they could see was light from the vehicle headlamps disappearing deep inside the dark chamber.

Tony glanced over his shoulder. Augie gave a thumbs-up from the second row. Jack offered the same hand signal from the third row.

"These are the container numbers of the three drums we need to find," said Tony.

He handed a piece of paper to Augie, then maneuvered the transport slowly into the unlit room, where an even deeper darkness sucked in the headlamp's weak glow. He had worked in confined spaces, but creeping through the vast salt mine where walls threatened to close in was different. White-knuckled fingers gripped the steering wheel. He crept forward, extra cautious, until he finally saw a familiar sight: industry-standard radioactive waste cans. Fifty-five-gallon black steel drums, lids secured with bolted rings.

On the left side of the room, drums stood erect, stacked three high. White bags resembling large flour sacks were packed around the steel containers. To the right, chunks of salt from the ceiling had toppled a few drums.

"Let's get to work," muffled Tony through the respirator.

Augie ran his fingers through the grainy material that had spilled from the bags. "What the hell is this shit?"

"Who cares?" replied Tony. "Jackie, climb around and check numbers on the far side. We'll work our way to the middle."

"I can't read the labels with all this shit covering them," said Augie, realizing immediately this was not the time to complain.

With his middle finger, Tony pointed to the forklift and shovels they passed on the way in.

After twenty minutes of flashlights and headlamps dancing on walls and containers, Jack returned with a thumbs-down. No sign of the drums.

Tony tapped his hip, prompting Jack to read the self-alarming dosimeter clipped to the Tyvek pocket.

Muffled profanity corresponded with a screeching *beeeep-beeeep-beeeep* when Jack flipped the switch on. A red LED flashed extra bright in the dark room, warning the trio that the radiation dose exceeded the safety threshold. Not imminently dangerous, but high enough they shouldn't stand around arguing about torn sacks that were slowing everything down.

Tony pushed Jack toward the transport. The tone decreased the farther they retreated from the drums.

Augie came out from behind the containers on the right side of the room. He bobbed a thumbs-up on one hand and displayed two fingers on the other, indicating he was pleased to have found two drums.

Tony held up three fingers and muffled, "Where's the third?"

An exaggerated shrug answered the question at the same time a gunshot rocked the room.

Pow!

The three men dropped to the floor. Dust puffed from a small hole in the ceiling.

"*What was that?*" yelled Jack.

Augie shined his light at wisps of dust trickling from a broken buttress. No other movement. No further noise. He scanned the light across the floor and found the culprit, a sheared-off hexagonal bolt head.

"A damn bolt sheared off," said Augie, getting to his feet.

Eyes on the buttress, Tony growled. "I'm sick of this shit. We need to get done and get outta here. We're gonna get dosed, so be quick."

The men double-checked labels on every drum. Tony focused on the area near the two drums Augie had found. The third drum of interest was definitely not in the group. Satisfied they had thoroughly checked the room, he gestured to the transport.

He stopped the cart at the entrance to check the clipboard hanging on the wall. The container layout showed their three drums in the back corner, exactly where they found two drums. Tony ripped the sheet from the clipboard and drove back to the elevator.

He snarled as soon as the respirator was off. "*Where the hell is it?*"

"It's the only drum missing, boss." Augie shrugged. "I dug all through that pile. So did you."

"And I climbed over the rest of them," added Jack.

"Yeah, with your dosimeter turned off."

Augie looked at the pager-sized unit clipped to the pocket of his Tyvek. He reached down and turned it on.

"*You too?* Dumbass. Let's get topside and figure this out."

The smooth hum of the elevator provided the only sound on the long ride up. When the doors opened, they each inhaled a deep breath of fresh air.

Tony's face turned deathly serious. "Dom has some explaining to do."

CHAPTER 19

NINE WOLVES

DAPHNE FOLLOWED BECCA to the Coyote Cavern, trading her brimmed hat along the way for a ball cap with a US Fish and Wildlife emblem. The group joined Fernie at their regular table.

Trip pinched a peck of fries from Fernie's plate. "Um, is that how you expected the meeting to go?" he asked Becca.

"Not exactly." She scrunched her face. "I crafted really good notes on stakeholders and harmony and sharing the land with native species, but my note cards got messed up. They all stuck together." She sighed. "It probably didn't matter. All the time I spent preparing was really just to keep from thinking about how angry everyone would be. How could they not be mad? The moment I said we were releasing wolves, it was over. At least nobody attacked the podium. In that sense, it wasn't so bad, actually." She popped a what-are-you-going-to-do shrug.

"Wasn't so bad?" Daphne's wide eyes also questioned the statement. She had been with Becca on a couple of assignments, but this was the first time the officer had observed the junior project manager in front of people. "That would suggest it could have been worse."

"Oh, definitely. I sat in on a meeting in Dallas where the crowd was super mean. They kept yelling at the speaker. Called him a liar and everything. Somebody even threw cow patties at him."

Brian's ears perked. "Who brings cow pies to a meeting? And how did he get them inside?"

"The cowboys at your meeting were ready to employ a more permanent solution," said Daphne. "Half of them had a sidearm. A little different than public meetings back east, that's for damn sure." She rocked her head. "They did not like you, DC."

Trip grabbed another fry. "Last week she told them you weren't releasing any wolves."

"I said nothing of the sort. Dr. Bradford lied to those people. Not me. I would have never done that."

Brian set his beer down. "Maybe not, but as far as folks around here are concerned, you're responsible. What did you mean when you said the relocation objective was thirty-four wolves? That's a lot of wolves."

"It is, but most have already been released. Those are the ones that died."

"I didn't hear you say that part."

She sighed again. "Because everybody knows that already."

Brian took another drink. "Yeah, I don't think so."

"Remember the meeting Saturday, when I mentioned the service initiated a reintroduction program in 2002? We've been doing this for years."

"I don't remember any wolves released back then," said Trip. "But I was only three years old. Mom probably didn't want to scare me."

Becca performed the quick mental math. Twenty years? No wonder nobody remembered the first release.

"We reintroduced a few wolves in 2002 and more in 2012. I guess it was a long time ago. This week we're only releasing three family groups. Six adults and three pups."

"Nine," said Trip.

"Yes, nine." She held up nine fingers. "What is so hard to understand?"

Another grin crawled across Brian's face. "In all that talking, you never mentioned the number nine."

"Ugh. How could I miss something so basic?" She turned to Daphne. "Tell me what you thought."

"Oh, no. Don't put me on the spot. I'm just a field brat. You headquarters people live in a different world, but I'll tell you this, DC, it might help to talk less and just give people the details. They don't care about all the whys and whats. They know the government has already decided to screw them over. Just tell them how many and when."

"Details." She closed her eyes.

"Don't worry about it," said Brian. "I don't think the number would have mattered too much tonight."

She buried her head in her hands. "For some reason, people either love us or hate us for reintroducing wolves. Those that hate us get a little crazy."

"I didn't feel any love in that room, DC. Gonna need to work on that if you ever expect to get a date at one of these meetings."

Hopeful ears perked on Brian.

"A date? That's the last thing on my mind. I'll be happy to get out of town without any cow dung on my clothes."

"The night's still young, DC."

"Why do you call her DC?" asked Trip.

"I got a name for everyone, Little Man. For Becca, it's like a term of endearment. Helps me remember the headquarters people who live and work in Washington, DC, are special."

"Like short bus special?"

Daphne sputtered a mouthful of beer. "No, Little Man. Though you might be right in Becca's case."

Becca forced a frown.

"The suits in DC are a different kind of special." She ran her hand along Becca's forearm. "They got soft skin. Live behind a desk. Don't get out much. Don't understand the people like some of us who spend our days in the field."

Becca planted elbows on the table and leaned her forehead into her hands. "Let's change the subject. That was my last public meeting for at least a few months. I just want to forget it." She sipped her beer, then glanced to Fernie. "I know Trip speaks Spanish from the last time I was here. Is it pretty common to be bilingual?"

"*Sí*," he replied, holding a toothy smile. "It's pretty common this close to Mexico. My parents are bilingual and taught my brothers and I. My grandmother helped a lot. She lives with us."

"Fernie and I were in the same French class in high school too," added Trip. "We're both bilingual in three languages."

Another sputter of beer. "You were saying something about a short bus, Little Man?"

"Dude," said Fernie. "We had two weeks of French and transferred out. That doesn't make us bilingual. It would make us trilingual, if we could actually speak the language. I barely remember how to say hello."

"Bonjour," said Daphne. She tapped Becca's arm again. "Go ahead, ask 'em."

The boys' eyes all zeroed in. Not helpful, considering the evening assault.

"All right. How do you guys feel about the wolves? I mean, I never really asked you. Do you care if wolves are released into the habitat? After all, they were here first. It is their habitat."

"That's the way, DC. Present the question with a direct lead to the answer you want to hear. Ever thought of being a reporter?"

Trip shrugged. "I don't know. Hadn't thought about it."

"When we go out shooting," said Brian, "I guess we'll need to be more careful."

Fernie sat quietly.

"What about you?"

"Me? No, I don't like the wolves." He shuddered lightly. "When we were growing up, my abuelita, Yolita, she used to tell me and my brothers to behave, or she would feed us to *el lobo*, the wolf. She connects with animals. I don't know how to explain it, but we all believe her, especially when she talks about *the wolf*." He leaned in and lowered his voice. "There is a legend about a wolf that traveled with families who made the long walk to America. It stayed in the distance, just out of sight, and howled every night. Some mornings, they would find bodies of banditos ahead. The wolf was protecting them. The people started to leave food for *el lobo*. These people had nothing, but every day they left food for the wolf. After the families arrived in America, they got jobs, and people were too busy working and taking care of their kids and celebrating. They stopped leaving food for *el lobo*. They forgot about their protector. One night, the howling returned, but it was a different howl. A hungry howl."

Their corner of Coyote Cavern was eerily quiet as Fernie shared a story that had not been spoken outside close family settings for a long time. "One day, the howling stopped. Men of the town found the wolf way out in the desert, dead. Its body emaciated. *El lobo* starved to death. Instead of burying the wolf with respect, the men celebrated with a big feast. Everyone in town went to the fiesta, but not everyone returned home. A small child was missing. The howling returned. An angry howl. Abuelita says ever since that night, the wolf is watching. Waiting for a child to wander from the family. When we were little, we could never play outside after dark, and whenever a child went missing, *el lobo* was blamed. Abuelita tells us she still hears the howling sometimes. I never heard it, but I believe the legend, *Fantasma del Gris*. Ghost of the gray."

The table remained silent for a full minute.

"*Ooookayyy,* then," said Daphne with a mocking roll of her eyes. "We'll put you down as against the release. But I'll tell you, we could use a legend like that in Atlanta. Crime would evaporate if nobody left the house at night."

A cold draft in the hot bar was all Becca needed to change the subject to anything other than wolves. "How come you weren't on the plane today?"

"Are you serious? Can you see me and all my gear on that little prop job outta DFW? I barely fit in the seat on a real plane. Wouldn't even want to try that little thing you came in on. Not to mention I needed to rent a truck for a month. The Carlsbad rental couldn't guarantee one would be available. I came Atlanta to El Paso and drove from there."

"There were three men on my plane bigger than you. I'm not gonna lie, I wasn't sure it would get off the ground. The flight attendant even made them shift seats to adjust the weight distribution. I was kind of expecting them to be at the meeting. Somehow I ended up with one of the guy's bags, and he got mine."

Daphne stretched a long leg to the side of the table. "How was security leaving DC?"

"Reagan is super easy. As long as you're not leaving Friday evening with all the weekly commuters, TSA is pretty quick. Ten minutes."

Daphne pounded her empty glass on the table. "*Atlanta sucks.* Has to be the longest security line in the country. Damn thing weaves all over the place. There's like six agents for every line, and they can't move people any faster? Took me an hour."

"Are they really like that?" asked Trip.

"You serious, Little Man? Have you ever been on a plane?"

The firm question elicited a nervous reply. "No, sir."

Daphne's hand shot out and grabbed the short hairs behind Trip's ear. "Do we have a problem, Little Man?"

He winced as she tugged the tiny hairs. "No. No. That just slipped out. Sorry, dude. I mean, ma'am, lady. What do you want me to call you?"

"*Daphne* will be just fine." She winked at him and waved for another round. "You've had a question in your eyes since the meeting. Spit it out."

"Were you in *Ghostbusters*?"

She tossed a wide grin to the kid who was not trying to be insulting but was doing a good job nonetheless. "No, Little Man, that was my sister."

Two beers later, anxiety and adrenaline finally subsiding, Becca pulled out a notepad.

"Remember the fur we found last week? Test results came in. It *was* wolf."

"But you said there weren't any wolves out here." Brian pushed his glass back. "They all disappeared or were shot by ranchers."

"I was under the same impression when I got this assignment," added Daphne. "Am I supposed to watch the nine wolves we release *and* keep my eyes open for wolves that are already out there?"

"That's not the weirdest part," said Becca. "The fur was radioactive."

CHAPTER 20

ESCAPE THE LAND
OF ENCHANTMENT

MEL ARRIVED AT the Carlsbad airport twenty minutes before the Tuesday afternoon departure. The tiny airport provided fast, friendly security and was still pleasant for travelers. He was on a first-name basis with both guards at the X-ray machine and friends with Karen Joy, the agent at the Cactus Air ticket counter, who was married to a forklift operator at WIPP. The only downside to the small-town airport was the size of aircraft able to land on the short runway.

After clearing security, Mel walked out the back door of the terminal, climbed the four small steps into the plane, and took his seat. The last afternoon flight leaving Carlsbad was wheels up at ten after five. Too early to sleep, but he tried anyway, bouncing in and out of consciousness in rhythm with the turbulence. Thoughts from a long career scrolled through his mind with vivid details of how he and Dom had made it to Carlsbad, and how they had planned to get out.

Simply leaving New Mexico was not an option. One must escape the Land of Enchantment. The town and the state had a way of holding on to people as tight as the caliche-laden soil, and Margaret was no exception. His wife had fallen in love with the desert. After they'd moved five times in twelve years, he could hardly blame her for wanting to stay put. She already warned him that if he was moving, he would do it alone. They had been drinking that night, so maybe she wasn't serious, though he wouldn't know until he played that card. But first, he had to get WIPP past the current mini-catastrophe; after that, he was prepared to retire. The time was right. Thirty-seven years of serving the man was more than enough, but he needed to get through the ceiling collapse for his and Dom's sake.

Bonus money from the upcoming midnight operation would be enough for Dom to catch up on his child support and pay off losses incurred in Aiken. After that, his friend was on his own. He could no longer be responsible for devising schemes and coordinating extra-curricular activities to cover Dom's debt. Vegas had hit both men hard, each leaving the Silver State worse off than when they arrived. Together, they lost their shirts on the gaming floor, their wives in the courtroom, and their sobriety.

Mel opened his eyes. A half-melted ice cube swirled in the bottom of the plastic cup on the tiny service tray. He gestured for another round and looked out the window thirty thousand feet above vast Texas ranchlands, where a cowboy could still ride a horse all day and not get to the end of his property.

During their time at Savannah River, he and Dom rode daily in the gorgeous horse country around Aiken, South Carolina. Dom took up pinhooking, buying yearlings at public auctions, prepping them for racing, and selling them as two-year-olds. Like the stock market, the concept behind pinhooking was buy low and sell high, and just like stocks, if it was that easy, everybody would be a millionaire. Dom bought and sold multiple horses, each time bumping up a notch in pedigree and a few notches in price, until a freak injury with a prized foal cost him everything.

Dozens of midnight misdemeanors over the years and the three drums entombed in Room 6 went a long way toward alleviating the debt. Another delivery, scheduled in two weeks, would provide a bonus sufficient to make Dom flush again. But that delivery could only be accepted if disposal operations were not shut down by the DOE.

The tiny airplane slammed down on the runway in Dallas, jolting Mel from the hazy slumber. His eight-thirty connection to Reagan National departed from a different terminal, but a frequent-flyer knowledge of the most direct route to the gate and masterful use of the

Skylink left plenty of time for a drink, or two. He landed in DC just before midnight, cabbed to the JW Marriott a block and a half from the White House, and was at a familiar seat in the lobby bar just in time for an expedited round before the bartender announced last call.

Mel signed the tab and staggered across the expansive marble floor of the chandeliered lobby. He pushed the elevator call button and entered the first conveyance that opened. Balancing against the rail in the back corner, he stared at the old man looking back at him in the mirrored walls. An infinite string of faces reflected from the left wall to the right wall and back again. An old face. His face. Deep inset wrinkles down each cheek. Horizontal canyons rippled his forehead. Droopy skin under the bushel of eyebrows that, along with his hair, were surrendering black to gray. Similar gray bushels protruded from enormous ears. Margaret always said the gray made him look distinguished. She lied. He looked like shit.

Mel stepped from the elevator car and walked the lengthy hall to his room. The nine o'clock meeting was going to come early, and there was still one issue he hadn't worked out: how to tell Joel that one of his drums was empty.

CHAPTER 21

SPECIAL DRUMS

AFTER A LONG night in the underground, the men occupied the same corner booth at the restaurant as they had the prior afternoon. The smell of stale sweat from three burly men barely masked the stench of moldy carpet and rotting kitchen garbage.

Tony sat on one side, brushing his hands across the front of his shirt and down his pant legs, puffing billows of salt dust with each swipe.

"This shit is everywhere."

No comment from Jack or Augie, whose salt-free clothes had been protected by the Tyvek.

"Joel's going to be pissed," said Jack, cradling a cup of thick coffee from a vintage percolator that hadn't been cleaned since New Mexico became a state. Perfect strength to wash down the salty metallic taste.

"Are you kidding me?" Tony growled. "You think that's our biggest problem? If that missing drum turns up in the wrong hands, how hard do you think it will be to tie this whole thing back to us? Joel's not stupid. He sent us out here, where we stand out like wolves in a sheep pasture. He's having dinners in DC, drinking wine with his crab cakes while we're eating at a dive that smells worse than you did on the plane. It's our asses on the line here."

Jack wiped salt crust from the corner of his mouth. "Well, yeah, but—"

"Shut up. Finding two drums and the inventory sheet that showed our third drum should have been right next to the others creates a whole new problem. We have to assume that our drum is missing for a reason. And if we assume the reason is someone peeked inside, then that 'someone' knows the contents."

"But why would somebody take our drum?" asked Augie. "Why that drum?"

"If I knew why, we wouldn't be here sitting on sticky seats slopping down cold toast and eggs." He lowered his voice. "That drum and those contents could send us to prison for life—or worse. Whoever has it knows that. We need to find the drum and find the asshole who stuck his nose into our business. Both need to be permanently disposed."

"And we need to know if they talked to anyone else," added Augie. "This could get messy."

"It's already messy."

Jack squeezed his cup to suppress trembling fingers. "I told you this was a bad idea when you took the job."

"The job is done," snapped Tony as though he expected the statement. "You didn't whine about the payday. Hell, you were laughing your ass off when we loaded those drums."

Jack had been laughing that night. A vivid memory, as it should be, since the memory returned to haunt every night since. He had drunk just enough to take the edge off and swallowed a handful of pills to put his body on autopilot. The only way he could muster the courage to accompany his friends through the dumbest decision they had ever made.

Six months earlier, Joel approached Tony about an opportunity to make real money. For years, the trio had taken side jobs to supplement their income doing work that was much more cost effective performed during off-hours, when regulatory eyes were sleeping. Making materials disappear under cover of darkness was one thing; making people disappear was a game with which Jack had no experience at the time.

A two-year proposal effort had just been completed for a major government contract. The leading contender, Wilmington Management, already operated three government research facilities. Well-publicized operational efficiencies had all but guaranteed WM the new contract — until three auditors, investigating beyond their charted assignment, identified significant noncompliance at a WM facility. Risk of losing a ten-year hundred-billion-dollar cash flow and risk of prison terms from impending criminal charges had to be mitigated.

Joel, who stood to do quite well with the new contract, agreed to take care of the problem. He sent Tony, Jack, and Augie to intercept the auditors leaving Idaho National Laboratory. They abandoned the auditor's vehicle in Grand Teton National Park, two hours outside of Idaho Falls, with enough evidence to make it appear the men got lost on a day hike in the Teton Wilderness. That night, three TRU waste drums from the massive INL inventory were replaced with three drums filled in the Grand Tetons. The following day, those drums were loaded into a TRUPACT-II container and on their way to WIPP.

The three drums, emplaced in Room 6 of Panel 5, deep in the bowels of WIPP, each contained an auditor. Though there were plenty of easier ways to dispose of a body, Joel thought it amusing to add insult to injury and entomb the men in a government facility run by the competition.

Augie caught a glimpse of the memories floating in his friend's eyes. "Come on, Jackie. Idaho's done. We're in cleanup mode now. That's our business, and we're good at it."

Jack sucked it up and put his game face on. "What's the plan?"

Chapter 22

Okay to Walk

Mel pushed the phone off the nightstand, silencing the seven-thirty wake-up call. He rolled to the edge of the bed and set his feet on the ground to keep from falling back asleep. Chin on his chest, eyes closed, his nose zeroed in on the stench, his breath.

Head pounding, he wobbled to the bathroom and readied himself for the day with a shave, shower, and four Tylenol. Twenty minutes later, a perfect Windsor knot around his neck, he was back inside the elevator headed up to the lounge for the free breakfast available to guests who earned sufficient points for the privilege. A perk for frequent travelers willing to trade the youth of their wives and children for powdered eggs and transparent bacon.

He nursed a hot cup of coffee at the window overlooking Freedom Plaza directly below. From his window perch, the elevated concrete pad inlaid with geometric stone shapes depicted a map of DC from the Capitol to the White House. A plaza he crossed on most trips but never stopped to read the text in the stone. Maybe this morning.

His eyes shifted from the Old Post Office clock tower to the Washington Monument a half mile down the street.

"Hmm."

"Excuse me?" asked a midforties woman to his right with shoulder-length blonde hair and angular cheeks dusted with half the makeup Margaret used.

"I was just thinking what it would be like, looking back at the hotel from the top of the Washington Monument. Always wanted to do that but never had the time."

"Well, you can't take your coffee up, I can tell you that. The glass windows are thick and a little too small to appreciate the view." She let out a relaxed sigh. "But looking out over this great city early in the morning, when fog is resting on the Potomac. There's nothing like it. Make the time. And if you can't do that, hit up the clock tower in the Old Post Office across the street. It's a hotel now, but you can still go into the tower."

"Never thought to do that."

"There's nothing better after a twelve-hour day than releasing stress at a monument or memorial. As soon as I get back from my meetings, I go for a run. Every day I head out in a different direction, always ending at something historic. I stop to catch my breath and think about how far this great nation has come and what it took to get us here. Washington, Lincoln, Roosevelt. It makes even my worst day seem not so bad, you know."

"Maybe I'll give it a try."

She glanced from his shoulders to his shoes. "It's okay to walk."

The slim woman in pinstripe slacks and a lavender blouse inhaled a deep breath, closed her eyes, and released the breath slowly, just like Margaret with her yoga. "I better get started. Windy Wednesday."

"Windy? It's gonna be hot, but I don't think there'll be any breeze."

"My pet name for the type of day." She ran an open hand down her blouse, pushing out a lone wrinkle. "Windy means I've got long meetings full of hot air. Yesterday was tornado Tuesday. Meetings on the hour. Ten straight."

"Good luck," he said, watching the much too perky professional refill her coffee and dash out the door.

Okay to walk? Was that an insult? Couldn't be. She was too nice. He picked the muffin from his plate and performed a fitness test, resting the sweet cake atop his protruding stomach. When did that happen?

Fresh cup in hand, he cut across Freedom Plaza, once again ignoring the text beneath his feet. He crossed Pennsylvania Avenue and took a shortcut through the Reagan Building courtyard, coming out at the backside of the Smithsonian museums. Heavy, warm air prevented deep breaths needed to replace the alcohol in his blood with oxygen. Underneath the navy sport coat, the sweat-infused cotton shirt was already sticking to his torso, courtesy of the humidity.

Though the temperature in Carlsbad was only a few degrees warmer than summertime temperatures in DC, the effect was very different. The Carlsbad sun baked and burned, evaporating sweat and leaving a salty crust on the skin. DC was more like a sauna with soaked foreheads and clothing.

"Shoulda worn a white shirt," he grumbled, stealing a glance at sweaty ovals spreading across the blue Oxford under his jacket.

He glanced at the sun gleaming off the large rotunda protruding from the top of the Natural History Museum as he passed between it and the American History Museum. Maybe after the meeting he would have time to take a quick visit. It was supposed to be a "must do" for DC.

As he crossed the National Mall, the gravel path crunched under his boots. At the Smithsonian Castle, he meandered through the rose garden and stopped at the curb of Independence Avenue. Across the street stood the James V. Forrestal Building, designed in the Brutalist style of architecture, appropriate for the internal power struggles of the current organizational network within her imposing walls.

He had spent the better part of his career working in Forrestal, supporting Department of Energy radioactive waste missions. As a cleared DOE contractor, he swiped his badge at the security portal and passed through the gate. Visitors in the adjacent line were funneled through a metal detector, their personal items examined on an X-ray machine much like TSA.

Mel rode the escalator down to the basement cafeteria to grab another cup of coffee and gather his thoughts before heading up to the fourth floor. Dave Parks, a longtime acquaintance from Idaho National Laboratory, stepped in line behind him.

"Ordered a new hunting rifle," said Dave, as though they were still in conversation from the last time they bumped into each other in the cafeteria. "Arrives in two weeks. That'll give me just enough time to break it in before deer season. You coming with us this year?"

"How you been, Dave?"

The tall, heavyset man with meaty arms chuckled. "Better now that rifle is on the way. Gonna join us or not?"

"First week of October, right? I might be able to get away."

"It's the third week this year."

"That would be more difficult. I'm leading a panel at the Waste Management Conference in Tucson that week."

He would resign long before the event, but now was not the time to discuss retirement and certainly not with Dave. A great guy, just a little too talkative. There was a good chance that before Mel finished his coffee, Dave would have informed a half dozen people on the upper floors it was a medium roast.

"Aren't you supposed to be on the Tucson panel? Hell, I'm only going because it's your turn to buy drinks."

Dave's perpetual grin widened, pushing heavy cheeks to the side. "Management tried to get me to go, but I haven't missed a hunt in thirty years. Hell, you know me, Mel, I still work for a living. Don't care how expensive the suit is that's asking me to do something. Happy to take on any job, anytime, anywhere—except the week I'm hunting."

Mel smirked. "That conversation couldn't have gone well."

Dave reached around and paid the cashier for two coffees. "Told the boss I was gonna be killing something that week, don't care if it's in Idaho or Tucson. He got the point."

"Good seeing you, Dave."

Mel sat at an empty two-top along the wall and opened the folder for one final review in case he needed extra data to distract anybody at the morning meeting. His cup looked lonely without the two fingers of calming he would have liked to add, alcohol forbidden in the government facility. He had pushed his luck many times in the past, swiping his badge and entering unaccosted with a pocket pint in his jacket. When an untimely glitch at security diverted him into the metal detector line, he learned quickly that DOE guards do not appreciate feeble excuses for violating policy.

After adding a few notes in the margins, he closed the folder and stretched his legs into the aisle. How many times had he sat at the same table, in the same cafeteria, preparing notes minutes before a meeting? Fifty? A hundred? How many times had he dreaded the impending meeting? Too many.

Thoughts turned to a retirement that couldn't come soon enough. He would buy a place in Aiken, where Margaret loved the greenery and the flowers. She hated the humidity, horseflies, and bugs, but with a little convincing, he'd have her on board.

Mel stepped into the elevator, cinched his tie, and pinched a professional smile. He was not looking forward to his version of Windy Wednesday with Carlton.

At eight-fifty, in a fourth-floor windowless office, Mel took one of three empty chairs. "How you been, Carlton? Diane and the kids?"

A curt *"Fine"* told Mel the meeting was going to be difficult. He adjusted his own demeanor to accommodate Carlton's frustration and slid two sheets of paper across the table.

"I've got what you need right here. This is the staffing log for last week."

"Good, Mel. I can use this. I'm catching a lot of heat here for not sending a team down yesterday." Carlton shuffled the papers.

"That list identifies employees on-site and those who are on vacation or were out sick last week. As you can see, only six people weren't at the site those days. Three staff were sick. I had my secretary call each. Two others went on vacation together. A trip to South Padre Island they'd been talking about for weeks."

"The report I received last Friday said a man was missing. That's why you're here." Carlton stared at the list. "You just identified six people away from the site and explained five. Is a man missing or not?"

Mel slid his hand across the desk, pointed to Chuck's name on the list, and feigned a snicker. "One thing about small towns, everybody knows everybody's business. Chuck's wife brought him to work, then went on to El Paso to catch a plane. She's visiting her sister in Austin. Nice lady, but a little overbearing. Kind of henpecks Chuck all the time. The wife, not the sister." Another less than convincing snicker. No response. "So whenever she leaves town, he takes advantage. He ducked out early last Friday and went hunting like he always does when she's gone. That's your missing man. Hell, half the men in Carlsbad, and some of the ladies, take off to go hunting. To tell you the truth, I'm a little pissed that someone made a big deal out of this."

The skeptical DOE senior staffer cocked his head. "I thought deer hunting was during October or November in most places."

"It is. Have you ever thought of joining us? I'm going with Dave Parks this year. He just bought a new rifle."

No reaction from Carlton.

"Chuck's a big bird hunter," continued Mel. "Duck, quail, dove. The guy is good. I've hunted with him a dozen times."

"And how the hell did he get there if his wife had the car?"

Mel needed to wrap up the lie before he started saying things he wouldn't remember later. "His hunting buddies picked him up at the gate. I personally checked the security tapes and watched him get into an extended cab pickup just before daybreak."

An uncomfortable pause followed.

Mel leaned back, forcing himself to appear calm. "I still don't understand why there's so much concern. We've been quiet at WIPP for months. Routine ops. No reportable occurrences. No injuries."

He waited for a reply, but Carlton was staring at the timesheet data.

Finally, Carlton broke the silence. "Someone told Donna that you had a radiological release last Friday. He told her that a man was missing, alarms sounded, and contamination was found in the elevator. The same person told me."

A gulp and quick regroup. "Hell, Carlton, I told you about the alarms on Monday."

"Uh-huh. When *I* called *you*."

"And your missing man is right there." Mel gestured to the staffing report. "Who called? Was it anyone you want me to talk to? Maybe help clear this up."

"It's not that easy. This wasn't WIPP staff or a government employee. It came from, well, let me just say, someone who has Donna's ear."

Mel's stomach turned, and it wasn't the powdered eggs. The details were accurate but nothing that Carlton hadn't already relayed when they spoke Monday morning. He had assumed Rip reported the alarms. The new twist was the call had not been made to DOE directly as he originally thought. The call had been placed to somebody who had the ear of the undersecretary, the one individual Mel had never been able to bluff. Rip was the only person smart enough to take that approach.

He forced a smirk. "Hell, Carlton. Are you saying I made a trip out here for a rumor?"

The senior staffer's eyes narrowed. "You told me your trip to DC was already scheduled."

Distrust in the room was thicker than morning fog on the Potomac.

"It was. It was. This trip's been planned for a couple-three weeks, but I always take the morning flight to arrive in time for dinner. With the extra prep for this meeting, I had to take the last flight out yesterday. Didn't get in until after midnight. If this was just a rumor, I'd have damn sure asked you to schedule our little get-together in the afternoon. I'm running on fumes here." Fumes he hoped were not wafting across the desk.

Carlton rocked his head slowly from side to side but didn't look up.

"So are we good here?" asked Mel. "I've got a meeting in the basement in a half hour, another upstairs at one, and I need to be in Germantown at three."

Had Carlton inquired about the meetings, Mel would have provided names of lifelong friends to validate the itinerary.

Carlton leaned back in his chair and interlocked his fingers across a stomach much too fit for a middle manager. "Rumors are something we deal with all the time. Depending on the administration, sometimes a whisper turns into a fire drill, and sometimes it's ignored as long as possible. But this one was different. Steve Simon informed Donna of a breach. A well-connected consultant telling my boss. That's not good, Mel. In a curious coincidence, our friend, Joel Weiss, met with one of my guys Sunday at the Health Physics Conference. You know Brendon."

"I told Brendon I would come in for that. Couldn't get away."

"I'm glad you didn't waste your time. Anyway, Joel asked him about our recovery plans for WIPP. He wanted to know what we would do if there was another release. He specifically asked about a release that might be caused by a ceiling collapse." Carlton leaned into the desk. "Why would he ask that, Mel?"

Mel's heart jumped into his throat at the same time his stomach fell to the floor. This incident was not going to be resolved with a falsified staffing report. If Steve and Donna were aware of the "rumor," they would be looking for substantive proof that no release occurred.

But the real concern was Joel.

CHAPTER 23

ARTURO'S FUNERAL

THE SUBURBAN WAS quiet, and the street seemed to have less traffic than normal for a Wednesday morning. The sun, usually beating the boys into submission by now, emitted a soft glow.

"I never saw so many people crying in my life," said Trip, driving to the motel.

Brian faced out the passenger window. "That's how funerals are. Everybody cries, but I didn't."

"Me neither." Trip adjusted the side mirror. "I can't believe everything went so fast. An hour at the church, and now he's gone. Forever. Doesn't seem right. We were all shooting Friday night. That was only five days ago. I mean, where did he go?"

"He went to heaven."

"How do you know? I mean, for sure."

"My mom told me. It's one of those things I remember from back when we used to go to church. That's where people go when they die. Good people. Arturo was good people. He always went to church with his folks."

Another mile of silence.

"Did you hear about his mom's sister?" asked Brian.

"Yeah. When I was getting a plate of taco rolls at the reception, Arturo's little brother was right next to me. He told me his aunt and uncle crashed their car Monday night way out near the Texas border. That's the accident I was telling you about yesterday. The one Fernie's brother, Benny, responded to. It was *their* rental car. His aunt texted from the El Paso airport that they were on their way, but they never checked into the Stevens. That was the last time anyone heard from them. Benny has been trying to track them down. He checked every hospital in El Paso and has to check the urgent care centers today. He said it's going a little slow because it's the first time he's had to work with the Texas State Police."

Brian pulled his head back, surprised at the level of detail and curious how his usually timid friend had struck up so many conversations. "When did you talk to Benny?"

"When I was going back through the line for seconds."

That explained it.

"If they got out of the car, then maybe they weren't hurt too bad," said Brian. "I'd sure go to El Paso first if I was in an accident that close to the border."

Trip rolled his hands on the steering wheel. "I kinda thought Arturo was kidding about the alcohol thing. I mean, about how bad it was, you know? About how it could kill him. We all knew he was an alcoholic, but hell, we all are. Right?"

Brian nodded. "He was pretty out of it for a few years, but when he quit drinking, he really quit. That's what gets me. Arturo wouldn't touch the stuff. Something isn't right about that. And freakin' Grady! Where the hell is he? His best friend should've been there."

Pulling into the parking lot at the Stevens Inn, Trip unclipped his tie and shoved it into the glove box. Inside, Becca and Daphne were sitting at a table next to the breakfast bar.

"Sorry about your friend," said Becca. "That's hard."

Daphne returned from the buffet line and put a hand on Trip's elbow. "You look real nice, Little Man. Grab a plate and sit down. Better hurry, they're gonna close up in a few minutes."

Trip's sun-scorched face reddened at the touch. "How much is it?"

"What do you care?" asked Brian with a disbelieving look. "We just stuffed ourselves."

"Free to hotel guests," answered Daphne. "You're with me. Don't worry about it."

Trip returned with an overloaded plate of instant eggs, thin bacon, and biscuits and gravy.

Daphne eyed the plate, wilting under the weight of a meal that could serve four hungry ranchers. "They let you go back for more."

"*Nice*." He stabbed the bacon with a flimsy fork.

"I don't know how you do it," said Brian. "You just ate."

"But this is free."

"You better not get sick. We're dropping the transmission on the Jeep tonight, and I need your help. That'll get us ready to install the new one Saturday morning so we can take it to look for Grady. I don't want to drive the truck in the desert until we replace the fuel pump. Engine was coughing again yesterday and stalled on me twice."

"What time Saturday?" asked Trip. "And you better not say seven."

"What kind of truck?" asked Daphne.

"An F150, but when we fix my Jeep, I'll be driving that more."

She set her plastic fork on the Styrofoam plate, casually covered it with a napkin, then looked Brian in the eye. "Are you sayin' you have two vehicles, and neither of them work? Tell me straight, Vidalia. Are they sittin' on blocks in front of a double-wide?"

Trip sputtered a laugh through his eggs. "The Jeep's on blocks."

"We were going to fix the Jeep last Sunday," said Brian. He looked down at his feet and took a breath. "But that's when we found... Arturo."

"I'm real sorry. I know how difficult that can be." An understatement if there ever was one. Daphne was a field officer for a reason. The position allowed her to work remote sites far away from Atlanta, but even Carlsbad wasn't far enough to escape the memories.

"Brian and I found him. Man, I'll...I'll never forget the smell."

Brian shuddered. "And his face. His eyes. I swear it looked like something scared him to death."

"How did he die?" asked Daphne.

"Well, he used to drink," replied Brian, "until he got some kind of liver problem, and the doctor told him to quit."

"It was an El Paso doc too," added Trip to emphasize accuracy of the diagnosis.

"But he stopped two years ago. Wouldn't touch the stuff. We found him with a bottle of vodka in his hand and an empty one on the chair next to him."

"Why would he start drinking? He had to have a reason."

"We don't know," replied Trip, gravy dripping down his chin.

Daphne extended a large hand and gently wiped the dribble, further enriching his red cheeks.

"Last time we were together, I offered him a beer. Just kidding, you know. He turned it down like he always does."

"When was that?"

"Friday. Right, Bri?"

"Yep. Last Friday. We had a few at the Cavern, then did some night shooting. Grady and Arturo left at the same time we did. Thought they just went home. We haven't heard from Grady since then either. We're gonna go by his dad's work today and ask about him."

"So the missing guy drove home with the friend that died, and you haven't seen him since that night. Do you think they started drinking together?"

Brian shook an emphatic negative. "No way. Arturo doesn't drink. Didn't drink, I mean. We made fun of him and all, but none of us would actually give him a beer. Especially Grady."

"Fernie wouldn't either," said Trip. "He went shooting with us too. So did Rich."

Daphne released a half laugh. "Fernie's the guy who offered to rent me a piñata. I'll tell you straight up, that dude is funny."

"Trip and I are going over to his house later to see if he has any other ideas on Grady. Do you guys want to come along?"

Becca looked to Daphne for approval. "We have all day. The release isn't until six. We want to let the wolves out while there's enough light for them to get their bearings."

"We need to make a few pickups first," said Brian. "That'll take about an hour."

"What do you guys do?" Daphne asked.

"They harvest the local honey," replied Becca before Brian could answer. "After Fernie's, can we find somebody to talk to about that fur we found where you were shooting? I read about a radiation dump around here in my research for this recovery effort. Maybe somebody out there would know why the fur is radioactive." She looked at her hands. "I was touching it a lot. I wonder if that's a problem."

Brian glanced at her pink fingers half the size of his. "Grady's dad works in some kind of health department at WIPP. He might know somebody who works with radiation out there. We'll go there after Fernie's."

*

Brian climbed into the Suburban. "Let's make this quick, so no horsing around today. We got five stops, all porta johns."

Trip drove to the office, a double-wide office trailer in a fenced gravel lot with four pumper trucks parked in front. Inside the empty trailer, Brian pulled a set of keys from a row of hooks hanging above the counter. He waved out the back window to Carla, who was hosing down equipment on a gravel pad.

The first two stops were regular customers scheduled for weekly pumps. Brian connected the green corrugated plastic suction hose to the truck, and Trip manipulated the nozzle to evacuate the tank. After the tank was empty, Trip brush-mopped the walls, floor, and seat inside the five-foot-square fiberglass potty. Cleaning finished, Brian dumped a cup of chemical mix in the tank, and Trip replaced the toilet paper.

"Last one, and we're out of here," said Brian, pulling the pumper next to a self-owned unit not on their regular route.

Trip dragged the suction hose to the dilapidated fiberglass shell. He opened the door to a blast of hot, acrid sewage fumes that smacked him in the face. A swarm of flies used the opportunity to escape.

He stepped back for a clean breath. "Damn, Bri. This one's nasty. We gotta tell Jenkins to stop cleaning tanks that he don't own."

"Just get in there. We'll be done in a couple minutes."

Trip hooked the door open and went back in, shirt covering his nose. "Not this one." His voice echoed in the thin-walled chamber. "Come look at the pile of shit in the bottom. Never seen anything like it. Gotta be a hole in the tank. All the water leaked out and left the shit on top. We got a pyramid of poop in here. Come see."

"I don't need to see another pile of shit," yelled Brian from the back of the truck as he clipped the quick-connect hose fitting to the pumper valve. He looked around the truck and saw Trip leaning over the opening.

"Don't lean too far!"

"*Shit!*"

"Dumbass."

"My sunglasses fell in."

Trip reached deep into the hole. Even with his head beneath the rim, he could hear Brian laugh.

"It ain't funny. They slipped out of my shirt pocket."

He backed out to get a lung full of clean air.

"Why the hell did you lean over the tank?"

Trip shrugged. "That pile is so weird, I had to look."

"I warned you about stuff falling out of your pocket. Lost two pair of sunglasses myself."

"But these are new. I think I can reach them. Plenty of light and they're sitting on top."

"On top of what?"

"The pile I told you about."

Brian waited at the truck, having seen enough piles that nothing in the bottom of a tank impressed him anymore.

Trip took a deep breath, leaned over, and reached his arm down as far as it would go, trying not to fall headfirst into the thick black pyramid. Each time his fingertips touched the plastic frames, he pushed the glasses deeper into the mud-like mix. On the third attempt, his dangling foot kicked the latch loose allowing the flimsy door to wobble closed.

Brian watched the shadowy movements through the translucent containment, shaking his head in disgust as his friend repeatedly lowered himself headfirst into the bowels of a shit tank.

After five minutes of foul language and shoes banging against fiberglass walls, a victorious "*Got 'em*" resonated from the chamber. Arms black to the elbow, Trip triumphantly exited the plastic potty. He wiped the glasses on his shirt and proudly positioned them in their rightful place—on the brim of his nose.

"There is *no way* that was worth it, dude."

"But these are new."

"Now I know how to get you to stick your head in a septic tank. I'll toss your sunglasses in."

Brian proceeded to spray the inside of the portable toilet, beating down the pyramid with a stiff water stream while the suction hose gobbled up the remnants.

"I gotta invent a stick that can grab things," said Trip, picking black muck from his arms and flinging it at Brian. "Something like that stuffed animal claw machine at the hardware store, but I'll put the claw on the end of a stick."

"Those claw machines drop everything. And you can already buy a claw on a stick. They advertise them everywhere for old people."

"Dang. Hey, if you know all about those sticks, why don't you have one in the truck?"

Brian snapped the metal hatch shut on the equipment compartment and opened the driver's door. "Because anything that falls into that hole is gone forever. I wouldn't touch it, even if I could reach it."

They dropped the pumper truck at the office, cleaned up in the restroom, and climbed back into the Suburban. A wry grin spread across Trip's face on the way to the motel.

"Don't get mad, but I forgot to reload toilet paper in that last unit. Some big-ass construction dude is going to be pissed."

"You ass. I think you do that on purpose."

The truck was quiet for a few minutes until Brian asked, "Hey, do you believe what Becca said about that fur being radioactive?"

CHAPTER 24

IN THE SHADOW

MEL LEFT WAVES of stress behind as he walked under the overhead section of the Forrestal Building toward the National Mall. He had escaped DOE without injury, without an immediate inquisition. Carlton pressed, but he defended his position well enough to stave off a visit from headquarters. The next and much more difficult issue was Joel.

His pocket vibrated as he crossed at the light. A text from his secretary.

MEETING WITH DONNA 8:30 TOMORROW

Mel replied.

MORNING OR EVENING?

With Donna, either was a possibility.

MORNING

A meeting with the undersecretary was the last thing he needed. Her underlings he could handle, but Donna's piercing blue eyes saw right through him. She may not know everything he was doing in the bowels of the desert, but she always seemed to know what he was thinking. He would have to make it an early night to get back to Forrestal for the morning mauling. Donna expected punctuality.

With nothing in his pocket to quench the anxiety that just bumped up a notch, Mel sat on a shaded bench along the graveled path of the National Mall and observed surroundings he always brushed by. Streets empty two hours ago were lined with cars and buses. Walkers and runners on the mall's rectangular circuit dodged business suits and tour groups vying for space on the gravel path. Families maneuvered steps and sidewalks, pushing and pulling children whining about everything being historical. Moms and dads with fat fanny packs, water bottles, and ever-present cell phones argued over itineraries. Children only steps away from the car complained of too much walking. Mothers replied to rapid-fire questions of when, where, why, and bathroom. Laser-focused fathers beelined it to the next museum in an imaginary competition to complete the most activities in a vacation day.

"Amazing," uttered Mel at sights and sounds he had observed a thousand times but never noticed.

He ignored a toddler's stare and proceeded to Joel's office on Fourteenth Street, a block behind powerful DC lobby offices. Exactly how Joel liked to work, in the shadow of those in charge. Mel entered a nondescript door in the center of a block-long stone office building and took the stairs to the second level.

Joel looked up from his desk in the exceptionally warm one-room office. "What the hell are you doing here?"

"Good to see you too, Joel."

He slapped his pen to the desk and sat upright. "You have one more job. Everything is on track. There is no reason for you to be standing in my office. What the hell is wrong with you?"

"We need to talk."

"We talked Friday. There's nothing else to say."

"Well—"

"You put me in a bad position, Mel. Again! We wouldn't be in this mess if you hadn't screwed up Savannah."

"I don't want to revisit that."

"Tough shit. When you get drunk and my job goes under, you'll damn well revisit it whenever I say."

In the lone visitor's chair, Mel begrudgingly accepted the admonition. Part of the nasally voiced berating was warranted.

"I know it was difficult."

"You want to talk about difficult? You were the only one to get out of that mess unscathed. You have no idea how much that cost me. Get the hell out of here. I got nothing to say to you."

Six weeks earlier, Joel had called in a debt, insisting Mel be the fourth man on a crew for midnight work at the Savannah River Site. At the time, things were not going well in Carlsbad. Margaret had gone to her sister's, and Mel disappeared on a weekend bender, something he was prone to do a couple-three times a year. During the bender, he called Joel and explained, as best he could under the circumstances, that he would not be going to South Carolina. Joel was forced to call in a last-minute substitute, and something went terribly wrong with the job. But that wasn't the reason for this visit. This meeting was to discuss three drums that arrived at WIPP months ago. Three drums that had been placed in Room 6 of Panel 5.

"Joel, when I called you Friday, that was in confidence. You told Brendon we had a problem last week."

The John Lovitz lookalike began to settle down. "I didn't tell him shit. He's guessing."

"He's guessing right. There's a rumor running around DOE that we had a ceiling collapse and a radiation release. You basically confirmed that rumor by asking Brendon questions about a *ceiling collapse and a radiation release*. You know damn well he works for Carlton."

"I didn't think he would put it together." Joel raised his voice again. "But that's not your problem. My guys are handling it."

Mel closed his eyes and puffed a stiff breath. Joel's guys handling anything was worrisome.

"Joel, if DOE thinks we have a problem, they *will* send a team to investigate. I told you Friday, Dom and I took care of it. We cleaned everything up and covered our tracks. If you hadn't said anything to Brendon, I wouldn't have to be here cleaning up your mess. You're not helping."

"Don't tell me little Brendon has you running scared. He's a classic burned-out desk jockey. Even if he mentioned our conversation, he's not the kind of guy to push it forward."

Vodka fumes were crawling out from under Mel's shirt as angered sweat glands activated. His favorite spirit did not smell nearly as good as it had the night before.

"Steve Simon told Donna the same story. Two sources, Joel. I nearly shit my pants when Carlton told me he had two sources. That's what has me on edge." An edge he desperately needed to take off.

"Aren't you getting a little too excited about all this? Granted, an investigation would not be ideal, but nobody can connect that release to our drums." Joel narrowed his eyes and leaned forward. "Or can they?"

Maybe now was not the best time to answer that question.

"Are you as dumb as you look? Alarms went off everywhere. A man is missing. That's a hell of a lot worse than a chunk of salt falling from the ceiling."

"What's going on with the missing man? You didn't mention that to me Friday."

"Friday, I thought Chuck had ducked out early, but we haven't heard from him since that night."

The same heat attacking Mel began to wear on Joel. A missing government employee at a secure facility had to be formally reported to DOE three days after the first absence. Combined with a ceiling collapse, the government would be forced to investigate thoroughly.

Joel interlocked his fingers. "What do you think happened to him?"

"I have no idea. To be honest, he's not my priority right now. I bought us a little time on his absence by saying he went hunting, but that won't last."

He leaned forward and placed his palms down on Joel's desk. "If DOE is poking around, they won't have to look far to figure out we have a waste characterization problem. The contamination released from those drums won't align with the inventory sheets. It won't be long before they want data on every drum in Room 6. I can fake data, but eventually they'll want to open drums. Today's problem, the real problem for you, is that they'll shut us down the second they confirm we had an unreported release. The special delivery scheduled two weeks from tomorrow will never get into the hole. We'll be ordered to check and double-check everything."

Joel cleared his throat. "There's been a change in the schedule. That shipment arrives tomorrow. You better damn well be there to receive it."

For the third time in three hours, Mel's stomach hit the floor.

"You moron. You can't just change the schedule. When were you going to tell me? What kind of operation do you think WIPP is, some redneck landfill where you back a truck up and push a refrigerator into a ditch? A dozen people inspect every load that comes on-site. You have to stop that shipment, Joel."

"Can't. I had some trouble with my temporary storage. The guys moved the drums sooner than I wanted. The truck is on the road."

Beads of sweat boiled on Mel's forehead. Heat and humidity in the confining office, and the fireball Joel had just slung, had his chest and armpits bleeding through the jacket. Logistics scrolled through his mind. He needed to call his secretary and get the truck arrival schedule. He needed to get ahold of Dom to make sure he would be on the dock when the truck showed up. Most importantly, he needed to send Rip somewhere to make sure he wasn't around when the truck arrived.

Joel sneered. "Did I lose you for a minute?"

"You think it's funny? *A game?*" Mel mopped his forehead with a moist handkerchief. "You said your guys were handling something. Explain."

"It's nothing. They'll meet with Dom today and give me a firsthand report on the three drums in the hole. If you've covered all the tracks like you said, they'll be in and out of the site in an hour."

"They're at my site? *You have men at my site?*"

"Don't get your panties all in a ruffle. These men are pros. They've worked a dozen DOE sites. They'll enter during off-hours. Nobody will ever know they were there."

Arteries in Mel's neck throbbed. Tony and the crew would surely report the missing drum back to their boss. He needed to have Dom get the replacement drum in place before Joel's men entered Room 6. Before they jeopardized any chance of getting through the incident unscathed.

"Do they have any role in the new shipment arriving tomorrow?"

"No. If everything checks out today, they'll leave Carlsbad before then. Nobody wants to be in that hick town any longer than necessary."

The size of the pile of shit sliding downhill in Mel's direction was almost too much to grasp. "Why didn't you just sink those new cans in a river near the site?"

"I have my reasons." Reasons that were no longer valid. After the last job failed, Joel disappeared for a week on his own bender. Not a crawling-through-desert-sand bender like Mel, but his liquid diet at an island getaway wasn't much different. During that time, acting on their own, Tony and the guys inserted the drums into a WIPP waste inventory destined for disposal. Removing them from that inventory was more risk than leaving them.

Joel leaned back again and stared at the blank wall as though he were looking far beyond the windowless room. He never liked Mel. He never trusted a man who depended on rum for resolve, bourbon for bravery, and vodka for valor. But now he was stuck having to pay Mel handsomely to get the new drums underground at WIPP because the drums were on the way.

"Let's go over this again," said Mel. "We can't miss any details or all of us are going to end up in prison. We have three drums underground, and tomorrow, three more will be offloaded topside."

"Two drums are on the truck."

"Two? What the hell, Joel?"

Another smirk. "Is that a problem?"

"The number isn't the problem. Three is the same effort as two, but when the hell were you going to tell me? The paper trail is the most important thing in all of this." Joel started to argue, but Mel was on a roll. "I have to get them underground ASAP. I'll call Dom as soon as we're finished here. He and I are the only ones who can touch those cans. We can't risk having one of your drums pulled off the pallet for secondary inspection. Sites RTR waste drums, Joel. If my waste acceptance manager picks one of your drums to review against the RTR, you, my friend, are screwed."

The smug attitude subsided. "What's an RTR?"

"Real Time Radiography. Like I said, this isn't some hick landfill. This is a complex nuclear waste repository. Sites place each drum on a pedestal inside a large X-ray machine. The drum spins and a video of the contents is recorded. Do you want to see a video of your drums, Joel? I could arrange that."

"Asshole."

"Of course, the site video won't show the real contents because the original drums were replaced with your drums. But if the shipping documentation indicates a drum of plastics and we have a two-hundred-pound drum of, let's just say, something else, somebody is going to ask questions. Dom needs to be there to make sure your drums get moved downhole before anyone has a chance to check them against documentation."

The situation was sounding far worse than Joel expected. He was unaware of the details related to offloading drums and had not considered the possibility of secondary inspection. He needed to call Tony and make sure everything was under control.

"What the hell are you doing here if you have work to do at the site?"

"First of all, your drums weren't due for two weeks. If I didn't make an appearance at DOE this morning, Carlton was ready to go to Carlsbad, and neither of us can allow that to happen. Especially now with *your* new delivery schedule. I was going to return today, but Donna wants to meet in the morning."

Joel's sweat-soaked eyebrows twitched. "What does Donna want?"

CHAPTER 25

RADIOACTIVE FUR

"WE CAN TAKE my truck," offered Trip.

"Truck?" Becca studied the camouflage paint job on the raised frame. "I don't know what to call it, but I don't think truck is the right word."

Daphne climbed into the front seat of the four-door Suburban. "Call it whatever you want, DC, but it's perfect for me. Lots of leg room up here, and my hair doesn't hit the roof."

"It's a truck, for real. Says so on the title and everything."

Trip reached for the registration in the glove box, bumping his hand against Daphne's leg in the process.

"You getting fresh with me again?"

He yanked his hand back and covered the hair behind his ear.

Brian climbed in the back. "Fernie's house is five minutes from here."

Trip pulled to the curb in front of a flat-roofed tan stucco home with gravel landscape and a meticulously maintained swath of native plants adjacent to the concrete walk. A ceramic desert tortoise and two white-tailed jackrabbits, distinguished by tall, oversized ears, were perched in the yard. A three-foot hand-carved wooden grizzly guarded the door.

Fernie opened the door, and before Brian could say hello, a short, wrinkled woman stepped from the kitchen carrying a plate of tortillas.

"Miho, don't make them stand. Come. Eat."

Trip didn't need to be asked twice. He barged past Brian, accepted a fresh tortilla, and went straight to the kitchen.

"Abuelita, this is Daphne and Becca. Some new friends we made." He turned to Becca. "This is mi abuelita. My grandmother, Yolita."

Trip and Brian slid into chairs next to the wall under a picture of the Blessed Mother. Becca and Fernie sat across, leaving Daphne at the head facing a crucifix on the opposite wall. Before Daphne could scoot her chair in, a bowl of pinto beans arrived.

While Brian and Trip peppered Fernie with questions about Grady, Yolita pinballed between the stove, refrigerator, and table with more energy than any young adult at the table. Daphne tossed a curious eye at a bowl of diced green something Yolita had set much too near.

"Green *chile*," said Fernie, pronouncing the *i* as an *e* and the *e* as an *a*. The New Mexican staple often found on the table for breakfast, lunch, and dinner. "Put some in your beans."

"And on the tortilla," said Yolita, instantly at Daphne's side. She glopped a heaping spoonful in the middle of Daphne's tortilla, spread it to the edges, and bounced back to the stove, next to which stood a small bronze statue of St. Francis of Assisi, bird on his shoulder, wolf at his side.

Daphne glanced at Fernie, who was devouring a tortilla loaded with twice the green chile than hers. She took a cautious half bite and chewed slowly. Just as she swallowed, the fire kicked in.

"*Ahhhhh.*" She opened her mouth and fanned her tongue. "*Water!*"

"*Oh, si.* It's not even hot." Yolita handed Daphne a small cup of ice water. She refilled Daphne's beans, then loaded a spoonful of chile straight into her mouth. "Fresh. We roast last week."

The demonstration did little to quell the heat. "*Ice. More ice.*"

After another round of refills, Yolita finally took her seat at the other end of the table. "Miho, you haven't told me about your friends."

"Oh, I'm Becca, and this is Daphne." She gestured to her partner who was still panting to cool a burning tongue. "I love your house and those wonderful animal statues out front. Daphne and I work for the Fish and Wildlife Service."

"The fish. Not so good on the Pecos." Her eyes found Fernie's. "Ahh, but your abuelito, mijo, he could catch the fish. Every day we eat fish."

"Oh, we don't work with fish," said Becca. "We work with wolves."

Yolita recoiled her head and gasped. She crossed herself with her fingertips, kissed her St. Christopher medal, and uttered, *"Fantasma del Gris."*

*

"Are you sure we can drive right out to a federal government radiation dump?" asked Becca from the back seat as Trip turned the wheel just outside of town. "It sounds kind of dangerous."

"WIPP's been here for a long time," replied Brian. "They had an accident back when Trip and I were in middle school. There's a lot of rumors about it, but nobody got hurt, and I don't think they've had any problems since then."

Trip squared his shoulders. "Getting on-site won't be a problem. We're out here twice a week. They have some portables in the back by the fence."

"Portable what?"

"All the guards know us," added Brian. "They just wave us through. Usually we're in the company truck, though, so they might ask us some questions today. But Fernie's brother is a guard, so we'll get in."

Daphne leaned her seat back. "Fernie's brother? Lucky stiff, growing up with a grandma in the house. That woman can cook, and I wasn't even hungry."

"Yolita cooks better than any restaurant in town. Bri and I stop by their house sometimes when we're starving."

"You're always starving," said Brian.

"I'd gain a hundred pounds if that woman lived near me," said Daphne. "She tried to spoon another load of beans into my bowl before I finished my second helping. Thought I was being polite with the 'no, thank you.' But that sweet little high-pitched *'you don't like it?'* forced me to take another helping. What else could I do? That reminds me." She loosened her belt a notch.

"I don't know if I ever had beans as a meal," said Becca. "You know, without a side or something."

Trip shrugged, not sure he ever had beans *with* a side of anything.

"The food was super good, though. Just a little spicy for me."

"No kidding." Daphne's smile disappeared. She turned back to Brian. "Lady kind of stressed out. Kissing her St. Christopher medal and running to the back room."

"Guess Fernie wasn't kidding when he told us his grandma hears wolves."

Becca leaned to the middle. "'*Fantasma del Gris.*' That's the legend Fernie told us about. I saw a picture with the same name at the Chinese restaurant. It means 'ghost of the gray.'"

"A gray ghost. As if we won't have our hands full as it is." Daphne rocked her shoulders and sang out, "I ain't afraid of no ghost."

"Oh, brother," muttered Becca.

"It's good that Fernie can look for your friend on Friday," continued Daphne. "Seven days is a long time to be gone."

"Fernie thinks he could be in Slaughter Canyon," said Trip. "That's on the way to the Guadalupes where he and Grady liked to fish. He told us that while you were—"

"Firefighting." Daphne stuck her long tongue out and examined it for blisters in the mirror.

"He might be right," said Brian. "Grady likes to camp near the cave in that canyon. I'll text Rich and make sure he goes with Fernie. That's no place to go alone."

Trip shrugged. "We've all been to Slaughter Canyon alone, Bri. It's no big deal."

"Not smart, Little Man. Especially a place called *Slaughter Canyon*. Kind of ominous. Sounds like the kind of place these ranchers would want to corral our wolves and take care of business."

"Is that where you're releasing the wolves?"

"You are so sweet, Little Man. Trying to get me to reveal the release location. Gotta do more than bat those pretty blue eyes to get me to talk."

Again, Trip's face transitioned to the color of his arm.

As the drive dragged on, Daphne found her eyes glassing over at the endless desert and the silent staccato of fence posts racing by just out of reach. A gust of wind swirled dust across the road in a half circle, fading to nothing as quickly as it arrived. The burst lasted just long enough to pop loose a pack of tumbleweeds, kick-starting them on a rolling journey to nowhere. Not a tree in sight, and just enough undulation in the landscape to give her trouble keeping an eye on the wolves after the release. Sage-green shrubs peppered the roadside, adding bland color to the sandy landscape. Sporadic cactus, yucca, and mesquite popped out of the dirt between patches of shrubs. Everything looked pointy, prickly, and thick. All potential issues if she ended up tracking on foot. Heat was another issue. The sun was already baking her skin through the window, though the AC was on high. This wasn't the most remote setting she had worked but definitely the warmest. Maybe the heat would finally sweat out the memory of that Florida night.

A transition from beige to blue snapped her back to the present. "What the hell?" said Daphne as they crossed a large shallow body of water. "Where did this come from?"

"Potash mines," replied Brian. "Most of the mining out here is conventional with heavy machinery and trucks, but one company started some kind of operation with water. They dissolve the potash and pump it up into these basins. After it dries, they go out and scrape it off the surface. Supposed to save money."

"And what the hell is potash?" asked Daphne.

"Just fertilizer," replied Trip. "We're like the potash capital of the country."

"Potash is fertilizer?" Daphne scrunched her face. "Like *manure* back home is fertilizer?" She turned to the window. "And you're the capital. This picture gets clearer by the minute."

"That's an interesting approach, though," said Becca, recalling geology studies in college. "Kind of like the way they mine lithium in Chile. I'm reading a book that talks about that."

"The approach might be interesting," replied Brian. "But look at all that water going to waste. We do live in the desert. Every summer, the city tells us to stop watering our lawns, then Trip and I drive out here and see all this water evaporating."

Becca pointed at a scattered herd of cattle beyond the water. "A lot of cows out there. Free-range grazing, Daphne. That's why you're here."

"Damn, that's a lot of desert," said Daphne. "How could anyone live here their entire life?"

Trip adjusted his hands on the steering wheel. "We haven't been here our whole life. Brian and I moved to Carlsbad after high school. Jal was too small, you know. But I miss it sometimes."

Daphne snapped her head from the desert to the driver. "Too small? You lived in a place smaller than this? Hell, I didn't think it could get worse."

"It's not so bad. Jal's just down the road. We're on the Jal Highway, actually. Jobs are better out there for some things. When Brian was a roustabout in the oilfields, he made real good money. I was a roughneck."

Daphne snickered. "Roustabouts and roughnecks. Not exactly the job titles we have in Atlanta or DC."

"I have to agree with Daphne. This place is pretty small, and everything is the same. Desert, desert, and more desert. I'm not gonna lie, it was super cool for the first couple of days, but now it's just the same thing mile after mile."

"But everything's not the same," said Trip. "All the towns around here are different. Artesia is border patrol. Alamogordo is Holloman and White Sands. Roswell is aliens and the military school. Clovis is the air force base, and Carlsbad has *everything*, like WIPP, the caverns, the potash. We even got a Walmart. I can't imagine living anyplace bigger than Carlsbad."

Brian stared silently out the window. His entire life, he'd imagined living somewhere bigger than Carlsbad. His mother had shared stories of Dallas, Phoenix, and Denver, places she'd visited and promised to take her children. A promise that ended on the same highway they were now traveling.

Daphne rolled her eyes at the much too excited reference to Walmart. "Since I drove into town, I've seen a dozen feral dogs, cats, and kids. From where I sit, these places are all the same."

"How can you say that if you haven't been to them?"

"Look, Little Man, we never release near a big city, so I've been in a lot of little places. When you drive through a town and all the signs tell you exactly what the business is in one word *or less*, those towns are all the freakin' same. We drove down Main Street in your town, and all I saw were signs that read, 'Laundry,' 'Tacos,' 'Gas,' 'Bank,' and 'Chinese.' Hell, one motel sign doesn't even say 'Motel.' It just flickers 'Vacancy' in the window, and only three letters light up."

"It's not that bad," said Brian.

"Maybe not, but it's close."

The cab was mostly quiet the rest of the drive with Brian imagining life in the city, Trip thinking about how great it was to live in a small town, Daphne thinking about how long she was going to be stuck there, and Becca thankful to be leaving in the morning.

At the WIPP gate, Trip chatted a minute with Julio, who pointed to the administration building and directed them through. They found Rip Anderson standing by the coffee pot talking to the secretary, Marsha.

Trip shook the man's hand. "Grady come home yet?"

"Not yet," replied Rip. His welcoming smile faded. "When I saw the beast pull up, I was going to ask you the same question. Been almost a week now. Three or four days, and I don't think much about it, but it's not like him to be gone six days without checking in."

"We were with him last Friday. You know, shooting and stuff, but we ain't seen him since. We can help you look for him this weekend if you want a hand."

"That'd be mighty helpful, boys. You know his hangouts in the desert better than I do. It's been a while since he and I went hunting and fishing. Need to do more of that." He took in a deep breath and lowered his gaze to the floor. "It was only a couple days ago I was fuming at him about something I can't even remember. Now I just want my boy back."

Brian gestured to the ladies. "Rip, this is Becca and Daphne. They're with the forest service. We have a question for you."

"It's Rebecca Olsen and this is Daphne Bender." They extended hands. "Actually, we're with the US Fish and Wildlife Service. I was hoping you could answer a few questions about some fur we found last week."

"Come on back to my office."

Becca explained the circumstances that led to her fur find as they walked down the pale hall. "When Brian and his friends were shooting, they saw a large animal in the dark but couldn't tell what it was. We went back to the same spot a couple of days later to try and identify the animal. There were a few tracks, but they had been eroded by the wind. I found a wad of matted fur stuck in a bush. A colleague of mine in DC told me it was radioactive."

"Let's take a look. I can do a quick analysis right here."

She scrunched her face. "I didn't bring it with me. I mean, he didn't give it back. And I didn't want it back. It was radioactive."

"I see." Rip pinched his narrow chin. "Dog fur, you say. What kind of dog? Like a shepherd or a Doberman? Long or short, I guess I'm asking."

"I didn't say dog, but it was definitely canine. Longer than a shepherd. We confirmed with a pretty high degree of certainty the fur was wolf."

Rip's attention refocused. "Didn't think we had wolves around these parts."

"You don't. Well, not yet." She deferred discussion of the imminent release. "We tried to reintroduce them in the past, but they didn't survive."

"Hmm. I worked at the Savannah River Site in South Carolina a few years before moving back to New Mexico. We had a deer problem at that site and a little bit of a radiation problem as well. There is a lot of forest in that part of the country. A lot of deer and a whole lot of water. All the old sites like Savannah River have legacy problems. You know, burying radioactive waste out in the backyard. That kind of thing."

Daphne's square hair spiked. "You are kidding, right? People didn't really bury radioactive stuff in the backyard?"

"Just a figure of speech." Rip leaned casually against the corner of his desk. "I don't mean in the backyard of a house, though some old-timers were known to take stuff home and play with it in the garage. At some of the older government sites, it wasn't uncommon to dump stuff in the forest just to get it out of the way and continue on with their mission. You have to think about it in terms of the Cold War era. Protecting the environment wasn't exactly our main concern."

He recognized familiar glassed eyes of a generation, who, like Grady, were scarcely familiar with the term Cold War and had absolutely no appreciation of the context.

Daphne shook her head. "Uh-huh. That makes it all okay?"

Rip passed on explaining the evolution of environmental protection and changing political priorities. "The buried drums and discarded material eventually found its way to the groundwater. Contaminants leached up through plant roots. The deer eat the grass and plants, and that's where we had our problem. To control the deer population, limited hunting is allowed on the site. Hunters apply for special permits and bring the animal organs to our lab. I've seen plenty of radioactive organs, but I never found radioactive fur."

"If they were only bringing you the organ meat, you probably never saw the fur," said Brian.

Rip pinched his chin again. "Fair point, son. We did some of our own testing on dosed animals, but not a lot on the fur. We mostly found issues with the thyroid and pituitary gland, depending on the type of radiation to which the animal had been exposed. We often found saturated pituitary glands to be cancerous, which caused abnormalities in some animals. Saw more than a few deer that were half-again as big as a normal deer."

"What do you mean 'dosed'?" asked Becca.

"That's a term we use when something receives a radiation dose. Like if you stand next to something that is radioactive."

Trip shifted away from the filing cabinet.

"We frequently recovered animals that had been trapped in old contaminated buildings where we stored radioactive material and other items. Sometimes those animals had been dosed for long periods of time. You ever see a squirrel the size of a house cat? Kind of catches you off guard the first time."

Back in the cab, Becca gazed out the window, lost in thought processing everything she just heard. A yellow subcompact car riding low to the ground drove through her line of sight.

✦

"That's the bitch who has my bag," growled Tony. "She's staring right at us. What the hell is she doing here?"

Augie pulled into a slot across from the admin building. The men scrunched as low as they could in tiny seats while the lady stared their way, pursing her lips and squinting her eyes.

"She's watching us," said Jack. "Doesn't even care that we see her. Tony, did you have anything in your bag that mentioned WIPP?"

A good question that forced Tony to run the contents through his mind.

"I don't think so," he lied, recalling a file folder that could get the team into trouble. "She probably connected the respirator and Tyvek on her own. Must have some affiliation out here to get on-site."

"A waste auditor, maybe?" asked Jack. "They travel in groups."

"In that piece of shit Suburban? Don't be an ass. And why the hell would an auditor keep my bag?"

"Just sayin'."

"If you're going to speak, try saying something intelligent." Tony stared hard at the Suburban. "FBI maybe? Undercover? Let's wait until they leave, then we'll go inside and find out who she is."

✦

"He didn't believe me," Becca finally said. "I can't blame him, really. It's super weird and everything."

Daphne put a hand on her friend's shoulder. "Are you sure your DC guy was right about the radiation?"

"Dr. Shanks is super good with bio analyses. I don't know anything about radiation, so I guess I don't know how good he is with that. He sounded pretty confident when he explained it to me."

"I've never heard anyone talk about radioactive animals like that. Maybe a dog or coyote ate something radioactive," said Trip, drumming up an image of a radioactive spider biting a dog.

"That's what I was thinking," agreed Becca. "Until he said all the radioactive stuff out here is stored underground. There's no way it can get out. I mean, he actually said it would be *impossible* to get out."

Trip smirked. "That's just the government talking. Things happen out here that people don't talk about. That big accident a few years ago didn't kill anybody, but it shut WIPP down for a long time. Just last week, Brian and I heard some workers talking about something they were afraid of down in the hole."

Brian glanced from Becca to Daphne. "Stuff gets out of this place. I don't know how, but it does. Don't take this the wrong way, but we think about things a little different out here in the west. You can't just believe Rip because he works for the government. You kinda have to assume he's lying *because* he works for the government. Even if he is our friend's dad."

"But they bury the waste over two thousand feet deep," said Becca. "How could it get out?"

"And they take it down in an elevator," added Daphne. "What the hell? Do you just push the call button for the basement? That's a long freakin' elevator ride. I'd get claustrophobic for damn sure."

"Can you drop us off at the hotel?" Becca asked Trip. "I want to spend some time on the computer before Daphne and I conduct the release."

Daphne cocked her head. "You make it sound like you and I are doing the work tonight. The release team takes care of everything. We just need to make sure the collars are synchronized before our little guys scamper off."

"Are you sure we can't go with you?"

"Afraid not, Little Man. A release is a pretty big deal for the service. We have some tight protocols that don't allow anyone at the release site. And with all Becca's pissed-off cowboys, we sure as hell can't risk it. If they get word of the release location, our babies won't last the night."

CHAPTER 26

HARDHATS

THE CONVERSATION WITH the Fish and Wildlife ladies left Rip perplexed. He had recently found clumps of fur that looked much like what the young lady described. Fur that most likely came from German shepherds, but until he could investigate further, he didn't want to bring it up.

Dom tapped twice on the doorjamb and stepped into Rip's office. "What was that all about?"

"I'm not really sure. Some park rangers asking about coyotes or dogs. They found some fur nearby and claimed it was radioactive. Didn't have it with them, of course. Without a sample, I don't know what to think. A week ago, I would have insisted that was impossible."

"What do you mean 'a week ago'?"

Before Rip could answer, they were interrupted by a dusty blast of wind as three large men entered the building. Men Dom recognized from Savannah River as the guys who came in late at night to remove troubling waste drums. Men who would not be at WIPP merely by coincidence.

"Can I get you gentlemen to sign in, please?" asked the student intern manning the front desk.

"It's all right, Katie. They're with me." Dom patted Rip on the back and gave him a gentle push toward the exit. "Some friends from way back, Rip. See you tomorrow."

"I'm out tomorrow. Going to spend the day looking for Grady. The receiving team will unload the truck and do the initial surveys when it arrives. I'll be back Friday to register the new shipment and coordinate placement underground."

"Good luck finding your son. This way, gentlemen." He led Tony and the big men to Mel's much larger office.

As Augie closed the window blinds, he watched the man who had just left climb into a large red pickup.

"Are you here to see Mel?" asked Dom. "He's out for a couple days."

"I need some answers," replied Tony in an ominous tone, enhanced by the darkened room.

"Okay. How can I help you, gentlemen? Coffee, anyone? Something stronger?"

Tony placed the crumpled, salt-laced inventory sheet on the desk. He allowed his dull eyes to do the talking, giving the man time to sweat. A silent intimidation technique that had a way of eliciting truthful answers.

Dom recognized the diagram immediately but had no idea how Tony had come into possession of a piece of paper from the restricted side of the underground. The large office, filled with oversized men, seemed to close in.

"Like I said, Mel's in DC. If that's for him, I'll be sure he gets it. Is that all?"

"Where's the drum, Dom? We found two. The third one is missing. Your job was to make sure those cans were safe." With Augie and Jack slightly behind and flanking the left and right sides, Tony looked like the godfather of a crime syndicate. He leaned his palms on the desk and snarled. "*Where's...my...drum?*"

"It's safe." Dom's voice projected a hint of tremor. "We had a collapse. Mel and I took care of it. There's nothing to worry about."

"I'll decide if there's anything to worry about. What do you mean, you '*took care of it*'? We were down in the room yesterday, and one of the drums is gone. Where did you put it?"

"Down in the...How did you get into the UG?"

"I'm asking the questions!"

"We had a ceiling collapse that triggered alarms, but Mel and I took care of it. We closed out the alarms and told the staff they were false readings. We went into Room 6 to make sure everything was okay with the special drums. If it was any other room, we would have never gone down there, but we know how important those cans are to Joel. We took care of them, like I said."

"Go on."

"The drums were a mess. Chunks of salt knocked half the pallets over and broke one of your drums open. Ruptured a big hole in the side. The collapse even busted a hole in the back wall of the room which surprised the hell out of us. We found a cave that nobody knew existed. It's not on any of our geological maps, and God only knows how they missed something like that in the drilling operations back when the site was assessed. We couldn't leave an open drum in the room, so we pushed it into the cave and fixed the wall with some large pieces of salt. Then we covered everything with bags of magnesium oxide."

"Magnesium oxide," uttered Augie. "That's the shit from the torn bags."

"Sounds reasonable," said Tony. "Except the part about a hole in the drum. What did you see?"

"Nothing. I swear. Just the yellow plastic rad bag. Looked like it had been pulled out of the hole, but nothing was in there. The drum was empty. I didn't even need Mel's help to get it behind the wall."

Tony had no doubt the man on the opposite side of the desk was providing honest answers. But the replies were not good. That drum was not empty when it had been shipped.

"Good answers, Dom. I knew we could count on you and Mel. Tell me about the yellow waste bag."

Dom exhaled a breath he had kept in much longer than normal. "Just a rad bag with a horsetail tie. You know, the opening twisted, folded over, and taped. The hole in the drum was maybe twelve inches in diameter." He held his hands up to approximate the dimensions. "Right in the side of the can. The bag was half shredded and hung out eighteen inches or so. A viscous goop had drizzled out. Not much light so I couldn't examine it to any degree, and we were wearing full-face respirators, of course, but the drum was empty, I'm certain of that."

"Interesting." Tony scratched his cheek. The goop was easily explained; fluid from a decomposed body could be substantial. The container being empty was more concerning. "If a chunk of salt fell onto the drum and breached it, how does the plastic protrude outward? And how in the hell does the drum get empty? Where did the contents go?"

Silence.

He turned to Jack and Augie. "You guys have any idea?"

Shrugs.

"Was anyone else down there besides you and Mel?"

Dom fidgeted in his chair and tapped a pen on the desk. "We're not sure. Chuck went missing the night of the collapse. He wasn't in the shaft when Mel and I cleaned things up. Everyone assumes he's out hunting and just forgot to tell us he left. He's done that before."

"That's it? Nobody else could have seen the drum with the hole in the side?"

"Maybe Rip. The guy that just left. He normally works the day-shift, but he filled in for a guy that night. Rip can be a little overly thorough. You know the type. Said he didn't go into the hole, but Mel and I suspect otherwise. Even if he went down, the second he saw the collapse, he would have followed procedure and backed out. Rip would never have walked up to the drums."

"Is he going to be okay?" asked Tony with a look that explained exactly what he meant.

"Rip's a good guy. He was asking a lot of questions today. Taking samples. Found some trace contamination but nothing reportable. We can expect him to submit the findings directly to DOE. That is his job, after all, but he needs to find his son. The kid's been missing almost a week. You heard him say he'll be in Friday."

"Submit to DOE." Tony pinched his chin. "That would be a problem."

"No, Tony. It's not a problem. It's procedure. Anything that deviates from procedure *is a problem*. With Rip out for two days, we have an opportunity to make sure we didn't miss anything. I've been doing all the surveys myself, and that's a lot of area to cover. Your guys can help. Maybe do some rapid decon if necessary."

"Dom, you don't understand. We're not here to decon. This has nothing to do with whether you missed anything, it's whether Rip found anything."

"I'd like you guys to keep Rip out of this. He's a good man."

"Uh-huh. We just saw some people out front. Were they meeting with Rip?"

"I have no idea who they are or what they were talking about."

Tony turned to Jack and Augie. "I think we need to go back down and look at the drum. If it is empty, then we need to find the contents." He turned back to Dom. "When the contents are located, then I'll decide if Rip is a problem."

Dom escorted the men to the waste hoist and down the shaft. When they stepped into the mine, he led them to the Lamp Room.

"We'll do this formal to keep the guys down here from asking questions."

Each man was issued protective clothing, a hardhat with a miner's lamp, a radio, and a brass badge.

Jack grinned and flipped the brass coin in the air. "Where's the slot machine?"

"You've been brassed," said Dom. "It's an old-school mine safety accounting system. If a fire burns your face off, that badge will let somebody know it's your body."

The grin slid away. Jack placed the coin in his pocket.

Venom spewed from Tony's eyes as they shot from the coin to Dom.

"Give me a little credit. I provided names of three guys who were here last month. This isn't traceable to you." He gathered the men's radios and set them behind a can. "But these babies are tracking devices, so we leave them right here."

Fifteen minutes later, four men dressed in white Tyvek and full-face respirators stood ten feet from the drums in Room 6. Jack carried the GM radiation pancake detector, that Tony verified was on.

"Follow me," muffled Dom, motioning toward the back corner of the room.

Pow! Dust puffed from the ceiling.

Jack dropped the meter and covered his head with both hands. "I hate that sound!"

"Buttress bolt," muffled Dom matter-of-factly. He exaggerated brushing dust from the custom plastic hardhat situated loosely on his head, leaving the other men second-guessing the decision to leave their hardhats with the radios.

With help from Augie and Jack, they promptly reopened the hole in the wall and stepped inside the dark chamber. Jack entered first and waved the meter around. When the staccato clicking decreased to silence, the men removed their respirators. Augie and Jack lit cigarettes and circled each other, shining flashlights at the geologic features protruding up from the floor and hanging from the ceiling.

Tony was dead focused on the drum that looked exactly as Dom had described. Remnants of a yellow plastic bag, which had originally contained an auditor, hung halfway out of a gaping hole in the side. Thick mucus dripped from the plastic. A wretched smell of decomposition emanated from the opening.

"It's empty. This drum is empty." He kicked the can as hard as he could, then jumped back, bouncing on his other foot, cursing the pain.

"What do you want to do, boss?" Augie flicked his butt into the dark. "Want us to put it back with the others?"

"I don't know," replied Tony, running his fingers through thinning hair. "I don't freakin' know. How the hell did this happen?" He limped around the drum. "You found it like this?"

"Just like that."

Tony sat on a stubby stalagmite to think. Decomposing four months in a sealed bag would have made the body pliable enough to be pulled through the hole. The bag had obviously snagged on the sharp metal edges, which kept it from coming out entirely. But who would remove it like that? How? Why? If somebody wanted evidence, unbolting the drum ring and removing the lid would have been much easier. Keeping the contents inside the bag would have been much cleaner.

Jack and Augie each lit another cigarette and moved farther into the cave, exploring like children. The cracking noises were not as loud but more frequent in the cavernous room.

"That noise you hear is salt pushing against this wall," said Dom. "Look next to your feet. You'll see little stalactites that fell. I told you to wear hardhats."

Another crack. A tiny stalactite shattered at Augie's feet, causing him to jump into Jack.

"Get off me, you puss. Every time we're alone in the dark. I swear."

Augie slugged him in the shoulder. "Ass."

"Will this be safe here?" asked Tony.

"Unless you want to take it into the desert, I'd leave it here. There's a nonzero probability that DOE is going to investigate the collapse. I have a dummy can already labeled. Just need to fill it. The tricky part is finding enough radioactive material to put in the new can. It's easier all around if the can gives off the same radiation dose as the one we're replacing. I'll bring the new drum into Room 6 later today and put it exactly where the diagram says it belongs."

Closing the hole took longer than opening it. Covered in salt dust and magnesium oxide, Jack, Augie, and Dom stepped back to admire their handiwork. They turned to the transport where Tony had been barking orders from the front seat. Another *crack* cut through the room.

"Salt shifts," muffled Dom, grinning at the big men cowering in their shoes.

Without warning, a massive salt chunk dropped from the ceiling, knocking Jack and Augie to the ground. When the dust cleared, a boulder of salt the size of a refrigerator sat inches from their feet—on top of Dom.

Jack and Augie jumped into the back seat. Tony stomped on the accelerator. The electric transport fishtailed out of Room 6, leaving a plume of dust all the way to the elevator.

Safe and secure behind the steel doors of the upward conveyance, Tony snickered. "At least he was wearing a hardhat."

With the WIPP gate in the rearview mirror, the three men finally breathed a sigh of relief.

Jack slithered to the middle of the back seat and pushed his head forward.

"Boss, we still don't know where the body is."

CHAPTER 27

RELEASE THE WOLVES

BECCA STOOD ON her tiptoes to peek inside the animal crates in the beds of two heavy-duty extended cab pickup trucks while Daphne, Sharpie in hand, busily circled various landmarks on a map spread across the hood.

"Checking one more item off my bucket list," said Daphne as she made final notations for the Wednesday evening release. "Always wondered what it would be like to stand in the middle of nowhere." Her eyes followed a two-track dirt road into the scorching desert. "Almost far enough," she uttered to herself.

"You've got that right." Becca shaded her eyes and peered into the distance. "Kind of hot, but that sure is a beautiful blue sky. You don't get skylines like that back east. I am a little surprised we're so close to that radioactive dump. Fifteen miles isn't far enough."

"I thought you picked the release location."

"Uh, no," said Becca as though the reply should have been obvious. "I sit in a cube writing reports, reviewing data, and making recommendations for Bradford to ridicule. When we were selecting this release site, I presented three options. Seven people sat around the table in the conference room. They left one chair open for me against the back wall. Bradford put a map on the screen with ten location alternatives, my three at the bottom."

"It's all about perspective, DC." Daphne hip-checked Becca. "Look at it this way. You made the top ten. Tell you what. Invite me next time, and I'll get you a seat at the table." She shaded her eyes and again looked out over the desert. "Might not be as far as you'd prefer, but there's a whole lotta nothin' in those fifteen miles, and I'm here for three weeks." She fought the map in a gust of wind, forcing it back to the original fold. "Three freakin' weeks while you're in DC sucking down venti lattes."

Becca pictured herself under a shaded canopy along the Potomac having coffee with Ashton. "Isn't that how long you're usually in the field?"

"Uh-huh, but usually I sit in the shade and monitor our guys." She wiped a bead of sweat from her brow and slapped the map against her leg.

"Paper map is super old-school. I haven't seen one of those in forever."

"In eight years of doing this, I've never lost the signal on a paper map. Battery never died on me, and I can even use it in the rain." The folded paper fell from her fingers to her feet. "Look at that. It didn't break."

"Smart aleck. Rain is the least of your worries."

The handlers removed the animal crates from the trucks and set them on the ground twenty feet from the vehicles. Daphne circled the caged canines, cooing as she calibrated her new government-issued tracking tablet.

"Don't know why they require separate tablets for tracking software and reporting. They're the same damn model." She held up twin tablets, one in each hand.

"You know why, Daph," said Gary, lead handler of the group. "Because the government can't pass up an opportunity to pay ten times face value for a custom piece of equipment. Look at these dog crates. Forty-nine bucks at any big-box pet store. Four-hundred bucks from our government supplier." He scoffed. "And twice a year, they ask me to cut *my* budget."

"I hear you, friend." She patted Gary's back. "My little brother could probably find the tracking software online and download it for me. I shoulda just had him do that in Atlanta, then I wouldn't have to carry one tablet to track the wolves and another to log every activity."

She finished another circle of the crates at a wider diameter. "I'm good to go, Gary. Got nine collars on the screen." She showed the tablet to Becca, nine dots clustered in a group. "Get a good look at our babies before they start terrorizing the neighborhood. A new top of the food chain just came to town."

"They better behave," said Becca. "As long as they don't roam too far, I think we'll be okay. But with open-range grazing, all we can do now is hope and pray they stay out of trouble."

Gary stepped next to Becca. "The government sure put a lot of money into all this only to *hope* it works out. And I'm pretty sure the service handbook doesn't allow you to pray anymore, so don't let them catch you." He moved back to the crates and removed the padlocks from each.

"This is the sixth release I've helped organize," said Becca, "but only my third time seeing them let out. I'll tell you, as long as I've been working with wolves, the adults still scare the heck out of me. I don't know how those guys do it."

"The Glock on Gary's hip has a way of boosting confidence," replied Daphne.

"Is that why he can call you Daph? I expected you to jump his ass."

"Gary's just being Gary. We were on a release in northern Idaho last year. Wolves usually shoot straight out, just like the dog races. Don't even look back. But our alpha female was acting funky, you know. She walked out of that crate with attitude. Real slow. Like she knew she was home and we were trespassing. That girl jumped on Gary. I mean jumped. Damn thing pounced like a cat and latched onto his arm." Daphne rocked her head as though she could hardly believe the story herself. "He was all calm about it. Kept his arm extended with the wolf pulling him until one of the guys tranked it. You might notice he's standing a little farther back today."

"Super scary."

"So Gary can call me Daph, but he's the only one."

"I'm surprised he still has an arm. Do you see the fangs on those things?"

"Idaho in the winter. We were all wearing heavy jackets. I'll bet he's a little nervous today. Ain't no jackets in this heat. Hey, Gary," she hollered. "Scoot a little closer. I want to get a picture."

"You know where you can put that camera," he replied in a soothing, calming voice, eyes never leaving the crates. He raised a hand to hush the team, then whispered, "Everybody ready? Release number one. Release number two."

Nine wolves scampered out of six cages. Three males, three females, three pups. Daphne watched the pack of Mexican grays all sprint away in one direction.

"Good job, Gary. Trained them to go west. That's a hell of a lot better than scampering out in nine different directions."

"Just for you, Daph. They don't call me the wolf whisperer for nothing."

She patted his back. "Gonna make my job easy tonight."

It took an hour for Gary and the men to load the cages and complete their paperwork. The team then stood around until well after dark, reminiscing about Idaho, Oregon, and other releases across the Northwest. As the team left, Becca climbed onto the tailgate of Daphne's rental. Dust kicked up by the exiting vehicles forced a cough.

"Look at that." Daphne showed her the cluster of dots settled down for the night. "If they stay close together, I can go in tonight and monitor from the hotel."

"At least this went right. I guess that's all that matters back in the office." Becca exhaled stress that had built to a crescendo over the last two weeks. "I've been working on this release for so long. Do you know this is my biggest moment with the service?" She exaggerated a look to the left and to the right, then placed a hand on Daphne's shoulder. "And nobody is here to see it."

The warm hand brought forth a memory of her mother's hand on the same shoulder. The night her mother insisted it wasn't Daphne's fault. Everything would be fine. But nothing was fine. Was now the time to talk to Becca? To share something so personal with a *friend*?

"I'm here," replied Daphne. "Just need to keep our babies out of trouble until you get back to the office tomorrow where you'll get credit for nine new wolves in the wild. Even Bradford will have to acknowledge how much these wolves enhance recovery of the gray." She cocked her head. "You know what that will get you, right?"

"What?" asked Becca with a hint of excitement at the thought of imminent recognition.

"Another reintroduction assignment."

Becca grinned. "Hopefully someplace cooler."

After a long, dusty drive back to town, they stopped at the Coyote Cavern, where Trip's Suburban was parked out front.

CHAPTER 28

PANIC ATTACK

INSIDE THE STAIRWELL down the hall from Joel's office, Mel reached into his jacket pocket, grasping only disappointment. He stepped out onto the Fourteenth Street sidewalk. What the hell was Joel thinking? Loading drums on a different truck could ruin everything. Nothing got by Rip. If he found the drums, he'd call DOE from the freakin' dock. Details like that had to be managed by ensuring Rip was off-site when the truck arrived. His only comfort, Dom was fully capable of keeping Rip out of the way.

Needing to stay an extra night to meet Donna in the morning gave Mel Wednesday afternoon to himself. Quality time to strategize the shipment and come up with a story to alleviate any concerns Donna had over site operations. He headed away from his hotel to avoid spirits in the business lounge that would haunt him if he tried to get any work done there.

He crossed the closed section of Pennsylvania Avenue between Lafayette Square and the front lawn of the White House, then turned on Seventeenth Street toward the Lincoln Memorial, another monument he had passed a hundred times but never climbed the steps. Along the way, he threw his jacket over his shoulder in a futile attempt to air out sweaty ovals under each arm. So many details to be worked. So many things that could go wrong in an industry where everything was traceable. He ran through a list of actions in his mind. At least a dozen activities needed to be completed discreetly to pull off receipt of the drums.

Anxiety, heat, and humidity made him flush. Hot, sticky air pulled Lincoln further away. Legs grew heavy. Strides turned to shuffles. His breathing accelerated. Sweat poured from his forehead.

Unable to make it to the bench, just ten feet ahead, he squeezed the black wrought iron fence surrounding the Eisenhower Building and lowered himself to the sidewalk. Behind closed eyelids, large dark spots danced with tiny white stars. Ringing ears drowned out surrounding traffic. His chest pulsed hard against his shirt. He pressed his head into the hot rail to keep from rolling to the sidewalk. A numbing tingle moved from his arms to his legs.

Heart attack! Help! Call an ambulance!

Tourists and locals passed the haggard man with hardly a look.

Why isn't anyone helping?

The tingle faded. Spots faded. A few deep breaths and he was almost back to normal. Flushed, sweating profusely, and shaky, he pulled himself up and looked around. Six men and two women, all of whom looked more derelict than he, had their arms wrapped around the same wrought iron along the sidewalk.

What the hell happened to this city?

Legs mostly cooperating, he staggered forward, ignoring gawkers and laughing off the near panic attack. Cutting across the park behind the Vietnam Veterans Memorial allowed him to avoid the crowd, shorten the distance to his target, and stay in the shade. Finally standing on the bottom step of the Lincoln Memorial, he looked upward into the white structure. The sun forced him to shade his eyes. He could barely make out Lincoln in the shadows behind the pillars of the marble temple. Energy that abounded from angry adrenaline at the start of the journey had evaporated in the heat. He plopped down on the step along with a dozen other senior citizens and gazed out over the reflecting pool and Washington Monument beyond.

Hordes of people crossed the pavement between the reflecting pool and Lincoln. A swarm of ants moving up and down tiers of steps, that he no longer had a desire to climb. Somewhere to his right, past the softball fields and Tidal Basin, the Jefferson Memorial hid behind the trees. If he walked through the Roosevelt Memorial adjacent to the

Tidal Basin, he could stay in the shade all the way to Jefferson. In forty minutes, he could conceivably knock three monuments off his list.

He glanced toward the Potomac and the tree-lined path he would need to take. A long way just to see statues, pictures of which were scattered around town in bars, hotels, and restaurants.

"Not today."

In ten minutes, a taxi had him in a corner booth at the Hamilton, a half block from the JW. The perfect bar for days when he had no desire to encounter a colleague because happy hour at the Hamilton was all about the sushi. Nobody in his circle liked sushi, and he wasn't there to eat.

Four hours of air conditioned ambiance had Mel refilled and refreshed. He walked the few blocks to Restaurant Row on Seventh Street, seeking to sink his teeth into a twenty-ounce porterhouse. With the evening sun finally barricaded behind concrete buildings, the temperature had finally subsided enough to make the walk almost pleasant.

At the lacquered bar in one of his favorite steakhouses, he ordered a filet and a tall something to wash it down. He glanced at each television above the bar. Ball games, a sports talk show, and a steeplechase somewhere in Europe. As his eyes bounced between the busy sidewalk and grand stallions, he texted Dom for the fourth time.

WHERE THE HELL ARE YOU? WE GOT A LOAD THAT NEEDS ATTENTION.

Again, no response.

He texted Margaret.

FIND DOM. HAVE HIM GIVE ME A CALL ASAP.

His wife promptly replied.

I'M DOING WELL. MISS YOU TOO.

Shit.

He had a bad habit of ordering Margaret to help before asking about her day.

He recalled the last time she traveled with him. He surprised her with tickets for the annual classic *A Christmas Carol* at Ford's Theater. She had a gleam in her eye rarely seen since the children left home. He got corralled into a meeting over drinks and texted her to go alone.

Later, he found the tickets in his jacket pocket. Margaret never said a word. He liked that about her. The woman never complained. She raised their children while he traveled. Cared for sick kids when he was away. Attended school functions alone. The perfect wife with whom he would spend a perfect retirement.

He tried calling his secretary again. No answer. He tried Dom again and even called Rip, whose phone went straight to voice mail.

Where the hell is everybody?

CHAPTER 29

JUST BECCA

"YOU THINK THOSE guys ever leave this place?" asked Daphne, her eyes adjusting to the dull yellow haze. As they approached the Seat Yourself sign, the raucous clamor reduced to a low hum. Trip waved the ladies over while Rich and Fernie grabbed extra chairs to accommodate the newcomers. The boys had spent the early evening reminiscing time spent with Arturo.

"Why'd they get so quiet?" asked Becca. "That didn't happen last time."

"Just the Wednesday night crowd," replied Brian matter-of-factly. "Five-dollar pitchers. They're a little drunk."

Daphne tapped her hip. "Thought it might have been my sidearm."

The third round, combined with exhaustion from two hours underneath Brian's Jeep, had loosened Trip's reserved female conversational skills. "Nah, half of them are carrying. It's probably because you're huge."

She reached for the short hairs behind his ear, but Trip whipped his head back.

"*Not me.* It's just these guys don't see a lot of ladies that could take them in a fair fight."

His crooked smile was melting something inside Daphne.

"He's right," added Brian. "Some of these guys don't get out much. New person in town gets everyone's attention."

Daphne cocked her head. "But not Becca. That right? She's okay?"

Trip struggled to explain. "I mean, you are huge and your spikey hair kind of draws attention. Becca is...I don't know, she's just Becca."

"*Just Becca.* Thanks a lot."

Rich, one beer beyond sober, added, "Yeah, Becca's the one they hate."

"Hate me? What the heck?"

He shrugged. "You told them you weren't going to release wolves. Then you let twenty of them bad boys loose to eat their cattle."

"I didn't say that."

"Sure you did. We were there Saturday. We all heard you."

Fernie nodded in quiet agreement.

"Bradford said that. Not me. And there aren't twenty wolves."

"Who's Bradford?" asked Rich with a hiccup.

"You mean there's more than twenty?" asked Trip before Becca could reply to Rich.

Brian rocked back, a wide grin on his face. "Told you nobody would remember the old guy."

"There are not twenty wolves."

"What happened to them?" asked Rich.

"Nothing happened to them."

"Where are they, then?"

"I can't tell you where they are."

"You lost twenty wolves? That can't be good." He clinked glasses with a less than enthusiastic Fernie.

"*There are not twenty wolves,*" repeated Becca, much louder than intended.

The room quieted once more. Local eyes bored into Becca, who buried her face in her hands.

"Now they're quiet because of you."

"Thanks, Trip. If you will excuse me." Becca left for the restroom.

Trip glanced at Daphne. "She seems a little sensitive tonight. Did everything go okay?"

"Everything's fine. She'll be better tomorrow when she's home sleeping in her own bed."

Becca returned while Cathy was distributing plates.

"I ordered you the burger," said Daphne. "It was that or the burrito."

"Good choice. I don't want to be on that little plane with a burrito in my belly."

Cathy placed the burger in front of Becca and a burrito, smothered in green chile sauce, in front of Daphne.

"I ordered *you* the burger. The burrito sounded way too good for me to pass up."

Becca eyed the swollen flour tortilla, beans and cheese inside, a thick sauce loaded with green chile on top. "It's a good thing you're alone in the truck tomorrow."

She grasped her hamburger bun with both hands and squeezed to keep the oversized patty from falling out. Bloody juice drizzled onto the plate in a glistening red pool. "This is the fourth burger I've had in three days. I can't keep eating like this or my arteries are going to harden in this chair. I'm going to die right here in the Coyote Cavern."

"You could have had the burrito," said Trip.

"What I'd like is something without all this grease. I'd give anything for sushi right now."

"We got a sushi place."

Daphne raised an eyebrow. "I am pretty sure I did not see a sign with the word 'sushi' on it. Do you even know what sushi is?"

"Raw fish," Rich and Trip answered at the same time.

"That's not actually correct," said Becca. "It's not raw—"

An oversized hand shot out like a school guard stopping traffic. "Wasting your time, DC." She looked into Trip's eyes. "Tell me, Little Man, where can we get sushi in this town?"

"They got a little refrigerator case at the gas station. I even saw somebody buy it once."

"There you go, Becca. If you want to leave town tonight, eat some of that gas station sushi. They'll medivac your ass outta here in an hour."

"Do you really want to leave?" asked Brian.

"It's not like I want to leave. I mean, it's my job, but this kind of place isn't what I'm used to. I've been here a lot longer than I expected."

Fernie drained the bottom half of his beer and set the glass down, amused he couldn't center it on the coaster. "You say that…like you're doing hard time." A belch slipped out. "It's not that bad."

"You should stick around," added Brian. "You might like it."

"Like it?" Daphne yelped a high-pitched laugh. "Vidalia, I just want to survive it. I got three weeks of this shit. Becca returns to civilization tomorrow. I'm the one stuck out here." She lifted a loaded fork. "At least I know where to get my survival food. Burritos, burgers, and beer."

"My kind of woman," said Rich. He gestured for Cathy to refill his glass.

"It's really great when you get to know the area," said Trip. "We could do stuff when you're not working. Like go fishing on the Pecos, hike in the desert, or do some shooting."

"I'm not on vacation. I head out in the morning to track the pack. As long as they don't get into trouble and rifle-wielding ranchers don't take potshots at them, I can come back to town at night. But if it looks like they're in danger, I sleep in the bush."

"Well, yeah. I mean, we gotta work tomorrow too. Then we're going to look for Grady."

"Fernie and I are going to look for Grady after work tomorrow," said Rich. "I think he's hiking the canyons by the caverns."

"His dad is heading out tomorrow too," replied Brian. "Said don't go to Slaughter Canyon alone."

"Old people." Rich scoffed. "I've been to Slaughter Canyon twenty times by myself."

"I think he's just worried with Grady gone and all. Keep your eye out for his red truck. He'll be somewhere around the Rattlesnake Trailhead, not far from the caverns. Trip and I can help Saturday, but we have to work until then."

"Hey, the caverns are something you could do if you have extra time." Trip's face lit up. "There's nothing like it in the whole world."

Daphne swallowed another bite, chasing the chile heat with a drink. "Saw the sign driving into town. Not a big fan of caves. Been to Meramec Caverns in Missouri when I was a kid. They turned the lights out on us, and let's just say I didn't care for it."

"I love the Luray Caverns in Virginia," added Becca. She passed

Brian her cell with pictures of underground stone architecture. "But I don't have enough time before my flight."

"Dang." Trip's shoulders slumped. "I thought we had the only caverns in the world."

An oversized hand settled on his undersized forearm. "You gotta leave this town, Little Man. See what's out there. You go east of here, up toward Dallas, and you'll see stuff we call *grass*. That green stuff you've probably seen on TV. It's everywhere from Dallas all the way to the Atlantic Ocean. Nothing like sitting in cool grass under a large oak and drinking a glass of sweet tea."

Trip glanced around at the wooden decor and inhaled a whiff of stale beer, unable to envision any place better. Across the table, Brian leaned back and closed his eyes.

Daphne tapped the tablet. A cluster of dots representing a twenty-year effort to reintroduce a species that had long ago dominated this land stared back at her. To Becca, each dot had a corresponding name. To Daphne, who had fostered and safeguarded animals since grade school, they were dots she was assigned to protect. Tonight, most of her babies congregated within a few hundred yards of each other, but one straggler was off in the distance. A lone wolf, much like she had become.

Fernie downed another beer and placed an unsteady glass on the coaster. His belch drew a disgusted look from Daphne who pushed her burrito aside.

"You okay, dude?" asked Brian.

"Wolves." Fernie shook his head back and forth. "My grandma told me to warn you. Stay away from the wolves." He belched again.

"I better take him home," said Rich. "Grab his other arm, Bri. Help me get him to the truck."

Daphne raised a mocking eyebrow. "Folklore, legends, and angry ranchers. Might have my hands full after all."

Trip's eyes zeroed in on Daphne's burrito.

"You gonna finish that?"

"Knock yourself out, Little Man. I got to get back to my dots. Something out there doesn't look right."

CHAPTER 30

BLOODY BELL

BECCA FORCED A last swallow of breakfast buffet coffee through lips that tried to refuse. The addition of four plastic cream capsules and a heaping spoonful of sugar did little to disguise the taste. As she cradled the warm paper cup, tension of the week drifted away at the thought of an afternoon brew at her favorite stop in Georgetown. Soft music, pastel paintings, and cushioned armchairs overlooking the Potomac. An aroma of beans roasted in the back, ground in the front, transitioned to a fresh-pressed cup only upon request. No resemblance to the muck she just swallowed.

Daphne's big legs knocked the small table askew as she joined her friend.

"Good morning, sweet thing. I'm glad you're here. I've been watching our little friends since five, and I've confused myself."

"Staring at that little screen for three hours would confuse anyone."

"Some damn train woke me up extra early, so I tapped the screen and ten dots popped up. I realized that was what had been giving me heartburn, not the burrito. Anyway, by the time I wiped my eyes, one dot disappeared. Kind of pissed me off, so I went into the field to see what the hell was going on. We released nine, right? Three males, three females, three pups."

"You've already been in the field and back? I'm impressed."

"Don't be. My little field trip didn't help." She stood back up. "Right now, I've got nine dots. Watch this thing while I get some food. See if my little rogue dot comes around."

Becca ran her finger over each dot and counted aloud. Nine dots. The dots were clustered too close to read the collar numbers, but there were clearly nine dots. What was the problem?

The screen faded as a blast of sunlight powered its way inside when the front door to the hotel opened. Shadows of three large men in cowboy hats, boots, and snapped shirts brought the screen back into focus as they neared the table.

"That's her," bellowed a gruff voice.

The men circled Becca, boots scuffing the mission-red Saltillo tile floor. Hands on their hips, shoulders wide, they glared down at the junior project manager.

"May I help you?" she squeaked.

"You government people have already helped enough," replied the gruff voice of the man standing in the middle.

He leaned forward, put his hands on the table, and moved in so close the brim of his hat bumped Becca's forehead.

Daphne's husky voice provided instant relief. "*Do we have a problem here?*"

She towered over the bent man with a look that made Becca cringe.

"Get your hands off of my table, and step your fat ass back."

She set her plate and coffee down and started eating, ignoring the cowboys.

In a less intimidating voice, the man on the left spoke up. "Yes, there is a problem."

Eyes on her plate, she replied, "Speak up. My food is getting cold, and waiting for you to talk ain't gonna make it taste any better."

"I lost two cattle yesterday. Bruce here," he gestured to the gruff voice, "lost two himself, and Cal lost three more. My brother lost five head. Your damn wolves are killing our cows."

Becca scrunched her eyebrows. "We fed the wolves before the release, and usually they're skittish for a few days after being crated. Attacking so quickly would be unprecedented. Your brother lost five. Where is he?"

"He didn't come in last night. Stayed out to protect the herd."

Daphne rotated a death stare across the three men. "That better not mean what I think you mean."

Bruce placed a bloodied cow bell on the table, closer to Becca than Daphne. "I found this yesterday. No sign of my cow."

Daphne growled, "Unless you want to add some of your own blood to that damn bell, I suggest you remove it from my table."

A quick hand pulled the bell back, clanging it once as it disappeared into a pocket.

"What time yesterday?" asked Becca.

"What does it matter?" spat Bruce.

Daphne repeated the question slow enough for the sound to penetrate the man's ear hair and in a voice that chilled the remaining food on her plate. "*What...time...yesterday?*"

"Three o'clock. Maybe four."

In an apologetic tone, Becca said, "We released the wolves at eight. It couldn't have been our animals."

"It was damn sure wolves," said Cal. "I found fur around the carcasses. Or what was left of them."

He placed a handful of matted fur on the corner of the table, quickly returning the pile to his pocket when Daphne's head swiveled.

"We see this every time we have a release," said Daphne flatly. "Somebody comes in with fur or bloody toys and blames our animals. There is no way our wolves did that. They were penned up until eight o'clock."

Bruce snarled. "You calling me a liar?"

Daphne screeched her chair back on the Saltillo tile, stood erect, and looked down on the man. "Is that hat covering your ears too tight? We released at eight. You found this shit in the afternoon. It's a pretty simple conclusion, even for a cowboy."

The men grumbled among themselves and turned around. "You ain't heard the last from us."

"Have you been watching that screen?" she asked Becca, sitting back down.

"No. I was pissing my pants until you got back to the table. What the hell was that all about?"

"Anywhere else, I'd tell you those guys killed a few of their own cattle and want the government to pay ten times market price for their trouble. Obviously, it wasn't our babies, but like I told you, those dots are confusing me. Sometimes I see an extra collar. Sometimes it's near our guys, and sometimes it's miles away."

"Well, the next time you see it miles away, write that extra collar number down. I can't make any of these numbers out when they're clustered. But even if that collar is a wolf, and it's not," insisted Becca, "a single wolf could never take down twelve cattle in an afternoon. They must have a cougar problem or something else."

"You could be right. Combination of a cougar and those guys killing their own cows could explain it."

"Explains everything but the fur," replied Becca. "That patch of hair he set on the table looked a lot like the fur I was telling you about. But like I said, attacking cows so soon would be super unprecedented. That would be like killing just to kill. It doesn't make any sense."

"Probably my fault." Daphne exaggerated a sarcastic face. "I was so focused on calibrating the collars I didn't give our babies time to read up on *precedent* before we opened the cage." She cocked her head. "Now, about those dots."

Studying wolf movements and reviewing archived data left Becca just as confused as Daphne. She finally gave up.

"My job is the public. Your job is tracking." She pinched a grin. "At one o'clock, I'm on a flight home."

"Wonderful. Leave me with the rednecks *and* an extra dot."

Becca picked her things up from the table. "I think it's a software glitch. Happens all the time. Custom software, built by the lowest bidder, purchased by the government. Sometimes I'm surprised we see any dots on that screen. Text me that errant number when you identify it, and I'll have someone look it up. Right now, I just want to get out of this place. Got my book, my headphones, and my bottle of water. I'm going to sit at the airport until my flight."

"Have a good trip. I'm heading out into the dirt. If cows are already dying, I'll be spending some quality nights in the desert."

An hour later, Daphne was sitting on the open tailgate of the

F-150 rental, tablet to one side, notebook on the other, bottle of water between her legs. She had watched the family of five for almost an hour. Mom and dad lay prone, alert, heads up, ears perked. Pups frolicked about.

She set the binoculars down, then swung her legs forward and back to get blood flowing and distract her from the monotony of watching canines sunbathe. A shadowy movement in a prickly bush caught her attention. She slid off the tailgate and inched her way to the bush. Something twitched under a thorny limb. She placed her hand on the soil, palm up, and waited patiently. A furry arachnid rose from its scrunched position and crept into the cradle of her hand. Spiny legs tickled as the tarantula settled into her palm.

"Hey, little guy," she whispered, raising her hand to eye level.

She placed her new friend on the seat to get acquainted with his surroundings when something else caught her eye. Something in the distance. Something large.

CHAPTER 31

WE KNOW NOTHING

TONY SLIPPED HIS cell back into his pocket. "That was Joel. He'll be here in a few hours. Wants us to stay out of sight until he arrives."

"Coming to Carlsbad. What the hell for?" asked Augie.

"Said he needs to check things out for himself."

Jack leaned backward, allowing his body to fall onto the bed with a heavy bounce. "What if he asks about Dom?"

"Listen close, both of you. We tell him Dom was right behind us after we finished. Said he needed to dress up the area. We left the site and never saw him again. We know nothing. *Nothing!* That's our story."

Jack rolled his feet to the floor. "Do we have to stay in the room? I could use a beer."

"*It ain't even eleven.* We can't start drinking this early. People will notice. All Joel said was stay out of sight. Don't do anything that draws attention. So while we're waiting, we're gonna find my bag. And when we find it, I'm going to ask that bitch why she's interested in us."

"But we already looked once," said Augie.

"*We're gonna look again!* There are only two hotels in this town where someone dressed like her would stay, and she ain't at ours."

In a timid voice, Jack asked, "Do you think Joel sent her to check on us? You know, because of the last time."

"I told you *never* to talk about that! Go get your shit from the room and meet me at the car."

On the way down the hall, Augie shoulder-checked Jack. "What's wrong with you? *Never* talk about the last job. You're lucky he didn't blow your head off. You need to be careful, Jack, or he's gonna leave your ass in the desert. Mine too."

Tony and the boys cruised the town, again to no avail. They confirmed the lady had checked out of her hotel, but her car was not in the rental lot at the airport and not at the WIPP site. She had disappeared once more.

"Maybe she's touring the caverns," said Jack. "We could do that since we need to lay low anyway."

"We ain't touring a damn cave, but drive out that way. We'll look for her car."

After searching multiple parking lots serving the caverns, Augie pulled to the side of the road.

"Over there." He pointed. "The red truck in the distance. I saw Rip get into it yesterday when we were meeting with Dom."

"Now you're thinking. Let's ask him what he knows about our drum."

A three-strand barbed wire fence blocked direct access to the desert, not that they could drive across it in the lemonhead car.

"How do we get there?"

"He found a way. Just drive. Take the first turn into the desert."

The subcompact scraped the bottom of every rut on the dirt two-track they found a mile down the road. Three plump heads swiveled back and forth the entire way.

"Where the hell did he go?" Augie asked, causing Tony to blow a gasket.

"*How could you lose sight of him? You got one job. Follow the red truck. One road, one truck, and you lost the son of a bitch.*"

While Augie was contemplating whether to remain quiet or remind Tony the passenger was supposed to navigate, the front tires dropped into a hole, popping Jack upward into the ceiling.

"Moron!" he shouted, rubbing his head. "I spilled coffee all over the seat."

"Nobody cares about your damn seat," barked Tony. "Just look for the truck."

The men dipped and dodged through arroyos and ruts for another hour. No sign of Rip.

"Bad news, boss. We're outta gas."

A tense Augie prepared for another flare-up, but instead, Tony seemed to have given up the fight.

"Head back to town. We'll fill up and eat. Wash some of this dust down our throats and come back. Bastard has to be out here somewhere. He's the only loose end."

In a corner booth, Tony leaned against the Coyote Cavern window, Augie to his left, Jack across the table, burritos all around, and an empty pitcher of beer in between the men. Tony watched a small blue car cruise to a stop in the parking lot. The female driver stared into the corner window of the bar.

"*That's her*," said Tony, in a harsh whisper.

"Who?" asked Augie.

"Who the hell have we been looking for? The lady who stole my bag. That's her. She's staring right at us."

Jack shook his head. "Can't be. Her car was white. That one is blue."

"Who gives a shit about the color? *It's her!*"

"She's just staring," remarked Augie.

Tony drummed his fingers on the table. "Something's up with that lady. She's too calm. Too confident. Just like yesterday. That bitch has got steel balls. Following us without even trying to be covert." He clenched his fists. "Steel balls."

*

Becca faced the smoky tinted windows of the Coyote Cavern, unable to see inside. Not that it mattered. Neither Daphne's truck nor Trip's Suburban was parked out front.

When she returned her rental, the attendant was unwilling to let her abandon the heavy suitcase in the trunk. She lugged it inside the small terminal, heels clacking on the tile floor as she made her way to a leather airport chair connected to a row of five empty seats. The only set of seats on the outer side of the locked security portal, closed until thirty minutes before the flight.

She placed her book and water bottle to her left and purse on the seat to the right. At the left end of the terminal, the gate agent disappeared behind the counter, having no other customers on which to wait. At the other end, a lone luggage carousel stood silent. The quiet terminal brought back memories of teenage years with preoccupied parents who scarcely spoke at home. In a few hours, she would be alone in her Georgetown studio apartment, which was much too expensive but came with a view of the C&O Canal.

She reached for her book and knocked the water bottle to the floor. As she bent over to pick up the bottle, her phone buzzed an incoming email. Thoughts of hot yoga and cold Froyo disappeared as Bradford's email described, in too much detail, his disappointment in her performance at the town hall and her treatment of the "gentlemen" who requested assistance in determining the cause of death of their prized cattle.

"*You son of a bitch,*" she said aloud, quickly glancing around. Her anxiety lowered when she realized there was nobody in the terminal to offend.

She directed the phrase first to her boss, who had been too lazy to travel to Carlsbad to do his job, then had the nerve to insinuate she failed with the presentation, a presentation he set her up to fail when he lied to the audience. Then she directed a plural form of the phrase to the "gentlemen," the angry cowboys who wanted money for cattle that died before the wolves were even released. They contacted their local congressman, who obviously had nothing better to do than track down Bradford.

The email instruction was clear. "Remain in Carlsbad until all issues are resolved."

Back she went to the rental car agency, lugging the overweight replica of her bag. The anal agent handed her keys to a blue subcompact, refusing to give her the full-sized vehicle returned thirty minutes prior. Needing a shoulder to cry on or at least an ear to listen, she found herself in the Coyote Cavern parking lot looking for her friends.

"*Get out! Get out of my way.*" Tony pushed Augie out of the booth and rambled to the door as fast as his thick legs would carry him.

Her friends nowhere around, Becca drove away just as the heavy wooden door flung open. She headed to city hall to meet Jen Lopez and review the list of attendees from the town hall meeting. Phone numbers from the sign-in sheet would be useful in tracking down the cowboys.

CHAPTER 32

OVER BEFORE IT STARTED

MEL ARRIVED TEN minutes early for his Thursday morning mauling. The voice of the undersecretary bled through the closed door. Donna had never been one to hold back. Sitting in the waiting area, he almost felt sorry for the poor bastard she was yelling at, but his turn would come.

The meeting was over almost before it started. He didn't get a single word in.

"Ten lousy minutes," uttered Mel as he left Forrestal. "I stayed an extra night just so she could bitch me out. Remind me she's in charge."

In the voice of a whiny woman, he argued with a planter at the front door. "*If things don't shape up, I'll have to make a change.*"

A guard shot him a curious look.

Mel stopped in the shade of the building to rip off his tie. Unsure how long the meeting would take, he had booked the one-thirty flight from Reagan. Not a bad choice considering the punctual prima donna had made him wait twenty minutes. An hour layover in Dallas, switching to the small plane to Carlsbad, would have him at WIPP by six. Too late to meet the truck. He shot a text.

DOM: ARRIVE CARLSBAD 6:00 P.M. NEED YOU TO TAKE CARE OF TODAY'S TRUCK. CALL ME!

No reply.

He stormed across the street, back through the rose garden to the National Mall. A left on the gravel path, he beelined it toward the Washington Monument. Four hours until he needed to be at the airport and nothing he could do to speed that up.

"To hell with everybody."

He kicked a pile of gravel into the grass in the direction of a group of young people getting in a game of kickball before the morning heat arrived. A booming homerun cleared the left fielder, bouncing Mel's way.

"Little help," came the voice of a man about the age Mel had been when he first crossed the grass expanse of the National Mall.

He pictured Donna's round head as he swung a leg, glancing the ball off the side of his wingtip boot, pushing it farther from the player. He hung his head in disgust. Nothing was going right.

A hundred trips to DC, and yesterday was the first time he felt the need to tour something. Anything. He should have climbed the steps to Lincoln and gotten it out of his system. He stopped at Fourteenth Street and turned a complete circle. The mall was lined with museums he'd seen but never noticed, walked by but never entered. A dozen flower and sculpture gardens between the Washington Monument and the Capitol served as refuse areas to toss his empties, rather than places of respite to rest, relax, and reflect.

The Capitol to his front, Washington Monument to his back, and museums in between. Hundreds of people walking, running, and playing all around the grand mall. Half a lifetime spent traveling to DC, and he stood alone. Gravel beneath his feet, dust on his boots, sweat on his brow. It occurred to him he had never enjoyed a single experience in the nation's capital.

What had the lady in the breakfast lounge called it? "This great city." Yet he had never smelled a cherry blossom, walked the Potomac, visited a monument, or toured a museum. His claim to fame in DC, joked about among colleagues, was an uncanny ability to name all the bars within ten blocks of the hotel that served free appetizers, offered extended happy hours, and didn't water down drinks.

"That changes now."

At the base of the Washington Monument, he stood in the long morning shadow of the giant obelisk, ready to finally tour the one monument he'd seen every time he visited the great city. He took his place at the end of a surprisingly short line and moved with the crowd to the park ranger at the entrance.

"Ticket, please."

Mel's puzzled look said it all.

"Sir, tickets are distributed in the morning for timeslots throughout the day. You can get them at the booth behind you or online. Daily tickets are usually gone by seven-thirty, so get here early."

No need to reply. He looked upward one last time, turned around, and plodded to the metro to wait for his flight in the airline lounge.

Perched comfortably at the bar in the frequent-flyer club, Mel reviewed the list of activities he had scribbled on the backside of a napkin at the Hamilton. Call Dom—again. Prepare substitute drums. Meet truck on arrival at WIPP gate. Stay with truck to receiving dock. Isolate new drums. Update waste manifest. Move new drums into Room 6. Tonight! Under each primary activity, he had listed additional tasks for Dom to complete discreetly. The final special shipment needed to be handled delicately. Particularly the paperwork. With Donna and Carlton breathing down his neck, there was no room for mistakes.

Moving the new special drums into Room 6 was preferred because he and Dom had left equipment in the room to open the back wall and dump the drums in the newly discovered chamber. Out of sight, out of mind. Once the drums were secure in the UG, he would override the administrative control to access the waste manifest and reconcile the inventory with the replacement drum details. If Dom would ever answer his texts, most of the work could be done before the plane landed.

WHERE ARE YOU!!

No reply. Margaret must not have found him either, or she would have texted. He wasn't about to poke that bear again.

Mel slid his phone under the barcode reader at the gate, prompting the machine to spit out an upgraded first-class seat assignment. At least something on the trip had gone right. With fewer available flights and so many weekly business travelers to the nation's capital, it had been two months since his last upgrade leaving DC.

He leaned his head into the window crevice and reclined two inches, recalling days of regular-sized seats that were more cushioned, leaned farther back, and were actually comfortable. A time when airlines prioritized passengers ahead of stockholders. He ordered a whiskey sour and was asleep before the drink arrived.

The plane lurched backward, jostling Mel awake to a warm drink on the armrest. Thirst overcame complaint. He tipped the glass to his lips with one hand and checked the time on his phone with the other. *Son of a bitch.* They had been sitting at the gate for sixty minutes and were just now backing out.

"Number nine for takeoff," announced the pilot. "Flight attendants, please prepare the cabin."

Wheels touched down in Dallas sixteen minutes before the Cactus Air departure.

"Come on. Come on," he uttered while the pilot took his sweet-ass time maneuvering into position at the gate.

He looked out the window at the empty jetway. *Why are they never ready when a plane arrives?*

Mel dialed the Carlsbad airport as a clearly inexperienced agent bounced the jetway toward the plane, missing the alignment on the first attempt. Karen Joy, the desk agent for Cactus Air, answered.

"Thank God!"

"Hello?"

"KJ! Hey, Karen. This is Mel. How you doin', hon?"

"Very well, Mr. Martin. You sound a little excited."

He faked a casual laugh. "I suppose you could say that. KJ, I just landed in Dallas, and I'm sitting at the gate."

"Excellent, Mr. Martin. Right where you need to be."

"Almost. I'm at my arrival gate, C12. Cactus Air leaves from A27. If they ever open the freakin' door to this plane, I can make a mad dash and be at A27 in fifteen minutes."

"Ouch. That is cutting it close. I'm not sure you'll make the connection, and we don't have anything else out of Dallas tonight."

"I hate to ask, KJ, but could you *please* call the Dallas gate and tell them I'm on my way? I'll hustle it up and cut the time to the gate to ten minutes. Just don't let them close the door."

"I'll give them a call, Mel, but you owe me for this, and I can't promise they won't leave without you."

"Thanks, darlin'. Door just opened. Time to see what these old legs still have in them."

The old legs only had an eighteen-minute mediocre jaunt left in the tank. The sprint out of the C12 gate quickly transitioned to a brisk walk to the Skylink, which gave way to a lumbering pace in Terminal A, when he saw the aircraft still on the tarmac.

"I can't thank you enough for holding the plane," Mel said to the gate agent.

"Glad to help, Mr. Martin. You're our only passenger this flight, but it's good you called, or we would have left on time." The young agent offered a friendly smile to his most frequent passenger. "An on-time departure with an empty plane is still an on-time departure."

Mel made his way down the jetway steps. Though his carry-on was small, the tiny aircraft had no overhead. He left the bag planeside and climbed the miniature steps. Leaning back two inches, he placed his feet on the seat facing him. One last text made its way into the cloud before he fell asleep.

DOM. LEAVING DALLAS. DID YOU OFFLOAD TRUCK? DRUMS SECURE??

CHAPTER 33

STUCK IN CARLSBAD

DAPHNE WHIFFED A fly off the steering wheel as she raised the clunky satellite phone to her ear.

"Hey, sweet thing. Did you have a good flight? Are you sitting by the water in Georgetown, eating crab cakes, and nursing a tall glass of something with an umbrella?"

"*No,*" replied a more-than-dejected Becca. "That bastard Bradford ordered me to stay out here. I've been making calls all day. I had to track down those guys from this morning and work out a premium price for their cows, just like you said. The tall one with the bell told me he lost two more head."

"Not possible. I've been watching our babies all day. No cows anywhere around. You coming out here to join me? Earn those big bucks you headquarters people make."

"I would, but they changed my car. This one is so tiny I scrape the bottom pulling into the hotel driveway. It would never make it on those dirt roads. By the way, I'm at the Towne Plaza now, Stevens Inn was full, but hey, I got a great view of a blue trash dumpster." Another dejected sigh.

"Perspective, DC. Can't complain about a view with color. Everything out here is beige, beige, and more beige." Daphne wiped sweat from her forehead. "Hotel probably filled up for a bull riding event or some other shit-kicking occasion in town."

"Shit-kicking? What have the locals been teaching you since I left this morning?"

"I'll come in and pick you up. We can go over these movement patterns again. Is an hour enough time to get ready?"

"Five minutes is plenty."

"Well, I have to get this damn fly out of the truck and pack my gear. It'll be at least an hour. That gives you time to slather sunscreen all over that little nose and chin. Sun is brutal out here. I ain't kidding. It's damn hot."

Daphne flicked the fly out, then went behind the truck and closed the tailgate. She caught herself staring at the truck bed. Two days ago when she arrived in Carlsbad, she felt as empty as the back of the pickup. A lot had happened in two days with Becca and the boys, good people who treated her like family from the moment they met. She turned her head east, toward Atlanta. Toward home. If the wolves were safe and stayed out of trouble for three weeks, she would return home to an empty apartment. An empty life. Eight years ago, she had accepted the field position because she needed to be alone. Was it finally time to put it all behind her?

An hour later, Daphne pulled into the hotel parking lot. Becca plodded out the front door, shoulders slumped, head hanging, ponytail lying dead on her back.

"Want to talk about it?"

"*No.*"

Daphne reached for the key.

"*Yes.*"

She started the truck, turned the AC to the highest setting, and left the vehicle in park.

Becca tilted her head back to keep tears from rolling down her face while she filled Daphne in on a turbulent relationship with Bradford that started her first day on the job. His constant criticism, berating, and lack of appreciation for her work. She paraphrased the email that instructed her to stay in Carlsbad, Bradford insisting she had failed with the locals. She left out the frustrating text from her boyfriend who was not at all pleased that she was spending so much time away from him.

Between the complaints and whines, Daphne gleaned that Becca was being manipulated by an overbearing manager who refused to acknowledge her expertise, insulted her at will, and sabotaged the few opportunities she had been given to succeed. Her friend didn't deserve such treatment. On projects they worked together in the past, Daphne had observed firsthand Becca's commitment to success. Projects Daphne always wanted to finish quickly, to move on to the next location, hopefully farther from Atlanta. A routine she wanted desperately to change.

Head tilted back, Becca dabbed welled-up eyes.

*

Tony had just finished another beer in the confines of the fourth-floor room. Jack and Augie sat on the edge of the bed polishing off their own while Judge Judy scowled at them through the television.

"How can you watch that crap?"

Augie snickered. "It's the only time Jack gets to see his family."

"Ass."

Tony peeled the curtain back and glanced outside at the low, still-blinding sun. He whipped the curtain closed.

"*What the hell?* There she is!"

He cracked the curtain and peeked out.

"She's staring at the window. Staring right at us. How does she know where we are all the time? How does she know we're in my room instead of yours?"

Augie and Jack peeked out the other side.

"Where?" asked Jack. "I don't see her car."

"She's in the truck. Don't open the curtain too wide."

"She's gotta have help," said Augie. "No other way."

"She's looking right at you, Tony." Jack sat back down on the bed. "Do you think Joel sent her?"

"I didn't at first, but I've been thinking about it a lot since yesterday. Who else knew we were on that plane? Who knew when we would be at WIPP? And who knows we're staying at this hotel? *Joel.* And who else could find a prissy-looking woman ballsy enough to tail us without even trying to hide it?"

"It can't be Joel," argued Augie. "He needs us to succeed. If Joel sent her, she would have shown up at the door with your bag."

"Yeah," agreed Jack. "She would have cut your balls off and told you to get to work."

"That little bitch doesn't scare me, but the driver looks like he can handle himself."

Tony released his side of the curtain. "Let's go see what they want."

Flanked by Jack and Augie, they took the elevator down and hustled their way out front, only to find the truck already gone.

★

Daphne passed Coyote Cavern on the way back to the desert. "There's the little guy's truck. We should stop in and get something to eat. Could be a late night, girl."

Brian smiled as wide as the steer horns over the bar when Becca came through the door.

"I thought you left town."

She slumped into a chair. "Long story. Not a good one."

"Couple of beers and it might not be so bad," said Rich. "Brian's buying."

"Thanks, but we're on the government clock," replied Daphne. "We just stopped in to eat before we head back out."

"Out where?" asked Trip. "Can you tell us yet?"

"Sorry, Little Man, can't talk about it for another week. But if you're around then, I'll let you know."

"Do you do, like, real classified shit?" asked Rich. "If you tell us you have to kill us kind of stuff."

"Something like that."

Rich glanced to Fernie, still pale from the evening binge. "We could follow them."

No reply from their usually animated friend.

"I find your ass out in the desert," said Daphne, "I might just kill you anyway. Who's to know?"

When the food arrived, Brian left the table to find Trip, who had been in the bathroom much too long, an indication that trouble may have followed him in. His friend's lanky frame and crooked smile had a way of bringing out stupidity in slightly inebriated wannabe tough guys. Sure enough, two sunburned, scraggly-haired field hands had cornered Trip in the bathroom corridor. One wore a backward ball cap, the other a ragged straw cowboy hat tipped too far back.

Cowboy Hat dug a finger deep into Trip's chest. "You gonna do something about it, *Little Man?* You like it when she calls you that?"

Trip glared back, doing his best to hold in tears and balance on jellied legs. He swallowed hard.

Cowboy Hat bumped his brim against Trip's forehead and raised his voice an octave. "Did you piss your pants, *Little Man?*" He drizzled beer over Trip's crotch just as Brian arrived.

"Back off."

Ball Cap pushed his chest out. "What are you going to do about it, asswipe?"

Brian shoved him into the wall and cocked a fist. Cowboy Hat slithered out of the corridor first, followed by his friend.

"I was about to hit him," said Trip, his voice trembling as fast as his legs.

Brian blamed himself for Trip's inability to stand on his own. He should have let Trip get out of his own mess a few times in high school. Instead, he stepped in to keep his best friend from getting beat, cheated, or embarrassed. In Jal, nobody messed with Brian, and by proxy, nobody messed with Trip. In Carlsbad, some kids still pushed their luck.

They returned to the table, where Rich was first to notice the wet crotch. "Little problem with your zipper?"

Brian slapped Trip on the back and laughed. "I bumped into him right when he was coming out of the john. Spilled my beer all over his front. Couldn't have aimed better if I tried."

Becca eyed the untouched beer in front of Brian as he sat.

"You sure that wasn't a little premature action?" Daphne placed a hand on Trip's forearm. "Men have a hard time controlling themselves when they sit this close to me. A real *hard* time."

His face flushed as red as the bull's-eye on the dartboard as he soaked in warmth from the hand covering the entire lower half of his arm.

"Speechless. Love it when I do that to a man." She stood to go, having quickly devoured her new favorite meal, a burrito smothered in green chile. "We're out of here. Long night ahead."

"Be careful," warned Trip. "It's easy to get stuck out there in the dark."

"You are so cute." Daphne leaned over and kissed him on the forehead. "Ain't nothing in the desert I can't handle."

CHAPTER 34

THREE LOOSE ENDS

THE YELLOW SUBCOMPACT pulled up to a disgusted look from Joel standing in a blistering early afternoon sun in front of the airport.

"Get in the back." He scowled at Augie as he loosened his red tie and unbuttoned his collar.

Augie grabbed the roof of the car to leverage his large frame from the small passenger seat. He released his hand as fast as his fingers would let go and fell out to the curb.

"*Hot! Son of a*—"

"Shut your ass up, and get out of the way."

Using his shirttail to protect his fingers, Augie pulled up on the handle to the back door, then squeezed himself into the rear seat. Jack occupied the seat behind Tony. Joel slid into the front. At five-foot-nine, his tiny head had plenty of clearance, unlike the other three men in the car.

"What the hell is this?" he asked, careful not to touch anything metal while he buckled in. "Why didn't you get a real car?"

Tony stole a glance at Joel, trying to size up why the man had traveled to Carlsbad and determine whether his anger was actually directed at the car.

"Small town. It's not like you get a choice out here."

"Just drive."

Though extra leg room was not needed, Joel slid the seat as far back as it would go, forcing Augie's knees into his chest.

"Give me an update."

Tony filled the boss in on both trips downhole, finding two drums in storage and the third drum empty. He identified Rip and Chuck as two loose ends who may have seen the drum contents.

"Three loose ends," said Joel. "Mel is trouble. He was totally out of it yesterday. When the time is right, we need to deal with him." Joel mopped his forehead with a handkerchief that was already soaked, though he had only been in town a few minutes. "But another shipment arrives today. That's our priority."

Jack's throat dried instantly in the summer sun. His voice cracked. "Another…shipment? While we're here? You never mentioned that."

"I'm mentioning it now! Dom is supposed to unload and make sure the new containers are secure. Maybe the truck already arrived and Dom's got everything under control. This one is too important." The one thing Mel had done in their meeting was make it clear how critical it was to control receipt of the arriving shipment. "That's why I'm here."

Jack rolled the window down to let the hot breeze dry his sweat-riddled face and ventilate body odor of four men much too large for the confined capsule.

Six weeks before the trio landed in Carlsbad, Joel hired the men to sabotage the TRU waste inventory at Savannah River. They were tasked with adding TRU waste drums to the existing inventory and tweaking the inventory tracking system, Jack's specialty. Adding drums would make it appear the company managing the site had deliberately underreported their waste volumes. A subsequent whistleblower phone call would inform the Department of Energy of the seemingly willful violations and cause the company to be removed from consideration for a large government procurement. Joel had invested everything with the only other company bidding on the multi-billion-dollar contract. But adding waste to an inventory was much more complex than making inventory disappear. Opening existing containers, removing half the contents, and filling twenty new drums required four men working three hours in full PPE.

Joel insisted Mel be the fourth, but Mel went off on a bender. Adam, a man without an ounce of muscle on his body but larger than

Augie, showed up instead. In the middle of the drum field, the new guy experienced a claustrophobic sensation that sometimes occurs when working in a full-face respirator. The fat ass flipped the filtered mask off his face and screamed that he couldn't breathe. In an anxiety-induced attack, he ran up behind Jack, who turned around at the commotion. Adam ran chest first into the steel shank in Jack's hand. His lifeless body fell to the ground. To add insult to injury, the next day, a site technician noticed the containers were not aligned in uniform rows and investigated the cause. In their rush to leave the site, Tony and the men had neglected to dress up the area. Site staff promptly reported the unusual occurrence, corrected the issues, and cleaned up the mess. Self-reporting saved the contractor from significant penalty, and they were subsequently awarded the procurement that Joel had spent two years trying to tilt in his direction. When the two drums containing Adam's body, the last evidence of that fateful night, were safely secure in the bowels of the desert, Joel could finally put the massive failure behind him.

"When Dom gets those two drums in the repository and reconciles the documentation, everything is finished. There won't be any traceability back to us. We need to work everything with Dom." He turned back around and grumbled, "He's the only dependable one in this entire operation."

Tony saw Augie in the rearview mirror shaking his head no and mouthing, "*Don't do it*." He cleared his throat. "That could be a problem, Joel." Tony then explained the one significant detail omitted from the status report. Dom was dead, his body splayed out beneath a slab of salt in Room 6.

Joel turned a dispirited head to the window.

"That could be a problem."

CHAPTER 35

AN UNEXPECTED NOTE

SHORTLY AFTER SIX, the small plane bounced its way to the lone gate at the Carlsbad airport. Mel bounded down the steps with a pulsing headache. He drove the thirty miles to WIPP and was in the admin building forty minutes after touchdown. The evening staff were doing their best to look busy.

"Would you like a cup of coffee?" asked the always bubbly Brandi. "Just made a pot."

"Thanks, but no. Had enough on the plane. Do you know where Dom is? He's listed as in, but I don't see him."

"He was pretty busy with some visitors yesterday, but I haven't seen him since."

Joel's men. Mel cringed. "Thanks. What about Rip?"

"He's out today looking for Grady. I hope nothing happened to the poor boy. Calendar says he'll be back tomorrow. I can call him and let him know you want to talk."

"That won't be necessary, Brandi. I'll be in my office. Two days in DC means three days of paperwork on my desk."

He made his way out the back door to the loading dock, where he found the drums had already been offloaded from the truck and removed from the TRUPACT-II shipping container; an eight-foot diameter, ten-foot tall stainless-steel container designed to protect the fifty-five-gallon waste drums in the event of an accident.

A quick walk around the pallets confirmed the drums had not been separated from the seven-pack configurations, which also meant that nobody had inadvertently discovered the two special drums somewhere inside the drum packs. Without Dom, separating the cans would have to wait.

He sent another text to the absent accomplice. No reply.

Mel left the site and drove by Dom's house. His truck was not in the drive. He could have kicked himself for not looking for Dom's vehicle back at WIPP. Maybe Dom was in the UG preparing the room which would also explain why he hadn't been answering his phone.

He texted Brandi and asked her to call when she found Dom. Then he headed home to eat a quick bite and put out the fire he was certain still burned in Margaret's ass.

Shoulda picked something up for her in DC.

Pulling into the driveway, relief replaced stress when Margaret's car was not under the carport. She was probably getting carryout somewhere in town, hating to eat out alone. That gave him at least a few minutes to relax and have a drink before she returned. Maybe she would bring him a plate as a peace offering.

He entered the front door to a dimly lit living room where the evening sun was pushing the last amber glow through the window. He placed a stack of papers on the entry table and poured a stiff drink.

"Quiet. Almost too quiet." He held the glass out and toasted himself. "I like it."

From the wet bar in the living room, something on the kitchen table caught his eye. A gulp and a refill, he ambled to the kitchen.

Margaret had left a note.

CHAPTER 36

SPIDERS AS BIG AS MY HAND

THE CLUSTER OF dots directed Daphne and Becca far out into the desert southeast of town. Daphne stopped the truck in the middle of the single-track road, both women in desperate need of a break from the bouncy, bumpy drive.

Daphne stuck her large index finger deep inside her mouth. "Think one of my fillings rocked loose."

"My whole head rocked loose," replied Becca.

The ladies climbed out and walked to the back where clumpy shrubs and cactus dotted the edge of the gravel track. Daphne dropped the tailgate and handed Becca the tablet.

"Knock yourself out, sweet thing. I've got to find a bush. That burrito's trying to make a run for it."

"That explains the smell in the cab. Didn't want to ask."

Daphne fanned her backside as she headed into the desert. "I tried to keep it quiet. Beans and cheese smothered in red chile sauce. Good eatin', but I'm gonna pay the price now. Always hotter coming out than going in."

"That is way too much information," replied Becca, her eyes focused on the screen.

While Daphne did her business, Becca studied what little movement the wolves were making. Nine dots bunched in a group roughly three miles away as the crow flies. No telling how far on the snaking rocky road.

She glanced at the ground between her legs and mumbled, "Hardly a road."

Daphne returned from the brush. "I've been on a lot worse."

"That was quick."

"Funny thing about spicy food. Shoots right out and—"

Becca flashed an open palm. "I do not need details. You were saying something about the road."

"Idaho was tough. We had desert *and* mountains. Tracking the wolves in the forest was almost impossible. At least here, if we get on top of a little rise, we can see forever. Let's get closer to our babies and put some distance between us and that burrito."

"Hold on a minute." Becca hopped down from the tailgate. "It's my turn."

Daphne pointed to a lonely clump of scraggly branches. "There's a good spot over there."

"I'll take that as a warning." She walked awkwardly in the opposite direction, heels and rocks not getting along.

Back in the truck, Becca monitored the tablet while Daphne crawled along the rocky road another thirty minutes. In the rearview mirror, the sun set the sky aglow with horizontal streaks of oranges, reds, and yellows blended together on a fiery canvas. Undoubtedly inspiration for the state's namesake, the Land of Enchantment.

"We're back to ten dots on the tablet, just like you said earlier. That's super weird to have more dots than collars. We're almost on top of them." She pointed straight ahead. "Maybe a half mile over that rise."

"Good. I need to get out and walk again. My knees keep hitting the dash every time we go over a bump, and every damn rock is a bump."

"Do you have anything to eat?" asked Becca, swaying with each tilt of the truck. "That salad at the cavern wasn't quite enough."

Daphne smiled at the DC professional, who, back home, was never more than a block away from a restaurant. "I always bring a couple sandwiches and granola. Got some bananas in there too. Check the backpack by your feet."

While Daphne was mesmerized with the array of colors in the side mirror, Becca reached for the plastic sandwich container on the dash and gave it a shake. The contents rattled like granola. The top flipped off with a *pop* and fell into her lap. A reflexive attempt to catch the lid diverted her attention momentarily from the contents. When her eyes returned to the container, they immediately zeroed in on a gargantuan furry spider with four legs on the rim of the plastic, fangs the size of a pitchfork, and too many angry eyes to count, all staring directly at her.

The bloodcurdling sound that Becca brought forth came with a shrill never before produced from her dainty lungs. Confinement of the cab exacerbated the unending upward pitch as she threw the container into the ceiling.

"*What the—*" Daphne tried to ask, but Becca was consumed in a rapid, repetitive, uncontrollable screech, grasping frantically at her seat belt and the door handle at the same time.

A flailing arm knocked into Daphne, who punched the brakes and turned the wheel. The truck skidded sideways, bouncing everything in the cab airborne and kicking up dust and rocks until it came to rest on top of a pile of boulders.

Becca burst out the door, brushing, slapping, and screaming. She shook every part of her body, constantly swiping her hands over her clothes and through her hair. Spinning in circles, she swung her head wildly, shrieking louder with each turn.

Daphne's inherent response was to jump out and mimic Becca.

"What the hell are we doing?" she asked when the dancing duo came together at the front bumper.

Finally able to enunciate a single word, Becca screamed, "*Spiiiiiider!*"

Daphne stopped bouncing. She put her hands on her hips and cocked her head. "Seriously."

She watched Becca dance halfway back around the truck before looking inside the cab and finding her furry friend backed into a crevice, scared half to death.

"It's okay, little guy. The crazy lady will be finished in a minute. Did she scare you?"

With a little cooing and coaxing, she moved the tarantula gently back into the plastic container and replaced the lid. She then walked around the truck to surveil the situation.

Becca continued the spasmodic dance moves, shouting a repetitive refrain. "*It's on me! Check my back. My legs. Get it off! Get it off!*"

"Slow down, DC. He's back in the container. Why the hell did you open it, anyway?"

Becca slowed the gyrating and passed a few more sturdy sweeps across her clothes to make sure nothing was crawling where it shouldn't be.

"Who the hell keeps a spider in their lunch box on the freakin' dash? I *hate* spiders. *I hate them!*"

She shuddered head to toe and wiped her hands across her blouse again. A creepy chill along her spine forced her shoulders upward in another shudder.

"This isn't a spider," cooed Daphne, raising the container in her palm and gently setting it back on the dash. "He's family. Named him Scooter 'cause he walks side to side. Like he's scooting across the ground."

"*Are you nuts?* Have you spent too much time in the sun?" Another shudder, less severe than the last.

Daphne ignored the remark. "We found each other this morning. Been training him to sit on the dash while I drive. I didn't get him out earlier because *some people* have uncontrollable phobias."

"My only phobia is spiders as big as my hand giving me a death stare."

"Well, that's not our biggest problem right now. Can you start the truck and put it in gear? I think we high-centered on these rocks."

"I am *not* getting into *that* truck with *that* spider."

"He's back in his container."

Becca stood as stiff and still as the boulder under the truck. "I'm not doing it." Another shiver coursed through her body.

"Damn, girl. Grow a pair." Daphne climbed into the cab and started the engine. "Watch the tires, and tell me which ones spin."

"The left rear is spinning. It's six inches off the ground."

"We're screwed, girl. There's no way to get us off these boulders without some help."

They climbed onto the tilted tailgate. Becca glanced at the tablet.

"Eight dots. Where's number nine?"

Daphne patted down a clump of Becca's wild hair, a result of the spider dance, then spoke to the tablet as though talking to an infant. "Where you at, little guys? Come out from hiding." She returned to a normal voice. "They usually reappear in a minute or two. Sometimes they're so close, the dots overlap."

"Now there's only seven."

"What? Let me see that." She counted the dots, zooming in for better clarity, but there were still too many overlapping numbers to read the individual collars. Seven. "It's been nine or ten since the release. Maybe we can see something from that hill. Let's take a walk."

"Shouldn't we fix the truck?"

"You are a funny girl, DC. We can't fix that. We're riding our *Chevrolegs* until we get some help. Come on."

"I'll try, but these aren't the best heels for walking in the desert."

"Heels? You DC people don't get into the field much, do you?"

"They're all I've got. I had a pair of brand-new sneakers in my bag." Her eyes mourned the loss. "They were so cute."

They walked to the nearby knoll that was just high enough to get a view, Becca slipping every time a heel landed on a smooth stone.

"I don't see anything," said Daphne.

"Can I take a look?" Becca peered through the binoculars, struggling to get any resolution in the fast fading sunlight.

*

A half mile due south, Tony stood on the hood of the yellow jelly bean car, looking through his own binoculars at the red truck they finally located.

"Nothing. Nobody around."

Augie strained to see in the distance as twilight was coming to a close.

"He's there. On foot. Look to the right a hundred yards from the truck. Two hundred, maybe."

"You got him, Aug." Tony zeroed the glasses in on Rip.

"Hey, Tony. Look another few hundred yards past him and farther out. What do you see?"

"What's wrong now?" asked Jack, sitting in the back seat, his legs out the door.

Tony adjusted the focus. "Son of a bitch."

He stared at a rapidly fading view of what appeared to be a large man and medium-sized woman. The woman was holding binoculars—directed straight at him.

"How the hell did she follow us out here? Nobody knew what time we left the hotel. I've been watching for a tail the entire drive."

"So have I," added Augie.

"Okay," said Tony, trying not to fall off the car. "We need to be smart about this. Let's catch up to Rip first. Then we take care of her."

"What were you guys looking at?" asked Joel, returning from a visit to the bushes.

The figures in the distance disappeared in the dark.

*

As hard as she squinted, all Becca could see was darkness.

"It's getting too dark to see with those glasses," said Daphne.

They climbed down the knoll and returned to the tilted tailgate, where Daphne watched the tablet and Becca scrolled through her phone.

"No service. I can't upload a picture of your furry friend on my social media."

"Seriously? That's your priority right now?"

"What else can we do?" asked Becca. "I'm *not* getting inside the truck, and you're not fixing the tire."

"The tire's fine. It just happens to be sitting a foot off the ground." She leaned over Becca's shoulder. "Okay. Let's come up with a caption for your pic. You could title it, 'Taking an unexpected shit in the desert,' or 'Doing the granola dance.'"

Becca tossed a mock smile and closed the app.

"Why don't you call your friends? Maybe they can help?" asked Daphne.

"Uh, no service."

She handed Becca the government-issue satellite phone, a compact device, complete with a GPS screen and stubby antenna. "I'm going up ahead to see what I can see. Sweet-talk the tall one. He's got a thing for you. Don't get any ideas with the sat-phone, it doesn't do social media."

Becca studied the phone screen. "It's not going to do much of anything. The battery is down to a half bar."

While Becca called their new friends, Daphne leaned her head through the window of the cab and explained in a much too normal conversation with Scooter that she would be right back.

"Trip said it'll take them half an hour to get here," Becca yelled to Daphne a hundred yards down the road.

"Took us three times as long to get this far," mumbled Daphne. "Hey!" she shouted. "You gotta see this. Bring the flashlight. It's behind the seat."

Ten minutes later, Becca handed Daphne the high-powered Maglite.

"Glad you could join me."

"You try walking on rocks in these shoes, and with that spider in the truck, getting this light wasn't easy. I had to find a stick and push the flashlight to the edge of the door where I could reach it."

Daphne focused on the issue at hand rather than comment on her partner's fashion faux pas and lack of stones. "Look at this, and watch your step. I found it the hard way."

She directed the light to a large pile of wolf scat.

"Whoever left that had a super big dinner," said Becca. "Looks like our wolves found a meal, and then they all crapped in the same pile."

Daphne squatted down to study the pile more closely. "Weird, right? What kind of seeds are these?" She poked the pile with a twig. "They look like squash or maybe a gourd of some kind."

Becca slipped on a nitrile glove and manipulated the excrement in her fingers.

"That's just gross, DC."

"Part of the job." She held a gooey piece of excrement up for closer examination. "Smells almost as bad as you in the truck. Hmmm. You know, I don't think these are seeds."

"Look like seeds to me."

Becca squished the sample, then flicked it off and jumped back. "Fingernails!"

A synchronized "*Eeeeeewww*" quickly transitioned to a whisper when a low rumble vibrated the ground underfoot.

Daphne swung the Maglite three hundred and sixty degrees, searching for the source. Something dashed away, crashing loudly through the shrubs.

"What the hell was that?" Daphne shuddered.

"The owner of this pile," whispered Becca. She leaned into Daphne. The touch forced her partner to jump.

"Damn, DC! Don't do that. It's gone, whatever it was."

Becca scooped part of the pile into a plastic sample bag, and they headed back to the truck. She opened the notes tab on her phone and logged the stool find. When she was finished entering the details, she popped open another app.

Daphne took the opportunity to close her eyes in the cab, hoping a short rest might relieve a growing unsettling feeling. After a few minutes, she called out, "You're pretty quiet back there."

Silence.

She peeled her sticky back off the seat and went to the rear of the truck, finding a teary-eyed Becca.

"That was pretty gruesome. It got to me too."

"That asshole," said Becca. "I can't believe he did it. I *hate* him."

"Sorry, sweet thing, but you're going to have to be more specific."

"Ashton. He just broke up with me."

"He what? Wait a minute. How did he do that? You don't have service."

"I opened my app on the drive out. Messages downloaded, but the road was so bumpy, I didn't read them. While I was sitting here, I scrolled through my open screens and found this."

She handed the phone to Daphne with an open picture of Becca and a wiry man smiling at each other on the edge of a lake. The picture faded out and a new picture appeared. The same guy with his skinny finger pointing to his watch. The caption: "Time to move on."

"Damn, girl. That's cold. And you can't even reply and tell him to kiss your ass. What's his name again?"

"Ashton. But I call him Ash sometimes, you know, when—"

"Whoa! I do not need details about an asshole who breaks up using a picture." A smile slithered across her face. "Hey, when we get back, let's send Ashton some granola."

CHAPTER 37

SMELLS LIKE FISH

A CLOUD OF dust kicked up when Trip skidded the Suburban to a stop in front of a salmon-colored, flat-roofed stucco house, where the dirt yard blended seamlessly with the dirt drive. The front door stood open. A remnant screen flapped outward, giving Trip a view of Brian's dad asleep in his recliner, television on.

He jumped out and yelled up to the roof, "Let's go. They need our help."

"Come up and give me a hand."

The rickety extension ladder wobbled with each upward step. At the top, Trip grabbed the parapet and pulled himself onto the flat tar and gravel roof.

"Don't step on the bubbles, dipshit." Brian pointed to raised nodules of tar that peppered the surface. "We don't want to crack those and get another leak."

"I know how to walk on a roof. What's wrong with the swamp cooler?"

"The belt slipped off again. Look at that piece of shit."

He gestured to the heavily frayed motor belt to his left that looked much like engine belts on the Suburban.

"Replaced it with an old one I found in the shed. It's not gonna last, but it might get us through summer."

Trip turned his nose away. "Smells like fish again."

"You should smell inside the house. It's nasty until you get used to it. Dad doesn't even notice anymore."

Trip snickered. "He's probably dreaming he caught a fish on the Pecos and brought it home for dinner."

"Hey, that would get him out of the house. Good idea. I'll take him fishing."

"Mom won't even turn ours on when it smells this bad," said Trip.

"The smell will be gone in a few minutes. I dropped a few chlorine tablets in the basin."

Brian smacked the back end of his screwdriver against the plastic pump housing, sending flakes of calcium jumping off the fifteen-dollar unit. The pump shaft kicked on, spinning fiercely, finally free of the crystalline binder.

"That'll get us a couple of months. Slip those panels in on the sides. I'll do this one. Keep your hand away from the squirrel cage."

"I know what I'm doing. I always leave the motor on when I work on our cooler. Get tired climbing up and down the ladder to turn it on and off."

Brian set the pump into the pool of water in the cooler basin. Water streams dribbled out of spider tubes positioned above the lou-vered side panels, three of which Trip had already closed up. Brian lifted the last thirty-inch square panel into place.

"Where we going?"

"Becca called," said Trip, a told-you-so grin across his face. "They got the truck stuck and need our help."

Brian climbed down the ladder facing forward, treating it like a steep set of stairs.

Trip sat on the parapet and pushed off, landing ahead of his friend.

"You gonna leave the ladder up?" he asked.

"Might as well. I'll be back up in a week for one thing or another."

Brian slid into the passenger seat. "How are we going to find them?"

"She gave me pretty good directions. They're out near the arroyos where we ride the bikes. Not far from where I broke my ankle."

"That's southeast of town," replied Brian, familiar with the location north of Slaughter Canyon. "Where the arroyos intersect that basin."

The boys had grown up riding dirt bikes in the desert, where summer monsoons turned rivulets into arroyos. A motocross wonderland. Though rain was infrequent, when it did rain, it dumped, providing little time for precipitation to soak into the ground. Heavy runoff eroded trails and washed debris onto paths, creating ever-changing challenges for riders and forcing split-second diversion decisions.

Always aggressive on the throttle, Trip popped high over a hill the previous spring. In midair, he saw a mesquite bush uprooted in the latest rain. The thorny thicket lay in the landing spot he hit a dozen times the prior week. He held his air long enough to clear the stump but couldn't clear the barbed branches that coiled in the spokes. The bike came to an abrupt stop. Trip kept going. He tumbled into the arroyo embankment and snapped an ankle. It wasn't their only near-death experience on bikes.

Brian grunted when the Suburban bounced hard over a rut, announcing the end of pavement and start of rocky dirt roads. "Do you mind?"

"Sorry. I told her we'd be there in thirty minutes."

"No way."

"We can do it. With the lift kit we installed, I got an extra six inches of clearance."

The higher clearance facilitated another hobby they shared with friends: nighttime four-wheeling.

"Extra clearance doesn't make the ride any smoother. Watch out for those boulders."

"Do you think she likes me?" asked Trip between bounces.

"Who?" Brian bonked his head again. "Watch the damn road!"

"Daphne. I think she likes me."

Brian rolled his eyes at the familiar conversation. Anytime Trip met a new girl, he instantly fell in love. "Did you talk to her?"

"A little. She gave me her burrito last night."

"That's a start. Try talking to her when we see them. Get her alone, you know. Walk out into the desert together. Tell her you like her."

"I can't just tell her I like her. She'll think I'm weird."

Brian choked a dust-filled laugh. "You ate half her burrito. She knows you're weird."

Trip pushed a CD into the refurbished radio he had installed and turned up the volume. Both butchered the words to "Rednecker" by Trip's new favorite singer, Hardy.

"*I got a bigger booger mess on my wall…*"

Brian stabbed a finger at the unit and ejected the CD. "*What the hell was that?*"

"I gotta great voice. You were the one off-key."

"We're both off-key. Those aren't the words, dumbass. He says, 'I got a bigger buck and bass on my wall.'"

"No, he doesn't."

"Dude, seriously. Do you think he says 'bigger booger mess'?"

"That's what it sounds like to me. Like on the wall by my bed. I mean, when I was a kid."

"You are *so* gross. It's 'bigger buck and bass on my wall.'"

He popped the CD back in, and the boys allowed Hardy to continue without the aid of backup singers.

"I hope they're okay," said Trip when the song ended. "I tried to warn her. Things happen in the desert. Especially at night."

CHAPTER 38

MAKES YOUR SKIN CRAWL

"IT'S PRETTY DARK," said Daphne. "How are they supposed to find us?"

"They know the area, but maybe we should leave the headlights on. You know, Daphne, I think Trip likes you."

"The little guy? That's sweet, but I'd squash him like a bug." She took a deep breath and let out a long exhale, unnoticed in the dark.

In their now normal position on the edge of the tilted tailgate, Daphne flipped on the tablet and checked the dots. The tablet's ghostly glow illuminated a scarlet hue on Becca's cheek.

"Looking a little pink, DC. Did you sunscreen?"

"As much as I could. My travel tube was almost empty."

"Got yourself some rosy reds there." She placed the back of her hand against Becca's soft cheek. "Feels hot."

"*Ow.*"

"Girl, with your pale skin, you gotta slather cream all over those pretty little arms and legs every day. I half expected your nose to be pasted white with zinc oxide."

Becca extended two red arms outward. "Maybe he won't notice."

"Excuse me? Sounds like you're the one interested in a local. Vidalia, right? I can see that. The boy's cute."

"How'd you pick Vidalia for his nickname?"

"He was easy. Got that sandy hair, a reddish-brown tan, and you just know everything underneath is a mild yellow, just like onions back home."

Becca rolled her eyes.

"My daddy always gave people nicknames. That and my height are the only things I got from him the way Mama tells it. She's a touch shorter than me. Played volleyball at Georgia State and fell for her college sweetheart. A six-ten basketball player. Guess he was pretty good. They had plans to get married after graduation, so she kind of let her guard down, you know. Got pregnant her last year of school. Same time he blew out a knee, ending any dream of playing ball. Mama said he was never the same. Couldn't adjust to being a regular guy."

Becca listened intently, not wanting to interrupt a rare personal conversation with Daphne.

"He didn't do anything stupid. No drugs or booze or anything like that. She said he was just different. No longer wanted to get married. He did his thing with child support for eighteen years, but I kind of stopped seeing him when I was about twelve." She closed her eyes and spread a genuine smile, relieved she had finally opened up.

Becca recalled her own teenage years. Her mother and father at the dinner table most every night, more often than not eating carryout. But they were never really there. Each on a phone or laptop, continuing whatever they'd been doing during ten-hour shifts at work, sacrificing family time to pay for her six years of college. The type of sacrifice few people understood. A sacrifice she promised herself to repay by excelling at her job and showing her parents that it was all worth it.

She gazed up at a million twinkling dots that filled the sky. Stars much more visible in the desert than in the light-polluted metropolis of DC. A momentary streak of light shot past, breathtaking at first, until realization set in. The falling star had burned out in an instant. How apropos. Her first professional opportunity to twinkle, to shine brightly on center stage, and she was stuck in the desert. If she and Daphne failed to keep the wolves safe, just like the star, her career would burn out in an instant.

"Must have been hard," said Becca when her thoughts returned to the truck. "Teenage years without a father."

"Oh, I had a father. A damn good one. Mama married Carl when I was eight. He's not my daddy, but he's damn sure my father. Took care of Mama like I want a man to take care of me someday. Took care of me too, but there's only so much parents can do when we're at school, right?"

"That's for sure." No one had been there to teach Becca how to handle school bullies and self-centered boyfriends.

Daphne looked at Becca. "Had one thing going for me. I was always the biggest kid in the class. Of course, sometimes that was a problem."

"A problem I would have liked to have."

"I had to get tough. Wasn't enough just to be big if I couldn't back it up. After I knocked a few heads together, kids stopped challenging me. High school was fine 'cause nobody messed with the jocks."

Becca patted Daphne's shoulder. "They never messed with those of us hiding in the library either. I wish I had half your strength and confidence."

The warm hand again triggered familial emotions. Had she found a true friend? "Be careful what you wish for. Size can get you into trouble, DC."

"Trouble? You've never had any trouble you couldn't handle."

Daphne took a deep breath and let out a long sigh. "Handling trouble is one thing, Becca. Living with the consequences is another. You want to be as big as me? It's a lot of responsibility. Everyone expects me to be the protector. Wears me out, having to always be alert. Always on. Ready for the next challenger or next asshole who picks on a friend. I'd give anything to blend into the crowd like you."

"How can you even think that?"

"I'm not a field officer by accident. I signed up for this gig because it allows me to work alone, far away from everyone. I don't tell a lot of people this." She hadn't told anyone, actually. "Just like you, I've loved animals all my life. Used to work animal rescues with my mama after hurricanes. You know, returning lost pets to their owners. You'd be surprised how many people just turn their dog loose when a storm is coming. We spent a couple weeks working a temporary shelter in Florida after one of the big ones." She took a sip of water. "Damn, it was hot that week. Atlanta's humid enough, but Florida humidity smacks you in the face first thing in the morning and stays the whole day. Come afternoon, we were getting on each other's nerves pretty good when some lanky dude came in looking for his dog. Mama left me to scoop shit into a barrel while she walked this guy through the pens." She tossed a derisive grin. "Rescue ain't as glamorous as it sounds. Halfway through, Mama catches my eye with a 'dude didn't lose no dog' look."

"Seriously? People claim dogs that aren't even theirs?"

"Just asking that question tells me you went to a private school and lived in a suburb. Am I right?" Daphne pulled her head back. "Don't answer. Of course people claim dogs that aren't theirs. That's how we place half the animals. But some people have a look that tells you they shouldn't be anywhere near a dog. This guy had the look and enough ink on his face and neck that Mama and I were convinced."

"Do they let you turn people away?"

Another are-you-serious look. "I'll turn away anyone I don't like even if it is their damn dog. But Mama and I'd been arguing, so I kept my distance while she and this guy cruised the cages." Her voice transitioned to serious. "Then I heard this grunt. That's it. Just a grunt, but the kind that makes your skin crawl. I look over and see this creep has Mama by the neck. I hurdled three rows of pens and came up on the guy fast. He turned around as my fist was flying. Crunched his chin so hard, teeth flew everywhere. Two of them stuck in my fingers. I never hit anyone that hard in my life."

Becca's jaw dropped. The story had taken a much different turn than she was expecting.

"Mama tells me all the time it wasn't my fault. When she told the guy he couldn't have a dog, he went all batshit on her. Hysterical. Found out later he was cracked out of his head. So, yeah, size can be a good thing, DC, till you put a man in a wheelchair for the rest of his life. Make him eat through a straw." She gazed back up at the sky. "The last few years, I've kept my distance from people. Can't hurt anybody when I'm alone."

"Daphne, you can't live like that. It wasn't your fault. You saved your mom's life."

"I'm trying, DC," she replied in response to phrases she had heard a hundred times from her mother. "That's kind of why I shared that with you. This trip feels different. Like maybe it's time to put some things behind me. Either that or I got too much sun today." She hopped off the tailgate and pointed to headlights in the distance. "There they are."

A cloud of dust announced the boys' arrival.

"Thanks for getting here so fast," said Becca. "Hope we didn't interrupt your plans for the evening."

"Not really," replied Trip. "I was helping Brian fix the swamp cooler."

Daphne glanced at Becca. "Okay, I'll ask the question we're both wondering. What exactly is a swamp cooler? I haven't seen any swamps out here."

"You know, it's just the air conditioner," replied Trip.

"Uh-huh. Well, *swamp cooler* is a new one for me. I grew up around swamps. The only way to cool them down is wait for winter. We got two kinds of AC in Atlanta, refrigerated air and a fan." She winked at Becca. "This place gets weirder every time you guys speak."

Brian studied the high-centered truck while Trip educated Daphne on evaporative air-conditioning systems and the occasional smell of fish blasting through the vents.

"How in the heck did you do this?" asked Brian.

Daphne tossed a sharp look to her partner. "Becca wanted granola."

"We can get it out," said Brian.

"Impossible." Daphne checked the tire again. "There's no way to get it off those rocks without a tow truck."

"This happens a lot actually," said Trip. "We'll jack the truck up on the right side. Once the wheels are off the ground a few inches, we'll push from the left to knock the truck off the jack. That'll kind of slide it over. Probably need to do it two times."

"At least two," agreed Brian. "It's sitting on a cobble bed. Placing the jack will be a little tricky because the ground isn't flat. We'll just have to be careful."

Trip headed to the cab of her truck. "I'll get the jack."

"We should hurry," said Daphne. "I was looking at the tablet. We're down to six dots."

Pop! Pop!

Daphne turned a full circle and pointed into the dark. "*That way! The ranchers are killing them off.*"

"Seriously?" asked Trip, his head swiveling in the direction of the shots.

"What the hell else would it be? We need to get over there now!"

"Let's take my truck. We'll come back for yours later."

"I'll get my pack. Becca, grab the tablet."

Becca climbed in the back with Brian. Daphne joined Trip in the front, setting her pack at her feet.

"Sounded like a handgun," said Brian. "Anybody I know would shoot a wolf from a pretty good distance. They'd use a rifle."

"I hope you're right," said Daphne. "We're getting close."

After bouncing back and forth for at least a mile, Becca grabbed the backside of Daphne's seat to steady herself. She glanced at the instrument panel.

"Your gas gauge looks low."

"I got dual tanks. Just need to flip the switch to the second tank."

Daphne reached over and flipped the nearest switch. "This one?"

The truck sputtered to a stop.

"Uh, what happened?" Her sheepish face hidden in the dark.

Trip gritted his teeth. "It's no big deal." He turned the lights off to keep the battery from dying. "You accidentally hit the kill switch. The dual tank switch is on the left. It happens."

He hopped out and popped the hood. Brian joined him in front of the truck.

"If I hit that switch," whispered Brian, "you'd have cussed me out. Now you have to prime it to get it started, and that's a pain in the ass in the dark."

"She flipped it before I could stop her. Have you noticed how smooth the back of her hand is?"

"Dude, just get this started, then you can lick the back of her hand all you want. I'll crank it when you're ready."

Brian climbed into the driver's seat. "He has to prime the second tank. Everything is automatic if the tanks are switched while we're driving, but killing the engine when the primary is empty requires a manual approach. He installed all this himself, even added an inline siphon to prime it from under the hood. He rewired the console too. It's pretty cool, really. Trip is good with all that stuff." Brian stuck his head out the driver's window. "You ready?"

"Almost."

Trip stood on the bumper and reached deep under the hood. His foot slipped, causing him to drop his cell, losing the lone light source. The phone clanked off engine parts as it fell through the metal maze and landed in the sand. He crawled underneath the engine to find the phone.

"What's that noise?" he asked, his body wedged against the right tire.

"I don't hear anything," replied Brian. "Just fix it already."

Back on the bumper, Trip again reached into the engine well. "I got it. Flip the switch."

"Which switch?" asked Daphne.

"*Wait!*" shouted Trip in a loud whisper. "There's the noise again. *Quiet.*"

A low-pitched growl, like a cross between a lion and a Harley Davidson, curled into his ears and pushed a cold chill up his spine. His legs jellied. His fingers gripped the frame so tight, metal cut into the skin. His brain froze.

"Is that one of your wolves?" Brian whispered to Becca.

"I hope not. They don't sound anything like that."

The muffled growl grew louder. Closer. Deep, heavy breaths crept out of the dark. A loud snap outside the passenger window. A dry branch broken by something in the dark.

Tears welled in Trip's eyes. Beads of sweat, not from the heat, dribbled down his forehead. A hot breath pulsed on the back of his neck causing every muscle to spasm. His sweaty hand slipped onto the hot manifold, burning him out of the frozen fear.

"*Flip the switch! Flip the switch!*"

Daphne stared at the row of toggles poking out of the dash. She had just flipped one that caused the problem and was hesitant to randomly flip another.

Trip's voice quieted again. "*Something's…moving.*"

The trembling whisper transmitted terror into the cab. Becca pulled her knees up to her chest in the back seat. Brian slid closer to Daphne. Concern in the eyes of the large officer was not helpful.

With neither occupant in the front seat taking action, Becca uncoiled, reached over the seat from the back, and flipped a switch. The tune of "Rednecker" blasted through the speakers.

"*Wrong switch,*" shouted Trip. "Flip another. *Now! Now! It's getting closer.*"

"*What's getting closer?*" snapped Daphne.

"*Flip the switch!*"

Becca flipped the next switch. The high-intensity LED light bar blasted a lightning bolt of white across the hood. A high-pitched yelp was followed by bushes rustling away from the truck. Whatever was out there bounded into the desert darkness.

Becca flipped another switch. Brian cranked the key. The engine roared to life.

Trip slammed the hood and jumped into Brian's lap in the driver's seat.

"What the hell *was* that?" asked Brian.

Hands tight on the steering wheel to keep them from shaking, Trip replied, "I couldn't see it, but I could hear it. I could feel its breath. Sounded huge, like a bear or a tyrannosaurus."

"You gotta lot of those tyrannosaurus in these parts?" asked Daphne, slightly less shaken by the ominous noise than the others.

"I don't know," he replied, his voice still shaky. "You know what I mean. I could feel its breath on my neck." He gave the back of his neck a hard rub.

"Something was so close you felt its breath, but you didn't see it?" asked Becca.

"It didn't seem so close. But the growl. You heard it. That low rumble." He shuddered. "Kind of like a Cummins needin' a tune-up."

Daphne knitted her brow, confidence having quickly returned in the safety of the Suburban. "What the hell does that mean? I warned them when they assigned me to New Mexico that I didn't speak the language. And *what the hell was that music?* Some dude said, 'I'm rednecker than you.'"

Brian got out and climbed into the back seat. "Are we really going to laugh this off? Use sarcasm to cover the fear? We nearly shit our pants. Does anybody want to tell me what the hell that was?"

Becca uttered a hushed, "*Fantasma del Gris?*"

CHAPTER 39

ROCKS AND RATTLESNAKES

THE TINY YELLOW car, carrying twice the capacity for which it was designed, scraped the top of every rock and bottomed out in every dip until the wheels spun, begrudgingly, in the sandy bottom of an arroyo.

"Are you kidding me?" growled a livid Joel.

The rhetorical question went unanswered. Jack and Augie jumped out to push. Free of the heavy burden, the car leaped forward. Though only stuck a few minutes, by the time they crested the shallow arroyo, Rip was gone. Tony continued in the general direction of the red truck, but with no buildings, trees, hills, or other landmarks around, confidence in the bearing diminished more with each mile into the dark desert. Aside from Joel's nasally whistle with every breath, the car was silent.

"*Stop!*" screamed Augie.

Tony hit the brakes, throwing the occupants forward.

"Shit, Aug! What the hell was that all about?" Joel's nasal voice was much less intimidating in angry spouts than eerie threats.

Augie stuck his arm forward, pointing spastically into the dark. "The truck! That's the white truck from the hotel."

Joel swiveled his head. "I can't see shit."

"To the right."

Tony crept forward through the plume of dust created with the skidded stop. "I see it. How does that bitch know every move we make?"

"What bitch?" asked Joel.

Jack stuck his head in between the seats. "The girl who took Tony's bag. She stole it at the airport. That's who we were looking at when it got dark."

"I don't like this. That lady is everywhere." Tony turned to Joel. "Is she with you?"

"I have no idea what you're talking about. What happened to your bag at the airport?" He narrowed his eyes. "And what did you have in the bag?"

Tony had been dreading this conversation. He had hoped to get the suitcase back, and he *never* expected Joel to show up in Carlsbad. Mistakes on Joel's projects were painful. Losing the respirator was bad enough. Losing the WIPP file, with Joel's name written on the inside cover, could be lethal. A detail he planned to take to his grave, hopefully not soon.

"Just some stuff, Joel. Nothing important. Do you see her, Jackie?"

"Augie's fat head is in my way. But, guys, this might be more important. Look ahead, I think that's the red truck. Hard to tell in the dark."

"Looks like our luck has finally changed." Tony sneered and accelerated in the direction of Rip's truck, leaving the white truck behind. "Jackie, you and Aug go find that lady. Joel and I will catch up with Rip and ask a few questions."

"You want to stop first?" asked Jack, watching the black desert expand between them and the white truck.

"I'm not losing Rip again."

Tony dipped through another small arroyo and stopped briefly at the top, Rip's truck in view.

"How are we supposed to get back there?"

Augie quickly made his way around to Jack's side and pulled him out an instant before the car lurched forward. "Don't ask stupid questions. We got this, Tony."

"Don't come back without my suitcase."

"Did you bring a flashlight?" asked Augie as the men, dressed in navy flex slacks, Oxford shirts, and patent leather shoes, started their trek into the dark.

"I thought you had it."

"Are you good for anything on this trip besides pissing us off?"

Jack thought for a moment. "Not really."

As Jack snickered at his own remark, his hard-soled shoe snagged a ragged rock, knocking him off balance into a mesquite bush. He cried out in the high-pitched voice of a teenage girl as he jerked a thorn-punctured leg from the bush with a *riiiiip*.

"*Fuuu—*" He never finished the word. His left foot slid between two stones that held tight, forcing him face-first into the dirt. With a busted lip and mouth full of sand, he screamed and rolled onto his back, revealing a prickly pear pad stuck to his gut. He instinctively grabbed the broad cactus leaf and hurled it into the dark, screaming louder from the needle-like thorns that impaled his palm. Punctures in his leg, stomach, and hand brought forth a profanity-laced wail.

Augie heaved a heavy howl until smoker's phlegm crawled up his throat and turned the laugh into a congestive cough. After hacking half his lungs out, he sat in the dirt next to Jack and helped pull prickly pear thorns from his hand and gut. Piercing stings remained even after they removed the last long thorn.

Jack held his hand under the cell phone light. "See any more stickers?"

"Just some furry shit." Augie studied the palm until the light faded away. "Did you forget to charge that?"

"We've been driving all freakin' day. When did you want me to charge it?"

"Give me your hand." He brushed his fat fingers across the furry spines, causing Jack to curse and yank the hand back. Augie cursed just as loud, having transferred tiny spines to his fingers.

After exhausting their saltiest vocabulary, Jack gently placed his hand on the ground to leverage his heavy frame up. A rapid rattle froze both men. Though neither had ever seen a live rattlesnake, the sound was unmistakable.

A half-coiled, very pissed rattlesnake was inches from Jack's hand, warning him to back off. The scaly reptile, two-thirds of its body on the ground, the other sinewy third swaying six inches in the air, whipped its tongue in and out. Jack could feel the spastic tail vibrating as the snake informed the intruders they were not leaving his personal space fast enough. When the angry rattle turned to a buzzing hum, Jack heaved his heavy body as fast as he could in the opposite direction. His center of gravity shifted, pulling him safely away from the snake but landing him ass first into the long spiny thorns of an ocotillo.

Yelling, swearing, and screaming resumed unabated until he was too tired to continue. He eventually leaned forward, hands gingerly on his knees, and waited for Augie to prove his friendship by pulling the thorny branch out of his buttocks.

They finally continued the trek to the truck, Jack walking awkwardly, pain shooting through his body with each misstep on the rocky road.

"I'm gonna kill that bitch," said Jack.

"You're going to have to wait. There's nobody here."

Jack opened the truck door with his good hand and climbed inside. Anyplace was better than outside in the dark, where everything wanted to prick, poke, or poison him. The dome light was just bright enough to see hairlike fibers still causing painful irritation, but his thick fingers struggled to grasp the stickers from his palm and stomach. He wasn't about to ask Augie to pull anymore thorns from his ass. Satisfied everything accessible was removed, he climbed out and limped around to Augie.

"They sure did a number on this thing. How do you even get a tow truck out here?"

"The girl must have been driving," said Augie. "Why don't you climb back inside? We'll rest up then go find them."

The dome light faded when the doors closed.

"Just between us, Aug, does Joel seem angrier than usual?"

"Tony explained it to me at the bar in Aiken. You were passed out in the booth."

"I had a rough day."

"You didn't kill him, Jack. Don't think of it like that. He ran into you."

"Yeah...but...if I hadn't been there."

"Joel is pissed because we screwed up. He lost his ass on that job and almost didn't survive the mistake, if you know what I mean."

Jack gave an understanding nod. Their efforts to make one of the competing contractors appear to be grossly noncompliant had failed miserably.

"But that night didn't go so good for us. I don't know Joel that well, but out here in the dark, in the desert, we need to watch our backs."

Another nod. "I'm starting to get stiff, Aug. Need to move around."

Jack left the cab and walked a few feet behind the truck. He unzipped and cautiously commenced to relieve himself with as little finger contact as possible to the one part of his body where he did not want to leave a stray barb.

"I hear something," he whispered over his shoulder.

"Yeah. A freakin' hose stream. Could you move farther away?"

"Not that. Get over here. Something's out there."

The large men stepped cautiously into the dark toward the noise.

"What the hell are we doing?" whispered Augie after ten minutes of walking.

"I'm sure I heard something."

"I don't hear shit. What the hell, Jack? You got us following a freakin' ghost."

Jack raised an open hand, stopping the duo. "There," he whispered, his voice tense. "Down there."

The soil gave way beneath their feet.

CHAPTER 40

THE OTHER TABLET

THE SUBURBAN CHOKED itself to a stop with the sound of an engine sucking the last fumes of gas from the tank.

Brian whiffed the back of Trip's head. "Doesn't do any good to have two tanks if you don't keep gas in both."

"Don't blame me. I added the second tank, but you never helped me put in a second gauge."

"Uh-huh. It's my fault that you didn't fill up with gas."

"All this bouncing is killing my kidneys," said Becca. "I'm not even sure where we are now." She pushed and held the sat-phone button. No response from the dead unit. "Well, this isn't going to help."

Daphne strained to see in the dark. "Based on the direction we've been going, I'd say we're pretty close to the spot where I saw two large animals this morning. Thought they were horses, but they disappeared before I could get a good look."

"Horses?" questioned Brian. "Out here?"

"Didn't get a good enough look to be sure, that's why I didn't say anything. When I was out here before breakfast, I saw two animals way out on the horizon. The sun wasn't up enough to zero in a distance with the rangefinder. I'd guessed maybe two miles from the release point. I watched for a minute until they shot off, straight toward our pack. It was unreal how fast they moved. Soon as they got to the pack, the wolves disappeared from sight in one of those gullies."

Becca raised unconvinced eyebrows. "Are you sure they were horses? Ungulates don't usually travel in pairs like that, at least not for very long. They prefer to be in a herd when they're out in the open. And horses would never run *at* a pack of wolves. They would—"

"Hold up," interrupted Brian. "What's an ungulate? We hunt everything out here. Trip, you ever heard of those?"

"Never. Probably can't eat them. It's not like a possum, is it? Do they look like rats? I couldn't eat anything that looked like a rat, but my mom did once."

Daphne snapped her fingers so loud they echoed. "Does a possum look like a horse to you?"

"An ungulate is a hooved animal," explained Becca. "Horses, pigs, sheep, that kind of thing."

"And you say we talk funny," mumbled Trip.

Becca ignored the remark and continued. "Horses would fight super hard if they were surrounded by wolves, but they would never take the offensive."

"That's my point," replied Daphne. "It was hard to see in the early dawn, and they were far away, but based on size, my best guess says they were horses. Once they were out of sight, I went back to the tailgate for a snack, and all the dots were together."

"What's the accuracy of your tracker?" asked Trip.

"Good to one meter."

"That's a yard, right?"

She looked at the lanky kid and sighed. "What do they teach you out here? *Yes,* it's a yard."

"Okay," said Brian. "So all nine wolves were really close together."

"Ten dots. There were ten dots at the time. They melded into a single black dot on the screen. Zooming in didn't even help."

"Are you saying a horse was the tenth dot?" asked Brian.

Daphne shrugged. "I don't know what I'm saying. That doesn't make sense either. Two animals join the pack, and I see one more dot. What the hell is that all about?"

"I can assure you we haven't tagged any horses," said Becca. "Must have been the errant dot that's been showing up now and then. Sometimes the signal gets funky when terrain is super weird. We had signal problems in Oregon last year. One of our techs told me the signal was bouncing off the trees."

"Do you see any trees out here, DC?"

"I'm just saying things happen with the signal. But there's another possibility I've been thinking about since we heard that noise. After we talked to Rip yesterday, I was super curious. So last night, I got on the computer and read a lot of publications about WIPP and the radioactive waste they put down there. Then I searched on thyroid defects caused by radiation, like Rip was telling us. There are quite a few papers on the subject. Peer-reviewed journal articles."

"Peer-reviewed?" questioned Brian.

"Research papers and journal articles that have a pedigree. Reviewed by peers, other experts in the field. That gave me some confidence in the underlying science. I was surprised how many studies have been done on radiation effects, particularly on the thyroid. The papers substantiated what Rip told us. Sustained low-dose radiation to the thyroid can cause enlargement of organs." She leaned to the middle of the seat. "And get this. In rare cases, it can cause extreme bodily enlargement."

Daphne smirked. "Sounds like you had another fun evening. I had a beer and watched some boxing."

"What I'm trying to say…Don't laugh because this is super specu-lation. But what if that *was* wolf fur we found last week? Dr. Shanks told me the fur was radioactive. What if it came from a wolf that was exposed to a lot of radiation?"

"Are we taking the ghost off the table, then?" Daphne asked sar-castically. "Get to the point, DC. What are you trying to say?"

"I'm saying Trip and Brian saw something last week that was very large and growled in a low rumble. We found wolf fur in a bush, right where the noise came from. What if the thing that growled at Trip was an oversized wolf? A real wolf. Not some transparent *Fantasma del Gris*. What if those horses you saw were actually wolves? Really big wolves. And what about the huge pile of wolf scat we found? Assuming it was one pile, the owner is huge."

"You guys found a huge pile of wolf shit?" asked Trip. "Where?"

"Not far, but let me finish. What if it was one of our wolves from the last release? We never found all the collars, remember? If she was pregnant at the time, her baby has been an adult for years by now, and it wouldn't have a collar." She leaned back. "That would explain one dot and two horses - or wolves."

"I counted a bunch of what-ifs in there and heard nothing to explain how a wolf looks like a horse. *What if* we find our damn wolves and just make sure the ones that are still alive stay safe?"

Trip gestured to the tablet next to Becca and asked meekly, "Um, where are the dots now?"

"Good question, Little Man. Hand me the tablet. I'll solve this mystery."

Becca passed the tablet from the back seat.

"The other tablet."

Becca's eyes widened.

"The...other...tablet." Daphne turned to the back seat. "You did bring the other tablet?"

"That's the only one I grabbed." Her voice jumped an octave. "We switched trucks so fast."

Daphne grunted but otherwise restrained herself. Given the events of the evening, the tarantula, high-centering the truck, gunshots, and whatever the hell happened when they were switching gas tanks, her friend deserved a little break.

"Guess there's only one way to find out if my horses are your wolves. Gotta go old-school. Tracks and night scope. The last bearing I had on the pack was southeast. At least one thing was in our favor." She glanced at Trip. "You were driving in the right direction. Let's do this."

"Do what?" asked Becca.

"Track."

Becca leaned deeper into the seat. "Not me. I don't mind driving around the desert, but I'm not walking out there in the dark. These shoes would never make it. You saw that when we only went a few feet from the truck. Not to mention there are *wolves* out there and whatever the heck growled at Trip. What if it followed us?"

"This is my job, DC. Tracking wolves. Of course, I would prefer to use the tablet, but *somebody* left it in the other truck."

Becca turned her head to the window. "You're making a super big mistake."

"I'll stay here with Becca," offered Brian. "Trip, you go with Daphne."

"How about it, Little Man? You up for a hike?"

Trip pretended not to hear the invitation, busily flipping random switches on the dash as though the right combination might start the truck.

"Get your butt out here," she ordered in a voice slightly more intimidating than the eerie growl in the dark.

He jumped out.

"We'll walk southeast to that little hill up ahead." She pointed to a shadowed mound in the distance. "From that high point, maybe we can see something."

Brian pressed the button to lower the glass in the tailgate, careful not to touch any other aftermarket buttons, switches, or knobs. He lowered the tailgate and climbed aboard with Becca.

"Trip!" Brian called out too late. They were already gone. He looked at Becca. "Sometimes I wonder about him. He's got a five-gallon gas can back here."

CHAPTER 41

TAZED

DAPHNE PLACED A finger across her lips, instructing Trip to stay quiet while two large men slid ass first down the steep dirt walls of the arroyo, cursing and complaining until they rolled to a stop at the bottom. Jack was first to his feet, circling himself like a coyote chasing his tail, pinching and pulling various parts of his body the entire time. The slide down had revealed more than one cactus thorn missed in the earlier hunt.

Augie pushed himself up and brushed a cloud of dust from his pants that forced Jack to cough and cringe at the same time. When the dust settled, he noticed two shadows. Gray stones in the arroyo bed reflected just enough moonlight to illuminate a rather large man standing next to a pencil-thin kid. As his eyes adjusted, he realized the taller of the two was a she rather than a he. The beefy woman stood with a familiar presence; she could handle herself.

He cursed under his breath and dusted himself off more casually, as though they entered the arroyo for a reason. "Where's your friend?"

"Are you the guy with the heavy bag?" asked Daphne.

Becca had whined so much about the guy who switched bags Daphne felt as though she knew the man.

Face to face with the female officer, Augie hardened his voice. "What do you know about that bag?"

Tired, dirty, hungry, and pissed over the night's misadventures, Daphne was in no mood for attitude. "Enough to know you need a damn good reason to be transporting that shit across country. And right about now, I'm thinking the contents are pretty freakin' important for you to hike your fat ass all over the dark desert looking for it."

Jack snickered at the female berating of Augie, another tidbit to color future barroom stories about the desert venture.

"Or are you out here for something else?" Daphne narrowed her eyes. "'Cause if you're the ones killing my babies, *I will take you out.*" *Killing babies? What the hell?*

Daphne watched a sardonic grin push the man's fat cheeks to the side. Not the smile of a new friend.

Augie looked left, right, and down the deep, dark, desolate arroyo, confirming they were alone. He swiveled his hip forward and cocked his right arm back, ready to unload.

From Daphne's perspective, the man's oversized body prevented any actual swiftness in the move he was attempting. With years of training and her own teenage experience surviving urban streets, she saw the right hook coming all the way from Atlanta. She also saw the butt-end of a nine-millimeter when the man's shirttail raised as he heaved a heavy punch in her direction.

Left leg firmly planted, she arced back and snapped her right leg forward, planting a boot in the center of Augie's face. The upward angle snapped his head with a *pop* and pushed him backward onto the rocky arroyo bed. She held the follow-through, then lowered her leg gently, content with the result.

From the corner of her eye, she saw Jack throw a blow. Her little friend's reaction was swift as he quickly covered his face with both hands. Not the offensive move she might have recommended. Jack jabbed solid shots into the back of Trip's hands, then buried a left hook into Trip's belly, freeing the most popular dish at the Coyote Cavern. A half-processed burrito spewed out, catching Jack in the chest and drizzling down his front.

Daphne pulled her stun gun from the utility belt and fired. The barbed probe caught Trip in the neck, causing him to twitch like a spastic six-year-old attempting to dance for the first time. The convulsions forced him to spew more vomit on his attacker.

"Piece of shit," she mumbled at the oversized toy gun.

She shot again. The second set of probes hit Jack square in the chest. The large man's face tightened. His body spasmed from a thousand volts coursing through the meaty mass. Somehow he maintained his balance. Quivering eyes were telling his body to reach out and kill the bitch, but his muscles only twitched and jerked.

As much as she enjoyed a little rough play, these men meant business. She hoisted Trip to her shoulder and dashed down the arroyo. After a hundred yards, she set him down. His wobbly legs maintained a slow gait back to the Suburban, where they found Becca and Brian sitting nearly atop one another.

Daphne directed the light. "What do we have here?"

Becca shushed her partner and ran a hand down her blouse to press out the extra wrinkles.

Daphne wrapped Trip gently from behind. "What do you think, Little Man? I'd say these two were about to get *busy*. Just like us, right?" She winked at Becca. "Soon as we were out of sight, Little Man here got frisky."

"You dog." Brian hopped off the tailgate as Trip's flushed jaw dropped to his knees.

"On a more serious note," said Daphne, her tone less animated, "we ran into your friend."

"My *friend?*"

"Fat guy. Owns a black suitcase that looks a little like yours."

"You found my bag!"

"Do I look like I found your bag? We found the fat guy who took it."

"Okay…So when can I get my bag back?"

"Yeah, about that."

"What's wrong with Trip?" interrupted Brian, noticing his friend's tousled hair and swollen face.

"I got into a fight with one of the guys," he replied as though the encounter was no big deal. "My hands hurt more than anything."

Impressed and a little shocked Trip was able to take care of himself, Brian helped him onto the tailgate. "I know the feeling. My hands always hurt after a fight."

"One of the big guys hit me pretty hard in my face and stomach."

"Then I tazed him," said Daphne, patting the yellow plastic-handled gun on her belt.

"Did you taze Trip or the other guy?" Becca asked as she wiped Trip's face with a rag.

A slight pause. "Well…" The pitch of her voice increased. "Both. The trigger on this POS is stiff. I missed the first shot. Kind of got Trip instead."

"She didn't mean to shoot me."

"There were two guys," said Daphne. "A big guy and a heavy guy. The big guy tried to get a little rough, and I had to settle him down. While I was doing that, Trip held off the other one until I tazed him. But those guys were serious dudes, Becca. One of them was carrying."

"Carrying what?"

"DC, we have got to get you out of the office more. He was carrying a nine-millimeter, and I'm pretty sure he was ready to use it."

"Daphne kicked his ass," said Trip, shuddering again, releasing residual voltage from his body.

"So where is my suitcase?"

"Would you quit about the bag already? Those guys were ready to kill us. We left them about a mile from here. If they try to come after us, we could be in deep shit, because I'm the only one with a weapon."

"But it's just a suitcase."

"Have you heard anything I've been saying? Those guys did not come all the way out here to return your bag. We've got to go back to the truck and get my tablet. With all the gunshots we've heard and those guys carrying weapons, this entire relocation could be in jeopardy."

"Let's go," said Brian, jingling the keys.

Daphne shot an angry glare. "Not funny. It's a long freakin' walk. We need to get started."

"We filled it with gas from a can in the back," said Becca, tossing Trip a wink.

"Oh, yeah. Forgot about that."

Brian brushed his hand up the back of Trip's neck. "Obviously, dipshit."

"Vidalia. If you keep giving my little man a hard time, I might need to peel a layer off your onion ass."

"He doesn't mean anything by it," said Trip, confidence riding high. "Let's go find the wolves."

CHAPTER 42

FLUKE FLIGHT PATH

RIP CREPT TO the edge of a deep arroyo and came to a stop. He flicked his high beams to assess the incline of the near and far bank and the width of the bottom. The truck would have no problem going down or climbing out, but the tires could bog down in the sandy bottom if he wasn't careful. He crawled down the embankment until the front tires reached the bottom, then punched the accelerator. A huge shadow dashed in front of the truck. He slammed on the brakes, throwing Sandy into the dash. The shadow was gone as fast as it appeared.

"Did you see that, girl?" He helped Sandy back into the seat.

The Cheagle anchored her paws to the worn leather and pinned oversized ears tight against her head. Ears and tiny stature provided the only indication she was part Chihuahua; the rest of the shivering lump, vibrating like an animatronic device with new batteries, looked purebred beagle.

"Great horned owl, maybe?" he asked Sandy, as though she were an active participant in the conversation.

No reply from the petrified pup.

Rip peered through the windshield, trying to convince himself the shadow had to have come from the fluke flight path of a great horned owl. The largest bird in New Mexico was relatively common in the desert. His headlights likely scurried a deer mouse into the open, presenting a ready snack for the feathered carnivore.

"What else could it have been?"

He placed a hand on the holster in the passenger seat. The

nine-millimeter was comforting and had already proved useful when he popped off two shots to encourage a wily coyote off the road. He pressed lightly on the accelerator to determine whether he had any traction. The rear wheels spun freely in the sand, exactly what he had tried to avoid.

"Well, girl, let's see what we've got."

A quick scratch under Sandy's chin, and he climbed down from the truck. The Cheagle jumped out and sped around front, happy to have feet on solid ground after the bouncy ride. She took the long route to meet Rip at the back tire.

"Just what I expected," he said with a frustrated grunt. "If you were a real dog, you could help dig this out."

Sandy curled into a ball and licked herself.

Rip climbed out from under the bed and checked his phone for the fifth time. No service. He thrashed through the glove box for the third time. No flashlight. Half his job at WIPP involved health and safety, yet he was in such a hurry to look for Grady he left town woefully unprepared. One bottle of water, no blankets, no food, no shovel, and nobody knew where he was.

"Dumbass," he mumbled with a self-deprecating snicker.

Hell, he'd been driving dirt roads since he could see over the top of the steering wheel and seldom packed any of that stuff. Shit happens in the desert. Not often, but it happens, which was why he carried a three-foot board in the back. All he had to do was slip the board under the tire and rock the truck out. Routine.

The expected routine changed slightly when he noticed the board was missing. He grinned at the thought of Grady using it for target practice.

Freeing the truck wasn't much more difficult without the board. Excavate around the tires. Fill the hole with stones, and kick them tightly against the rubber. Rock the truck back and forth to build a little momentum, then gun it and don't stop until cresting the far bank.

In five minutes, he gathered enough jagged rocks to do the job and started placing them under the tires. He lay on his back and kicked the first pile into place.

"This isn't going to work, girl."

He returned to the cab and turned the engine off, along with it the lights.

"Can't be sucking in exhaust while I'm kicking on these."

Still no reply from his faithful partner. Returning to the horizontal position, he kicked another batch into place.

Thwump! The truck kicked back.

"*What the hell?*"

A puff of dust billowed under the chassis.

"Sandy?"

Nothing. The pup probably kicked up dirt chasing a lizard.

He grabbed the rear bumper for leverage, thrust his legs under the back end, and compacted the stones against the tire.

Thwump!

Something bumped hard against the driver's door. A low-pitched rumble crawled around from the front. An eerie sound mixed with a slow, rhythmic scratch. Heavy pawing in the dirt. Dust puffed again.

Rip squeaked a hopeful, "*Sandy?*"

He strained to see in the dark. Something was out there. More pawing. Louder. Closer. He leaned his head around the tire and looked toward the front just as a beam of light flashed over the edge of the arroyo. Another burst of dust. The rumble ceased. Footsteps skidded down the slope, accompanied by cursing in a thick Brooklyn accent.

Rip looked toward the high-intensity flashlights walking his way. Blinding beams zeroed in on his face.

"Who's there?" he asked.

"Good evening, Rip," replied the nasally voice of a confident man.

"Mind turning those off?"

Joel turned his light off. Tony redirected his beam to Rip's midsection.

"Do I know you?" Rip asked the shorter man, who was dressed in a sport coat and tie in the middle of the desert in ninety-degree heat. Red flags that did not register concern because his mind was still on the stuck truck and the rumble.

"I'm Joel. This is Tony." No offer of a handshake.

Tony tossed a what's-with-the-names glance at Joel.

"Looks like you got yourself a problem, Rip," said Tony, revealing which man had the accent.

"Just a little sand. Mind giving me a hand?"

"We need to ask you a few questions first," replied Joel.

"Questions?" Rip raised an eyebrow. "I'm sorry. I'm usually good with faces, but I'm not sure I know you. Have we met?"

"We just did. I'm Joel, this is Tony."

"I saw you at WIPP yesterday, right? Meeting with Dom."

A concurring nod.

"What the heck is this about? You guys are pretty darn dedicated, coming out in the middle of nowhere to ask me a few questions."

"We're investigating the problems at WIPP," said Joel. "I understand you were there during the accident last week. We just need to know what you saw in the underground."

Rip leaned against the taillight and cocked his head. "You can't be serious. You came all the way out here to ask me what I saw a week ago? If you give me a push out of this sand, we can go back to the office and review my log. I write everything down."

Tony covered his mouth and choked out a whisper. "That's a problem."

"The situation has grown in complexity," continued Joel. "We need some answers. Now."

Rip considered the curious situation. Two men had tracked him down in the middle of the desert, in the dead of night, wanting to know about the ceiling collapse.

"Who are you with again? DOE? DNFSB? Got any ID?"

"That's right," replied Joel. "We're with the Defense Nuclear Facilities Safety Board. ID's in the car."

That explained the sport coat and tie. DNFSB always came from back east and generally maintained East Coast attire.

"I gotta hand it to you, for feds, you take your job pretty serious to be out in the desert at this hour." He dropped the tailgate and hopped on the edge. "What do you want to know?"

"Let's start from the beginning."

"Okay, but I have to qualify whatever I say based on the fact I don't have my notes in hand. Please keep that in mind."

Rip's voice transitioned from curious to authoritative as he explained events of that odd evening. "Thursday night. Actually, Friday morning, around two or three o'clock. I had finished taking swipes and readings on a truck we unloaded earlier that evening. It's not uncommon to offload at night and leave the drums up top until the dayshift comes in to review everything, then they take the containers down. I usually work dayshift, but that night, I was asked to come in because Steve called in sick. Lucky me."

Joel sighed. "Can you get on with it?"

"The truck had come in late, and we offloaded. Left the packs in the temp area to take down the next day. I knew the driver, and we stood around catching up. Hadn't seen him in about a year, maybe a little less. So I was outside near the gate when I heard the alarm. I observed the flashing light on the Waste Handling Building, which told me we had a problem over there. At the time, I didn't know if the problem was topside or in the shaft. In accordance with procedure, I went to my office first to check dose levels remotely on my computer. We do that to keep staff from running into a burning building, so to speak. You know the ALARA principle. As low as reasonably achievable."

Tony was fully aware of ALARA. Joel couldn't care less.

"I don't recall the alarm readings offhand, but those are archived, and I made a separate list for my file. Per procedure, I silenced the alarms but did not reset them. That's an option, and the procedure gives me the authority, but I had a gut feeling. I can't explain why. Late hour, nobody around. That's when stuff happens sometimes. Kind of like my truck here."

Joel scowled at the slow progress of the information dump.

"Readings were definitely elevated but not high. So I went to the Waste Handling Building with my GM meter to confirm nobody was inside. They shouldn't be, you know, with the skeletal evening shift and, of course, the blaring alarm, until I silenced it."

He thought for a moment, fingers pinching his chin, wanting to get the chronology correct.

"The sensor in that area is a radiation area monitor. So the dose could be coming from anywhere in the vicinity of the meter. I entered the room cautiously and scanned systematically in each direction. You know the routine. Roughing out a grid to make sure the complete area was surveyed. Obviously, I eyeballed the grid and swept through pretty quickly."

Tony rolled his eyes to Joel and mumbled under his breath, "Obviously."

"I was unable to confirm an elevated dose. That was odd. Given the dose I observed remotely in my office, I expected to find something."

"What could cause the alarm if there was no radiation?" asked Joel.

"Hard to say, really. If somebody wheeled a hot drum through the area on a dolly, the radiation area monitor would alarm, but the drum wouldn't leave any contamination behind. The area would be clean upon examination. Of course, that's not a real scenario. At that hour, nobody should be moving a drum."

Tony scratched his chin. Why had Rip offered *that* explanation? Had the body been repackaged in a drum and moved?

"Anyway, with no dose concern, I proceeded farther inside. When I got to the shaft elevator, my meter started to sing pretty good." He paused again, regretting use of the word "sing." He didn't want to piss off the DNFSB with cheap slang. "I pushed the call button to see if there was anything inside the car that might have contributed to the elevated reading. The elevator door started to open at the same time the emergency speakers notified all personnel to report to the muster point."

He stopped, hoping the men would ask a question and allow him to skip the next part of the story, the part where he violated procedure. He had lied to Mel, saying he immediately reported to the muster point. But that was Mel, a drunken ass who had never followed a procedure in his life. These men were DNFSB. He couldn't lie to feds.

"The elevator," prompted Joel.

Rip placed his forearms on his thighs, leaned forward, and took a deep breath. He wasn't going to get out of this one. Everything was in his notes anyway and would turn up in a formal review. Willful violation of procedure could cost him his job, but what he had seen that night in the elevator and in the underground was so odd.

He clapped his hands together and sat back upright. "Okay. I admit it. I violated procedure. I'm sorry, guys. I always go by the book. Ask anyone. The guys poke fun at me about how anal I can be, because I never deviate from procedure. Hell, I wrote most of them."

He waited for the admonition, somewhat surprised at the lack of concern over a protocol breach. He also realized neither man was taking notes.

"The elevator doors opened. Guys, I don't know how else to say this. The back corner was covered in blood. I found a clump of hair in the railing, at least I thought it was hair at first. When I looked closer, I realized it was fur, like from a dog or something. My meter was showing a pretty good dose, and I thought the blood or fur might have something to do with it. I bagged it and took some swipes to analyze in the lab. Not a blood analysis. We don't do bio."

Joel glanced at Tony. The contents from their drum could be the source of the blood. Fur was an unexpected twist, but the man in front of them was not a biologist. He may have mistaken human hair for fur. On a decomposing body, hair could fall off in clumps.

"How would a mess like that get inside the elevator?" asked Tony. "Do you have any ideas? Do you think a drum popped open?"

"A drum? No way. We don't accept bio waste or free liquids. That much blood would definitely be considered free liquid. I had no idea what it could be at the time."

Tony and Joel looked at each other's feet.

"But later, after talking to Mel, it came to me. We have this staff member, Chuck. He raises German shepherds and has been known to bring them to work. Leaves them in his truck, but it's still not allowed. I've written him up for it a few times. That's just the kind of guy he is. In fact, I gave him a verbal warning last month for bringing the dogs into the Waste Handling Building. It's a short walk from there to the elevator. That scenario satisfied Mel, and I don't have a better one. I've been too preoccupied with finding my boy to investigate any further."

"You're pretty sure you found fur?" asked Tony. "If I found hair in an elevator, I'd think somebody slipped and knocked his head against the rail, leaving a patch of hair behind. Head wounds bleed pretty good. That could explain the blood."

"I'm confident the sample I bagged was fur. At least I was sure at the time. I'd love to look at it again if I could find it. Even if it was hair, who put it there? Chuck didn't have much hair left, and what he did have didn't look anything like what I found. The other piece to all this, Chuck hasn't been seen since that night. Everyone keeps telling me he's on a hunting trip, but it's not hunting season. I don't know what to think, guys. He was working alone that night, like he usually does. Maybe he did bring a couple of his dogs into the underground. When the alarm started blaring, maybe they got skittish and turned on him. It gets pretty loud down there. Somehow he got to the elevator with the dogs. Hell, guys, this is all speculation, but maybe one of them bit him or they mauled him on the way up. Chuck would never report it because it would cost him his job. He would pack the dogs up and leave. Knowing Chuck, he's off somewhere licking his wounds until they heal. He'll return in a few days with some kind of story about injuring himself on a hunt and forgetting to tell anyone he was on vacation. That's the best theory I've come up with."

Again, he waited for questions. Nothing. He was desperate to end the conversation before they forced him to tell the whole story.

"I had to report to the muster point, so I returned to the admin building and put the swipes and fur in my sample cabinet. After we were released from the conference room, I went straight to my office, but the samples were gone."

"Gone? What do you mean 'gone'?"

"I mean gone. Not there. We were all waiting in the conference room while Mel checked out the alarms. That took him a long time which would be expected with so many units to check. When we were released, the swipes and fur were gone."

"And nobody else left the room?"

"Nobody, but we never talked to Chuck. He's the only one who would benefit from that stuff disappearing if it was from his dogs."

Joel bit the inside of his lip to maintain self-control. The nervous man on the tailgate was taking his sweet-ass time explaining the incident, but he was providing exactly the information they needed.

"Chuck? That name hasn't come up in our investigation." The name had come up plenty, but nobody had provided useful information on the missing man's activities in the underground or where he might be found.

"Not surprising. Mel and Dom aren't always forthcoming about information."

"I want to hear more about the elevator," said Joel. "And tell us about Chuck."

CHAPTER 43

WALKING IN CIRCLES

JACK PUSHED AUGIE with his foot. "Get up."

"What the hell happened?"

"A girl kicked your ass." He bellowed a coarse laugh, cut short when a residual spasm twinged his diaphragm.

"Where are they?"

Jack rubbed his chest. "Bitch tazed me."

"And you let her get away?"

"You weren't a whole lot of help yourself, asshole. Let's get out of here, before she comes back."

"Tony's gonna be pissed," muttered Augie, tenderly touching the bridge of his broken nose. "*Ugh.* Step back, ass. Even with a busted nose, you smell like vomit."

"That little shit threw up on me. It's sticking to my pants."

The men lumbered down the arroyo in silence. After a few hundred yards, Augie looked to Jack. "Hey, buddy. Friend. You're not going to tell anyone she kicked my ass, are you?"

"You don't even need to ask, Aug. We been friends a long time. I'm not gonna tell *anyone*. I'm gonna tell *everyone!*" Another coarse laugh was cut short by the pain.

While mumbling obscenities, Augie searched for a way up the bank of the arroyo. He found a crevice in the vertical dirt wall and started to climb. A sliver of moonlight reflecting off gray cobblestones protruding from the earthen wall gave him just enough light to see footholds. He placed the toe of his shoe on a rock then pulled on scrub brush growing out of the earthen wall to assist the vertical ascent. The slick leather sole of his shoe slipped off the rock.

"Stop knocking dirt in my face, asshole," said Augie. "And you still smell like vomit."

"Hey, dumb shit. I'm down here, *beneath you*. You're the prick knocking rocks on my head."

Augie reached over the top edge and grabbed the soft trunk of a small tree.

"Then who's kicking shit on me?"

"*Grrrrrrrrrrrrrrrrrrrr.*"

Massive fangs, inches from Augie's face, glistened in the moonlight. The monstrous animal peeled its lips back, displaying two rows of stained teeth. Augie's fingers finally transmitted a signal to his brain; the soft tree trunk was the leg of an animal. A very large animal.

A rumbling growl rolled down the embankment, spiking the hair on Jack's neck. Looking upward at Augie's backside, he couldn't make out exactly what was going on, but something was definitely wrong. His friend was stone stiff.

Foul, moist breath peppered Augie's face with spittle. He let go of the leg and tumbled down on top of Jack, screaming at the top of his lungs.

"*Shoot! Shoot! Shoot!*"

Both men reached for their guns, but Augie's had fallen to the side in the tumble. Jack fired a dozen quick rounds upward into the darkness; at what, he was not certain.

Augie fumbled with his cell phone, certain his fingers were consciously avoiding the flashlight function. He had no desire to see whatever owned the hot breath and the growl strong enough to shake the earth, but he needed to find his gun.

A high-pitched shrill pierced the night air.

Fat fingers finally manipulated the phone light. Augie directed the beam at Jack.

Two animals, one with Jack's leg in its jaws, pounced almost vertically and charged off into the night.

He crawled over to Jack, who was rocking back and forth holding his leg. Both men clung to each other, shaking uncontrollably. The noxious smell of Jack's clothes no longer offensive. After too many minutes of huddled nonmovement, the big bodies began to stiffen.

"We gotta move," said Augie. "Can you walk?"

"I'll need some help getting up."

Jack wrapped an arm over Augie's shoulder, and they hobbled down the arroyo. Blood draining from Jack's leg into his shoe squished with each step.

"It hurts, Aug. It hurts real bad."

Augie took a knee and examined Jack's leg. "That don't look so good. You're losing a lot of blood."

The cell phone light faded.

"Damn phone." Augie smacked it against his leg.

"Did you see them?" Jack shuddered.

"I didn't see anything."

"Come on. You were right next to me."

"No. I was moving my ass away from there like you shoulda been doing."

"They were dogs. Big freakin' dogs."

"Wolves."

"You did see them! I knew it."

"I don't know what I saw. They were too big to be wolves."

"Why didn't they finish me off?" asked Jack.

"You asking me? Do I look like a wolfologist?"

Walking endlessly up and down arroyo banks and through the sandy desert, anxiety eventually turned to frustration.

"What the hell, Jack? We were just here. Where are you leading us?"

"I was following you."

Augie kicked the dirt. "This is right where I fell."

"Can we rest here? My pants are wet from that kid's vomit. They're starting to chafe, and my leg hurts."

"Stop complaining. You're not the only one injured. I got a blister on my foot from these shoes. It's killing me."

"You got a blister? I got a wolf bite on my leg, cactus in my ass, and vomit all over me. *And you're bitchin' 'bout a blister.*"

"It hurts, damn it." He pushed sand aside with his uninjured foot. "Let's find my gun. It fell out around here. I think we're gonna need it."

Jack kicked a hunk of metal in the dark. "Here it is."

Augie picked the gun up and chambered a round. "Let's see that overgrown mutt mess with me now."

"Aug," whispered Jack as he slunk backward.

"I'm not screwing around, Jack. I'm gonna—"

Two wolves pounced on Augie, gnashing teeth through the big man's throat before he could finish the sentence.

Jack's legs pushed backward on autopilot until he tripped and landed on his ass with a yelp. The wolves turned their heads. Augie's flesh hung from clenched teeth. Blood drizzled from jowls the size of a bear trap. Jack tried to steady the gun between his knees and take aim.

Pow! Pow! Pow! Three shots in rapid fire.

One wolf yelped and tumbled. It yelped again and hobbled off into the darkness. The second wolf growled.

Hands shaking uncontrollably, Jack squeezed the trigger again. *Click.*

CHAPTER 44

BREACH OF PROTOCOL

TONY WINKED AT Joel when a dozen shots rang out in the distance. The guys found the bag.

"That could be my boy," said Rip. "He's been out here a few days. He and his friends like to spotlight, you know."

"Spotlight?" questioned Tony.

"The kids shine their spotlights at rabbits and coyotes, then pick 'em off."

"Can we get back to the elevator?" asked Joel, confident the shots were not from kids.

"Like I was saying. Blood was all over the floor and smattered around the chain-link cage. A lot, actually. I really can't explain it. I was still getting a pretty good reading on my rad meter, but there shouldn't have been any reading at all in the elevator. The waste car is below the personnel car. Containers are surveyed before they're moved to the hoist, and they're never opened inside the conveyance. I was at a loss."

With Rip taking way too long to get to the critical point. Joel asked flatly, "Did you go into the repository, Rip?"

"Listen, guys. I know I'm not supposed to go into the shaft alone. We have a two-man rule, and I always follow it. But this was weird. Two of the alarms came from Panel 5. I know I just told you that I went back to the muster point in the conference room, and I did, but I left out one thing. I went downhole first to check things out."

"What did you find?" pushed Joel.

"There was no blood on the salt when I got out at the bottom, but I swear there were paw prints on the floor leading straight into the elevator." Something he hadn't mentioned to Mel because he preferred to confront Chuck first. "I've done my share of tracking. I know what I saw. These were large. Too large. It looked like one or two big dogs had run into the elevator."

Three additional shots rang out. Joel checked his watch. They'd been talking to Rip for almost an hour.

"I'm telling you. That's the local kids shooting rabbits. I'd appreciate a little help with the truck now. I need to see if my boy is with them."

"The truck can wait. You were saying."

Joel's tone was beginning to irritate, but Rip also felt self-preservation nerves tingling and wished his gun wasn't sitting on the seat in the cab. Something was not entirely right with these men.

"Like I said, we all know Chuck raises German shepherds. He's brought them in his truck before. I can't believe he would take them into the underground, but how else do you explain paw prints? Night shift. Nobody around. I wouldn't put it past the guy. Once I figured out his dogs were there, that explained the blood streaks in the elevator. Like the dogs licked up the blood after they bit Chuck. It's a long ride up."

"I get it," barked Joel. "He brought his damn dogs. What did you see in Room 6?"

"I saw the ceiling collapse. That's when I knew the alarms were real. Until then, I was hoping we had false readings." He shook his head in disbelief. "A large block of salt had fallen from the ceiling and crushed some drums. I only drove into the room far enough to see the collapse, I swear."

"And how far would that be?" asked Tony.

"The room is three hundred feet deep. I drove in about two hundred feet and stopped when I saw chunks of salt on the floor at the back end of the room. I shined my light across the drums. As soon as I noticed breached containers, I turned around and got out. That's one protocol I would never break. I don't usually break any of them, but that night, you had to be there to believe it."

"Tell me about the drums that were crushed. Describe what you saw."

"Most of Room 6 is empty. The only waste is in the back, up against the wall. I drove down the right-hand side and stopped the cart a little more than halfway, like I said. My meter confirmed a slightly elevated dose, but the reading was a little confusing. The dose I was seeing in Room 6 was lower than in the elevator. Of course, I wasn't right up next to the cans. From where I was standing, I could see some drums on their side, one with a pretty big hole in it. The plastic rad bag was hanging out. Like someone had tried to pull it through the hole and quit halfway." He let out a nervous laugh. "Add that to the list of things I can't explain."

"From where you were *standing*?" Joel cocked his head. "You didn't mention getting out of the cart."

"I, um." Rip stuttered at the man's tone and began to wonder if the only thing at risk tonight was his badge. "I got out for a second, just to wave the meter around. I didn't go much closer to the drums."

"You're telling me you never saw the contents of that drum?"

"Guys, for a repository incident, you sure seem focused on one drum. No, I did not see any contents, just the yellow plastic bag hanging out the side and the slimy stuff dripping into the salt. I don't know how we let free liquids into the UG, but we'll get to the bottom of that during the investigation."

Rip paused, waiting for participation or more questions. Joel seemed to be thinking.

"That's why you're here, right? To start an investigation?"

After telling his good friend Steve Simon what had happened, Rip had been waiting all week for the cavalry to arrive. He expected DOE to be on a plane Monday morning to start cleaning house, beginning with Mel. But the cavalry never came.

Tony's voice turned ominous. "And now, here you are, all alone, stuck in the sand."

"I'm not alone. Sandy came with me. We go everywhere together."

Eyebrows shot up on Joel's forehead. "Sandy?"

"She's over there." He pointed into the darkness. "Going to the bathroom and probably looking for sticks or a rock to bring back and show me."

Tony and Joel huddled together.

"Thanks for your time," said Joel.

They climbed up the arroyo embankment, slipping so much with each step they had to use their hands to assist.

"Are you guys gonna give me a hand?" shouted Rip.

The men didn't look back.

"I don't know, Joel," said Tony when they were out of earshot. "I think we should have taken him out right there. Make it look like an accident."

"How are we going to make it look like an accident with his wife out there? You shoot him and then what? We don't have a shovel. We don't know this area. Somebody could find him tomorrow or never. We're not going to start getting careless now."

"I was thinking I could bash his head in with a rock, then jack the truck up and set it down on his body. Like it fell on him when he was trying to dig himself out."

Joel stopped. "That's not a bad idea. We might have to do the same with his wife if Sandy comes back before you're finished. Are you up for killing a woman?"

Tony's stomach tightened like a vice, but he said the only thing he could. "I'll do what I need to do."

The men skidded back down the embankment.

Tony shouted, "Rip, sorry about that, man. We were just kidding around. Sure, we can give you a hand."

Silence.

"Rip," repeated Tony. "Hey, Rip, where are you?"

"Quiet!" shot Joel in a loud whisper. "Do you hear that?"

An unusual noise from the front of the truck stopped the men in their tracks. Sloppy, crunching sounds. Sloshing. Slurping. The noise of four-inch fangs ripping flesh. Eighteen-inch jowls crushing bones. Thirty-inch necks gulping down—the appetizer.

"What the hell is he doing over there?" whispered Tony.

The slurping stopped.

A guttural growl crawled from their feet to their ears. The rumbling increased. The men backed up and turned to run. The quick sprint and the embankment proved too much for Tony's heavy legs. Halfway up, he lost his footing and fell to his knees, catching the sharp edge of a rock between his patella and knee bone. He let out a screech more befitting of a tiny woman.

"*Give me a hand! Pull me up!*"

Joel had his own struggles, pushing piles of loose gravel downward with each upward step, making slow but steady progress to the top. He ignored Tony's pleas and kept moving.

"Get back here. You son of a bitch!"

Tony pulled his gun from the inside of his waistband and fired a shot at Joel that missed and zinged off the rocks.

Joel disappeared over the rim of the arroyo, picking up the pace as fast as stumpy legs and cholesterol-filled arteries would allow. He stopped to catch his breath, leaned forward, hands on his knees, and sucked air into tar-laden lungs. He needed a cigarette.

Tony turned the gun toward the truck. He could barely make out two large shadows in the darkness, creeping around the driver's side, heads of each creature level with the truck bed.

"*Grrrrrrrrrrrrrrrrrrrrr.*"

Two huge wolves uttered an unending growl, bared bloodstained teeth, and glared at Tony. They crept forward. One with a heavy limp, revenge in its eyes.

Tony tried to raise the pistol, but jellied fingers, much like his legs, had left him immobile. Defenseless. The gun tumbled from his hands and discharged. He shrieked another girlish scream that carried out into the night, ending abruptly when massive jowls clamped around his head.

Joel heard the shot and the scream but never looked back. Gasping for air, forcing one leg in front of the other, he made it the short distance to the car. Safe at last.

One problem. Tony had the keys.

CHAPTER 45

SOMEBODY'S SHOOTING
MY BABIES

"*STOP THE TRUCK*," yelled Daphne at the sound of gunfire.

She spun the window crank and stuck her head out. Silence. She jumped out and ran forward into the headlights.

"That was a lot of shots." She turned in a full circle. "I didn't get a bearing."

Brian joined her. "I counted twelve."

"*Somebody's shooting my babies!*"

Trip and Becca approached. "Where did they come from?" asked Trip.

Brian shrugged. "We couldn't tell."

"Let's split up," said Daphne. "Walk out in each direction. Try to hear something."

"Alone?" Trip shuffled a step back. Thoughts of a hundred movies ran through his mind where people in the dark had decided to split up. Movies that never ended well. "I mean, what if that thing comes back?"

"The tyrannosaurus? You just holler, Little Man. I'll come over and kick its ass."

Large, determined strides carried Daphne into the dark. The others moved much more tentatively, keeping the Suburban in sight.

"I didn't hear anything," said Trip, the first one back inside the vehicle.

Becca was right behind him. "Me either."

Brian took a seat on the front bumper. "Guess we wait for Daphne."

A few minutes later, three more shots cracked the night air followed by a faint screech, too far away to distinguish the sound. Daphne came sprinting out of the dark with her arm extended east.

"*That way.*"

"Sounded about a half mile away," said Brian, closing the driver's door. "We're close."

"Those bastards are shooting our wolves. We gotta stop them. Head back to my truck first. The shots will have scattered the pack. We need that tablet."

Dust and gravel kicked up as Brian peeled out.

"Maybe the ranchers who came into the hotel this morning hired someone to kill the wolves," suggested Becca, slamming a shoulder into the driver's seat when the truck hit a dip.

"Not in this town," replied Trip. "A rancher might send his kid out to shoot them or do it himself, but nobody in these parts would ever pay someone to shoot a wolf."

"You don't understand. Killing a protected species is a felony. The kind that sends people to jail. Judges let drug smugglers, burglars, and rapists off with a slap on the wrist; kill one of these wolves, it's a minimum five-year sentence. I've never seen a judge go easy on anyone." She paused for a moment. "Kind of weird, now that I think about it."

"To folks out here, they're just wolves," replied Trip. "Big dogs that kill livestock. Our friends are always shooting wild dogs 'cause they're a nuisance. A wolf is just bigger."

Daphne gripped the dash with both hands. "Guys, we need to go faster. We're blind out here without the tablet."

In fifteen minutes, they were back at the pickup. Daphne jumped out before Brian stopped.

"Got it!" She tapped the screen. "There you are, my little one. Now, where are your friends?"

The other three gathered around the glowing screen while Daphne scrolled a thumb along the glass face.

"This isn't right. I got one dot. One freakin' dot, and it's that weird one I've been seeing since yesterday." She let out a heavy sigh and passed the tablet to Becca. "Can you look at this? I'm lost here. One dot, and it's moving as fast as a car."

Becca watched the dot make its way across the screen at a rapid pace. "With the other dots off the screen, we can finally make out the collar number. Hey, this identifier is all wrong." She zoomed in to enlarge the collar descriptor, 12-A10. "See the first number? It's a twelve. All the new collars start with 22 and a dash."

"Is 22 for the year?" asked Trip.

"Exactly, and 12 was for the pack we released in 2012. Those wolves were all killed, but the thing is, they never found one of the collars. That makes me think that what I was saying earlier might be correct."

"The dot stopped," interrupted Brian. "Why don't we just follow it? See what it is?"

"Let's go," said Becca. "Maybe we can figure all this out on the way."

Daphne clipped her seat belt. "I already figured it out. Somebody killed my wolves and destroyed the collars. That explains the gunshots and missing dots. The only thing left to figure out is where I'll be working next week. I'll be lucky if they don't make me walk my ass back to Atlanta."

CHAPTER 46

GOT WHAT HE DESERVED

JOEL SLAMMED THE car door closed and pounded the lock repeatedly. His chest pushed against the steering wheel with each heaving pant. Eyes burned from sweat pouring down his forehead. He wiped an arm across his face, soaking the jacket sleeve. He needed to gain control of the situation but couldn't stop shaking. Rapid breaths refused to slow.

He tried counting to ten, stopping at five when he realized the driver's window was down. Tony had lowered it to anchor his fat elbow on the door while they drove. The gaping hole increased the tempo of the panting, but he wasn't about to get out and move to the passenger seat. He climbed awkwardly over the center console, eyes never leaving the open window.

Moments passed, then minutes. Quiet settled in, revealing the sound of his heartbeat. Could those things hear the pounding in his chest? His eyes played tennis with the windshield, darting left to right and left, again. Sweat continued to drain down his face. His clammy palms were soaked in muddy sweat from clawing at the dirt to get up the embankment.

"Calm down," he whispered so quietly he barely heard the words. "Calm down."

More than once he had been rushed to the hospital for panic attacks, believing at the time they were heart attacks. His therapist had taught him to take deep breaths in stressful situations. He grinned at the thought of the next session. A growth of goosebumps wiped the grin away. Alone, in the desert, in a car, in the middle of nowhere, the calming techniques designed to help a desk jockey who had a rough day at the office were not working. His hands shook like leaves. Short, raspy breaths were so loud, Jack and Augie could probably hear the breathing, wherever the hell they were.

Head on a swivel, he looked out in every direction. Scarce moonlight illuminated surroundings in a ghostly gray. Dark shadows cast off cactus and shrubs as though he were in a black-and-white horror movie. With every twitch, he was certain he saw the beasts.

After more moments, more long minutes, the safety of the steel vehicle began to feel real. His chest pulsed slower. He was finally able to suck in deep, calming breaths. Maybe they hadn't followed him. Maybe he got away. Maybe he would get out of this alive. Courage crept in.

"Fat ass got what he deserved," he mumbled in a whisper, wiping his forehead again. "What a way to go."

Flicking the seat lever, he tilted back and allowed a wry grin to crawl across his face. "The boys back home are never gonna believe this."

Exhaustion pushed his eyelids down.

With no cell service, Joel had no idea how long he had been asleep. A minute? An hour? It didn't matter. He awoke to isolated silence and an uncomfortable realization of just how alone he was. Unable to see anything but moonlit shadows, he focused on sound. His heartbeat. Ringing in his ears. The gentle scrape of polyester rubbing against his body with each breath.

Something outside moved.

A single rock clicked lightly against another. A delicate whoosh of a branch bent and released without breaking. Sand pushed aside as padded paws crept toward the car.

His eyes revealed nothing. His ears told him they were getting closer: brush crackling, branches breaking, rocks clacking, coarse panting.

Joel stared out the windshield, not wanting to believe the image his mind was attempting to process. The massive animals made the tiny vehicle feel even smaller. Two wolves, the tips of their ears higher than the car. Deathly glaring eyes. Darkened fur on the shoulder of one revealed a glint of moisture in the moonlight. Blood. Tony had hit his target.

The canines circled slowly, ominously. After three rounds, their eyes never leaving his, the uninjured wolf charged the passenger door, lowering its head and crushing into the steel. The car shook. Metal crunched. The window shattered.

Dazed from the concussive impact, Joel tried to scramble back over the console. With both hands grasping the driver's seat, his nose on the cushion, he pulled hard, but his body made no forward progress. His feet were supposed to push against the door to assist the arms in pulling his gut over the shifter. His mind was confused at the nonresponse of lower appendages. An odd sensation coursed up his legs. Searing pain made its way from his shins to his brain. Jaws clamped tight.

He just had his shoes polished at the airport. A ridiculous thought, but he had no control over his mind.

Crimson blood dripped from the enormous mouth. Joel arched in pain, raised his head, and opened his mouth. The bloodcurdling scream knew better than to exit, hiding deep in his throat, forcing his chest to spasm in silence. The head of the second wolf entered the driver's side window.

His brain, slow to recognize pain in the legs, moved even more slowly, registering an itemized list of violations from the second beast. Piercing fangs. Two in the scalp. Two under the chin. Teeth shifting to the side to make room for the intrusion. A migraine sensation from the top combined with a root canal from the bottom. Below the knee, six teeth anchored deep into the bone. Each tooth registering an individual pointed pain as, together, they sheared away the lower eighteen inches of his body. The tugging more uncomfortable than painful. A final obscure thought: he was about to be even shorter. Darkness arrived.

Each wolf pulled its half through the window on respective sides of the car. They crept away into the darkness, one to the left, one to the right.

CHAPTER 47

KILLING MACHINES

"CAN I CUT across here?" Brian asked Trip. "You know this area better than me."

"Turn at the rock outcrop. You'll run into another two-track in a quarter mile."

The Suburban bounced hard when Brian cut into the desert.

"Turn on the light bar," said Trip.

Daphne slapped Brian's fingers when he reached forward. "*Don't touch shit on that dash.* You reach up here and flip the switch."

Trip leaned over Brian's right shoulder and toggled the fourth switch. A blast of light illuminated the desert.

"There's the road."

"What the heck," said Becca. "Look over to the right."

"Good eye, DC. Looks like somebody beat the shit out of an oversized lemon."

"That car was at WIPP yesterday," said Trip.

"At WIPP?" asked Becca. "Are you sure?"

"Yep. Had a bunch of big guys in it."

"Guess I missed it. The guy with my suitcase got into that car at the rental lot."

Daphne was out first, the others right behind. Shoulder to shoulder, they chorused, "What the hell?"

Becca gagged. "Is that…?"

Daphne shined the flashlight across the bloody car, revealing shattered glass on the passenger seat and ground. A swath of blood painted the yellow door. A similar stain coated the driver's door. She passed the light over the center console.

"There's a pile of something between the seats. Looks like…, entrails. *Shit! Intestines. Guts. Shit!*" Daphne backed up fast, tripping over something in the process. An obscenity-laden tirade followed.

All eyes turned to the wildlife officer crab-walking rapidly away from a bloodied shoe still connected to a shinbone.

In three seconds, four bodies were back in the truck, doors locked, windows up.

The truck trembled as they all released spasmodic shudders.

"What the hell was that?" asked Daphne.

Nobody spoke. An eerie silence settled in. The only sound, Trip's chattering teeth competing with Becca's for the fastest vibration.

"It was a leg," Daphne finally admitted. "Somebody's leg, and the shit in the car was his guts. Somebody died out here."

Trip muttered what everyone else was wondering. "Where's the rest of him?"

"Did your wolves do that? " whispered Brian, his voice vibrating as fast as Trip's teeth. "Do wolves *do that*? Nothing else out here could tear a man apart."

"No," replied a defensive Becca, curled in the corner, arms wrapped tight around her knees. "Impossible. Our wolves couldn't do that. They wouldn't do that."

"One way to find out." Daphne scrolled through the archives of animal movement. "Son of a bitch. It's the weird number, 12-A10." Her eyes doubled in size as she looked at the others. "The collar number we can't identify was right here eighteen minutes ago."

"You mean, you can check the location of where your wolf was?" asked Brian.

"That's not one of our wolves," insisted Becca, wiping teary eyes. "They wouldn't do that."

"Check to see if the same collar was by the truck, when Trip, *when we all*, heard the growl."

Daphne's fingers zipped across the screen.

"You're not going to believe this. That collar spent ten minutes straight ahead of this spot. What the hell would it have been doing for ten minutes? That's too short for a nap and too long to take a crap."

"We should go back to town and call the police," chattered Trip.

"Let's see what the collar was doing up ahead first."

Becca leaned forward, looking for dots on the tablet. "Before we do anything, you need to tell us where that collar is *right now*."

"North. The collar is a thousand feet from here. The pace is slow."

"He's probably full," added Trip, not realizing the magnitude of his comment.

"*Auuooooohhhhhh.*"

"Shit," whispered Becca.

The cab went silent again.

"*Auuooooohhhhhh.*"

Daphne pointed in the direction of the bloodcurdling howl. "It came from over there."

"That's east," said Brian. "You said the wolf was heading north."

"Can we just go?" pleaded Trip. "I need to get home."

"Howling is a good thing, Little Man."

"Uh-huh," he replied, not as convinced.

"She's right," said Becca. "The howl came from a long distance, and it sounded injured. You can tell by the higher pitch and kind of warble at the end. None of the other wolves responded."

"Their mouths are probably busy," muttered Trip.

Becca placed her hand on his arm. "It's okay. They howl to locate each other. If there is no reply, it's probably because there aren't any wolves left except the injured one that howled and the one heading north."

"I want to look for tracks." Daphne opened her door. "See if our collar left us any other information."

Brian inched his way out, hugging the driver's side fender.

"These prints are huge," whispered Becca, nearly connected to Brian's hip. "Like the prints we saw last week where you guys were shooting rabbits. This one is bigger than my hand."

Brian stepped into the light. "Bigger than mine too." He stood and peered into the distance. "These tracks are heading north—directly toward town."

"Look at this." Becca moved a few feet and got down on one knee. "The same size tracks over here but they're heading in the opposite direction. A lot of blood with this set. She's injured. Heading back to the den." Becca stood back up and moved next to Brian. "One wolf is heading to town. One is going home."

Trip moved next to Brian. Daphne moved over to Becca. The foursome stared in the direction of Carlsbad.

"We need to get ahead of her," said Daphne, "so we can warn people, 'cause that ain't no ghost heading to town."

Becca wiped a lone tear, her voice somber. "We're no longer saving our wolves from the public. We have to save the public from our wolves."

CHAPTER 48

NOBODY LEFT TO LEAVE

MEL'S PHONE BUZZED.

"Hey, Mel," came Brandi's cheerful voice. "I just went outside for a smoke and some fresh air. Dom's truck is behind the Waste Handling Building, so he's gotta be here somewhere. I paged him, but he didn't answer."

"Thanks, Brandi. I'll head back out in a few minutes. It's late, but he and I have a ton of work to do."

Mel downed three fingers of bourbon, stuffed Margaret's note in his pocket, and left the glass on the table.

Forty minutes later, Julio rested an elbow on the window of Mel's truck, the hood gleaming from the overhead flood lights. "Another late night?"

"It never ends, Julio. Looks quiet, though. Maybe I can finally get some work done."

"Yeah, it's been quiet, Mel. Almost too quiet."

"You keep it that way. See ya."

Mel cruised around back and parked next to Dom's truck. He made a quick pass through the office to see if his friend was sitting at the desk. No Dom.

"Gotta be in the shaft getting things ready," mumbled Mel.

The elevator door opened to the dimly lit salt cavern. Mel took another swig and stepped into the mine. No PPE. No respirator. No dosimeter. Between the alcohol and Margaret's note, he was long past caring.

He drove the transport to Room 6, turned inside, and stopped three-quarters of the way in. A massive block of salt sat on the floor just ahead.

That wasn't here last week.

He grabbed the flashlight and stumbled out of the transport. Something shiny reflected in the headlamps. A glimmering dome-shaped object. Dom's custom aluminum hardhat sporting the logo of his favorite team.

He circled the salt block. Half a leg protruded from one side. Dom's tan Tony Lama cowboy boot on the foot.

"You bastard." His throat choked up. "We were supposed to leave together. *Later.* Not now. Not tonight."

Mel dropped to the floor and placed a hand on the boot. Tears from a man who hadn't cried in thirty years dissolved salt crystals between his legs. He pulled Margaret's note from his back pocket and read it again. She was right. She was always right. He drank too much, was tired all the time, argued about everything, and was gone too often. *You're not the man I married.*

He staggered to the back wall, kicked a block of salt out of the way, and climbed into the cavern. Along the narrow path, far from the opening, he found a niche in the wall and plopped down. A comfortable fit. Cool limestone against his warm, alcohol-infused body. Finally, a place of solitude. A place to rest. Nobody around to bitch at him, insult him, threaten him…or leave him.

The light beam from his headlamp formed a white oval at his feet as thoughts of the week streamed angrily through his mind. Carlton, Joel, Donna. Every one of them wanting a piece of his ass. Tipping the flask to his tongue, he licked the last few drops from the rim and discarded the much-too-small silver container. He crumpled the note, tossed it into the darkness, and closed his eyes, exhaling a long, deep breath. Peace. Quiet. Rest.

A single wet stalactite dripped a soothing steady *tet…tet…tet* in the dark. A whiff of air passed by, escaping a thousand years of confinement as it made its way to freedom through the hole in the wall of Room 6 and out the repository exhaust.

Sleep overcame exhaustion.

"*Auuooooohhhhhh!*"

CHAPTER 49

SLAUGHTER CANYON

DAPHNE THRUST HER arm forward. "Let's see what that thing was doing up ahead before we follow the tablet."

"Do we really need to know what it was doing for ten minutes?" asked Becca, curled tight in her corner.

"I agree with Becca," said Brian. "It couldn't have been doing anything good."

"Someone might need our help. Or there might be evidence of the wolves we released. I don't know what we'll find, but we're already here. We have to check it out."

Brian flipped the light bar on and maneuvered around the tiny yellow car. A short thirty feet up the road, he stopped at the arroyo edge.

"Guess we didn't need to drive," said a timid Trip.

Brian pointed into the arroyo. "That's Rip's truck."

Trip locked his door and burrowed into the seat corner.

"I need you to stay here, buddy. Keep the engine running. Daphne, are you sure that thing isn't around here?"

"The tablet still shows her heading to town."

"And the injured one that howled would probably be back at the den," added Becca. "But you still need to be quick."

"Why?" asked Brian. "If one is headed to town and the other is going to the den, we should be okay."

"We don't know where the den is. The injured one could be any-where in this desert."

Feet sliding with each step, they made their way down the

embankment, nearly stepping on what was left of Tony concealed in the shadows.

"I'm going to be…" Becca turned her head and hurled.

Brian repeated the action in the opposite direction.

"*Fu—*" Daphne stepped in a pool of mud. "*Guys.* Get over here."

"*What now?*" snapped Becca, wiping her chin on a sleeve. "I can't take any more of this."

A lone cowboy boot lay in a circle of red-tinted mud. The foot still inside.

"That's Rip's boot," whispered Brian. His chest heaved, but there was nothing left to expel. "Let's get out of here."

Halfway up the embankment, the sound of rapid feet running toward them caused arms and legs to move faster than they ever had before. Brian pulled Becca up the last few steps, and together the three sprinted to the truck, the sound getting closer with each stride.

Daphne jumped in first, followed by Becca and Brian. Sandy leaped inside just as the door closed.

"What did you find?" asked Trip, cradling a panting Sandy. "Hey, little girl."

"Rip's down there," replied Brian solemnly. "It got him."

Tears slowly fell from Trip's eyes onto Sandy's fur. He squeezed the steering wheel with both hands for a long quiet moment. "Who's gonna tell Grady?"

"I think the other one was the guy who took my bag," said Becca.

Daphne shook her head, anger overtaking despair. "What the hell, people? *I'm pissed.* We can't let that thing kill anybody else. We're the only ones who know where it is." She pulled her gun from the holster and chambered a round. "Let's get that bitch."

"Hold on, Daphne. We're only guessing *what* it is."

"Well, we sure as hell know *where* it is. After I put a bullet in its head, then we'll figure out *what* it is."

Brian turned from Daphne to Becca. "What *exactly* do we know? I can tell that you recognize the 12-A10 number. What does the number mean?"

Becca hesitated.

"You holding something back, DC?"

"No. Not really. I mean, I've been thinking about this all night. I have a guess, but that's all it is, *a guess*."

"A guess is better than anything else we've got. Let's hear it."

"Like I said before. What if a wolf got radiation on it and that made it grow really big, like Rip told us? We know those collars were all coded with 12-A followed by a number designating the specific wolf. I think we can agree this has to be one of our collars from 2012. When a wolf goes off grid for so long, the project manager has to decide whether to keep the case active and continue searching or declare the animal dead. All the wolves from the 2012 release were declared dead, but I think this one must have been living in a place where the collar couldn't send a signal."

Daphne nodded partial agreement. "Okay. But explain how a wolf took the elevator down 2,150 feet into that radioactive dump and got itself radiationed, irradiated, radioactive, or however the hell you say it."

Becca pulled a wadded hotel brochure of Carlsbad Caverns from her pocket.

An understanding grin slid across Daphne's face. "That's why they keep you smart people in DC."

"I don't get it," said Brian.

"I'm saying I think the alpha female from the 2012 pack made a den deep in the caverns in a branch cave somewhere close to the WIPP site. She bedded down, had a baby, and both were exposed to enough radiation over many years to cause abnormal growth. That explains two big wolves and one collar. When our new wolves started howling the first night we released them, I think the alpha female heard the howls. She and her baby, well, it's full grown now, found a way out to link up with the pack."

"Trip, do you or Brian know how far the caverns go?" asked Daphne.

"A long way," replied Trip. "They've never mapped the whole thing. Park rangers tell you that on every tour. Grady and Arturo have been in the caves more than the rest of us. They're always looking for unmapped entrances and found a few tight openings not far from Slaughter Canyon."

"That's exactly what the brochure says. The caverns splinter into a thousand smaller caves that go for miles. Most of the caves have never been mapped, and nobody knows where they go."

Daphne hit the light bar switch, illuminating a wide swath of desert. "What are we waiting for? Drive." She scrolled across the tablet, switching between screens to review archived data. "*Whoa.*"

Trip slowed down.

"Not you. Keep going and speed up. I just searched the archive track for A10. That bitch was at our truck when you were fixing the engine. That's what you heard breathing down your neck. The wolf was right behind you." Her wide eyes moved from the tablet to Trip. "Little Man, when you said a tyrannosaurus, you weren't too far off."

"How far back does the archived data go?" Brian asked. "Can you see where that wolf was last Friday?"

Becca leaned forward to help Daphne with the location. "There. Close to that intersection is where I found the radioactive fur."

"Damn, DC. She was right there, left for a while, then came back."

"That doesn't make a lot of sense," said Becca. "Unless she had become familiar with the area, or there was food over there."

Trip gulped. The others remained silent.

"Will somebody say something?" barked Daphne. "It's scary enough out here to have you guys getting all eerie on me."

In a hushed voice, Trip replied, "We found Grady's hat right where the wolves were standing."

Brian reached over the seat and put a hand on Trip's shoulder. "Dude, are you thinking what I'm thinking?"

"*Watch the road,*" shouted Daphne, reaching for the wheel a second too late.

The front end of the Suburban dipped deep into a drainage crevice cut into the dirt. Four heads bounced into the ceiling, followed by a chorus of foul language, each seemingly attempting to outdo the others. The truck lurched to a stop.

When the dust settled, Daphne glared back at Brian. "What was so damn important?"

"The hat and Arturo. I mean, it all kind of makes sense. Arturo and Grady went back that night. Grady got killed by those wolves. We know how gross that is. Somehow Arturo got away. But dude, that would drive anyone to drink. I think Arturo went home and drank himself to death."

Trip opened the door and wretched clear bile onto a bush. He took a few deep breaths, regrouped, and gunned the engine. The truck stayed put.

"Dang it."

He opened the door again and checked underneath. "It's not bad. Brian, there's a board in the cargo area. I'll turn the wheel hard to the right, and you slip the board under it."

Brian reached over the back seat and grabbed the board, that, for locals who drove daily in the sandy desert, was almost as important as a spare tire. He also grabbed Trip's thermos.

"In case one of you gets thirsty while I'm out there."

The stillness of the night became eerily apparent while he lay alone in the dirt positioning the board under the tire. "Is there a reason none of you will come out here with me except Sandy? Did something show up on the tablet?"

"Vidalia, don't go getting your pretty panties in a ruffle again. I would never send you out there if something was on the tablet. Well, almost never."

"*Almost never?*"

She winked at Trip and climbed out.

"Everything looks good," she whispered, mostly to steady her own nerves.

"Why are you whispering?" asked Brian. "You said one wolf headed toward the caverns and the other is on the way to town."

Trip cranked his window down an inch. "Because one wolf doesn't have a collar."

"And it is just a theory," added Becca. "I mean, they could have made more babies by now. Lots, really."

Daphne stilled her position, eyes trained into the dark, searching for any sign of movement.

"I really think we can relax a little," said Becca, sliding out to join the others. Trip followed. "I'm sure the injured wolf would have gone to the den and bedded down by now. He was losing way too much blood to stay out prowling."

"Got it," said Brian. He climbed in and rocked the truck forward and back until the tire grabbed and pulled the heavy Suburban out of the rut.

"Is the coffee fresh?" asked Daphne when they were all in the truck, Trip and Becca in the back seat.

"Fresh?" asked Trip.

"*Fresh.* Like you, Little Man. Is the coffee fresh?"

"Not too fresh."

"Pour me a cup anyway. It's been a long night, and I feel like things are gonna get real serious real soon."

CHAPTER 50

NUMB NUTS

"WHAT THE HELL, numb nuts!" yelped Daphne when cold coffee sloshed into her lap.

"*Numb nuts?*" Becca repeated, again questioning her friend's application of the local vernacular. "Girl, you're going to need some of that transition therapy when you get back."

"One night with these guys, and I'm talking like a hick. Who the hell puts railroad tracks in the middle of the desert?"

"There's a lot of railroad tracks out here," said Trip, pointing south to raised tracks barely visible in the dark that was slowly fading to dawn. "Mostly for the potash. That's how they ship it out of Carlsbad."

"The rail yard is on this side of town, away from your hotel," added Brian. "You might have heard the express this morning. Yesterday morning, I guess, since it's almost this morning now. The express is the first train of the day. The only one that hauls through town without stopping. Goes straight through to El Paso."

"Every morning the whistle blares around five thirty," said Trip.

Brian glanced over his shoulder. "How would you know? You'd sleep till noon if I didn't wake you."

"I heard it," grumbled Daphne. "Damn thing woke me yesterday. I was wondering who to thank for the wake-up call. At least those tracks mean we're close to town."

She gulped a mouthful of coffee and spit it out on the dash. "What the hell is this? There ain't supposed to be anything chewy in coffee."

She ran a finger along the bottom of the cup, captured a tiny carrot cube, and flicked it at Trip. The mushed brownish-orange vegetable stuck to his forehead.

"I don't know," he replied apprehensively as he wiped it off. "I mean, I use the thermos for everything. It might have had soup in it before I filled it with coffee."

"You ever try washing it before you refill it with coffee?" She wiped her tongue on her sleeve. "Take this back. That's about all of *your* coffee I need. Vidalia, are we there yet?"

"Less than a mile. I used to live on this side of town when I first moved here. Before my dad came. Lived in a trailer park not far from the rail yard."

Daphne rolled her eyes. "Does everybody in this town live in a double-wide?"

"I wish," uttered Trip.

When the dirt track finally transitioned to pavement, Brian pointed to a long, narrow building off to the right. "The streets are a little weird behind the train terminal, and there's a lot of stray dogs in the area. They eat pigeons that flock by the railyard. Do you think the wolf would smell the pigeons and go after them?"

"More likely she'll smell the stray dogs and go after them. Let 'em know this is her town now. DC, check the tablet. Find out where that bitch is."

"How can you be so sure it's a girl?" asked Trip.

"Because the only collar unaccounted for in 2012 was a female," replied Becca. "It's her offspring we should be worried about."

"Why?"

"Because wolves usually have four to six pups in a litter. If she was stuck somewhere in a cave, maybe she couldn't nurse her first litter and a few died. But if a male survived, you can bet there were a few more litters since—uhm, guys." Becca's voice turned to a firm whisper. "She stopped near here and hung around for sixteen minutes."

"That can't be good," said Daphne. "Every time she stops somewhere, she leaves a mess."

"Turn down there." Becca pointed. "She's close."

Brian navigated the narrow alley, slowing when he came upon a bloodied mess at the far end.

"Make a left at the next street," continued Becca, the bloody mess having no effect on her focus. "She's moving but not fast, and I am not about to lose her again."

Daphne rocked her head, proud of her friend's newfound stones and sensing imminent engagement.

"How do you want to do this?" Brian asked Daphne, her window down, service pistol in hand. "Stop and get out, or shoot from the window?"

"Stop at the end of the street. I'll get out. You stay in the truck."

Calming words to Trip, who had resumed trembling in the back seat.

"If she takes off, follow her. Ram the beast if you have to." She turned to the back seat. "Trip, you come with me."

He forced hot bile back into his gut and slid out.

"You'll be my other set of eyes. This girl is fast. We need to see her before she sees us."

With a stride more than twice his own, Daphne's boots clomped loudly on the pavement, raising doubts about sneaking up on anything. She rounded the corner, Trip attached to her left shoulder.

"There she is," whispered Daphne, halting so fast he bumped into her.

Across a wide street, the gray beast blended in with the weathered wooden siding on the old train depot. The animal that wreaked havoc and death throughout the night stood solitary at the edge of a graveled loading area. Characteristic pointed ears, long nose, and narrow eyes. Behind the wolf was the town. In front, an expansive graveled loading area through which passed four sets of railroad tracks. The desert lay just beyond the tracks. The wolf appeared to be contemplating whether to return to the safety of the desert or slaughter every living soul in town. Daphne had a gut-wrenching feeling the stately animal before her could do whichever she chose.

"It's just standing there," whispered Trip.

Daphne lowered to one knee. She leveled her pistol and took aim.

A slight adjustment of her foot to steady the leg scratched the gravel surface so lightly Trip barely heard it.

Ears twitched. The gray head rotated, coming to a stop with small black pupils of large eyes glaring angrily at Trip.

"If we don't move, she can't see us."

Daphne restrained from smacking her new friend for yet another dinosaur movie reference not at all applicable to wolves.

Boom! Boom!

She fired two shots in rapid succession. The first bullet hit low, kicking up dust behind the beast. The gun barrel rose with the recoil, causing her second shot to hit the building two feet above the animal's shoulders. The wolf leaped straight up and dashed off the instant her feet returned to earth. Daphne was right behind, jumping out of her position like the high school track star she had once been. Trip followed, losing distance with each stride.

Becca watched in silence, a tear crawling down her cheek.

"Let's go," said Brian. He gunned the engine. "We need to keep them in sight. If it doubles back, we can…"

"All we can do is pray."

CHAPTER 51

EL PASO EXPRESS

THE WOLF DASHED behind the train station, clearing the length of the building in eight strides. Daphne and Trip arrived just in time to see her turn into town.

"*Shit!*" shouted Daphne, turning on an extra gear.

She cut along a parallel street. A billow of dust at the next corner told her to turn right. The large officer dug deep. She kicked into an accelerated sprint. Bell Lap. She barreled down the next street, turning the corner way ahead of Trip, just in time to see the wolf leap straight at her.

No time to scream. No time to move. No time to react. The impact heavy and hard, like getting hammered in the chest with an unexpected medicine ball. Enormous paws anchored on each shoulder slammed her backward.

On the way down, time slowed to a crawl. Her brain sensed every detail. The athletic officer's first thought; the big girl could probably hold a basketball in that mouth. Her nose processed liver-scented breath. A mist of spittle sprayed her face. A feeling of sorrow for the large animal, badly in need of a teeth cleaning. Her last thought, before the back of her head smacked the pavement: Why hadn't her life flashed before her eyes?

In the second and a half it took the wolf to knock Daphne flat on her back and open its mouth wide enough to suck in her head, Trip lowered his shoulder and broadsided the beast with every ounce of strength he could muster. Just like he learned in football, he maintained his directional force to push through the opponent and knocked the beast off his friend.

The surprised animal landed on its back, rolled over, and was on her feet in an instant.

Trip scratched his arm and face on the pavement in the tumble. He rolled to his hands and knees.

"*Grrrrrrrrrrrrrrrrrrrr.*"

Narrow eyes radiated hate. The wolf's ears were pinned to her head. Quivering lips peeled back, exposing enormous fangs and rows of razor-sharp teeth. Bloody teeth that had killed his friends. The growl grew just as it had in the dark when Trip was working on the engine. This time, the hair on his neck did not rise. Legs did not shake. Bowels did not threaten release.

Trip growled back. "*Grrrrrrrrrrrrrrrrrrrr.*"

He shifted his feet shoulder width and assumed the posture of a defensive end, ready to wrap the wolf and take it down the instant it moved.

The beast crept forward. Trip inched backward, stopping when his foot bumped Daphne's body. This was it. There was no way he was going to allow the wolf to get past him to Daphne.

The wolf shot forward so fast, all Trip could do was watch as the huge mouth snapped at his leg. As fast as she leaped forward, she bounced back into the shadow with the cuff of his jeans in her mouth. A sliver of sunlight streaking between the buildings glistened on her gray paw. She shook her head wildly. She approached the beam slowly, cautiously, growling with avenging anger. She nudged her nose into the light. The beam crawled up the snout until it hit her eyes, forcing her to bounce back and bark at the invading beam.

The wolf pushed her gray head into the sunlight a third time, yelped, jumped, turned in the air, and bolted away.

Trip rocked back on his butt, staring in awe at the bounding beast that ran with the grace of an antelope toward the open desert. She passed the train depot in six strides, sprinted across the loading area, and leaped over the first set of tracks in front of a parked train. She landed cleanly on the second set of tracks, knees bent, ready to spring forward into the desert, where she could live free and wreak havoc for years.

Whoosh! Chug-a-chug-a...chug-a-chug-a...chug-a-chug-a... chug-a-chug-a.

The El Paso Express slammed into the wolf, bursting the beast like a birthday piñata, obliterating the massive canine in a red spray of blood.

Trip watched in disbelief as the rumbling freight train sped onward to El Paso, unfazed by the impact. The wolf that terrorized the night lay shredded along miles of track.

Brian pulled to a stop at the corner. He and Becca jumped from the truck.

Trip crawled to Daphne, who had shifted to her side and rested her head on an elbow. Adrenaline faded fast as his mind caught up to the actions at hand. His body trembled. He swallowed hard and sucked in short panting breaths.

Daphne reached up and dabbed the corner of his eye. "Are you okay, Little Man?"

CHAPTER 52

COFFEE WITH PERSONALITY

AFTER TWO HOURS of too many flashing lights to count and nobody believing their story, the four friends slipped away from the huge crowd gathered at the railroad yard. Though everyone from the city manager to the mayor was skeptical of the story, large tracks left by the beast gathered a lot of attention. With Benny on his way to the arroyos south of town, it wouldn't be long before the crowd moved into the desert and blame moved to the nine wolves released Wednesday evening, only thirty-six hours earlier.

"Cavern or the restaurant, your choice," Brian said to Daphne.

"Cavern. Give me a chance to piss off a few more locals before I leave town. Maybe your waitress friend can make an ice pack for my head."

The four occupied their regular table in the almost empty Coyote Cavern.

"I just need a good cup of coffee," said Becca. "Preferably a dark roast."

"Coffee is coffee, girl. You DC folks turn everything into a specialty."

Becca slid Daphne a grin. "You didn't care much for the coffee last night."

"I don't know what the hell that was, but it was not coffee." She stuck her tongue out. "Bleh! Nasty."

"I just like my coffee to have a little personality," explained Becca. "Nothing wrong with that."

Trip glanced at Brian. "Do I like coffee with personality?"

"Just order, dickhead."

After the first cup, Daphne and Becca excused themselves and stepped outside with their cell phones, each calling their supervisor to explain the evening adventure.

Trip placed his elbows on the table and rested his chin in his hands. "Daphne said I could go with her to Atlanta."

"*Dude, you have to go,*" exclaimed a wide-eyed Brian. "You'll never get another chance like that. Escape. Get the hell out of here."

"How can I leave? I love Carlsbad. How can I leave my mom? And what about you and the company? When you get your own truck, you're gonna need help."

As much as Brian would miss his lifelong friend and desperately needed a trustworthy partner in the new company, he couldn't allow Trip to miss a true opportunity of a lifetime; an opportunity Brian would never have with a father who required daily assistance.

"I was doing all the work by myself before you started. I can do it again. Besides, when I get my truck, it'll be hard to pay for an assistant until I get some accounts." He tousled Trip's hair. "Don't worry about your mom. She'll be excited to see her little man get out into the world."

Cathy set plates around the table, licked two fingers, and patted down Trip's cowlick. "Were you guys out all night again?"

"How can you tell?"

"I'm not gonna lie." She scrunched her nose. "You smell a little. Like, more than normal. Don't worry. I won't sit anybody near this corner."

Becca returned first. "Well, that was interesting. Boy was Bradford pissed. He started yelling at me. Then I told him about the extra collar. Turns out he was in charge of the 2012 release. He was the one who officially declared the entire pack a dead reintroduction. Once he admitted those were his wolves, I climbed up one side of his back and down the other. The wolf that haunted us all night was his freakin' wolf. I blamed *him* for everything that happened with this release. He should have sent a task force out in 2012 with more sensitive tracking equipment. Who knows, they might have picked up a weak signal. They might have prevented all this if he had done his job better. By the end of the conversation, he was apologizing and thanking me for finding his wolf." She shook her head. "It's not like he had a huge change of personality. Our archived data will prove his wolf lived ten years. Now he can claim his release was a huge success in the recovery of the Mexican gray. Asked me to get back soon because he has a wolf pack assignment for me in Wyoming." She beamed a smile. "Yellowstone! That's like the pinnacle position at the service."

Daphne dragged her chair back from the table and sat down. "That went better than expected. Boss said they should have sent three officers on this assignment, knowing how ranchers in this part of the country like to protect their livestock. He kind of blamed himself. Just wants my report by Monday. I told him we encountered other wolves, but I didn't mention the beast. Not sure how to fold that in just yet." She put her hand on Trip's forearm next to the bloodied road rash that stretched from his wrist to the elbow. "Why didn't that wolf eat me?"

"'Cause you're huge and you got spikey hair." He slapped his hands over his ears for protection.

"I'm gonna kick your ass all the way to Atlanta."

Brian wrapped an arm over his best friend's shoulder. "You should have seen it. Trip broadsided the beast like a linebacker. Slammed it to the ground. That's why it didn't eat you. I don't know why it didn't eat Trip, though. That wolf had venom in her eyes. I thought Trip was a goner, and we were too far away to do anything."

"It was the sun," said Becca. "There was a beam of sunlight between you and the wolf. She was afraid to cross it. I must have been right about those wolves living in a cave. Her eyes were super sensitive to light. That also explains why they ran away so fast when we turned on the light bar last night."

"Well, you were right about one thing, Vidalia. That El Paso Express don't stop for nothing."

"So what's the plan?" said Brian. "Sounds like Trip is going with you. Becca's heading back to DC. I'm going to work."

Becca shrugged one shoulder as if the reply were obvious. "We'll be cooped up on a plane all day. You're the lucky one. You get to pump honey and breathe in the sweet aroma. I wish I could stay an extra day and go around with you. That would be super cool. I'm not afraid of bees or anything."

Brian spread a sweet smile. "Maybe we didn't explain our job so well."

"You drive a honey wagon," she replied matter-of-factly. "What's to explain?"

Trip covered his grin with both hands.

"A honey wagon is...well...it's another way of saying a septic pumper truck. Trip and I pump septic tanks and porta johns all day."

The Fish and Wildlife workers pushed their chairs back in unison. "*Eeeeewwww!*"

*

Forty miles from the El Paso airport, the cab of the pickup was quiet, Daphne driving, Trip in the middle, and Becca at the window.

Trip held up a CD. "Wanna listen to some music?"

"Let me see that." Daphne read the title track. "Well, I'll be a son of a gun. Rednecker." She rolled the window down and held the disc in the turbulent air. Trip's eyes widened. "I couldn't do that to you, Trip. Need this for evidence. Nobody back home is ever going to believe a song like this exists."

"They might," said Becca. "When they meet Trip."

"You both called me Trip."

"Little Man was gone the second you saved my life. You '*the man*' now."

A satisfied chill crept through him unlike anything he had ever felt. A calmness filled his body, knowing he was among friends.

"I'm hungry. What do you have to eat?"

Trip reached for the plastic container on the dash.

*

The screen door smacked against the wood frame, announcing Brian's arrival.

"Mornin', Dad. What do you say we go fishing today? And have I got a story for you!"

CHAPTER 53

BUREAUCRATIC BUREAUCRACY

CARLTON KICKED THE dust off his shoes and climbed into the aircraft with Donna. The only two passengers on the DOE Learjet leaving Carlsbad Sunday afternoon.

"That was the most gruesome meeting I've had in my entire career," said Donna, sitting erect, attempting to conceal unprofessional feelings. "Thanks for handling most of the conversation with that deputy. I had to get some air."

"I can't even begin to imagine what happened in that desert," replied Carlton. "Five bodies. Some mauled so badly they don't even know which parts go to which bodies? What the hell happened out there?"

"It's clear to me that Fish and Wildlife screwed up and released a pack of wolves too close to town. What the hell were they thinking, turning nine wolves loose on a community? They hunt in packs, you know. What I can't believe is Fish and Wildlife trying to blame us. A big bad wolf got irradiated and went on a rampage. They can't be serious."

"I've known Rip and his family for years." Carlton looked out the window at the cactus and mesquite landscape. "He's as outdoor a guy as you'll find. All he did was take a couple of days off to search the desert for Grady and look what happened. I'd do the same thing if my boy was missing."

Donna eyed Carlton's Brooks Brothers patent leather shoes.

"His truck gets stuck and a pack of wolves attack. Of all the luck.

He would have never expected wolves in a desert that he's hiked hundreds of times." He closed his eyes and took a deep breath. "Deputy Montoya described that scene in more detail than I needed. Showed me pictures of Rip's truck and a beat-up yellow car nearby. Two bodies at the car. Well, most of two bodies, the way the deputy described it. Thank God he didn't flash those pictures on his phone or I might have lost it. Tony Valastro's name was on the rental contract. The name matched a DOE contractor badge they found in a jacket. Deputy Montoya said parts of a second man were found around the rental car along with another contractor badge. Marsha had no record of either man coming on-site, but she'll check with the rest of the staff tomorrow."

Donna huffed lightly. "And where the hell is Mel during all this? He and Dom both gone. I read him the riot act a few days ago but nothing I haven't said to him before. Hell, I've yelled at Mel so many times, you'd think he would be used to it."

Carlton shook his head half in disgust, half in despair. "He wasn't at his house when we went by. Katie spoke with him Thursday night. Said he was looking for Dom and sounded exhausted. His and Dom's trucks are both parked at WIPP, which suggests they left with somebody else."

"Did anyone see them leave with Rip?" asked Donna.

"Nobody I spoke with, and I hope that's not the case, because those other two bodies were found a mile from Rip's truck. Not enough remains to identify. The deputy described it as a shredded mess with parts that added up to two men." He glanced back out the window, both passengers thinking the same thing, Mel and Dom. "It'll take time to check dental records or DNA, if it comes to that."

Donna opened her satchel as soon as they were airborne. "At the risk of sounding insensitive, I want to make sure we stay aggressive on this. Walk me through the path forward again."

"The acting site manager inspected Room 6 yesterday at my request. He could see from the entrance that a third of the room was filled with salt. He reported the ceiling was unstable and had the room sealed with a temporary closure. Radiological surveys completed in the corridor revealed no residual contamination." He flipped to the next page. "Corrective actions will have to include increased management oversight and training enhancements with regard to immediately reporting collapses. Nobody will enter Room 6 until a formal reentry plan is developed and approved by us. The contractor will submit a cost for developing those plans. I'll do the independent government estimate to compare with their estimate. We all agreed six months was reasonable to put the plan and the numbers together, but honestly, I'm pretty busy, so that date might slip."

She nodded. "Don't let it slip too much. I need that estimate to submit with the fiscal year budget request."

"That will get us the funding to complete reentry planning the following year," said Carlton. "We should be able to start decontamination of Room 6 a year after the planning and complete the cleanup in a year. Recertification and compliance checks will have us fully operational in four years."

Donna set her coffee on the armrest table next to a chocolate éclair. "That's unacceptable. We just restarted the damn facility. I can't justify a four-year delay. What's plan B?"

"Plan B? I suppose we could say the temporary closure of Room 6 is permanent. Abandon that room and never reenter. That would allow us to restart operations in the rest of the facility immediately."

Donna closed her eyes and leaned the seat back. A wolfish grin crept across her face.

"Plan B it is."

ACKNOWLEDGMENTS

First and foremost, thank you to my wonderful wife, Belinda, who is the first to see any manuscript and as my front-line editor, the first to point out embarrassing mistakes and offer suggestions. A personal and special thanks to my friend and former boss, Dr. Rip Anderson, whom the *Wall Street Journal* referred to as "arguably the world's top expert on long-term disposal of nuclear waste." In support of this novel, Rip described the WIPP underground to me in vivid detail.

Thank you to Dora Walker, Mary Baligad, and Debbie Baligad, readers I trust to provide honest critiques as they trudge through early drafts. Special thanks to Chris Aas, a longtime friend who provided candid feedback, technical advice, and excellent suggestions, all of which made this book better. Thank you to my friends and technical experts J. D. Smith and Dr. Joe Schelling, who provided critical and accurate comments that improved the finished product. My brothers Jim and John, thank you for positive reinforcement along this journey. A special thanks to the late Dave Parks; the story herein actually happened and was one of a hundred I'll remember always.

Thank you to staff at the Carlsbad WIPP Experience Exhibit who took the time to describe repository operations and characteristics, which I then painted with attributes not founded in the reality of such a well-operated, highly regulated, extremely secure facility. Special thanks to all radioactive waste management professionals who make our lives safer through proper disposal of radioactive waste.

Writing this novel gave me the opportunity to return to the friendly city of Carlsbad. I chose to describe the Carlsbad of my youth, a small New Mexican town where good people work hard on hot summer days. Thank you to the editors and staff at Elite Authors and

Kevin Anderson and Associates who provided professional editing necessary to turn a manuscript into a product.

I also thank you, the reader, for making it all the way to this page. I hope you enjoyed *Ghost of the Gray* and are looking forward to upcoming releases. I appreciate any reviews on Goodreads, Barnes and Noble, Amazon, or other platforms.

ABOUT THE AUTHOR

J. Jones is a retired engineer who has managed and characterized trans-uranic waste for disposal at WIPP, experience that helped immensely in writing *Ghost of the Gray*. He is in an international expert in radioactive waste volume reduction and has authored or co-authored numerous technical guidance documents on emergency response for nuclear power plants—documents he insists are page-turners, just like *Ghost of the Gray*.

Made in the USA
Monee, IL
06 November 2023

45856829R00173